GUNMETAL GODS

ZAMIL AKHTAR

Cover by Miblart

Edited by Fiona McClaren

Special thanks to Salik, Tim, Sophie, Chirag, and Colton

This book is a work of fiction. Names, characters, places, and incidents are the product of the author's imagination or are used fictitiously. Any resemblance to actual events, locales, or persons, living or dead, is coincidental.

FREE BOOK

Get *Death Rider*, a prequel novella to Gunmetal Gods, for FREE by
joining my mailing list at ZamilAkhtar.com!

For my wife Jenalyn

CONTENTS

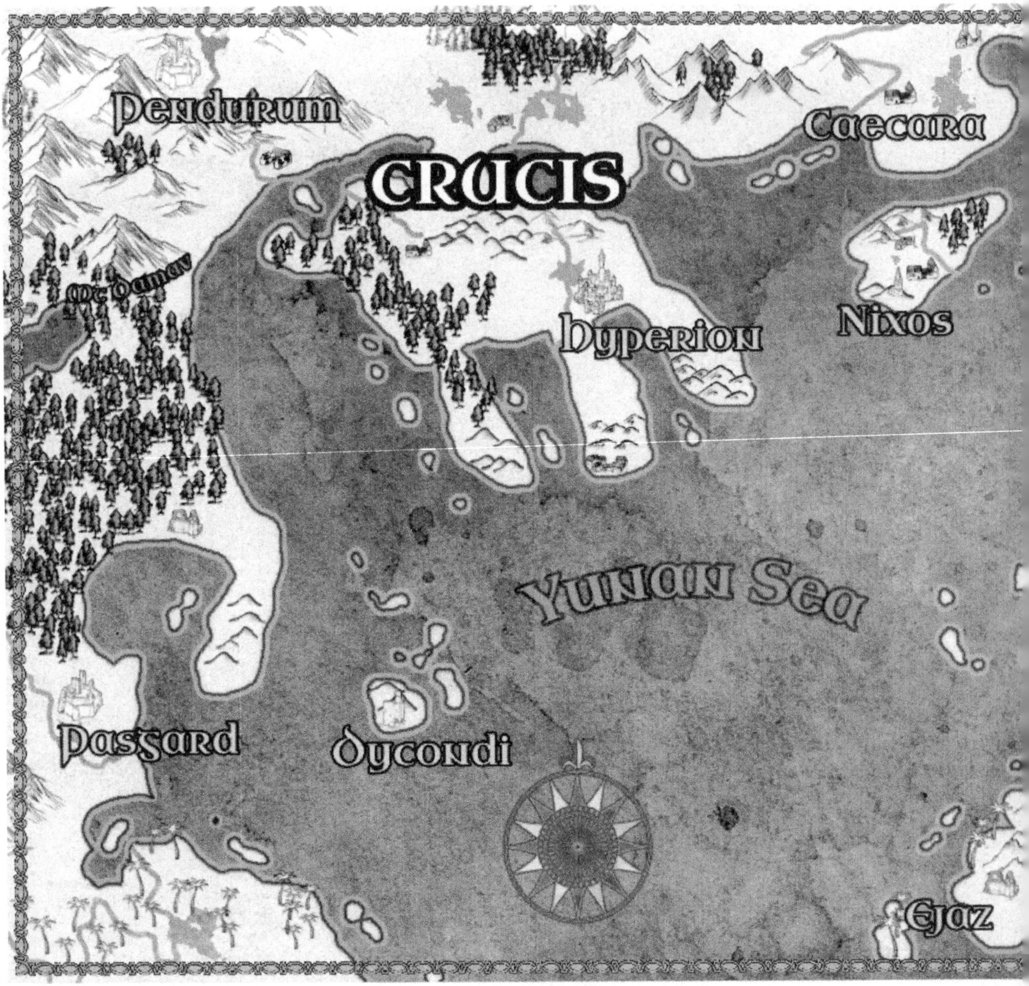
Penduirum
Caecaura
CRUCIS
Mt Damav
Hyperion
Nixos
Yunan Sea
Passgard
Dycondi
Ejaz

Rastersan
Siyah Sea
Noepla Mts
Shrunken Strait
Zari Zar Mts
Taskalay
Kostany
SIRM
Syr Darya
Demoskar
Lyskar
Zelchuriya
Karmaz Mts
ALANYA

1

KEVAH

YOU DON'T REFUSE A SUMMONS FROM THE SHADOW OF GOD, EVEN IF
you're a veteran of twenty battles, with a body count longer than
a sheikh's beard. I'd left my anvil weeks ago and journeyed by
carriage to Kostany, the Seat of the King of Kings. Finally through
the gate, I recoiled at the fishy stench of the streets. But when it
didn't smell like fish, it smelled like home — like the city I'd
grown up in and come to love and hate.

The walk through the grand bazaar left my ears ringing, such
was the clamor of folks rushing to buy geometric carpets from
Alanya, colorful Kashanese spices, and ghastly metal idols. The
hollering and running and bumping awakened memories of
clashing armies; already I wanted to flee to the countryside. To
relieve the strain, I considered stopping at a coffeehouse to smoke
cherry-flavored hookah and down a thimble of their strongest
black, but I feared the Shah had waited long enough.

The Seat of the Sublime Palace was not the highest point in
the city; that honor went to the Blue Domes. But the Seat sat on a
hill and looked upon Kostany the way many imagined god

would. It wore its green dome like a turban, and the rest of the palace shimmered like pearls under the midday sun.

The plaza was all fountains and gardens and white marble. Imposing spires overlooked the gates. They were watchtowers for the Shah's *loyal* slave soldiers: the janissaries. But the young janissary guarding the gate in flashy yellow and rose-colored cottons didn't believe I was the great hero Kevah, answering a summons from the Shah.

"You're the janissary who jousted twelve armored cavaliers while on foot?" he asked, disbelief bulging from his eyes. "Were they drunk?"

"No, but when your mother sees what I'm going to do to you, she'll drink herself into a stupor." An old janissary taunt — harmless since we didn't know our mothers. "I was guarding this gate at sixteen. By eighteen, I'd left bits of my flesh on seven battlefields. At twenty — you get the idea. I won't waste breaths on you while the Glorious Star is waiting."

The young janissary bit his quaking bottom lip, forced a smile, and said, "The legend returns. His Majesty has been expecting you."

He ushered me into the great hall, where the Shah sat upon his golden divan. And above it, the golden statue of the Seluqal peacock stared down with its ruby — literally ruby — eyes.

"Kevah the Blacksmith," the Shah said. "I've met eunuchs with better titles."

He wore lavender brocade with the imprints of peacocks, the sigil of House Seluqal. The plumes of real peacocks augmented the crest of his golden turban, which he'd wrapped just above his shaped eyebrows. At least he had the beard of a warrior — trimmed but thick enough to evoke respect. Beneath the pomp, he still had the hard way about him.

"Your Glory." I bent my neck. "A former slave ought to appreciate whatever title he can get."

"Oh shut up." The Shah rose from his divan as the whine of a cicada punctured the air. "I freed you and gave you enough gold so you wouldn't have to lift a finger, and yet you bang a hammer in the heat all day. You're an ingrate if I ever saw one."

"I could say the same for you."

The Shah laughed, his belly shaking. "That's the Kevah I know. Sharp blade and sharper tongue."

"It's good to see you again."

"But it's not. I wish I never had reason to call on you." Shah Murad's sigh was like air escaping a leather sack. "Another magus is stirring up trouble. I'd like you to bring me his head."

Not what I expected, but I kept my back straight and tone even. "No 'welcome home' feast. No parade. Just straight to business."

"Apologies, I mistook you for a soldier. But if it's a powdering you want, let's walk."

We left the great hall and strolled through a pleasure garden. A breeze blew against the pretty flowers. A hornbill fluttered above the veranda — its green and gold wings flapping too fast for the eye.

The Shah said, "I require every ambassador to gift a native bird from his kingdom. Now songbirds from the eight corners make a home here."

The spear-like beak of the fluffy, round one on the branch above could poke an eye out.

"Can't they just...fly away?" I asked.

"Hah! Even the birds know there's no place greater. They've far more sense than you."

"I hope you've the sense to find another plan," I said. "I can't kill a magus."

"But you did kill one. You're the only man alive who has."

"I got lucky."

"Luck doesn't behead a sorcerer." The Shah studied me. He surely saw hair that had thinned with years and a belly that my tightest belt couldn't hide. "Tell me, Kevah, what is it you want?"

3

"I have everything I need, thanks to you."

"It's been almost ten years since Lunara. You should take a new wife."

"We're still married."

"You can't be married to the dead."

I made a fist behind my back. How dare he say that? "She's not dead."

Black birds with silver beaks flew overhead, their dark pupils bathing in red. The Shah raised his eyebrows and looked upon me with pity. "A woman doesn't show for ten years, she might as well be. The Fount have decreed a husband need only wait five years, and you've doubled that. You're almost forty, aren't you?"

"I'll be forty in seven moons." I unclenched my fist, hoping he'd get to the point.

"Gray hairs in the beard and no children. You need a young, fertile woman. I've got dozens in my court, from this tiresome family or that. You kill this magus, and I'll let you choose whomever you like."

"I don't need a reward to fight on your behalf. You need only ask."

Shah Murad's snicker wasn't very royal. It reminded me of a younger Murad, who ate the leather off his shoes during the siege of Rastergan. "You think I'm sending you to your death."

"I'm ready to die for your house. Always have been."

"Fucking imbecile — I don't want you to die for me. I want you to be the Kevah of ten years past and kill another magus."

"Truthfully, I don't know how I killed that magus," I admitted. "Never have, really. I think about it all the time. The magus opened the clouds and rained hail upon us, each hailstone sharp as a diamond. One sliced into a man's helmet and down through his groin, carving him in half. So many died." I suppressed a shudder. "Then Lunara distracted the magus while I swung my sword. The next moment, his severed head and mask were at my feet." Describing it was reliving a nightmare. One I'd never woken from.

"No-no-no." The Shah glared at me with royal disdain. "I remember you boasting how you'd cut his head clean. You showed off that magus' mask like it was an ear you'd cut off and hung around your neck. It's too late to be humble."

"That may be, but I was faster and stronger back—"

"You're afraid!" The Shah's shout startled a flock of parrots, sending them fluttering into the sky. The janissary guards straightened their backs. "I don't ask. I command. You will kill this magus. Afterward, you will come to my court and choose the youngest, fairest, biggest-breasted girl and put Lunara out of your mind for good. Refuse either command, and I'll feed your head to my birds."

Had I left my countryside cottage and journeyed hundreds of miles to die?

I forced my neck to bend. "I've never refused a shah and won't today."

I COULDN'T JUST MARCH to the magus and lop off his head. I had to train. So I sought the man who had trained me when I was a boy.

Tengis Keep looked as I remembered: three floors of sandstone, a dusty courtyard, and the barracks with all its sour and sweet memories. Save for pigeons fluttering overhead, it was quiet. No janissaries trained in the courtyard, and no one fished at the lakeside. I swallowed nervous dread, which poured through me at the thought of seeing the family I'd abandoned ten years ago. I dusted my caftan, hands jittery, then pounded on the large wooden door.

I inhaled deeply and prepared to see Tengis' shocked face, but a young woman answered instead.

She covered her mouth. "Papa?"

I had no idea who she was.

"It's me, Melodi," she said.

Now I saw it: how those cheekbones became lean and that stub nose grew pointed. She hugged me before I could say a word.

Then she reared back and slapped me so hard my ears rang.

"You never visited. Never wrote. And then you appear out of nowhere and fail to recognize the girl you adopted."

I rubbed my raw cheek as the sting receded. Melodi stomped her foot and disappeared into the interior of the keep. I slipped inside before the door shut. The front hall was not as I remembered: faded, tribal carpets covered the floor. Dust kicked off them as I walked. A musty odor made me cough — was no one maintaining this place? A calligraphy-covered matchlock hung on the wall next to an unpolished scimitar. The stairs creaked as I climbed.

Tengis was in the solar, sitting on the floor at a low table and banging on a printing press. They imported them from the Silklands and were faster at transcribing than feather pens. He'd strewn metal trinkets and contraptions around the room — what a mess. The ancient man stared at me, mouth agape, and said, "You miserable goatshit."

"Ancient" was a mild way to describe him, but all words were shade when it came to Tengis. His skin had so many spots, it resembled a carpet woven by a blind man. "How can you just stand there, gawking?" he said. "Are you a ghost? If so, know that fat ghosts are not welcome in my keep." He stood and wagged his finger at me. "Get out, or I'll fetch the exorcist this instant!"

After convincing him I was real, we went to the terrace for relief from the musty air. I took a seat on a floor cushion.

"Lunara was too good for this kingdom," Tengis said. He gave me a mug of fermented barley water and plopped next to me. "Perhaps she's better off...wherever she is."

"I couldn't keep her safe."

Sitting in the house where I'd grown up, nostalgia flowed through me like poison.

"She didn't need you to." Tengis grunted in disgust. In ten years, his tangled hair had gone from gray to white. "I trained and tutored her for the same reason I did for you. Strength and intelligence are ladders for slaves. A girl as beautiful as her would've ended up in the harem had I not taught her how to think and fight. And where would you have ended up with those big arms of yours…a blacksmith?"

The sarcasm stung. "Come on, it's not a bad profession."

"I saw so much in the two of you. The day you married was a day of endless happiness for me. Melodi is lovely, but I wanted more grandchildren."

"Sorry to disappoint."

"You don't disappoint me," Tengis said. "Lat does. Though we may pray ceaselessly for her blessings, she gives and she takes."

"She mainly takes from me. She may take my life soon enough."

Tengis took a deep chug, then sat back on his floor cushion. The crust around his eyes seemed permanent. "In the ten years you've been gone, the Shah has become…restless, to put it mildly. This dispute with the magus should be resolved in peace. The *unholy* Imperium of Crucis masses its forces to the west, ready to invade at the slightest unrest. A conflict with Magus Vaya and his sycophants would ripen us up."

"So I shouldn't kill him?"

"Kill him? Even you'd certainly not succeed. This magus is said to be far more terrifying than the one you killed."

The chill of the hailstones that cut through my platoon ran through me. What could be more terrifying than that?

I rubbed my arms. "How do you expect me to disobey a command from the Shah of Shahs and walk out of Kostany with my head attached?"

"Say you're training with me and let his viziers talk sense into him. A moon passes and he'll rescind the command."

"I hope his viziers are up to the task."

Tengis nodded. "Grand Vizier Ebra is a prudent man. He's vehemently opposed to conflict. Last year, Shah Murad wanted to invade the isles of Jesia because they stopped exporting his favorite cheese. The man is prone to impulses, which his viziers have learned to reign in."

"Ebra is Grand Vizier now? That was quick." I gulped barley water. "Did we put the wrong man on the throne?"

"Certainly not. His brother would have been the end of us. I'd take a bit of imbecility and impulsiveness over cruelty and lunacy any day."

"So," I said, "I'm on leave for a month with you and Melodi."

"Oh no, this won't be leave." Tengis could dismiss your entire world with his snigger. "We're going to train. War is never far. You're not old like me. You've no right to be weak."

MELODI STOOD in a bog by the lake, which I now noticed had receded and was barely more than a muddy pond. The soil used to be harder, too. My adopted daughter wore the same yellow dress as when she'd answered the door — except now she held a shamshir in high guard above her head. The blade was thicker than both her arms. Her stance seemed to compress the ferocity of an army into one teenage girl, and her menacing glare the anger of a hundred forsaken daughters.

"You can't expect me to fight her," I said with a cockiness that failed to disguise my fear.

Tengis' conniving laugh unnerved me. "I've trained her with sword. I've trained her with spear. She's learned the mace and crossbow. And even the matchlock, something you never cared for."

"I hate guns."

"Guard up!" Melodi soared. Steel rang as she slammed my high guard and pushed me back. My adopted daughter was freakishly strong.

"Melodi, go easy," I said, breathing fast, "I haven't dueled in years."

"Grandpa always said you were a complainer." She charged, slammed into my middle guard, and staggered me. Would have drawn blood with her thrust had I not stepped back.

Wielding a sword in battle felt so...unfamiliar. It might as well have been a giant cucumber. Had I really regressed so much in ten years? What happened to the skills that made me a hero among the janissaries?

Tengis stood like a dervish in meditation, hands crossed. "You proud of your slowness? A pregnant woman would make a more fitting opponent."

Melodi slid and swept my feet with her shamshir. I jumped and landed on half a foot, just missing an anthill. Instead I fell on my knees into mud.

"Can we do this somewhere with solider ground?" I said as Melodi put her sword to my neck, concluding the duel.

"You must be tired, Papa." She clanked her sword into her scabbard and tousled her inky hair. "Hope you'll do better tomorrow." Her disappointed sigh sealed my humiliation.

Minutes later, I was scrubbing my boots at the lakeside.

"What the hell kind of girl did you raise?" I asked.

Tengis watched me, his nose ruffled in disgust. "A girl who wouldn't care if her favorite shoes got some dirt on them."

I chaffed at the boot's sole. "I just had these made. Do you want me to trail mud through the Sublime Palace?"

"You're a soft, well-fed ninny. When is the last time you fasted?"

I almost retched at the question. Tengis would make us fast from sunrise to sunset, in the way of the saints, at least ten days of the month. There were few things I hated more. I blamed

9

fasting for why I was fat now — I had to eat enough to make up for all that. "I once went three days without eating in the caves of Balah."

"So ten years ago, like every accomplishment to your name."

"Saving a shah. Killing a magus. Deposing another shah, ending a war of succession, and crowning his brother. I'd say I accomplished enough for a lifetime. It's charitable to let someone else have a bit of glory. Who knows, Melodi could be the next me." My eyes were closing. I needed sleep. I'd paid eight gold coins to the coachman to get to Kostany, and all that bought me was a bumpy carriage. Bed bugs plagued the caravansaries along the way, so I'd woken each night scratching. "Tengis, is she your last one? Will there be more like Melodi?"

The old man sighed and squatted by the lakeside. "The Shah retired me from training janissaries, and the Fount has disallowed women to serve in the corps, so Melodi can never take the vow. What to do with her, I wonder…"

A family of ducks floated by, quacking at the boot I doused in the water. The mother duck pecked it; I pulled it away before she could do any damage. My shoes would not be harmed by such a tasty bird. My stomach grumbled. There wouldn't be any decent grub in Tengis Keep, and I wasn't going to eat bone broth with barley. I'd have to catch something sumptuous at the bazaar tomorrow.

I smacked my boots together to dry them. The red leather was discolored at the base, but the green and gold embroidery glistened like new. They smelled funny though. Like the rest of Kostany — of fish and shit. A boiling bath could cure that. Another thing to do tomorrow.

Tengis told me to take the guest room upstairs: the softest place in the house, with a feathered mattress and cotton sheets instead of a bit of straw and hide like the barrack chambers I used to sleep in.

Melodi was sitting on the staircase in her yellow dress, still dirty from our bout. It was the most colorful thing in this dank keep. Her eyes said she wanted to talk, and I couldn't ignore the daughter I hadn't seen in ten years. We were all sons, fathers, or brothers to someone at Tengis Keep — blood didn't matter to janissaries, and we bonded fiercely because of it.

She sulked. "Can I...ask you a favor?"

I craved a hookah pipe. Smoking cherry-flavored hashish before bed would've been the perfect release.

"Get me the hookah and I'll give you the world."

"Grandfather quit years ago. Threw them all out."

I sighed. "Well, another reason to be disappointed."

Melodi picked at the fake topaz in her bronze bracelet. "Are you sad to be here?"

I sat a step below her and reclined against the wall. "I'm sorry I didn't visit or write. Truth be told, I've not been myself for a long time."

"I know, Grandpa would always say it wasn't your fault. That it hurt you too much to be here. I'm sorry I slapped you." She took my hand. "I miss Lunara too."

Tengis hadn't painted his walls since I'd left. What was once white was now gray. I supposed houses got old like the men within them.

"Lunara loved to mother you," I said to lighten my mood. "I'm surprised you even remember us. You were only five."

"She should be here. Then it could be like old times." Melodi squeezed my hand. "Do you pray for her?"

Grit roughened my voice. "I used to stand in vigil from dawn to the zenith hour and beg Lat to bring her back. All I got were swollen feet. Actually, they were already swollen from how long I'd been looking for her, through the forests and mountains in the countryside. When someone disappears in the night — not a clue, not a hint of where they went...there's nowhere to look."

"And yet, there's everywhere to look."

I pulled my hand away to scratch my beard. "So...what favor would you ask of me?"

Melodi gulped and pulled on her thin, dark hair. Whatever it was, it made her hem and haw. "Teach me everything you know."

I laughed. "You're better than me now."

"I'm younger, faster, maybe even stronger. But I'll never be as clever or experienced. I grew up in peace, mostly. You used to sleep with a dagger under your pillow, remember?"

Thinking back, it was a miracle I hadn't cut myself turning in my sleep. It was easy to grab the dagger under my pillow and stab whoever was sneaking up on me. And during the conflict between Shah Murad and his brother, often fellow janissaries were trying to gut me as I slept, so divided were loyalties.

"I hope I never have to again," I said. "Peace is its own reward."

"Peace makes us weak."

"You're just saying that because you're bored." I rubbed her head.

"No, I've seen how people act in this city. Everyone just wants an easy time — without earning it." She grimaced and swatted my hand. "Why'd you move so far from everything?"

"Because I earned my easy time. And I like being bored. After what I've been through, boring is the best I can hope for. Boring means no war, no fighting. It means the ghosts of those my blade bloodied won't come back to dance."

The glint faded from Melodi's eyes. I hated seeing her sullen.

"Listen, Melodi." I patted her back; her shoulder blades stuck out. I'd have to take her to the bazaar for a feast of pheasant marinated in yogurt or fermented dough stuffed with beef. "That old man made sure that if you want something, you have the strength to take it. He's taught you everything you need." I got up to go to bed.

"And what about you, Papa? What do you want?"

"I want a soft mattress for the rest of my life." I'd have one tonight, at least.

My hope as I reclined on the mattress was that the Shah would see his error, make peace with the magus, and send me home. I prayed to Lat that I'd spend my days hammering trinkets and horseshoes and die with wrinkled skin and gray hair. And yet, as I stared at the guest room's unfamiliar gray ceiling, I knew it was another prayer she would laugh and wave away, like a hornbill flying past her verandah in the heavens.

IN THE MORNING, I was devouring almond soup with buttered beef at the grand bazaar's most overpriced establishment when some flashy courtier summoned me to the Sublime Seat. The warrior-poet Taqi called it the "Palace on the Shores of Time" because it outlasted a dozen dynasties and conquerors. I felt its green dome clashed with the white marble. Nevertheless, I trailed my slightly muddy boots through the Shah's garden, where marigolds perfumed air cooled by a stone fountain. Black-feathered drongos chirped atop the trees that shaded me.

Flanked by janissaries in their colorful cottons, a slim man sat on the wooden divan beneath the veranda in the center. A glittering turban patterned with the eight-pointed star of Lat adorned his head. His beard and mustache were more manicured than the garden and evoked fashion rather than ferocity. I almost coughed at the astringent scent of myrrh flowing from his gown. Ebra, the Grand Vizier, was a far shade from how I remembered him in youth.

A yet more ostentatious man stood across from him, his head bowed, a pound of purple kohl around his eyes. His maroon silks were foreign, patterned with spades, and, dare I say, finer than the Grand Vizier's.

"We'll do something about those ruffians, rest assured," Grand Vizier Ebra said to the man. "The Shah will compensate you from his own purse for the loss of your...what did you call it?"

"Palace of Dreams, Your Eminence. A place where no man could leave without a smile, his every yearning fulfilled. And now it's just a husk. Boiled and blackened and burned. A dream in smoke. My fortune — ash." Kohl streamed down his face with tears as a trembling overtook him. "We had twelve varieties of card games, wines from as far as Lemnos, beardless boys and pleasure girls versed in the techniques of Kashanese sutra. You would have loved—"

"No-no." The Grand Vizier flushed and shuffled on his divan. "I am a worshipper of Lat and follower of the Fount. While it sounds lovely for some, such a den would be forbidden to me." He crossed his legs and swallowed. "No one was killed, so there's no blood money to be paid, but restitution there will be. For you and all others who have lost such *fine* establishments to these rabid fanatics. The Shah does not let criminality go unpunished." Ebra looked to me and raised his eyebrows, a false smile spreading across his face. "And here is the legend who will make it so. It is with the grace of Lat that we meet after so long, Kevah. You're a man who has done so much, and I now expect much of."

"Your Eminence." I bent my neck. "As I told His Glory, I'll do as commanded."

Ebra gestured for the pleasure house owner to leave. Once the tearful man had sauntered away, Ebra said, "After much cajoling on my part, the Shah has wisely rescinded that command. Instead, you are to parley with Magus Vaya."

Somewhat of a relief. I hunched my shoulders. "Parley? I'm no diplomat."

"You are a respected and feared warrior. You are worthy to carry the Shah's terms because you are one who can enforce them."

"I'm sure there are many respected warriors in this city."

"But only one who has killed a magus."

A boast always catches up with you. I sighed with regret. "Your Eminence, the man who killed the magus ten years ago is gone today. I am not the warrior I once was. Yesterday during training, I was defeated by my daughter, a girl I once carried on my shoulders. Parleys can get messy, and as my father put it, you are sending a 'well-fed ninny' against the most powerful sorcerer in the kingdom."

"Ah, us janissaries are so fond of calling those we love daughters and fathers and brothers." The Grand Vizier laughed from high in his throat. "Perhaps one day I'll call you 'brother.'"

Ebra had trained under Tengis. I'd known him in those days, but he was shy and we didn't speak much. Afterward, he was sent to a palace school for elite janissaries to be trained not in warfare, but statecraft.

"Did you not love the man who trained you and taught you everything you know?"

"Unlike most janissaries, I remember my real mother and father," Ebra said with venom. "I remember the day they sold me for a pouch of silver. So…I find it difficult to call anyone else by those words."

"And I find it difficult not to. What is a man without family?"

Ebra sipped the red liquid in his bejeweled goblet, then wagged his finger at me. "You're blunt and persuasive, perfect traits to deal with a man like Magus Vaya. You leave within the hour."

Before the guards could usher me out, I said, "You don't need me to make war, and I doubt you need me to make peace. It was a long carriage journey from Tombore to Kostany. Tell me truly, why was I summoned all this way?"

Ebra seemed so comfortable on his divan; it surprised me that he got off it and came close to my ear.

"The Shah has his eccentricities," he said in a hushed tone, as if we were court gossips. "One day he wants this, the next day that. I don't claim to understand it. Play your role, and you'll be a passing fancy that he'll toss aside and forget."

Ebra sat upon his divan with a straight posture and high chin. He dismissed me with a backhand wave.

MAGUS VAYA PREACHED at the shrine-town of Balah, ten miles east of Kostany. I traveled by carriage through the Valley of Saints, which was surrounded by the Zari Zar Mountains. It was also where I'd survived a hailstorm and killed a magus. I shut my eyes so I wouldn't be reminded and to get a bit more sleep. The Fount insisted the hardships of the saint's road be preserved, so rocks and broken patches jolted the carriage the whole way. I'm sure the horses hated it as much as I did.

After an hour, the hovels of Balah began to wrap around the mountainside. The path to the shrine of Saint Nizam, the only impressive sight in this pile of rocks, ascended the mountains. Too steep for carriages, so my janissary escorts and I continued on foot. We passed the cave where Saint Nizam had hidden, which some obscure scholar named the Bath of Stones. By the time we stood before the Shrine of Nizam, I realized I knew too much about this topic. It was thanks to Tengis, who made sure we had a thorough education and that our wits were as sharp as our skills.

At the shrine, the wailing of supplicants never ceased. While holy men chanted prayers, beggars cried for Saint Nizam's intercession. All who entered the shrine wore white, except for me and the colorful janissaries.

The incense pots couldn't cover the human smell of the place; skin-stench and sweat shot up my nose and burrowed in my brain. The janissaries clutched their matchlocks as we waded through the sea of worshippers. I'd neglected to even bring a sword.

We passed the mausoleum of Saint Nizam, where his shroud

rested within a metal cage. Supplicants clung to that cage and pushed their arms through it, seeking closeness to the saint. I whispered a quick prayer, asking only for Melodi's good health.

Stout men brandishing maces guarded a room behind the mausoleum. So these were the ruffians bringing disorder to Kostany — burning taverns and pleasure houses — supposedly on the orders of a magus. I displayed the Seluqal peacock seal and they let me pass.

A young man sat on the floor of the empty, tiled room, his face fresh and fair. Prayer beads in his right hand *clack-clacked*, and he whispered praises to Lat under his breath. In his cross-legged posture, he looked as unshakable as an anchor at the bottom of the sea. His hypnotic breathing seemed to inhale time, slow it down, and exhale serenity.

The young man gestured for me to sit. He snapped his fingers, and an elderly servant brought small, stone cups of tea.

"So you're Magus Vaya." I sipped the tea. It was so diluted, it might as well have been hot water. The faint taste of cumin did nothing to perk me up. And yet...the room seemed to tilt when I sipped. "Tell me, are you a man of peace?"

The young man locked eyes with me. I couldn't read whatever lay behind his blank expression. How easily would he see the trepidation that hid behind mine?

The magus closed his eyes. "Anyone who claims to serve Merciful Lat must strive for peace."

"Then let us guarantee the peace."

"Without justice, how can there be peace?"

"And what injustice has been wrought?"

The magus sat up and straightened his back. "Below the Sublime Seat, in the place they call Labyrinthos, our sheikha is kept prisoner. Every Thursday, I used to visit her to record her sermon. And then on Friday during the prayer, I would recite that sermon, as if from her mouth. Tomorrow will be the third moon since we have not heard from our sheikha."

I perked up in surprise. No one had briefed me on any of this. Was I sent here just to show that the Shah possessed a magus killer? Did my life matter so little that I'd been summoned across the country for such a paltry display? I hoped the magus didn't notice the surprise and indignation in my eyes. I pushed those feelings down deep. "Why not seek recourse the proper way? Why agitate?"

"Have you been to Labyrinthos?"

I shrugged. "Can't say I have."

"When they put you there, they give you a torch and tell you to find your way out. The historians say that a Crucian imperator built Labyrinthos to confuse the demons coming out of the gate to hell. The tunnels go on forever, deeper, deeper, and twist in such ways that men go mad trying to get back to where they started. In the darkness, you hear the whispers of jinn as they prick your forehead with nails as sharp as knives. No one survives Labyrinthos...and yet our sheikha endured it for ten years."

When I was a child, Tengis would scare us with tales of Labyrinthos. Hearing the magus describe it, a childhood fear jittered through me. "How did she survive in a place like that?"

The expressionless magus pointed to his face, then covered it with his hands and opened his fingers so his eyes would show. "The wonders of our invisible masks and training allow us to survive without food, without water, without sleep — forever unaging." He brought his hands back to his lap and clasped them. "But what kills in Labyrinthos is not the absence of those things. It is a madness that creeps like an assassin. Sheikha Agneya resisted it. She stayed by the entrance and never explored more of the cave."

"Agneya...I met her once." I recalled the pale girl, her hair wrapped in a bright scarf and body covered by a rough wool robe, standing before the throne in the great hall. "Twenty-five years ago, about. She looked younger than you. She refused to help Murad's father campaign across the Yunan Sea and also to war against the Alanyans. Shah Jalal smashed a goblet or two but had the good sense not to throw one at a magus." I could never forget her kind eyes as she walked toward me with the grace of a cloud. "I was fasting that day and sundown was far...she came up to me while I was guarding the palace, reached into her cloak, and took out the softest and whitest piece of bread that, till this day, I've ever eaten. Sometimes I wonder if I'd just dreamt it."

"Our sheikha loved to feed the destitute. She was succor for the weak, wherever she went, in the spirit of Saint Kali."

I grunted in dismissal of his platitudes. "And in whose spirit do you act? Name the saint that liked to burn things down. Tell me, magus, what is it you want out of this?"

There was elegance in the way the magus cleared his throat. "In the darkness of Labyrinthos, our sheikha heard the voice of Lat, like a breeze from paradise. And without her sermon, we are deprived of that heavenly breeze. Restore our right to see and speak with Grand Magus Agneya — that is all we ask."

Reasonable enough, but I'd only heard one side of the story and was eager to hear the other. "I will convey your request to His Glory." I got back on my feet. "Show good faith in the meantime. Have your followers take a break from assailing the card dens, taverns, and — yes — even the pleasure houses in Kostany."

"Everything has a reason." The magus gazed through me. Staring back, I was almost entranced. "Even a piece of bread given in kindness to a palace guard."

I shuddered and returned to the janissaries waiting at the doorway.

AN HOUR into our journey back to Kostany, the Balah stench finally left my nose. I could breathe air that didn't stink of poorly washed, sweaty men. We rolled through the eastern gate toward the Sublime Seat. The smooth roads of Kostany let me doze off. It didn't last — my carriage driver shook me awake.

"This isn't the palace," I said as I looked at the narrow street outside my window.

Yellow mud houses two-stories high lined the cobbled street. But why was it empty, save for our carriage?

My carriage driver beckoned me into a nearby coffeehouse, with its soft cushions and wooden floor tables, and guided me to the staircase. Upstairs, in a colorful room with two floor cushions and a hookah pipe, sat Shah Murad.

"Sit down and dispense with the courtesies," he said. "We are here to talk frankly. You will be as straightforward and honest as with a dear friend."

"Dear friends?" I chuckled with all the bitterness I'd been swallowing. "Would a dear friend send you to parley entirely disarmed of knowledge on the matter?"

"You misunderstand me." Murad pulled the pipe out of his mouth and glowered. "I am the Shah, and you will tell me what happened, janissary."

"Have you forgotten? You freed me from the janissary vows."

"You're still my subject all the same!" The Shah looked ready to strike me with the pipe. Instead, he puffed on it and closed his eyes. His breathing slowed. "I apologize, Kevah. It has been a trying few moons. Grand Vizier Ebra was supposed to brief you. You are a free man, one whom I respect, and that list gets shorter by the day. That is why you're here. Now, please tell me what happened."

"All right, I'll give you your due." I sat on the floor cushion and relayed what happened with the magus. The Shah kept silent and reflected. Hogged the pipe, too.

"Peace is a disease," Shah Murad said after I concluded my report. Confounding words.

Finally, he passed the hookah pipe. I inhaled deeply. Cherry-infused smoke billowed in my lungs and out my mouth, calming me.

"Peace. Peace. Peace," he said. "That's all everyone wants. But I'm telling you, it's a disease. Like leprosy or the pox."

"Would war be better?"

Murals of lilies covered the walls. It seemed strange to talk about war in such a flowery room.

"Better or not, it's coming." Shah Murad let out a dry cough. "My spies tell me that a Crucian armada of five hundred ships and fifty thousand men has landed on the island of Nixos, only a few days away — with fortunate winds — from where we sit. Where do you think they're going?"

One of the janissaries on guard handed the Shah a waterskin — the kind we'd use on campaigns. Murad guzzled from it like a warrior thirsty from battle, wiped his beard, and handed it to me.

"Demoskar, I'd imagine." I chugged. It was just water. Even when we were young, I'd never seen Murad drink anything other than water and milk. So unlike his father and brother. "With five hundred ships, they'd take the port city in a day and march for a few more days through the lowlands to Kostany."

The Shah winced as if pained by the picture of my words. "Our army is a shadow of what it was under my father. I was a fool to listen to my advisors, cowards like Ebra. 'Build ten hospitals instead,' he'd say." The Shah heightened his pitch and spoke from his throat — a crude imitation of the Grand Vizier. "'You'll be the hero of the masses. The people will love you.' The people are really going to love the Crucian imperator when he forces them to bow before cursed idols."

I took this chance to puff out a billow of cherry-flavored smoke. "They'd never get to Kostany. No one wants to bow to Crucian idols. We would fight to the last man."

"But what is a man worth these days? When my father was shah, everyone was a warrior. He led us across the Shrunken Straight into Yuna to conquer Crucian cities, and south beyond the Syr Darya to take Alanyan ones. The thought of a Sirmian warrior made Crucian imperators soil their sheets."

Each word he spoke evoked memories of my service to Shah Jalal — some sweet and others sour. But too often, remembrance left me sullen. "And then when your father died, those great warriors killed each other."

"Better someone was being killed. Better swords be sharpened daily for killing. You think I'm bloodthirsty? I say it to prevent worse bloodshed — the kind we'll experience when the Crucians invade. Look at us. The magi stay in their holy shrines and obscure their minds by chanting and whirling. I hope to Lat you didn't drink their tea."

I held my tongue.

"And the warriors, look at our warriors." He pointed to me with an open hand. "Our greatest one hides in a village on the edge of nowhere and distracts himself by banging on an anvil. What we need, Kevah, is a reason to fight that eclipses theirs. Never forget that Kostany is holy land to the Crucians." Gray riddled Shah Murad's beard. He tugged at its end, fingers tight. "Your wife Lunara was the kind of warrior we need today."

Just hearing her name stopped time. Talking about Lunara was like bringing her back. "How well did you know her?"

Shah Murad smirked and nodded. "Don't strike me, all right? I would have taken Lunara as a concubine, had I any sense. She was a lioness, and together we could have raised a litter of warrior kings, like Utay and Temur, who crafted this kingdom with blood and iron."

My temper simmered. "You are a king. Why didn't you?"

"Because I saw the way you looked at her, and I saw the way she looked at you, and realized I couldn't rule without my head."

I chuckled. The way he spoke about Lunara vivified her in my mind. What a strange woman, as if Lat made her from the clay of another world. Her hair outshone pure gold, yet she was tan from

22

training under the sun and her small hands roughened from squeezing sword hilts.

A janissary went about the room and relit the candles on the ornate hanging lamps, giving us a bit more light.

"Kevah, she died."

"How can you be certain?"

"Because she looked at you as if you were her prize. As if all the suffering and fighting were for you and the life you would build together. No way she ran from that."

To the Shah, I must've seemed a feeble man forced to hold his tears.

"As I recall," the Shah said, "she went missing mere days after my ascension. We all had too many enemies to count. Someone could have taken her unaware in the night, slit her throat, thrown her body in a pit."

"No—"

"Wake up!" Shah Murad pounded the floor, almost toppling the hookah. "I'd strike you, but I've too much admiration for the man who got me where I am. This sulking will not do, not now, not when so much is at stake. If we don't unite, the Crucians will roll us. That is what I want you to focus on — not some dead woman!"

The Shah could command my body, but not my heart. I didn't want to care. I didn't want to wake up. All I had was a dream of happiness.

"Why did you bring me here, to this abandoned coffeehouse, of all places?"

"Because Ebra controls the Seat. To the court and the janissaries, he's painted me as an impulse-driven fool and himself as the wise and steady hand that steers the ship. That's why he didn't brief you — he wanted you to fail, so I would have no one to rely on but his underlings." The Shah took a moment to breathe. "When Crucis lands fifty thousand paladins on our shore, we'll see who's the fool then."

"If you don't trust Ebra, depose him."

"Everything's so simple for you, isn't it? Metal isn't straight," the Shah pounded the air as if he held a hammer, "so *bang-bang* until it is. If I stripped Ebra of rank and privilege, he would throw off his silks and wrap himself in carded wool, then join the agitators. And if I executed him, his janissary faction would hang my head from the Seat gate and put the crown on my son. He's been outmaneuvering me for years and must be dealt with carefully."

I shuffled on my pillow; my behind ached. What did I care about the power games of the palace? These feuds were why I'd moved so far away. "What do you want from me?"

"I realize you are fat and soft and can't kill the way you could. Truth be told, I asked for the head of the magus to test your loyalty. To fight our enemies, within and without, I need steadfast men — not sycophants. There's a fine line."

Not so fine. A loyal janissary knew the difference between a true tongue and a brown tongue.

"Here's a way to solve your problems," I said. "Let those pungent folks from Balah see their sheikha."

"Oh, Kevah." The Shah crossed his arms and sat back. "Do you think I'm such a fool? I would even free her…if I knew where she was."

I stiffened my posture. There was more to this story. "Is she not imprisoned in Labyrinthos?"

The coals in the hookah had gone cold. Shah Murad puffed, but the smoke he blew out was like gray hair. "Labyrinthos is the end of all. Sooner or later, they succumb to the whispering jinn that climb out the gate to hell. The Fount throws the worst offenders in there, as a punishment worse than death."

The Shah puffed again but exhaled no smoke. He reached inside his silk vest, took out a yellow scarf, and tossed it in my lap. It stunk…of decayed trees and grass. I stretched it out: a Zelthuriyan hex pattern, the kind worn by pilgrims returning from the holy city.

"Other side," the Shah said, twirling his finger.

I turned it around. Words…written with…tar? Indecipherable because I didn't understand Paramic.

"Well?" The Shah peered over it and glared at me. "Don't tell me you can't read it."

"I was never good with foreign tongues."

"Dear Lat, you trained under one of the greatest polymaths alive and you don't know the holy tongue?" The Shah coughed smoke and soot with each laugh. "You're as single-minded as they say. Allow me to translate…"

I drank from the cup.

And now I hear the hymns.

They say: Remake the world.

With the demons on your sword.

A shiver spread through my back and arms, as if I'd been pricked by a jinn. "Poetic…but dark. Let me guess — you found it in Labyrinthos."

The Shah nodded. "Had my bravest janissaries search the entrance. They pulled it from under a rock. One of Grand Magus Agneya's scarves. You love the warrior-poets, don't you? This any verse you know?"

Taqi and the other warrior-poets never used words like "hymn" or spoke of "demons" and "remaking the world." Neither did the saintly recitals. I shook my head. "It sounds more like an Ethosian verse."

"Aye…that was a thought as well. But the Ethosian bishop swears it's not in their books." The Shah crossed his arms, made a fist, and rested his forehead on it. It was his thinking posture, as I recalled. He used to meditate like that for hours. "Kevah, something truly frightful is coming. My bones haven't ached like this since the war of succession. Ten years of peace does not go unpunished. I need true men to see this through. Men that can do more than just obey orders and swing a sword." The Shah stood and brushed soot off his silks. "You're right — you are a free man.

I may jape about feeding you to the birds, but I'm not my brother. Walk out that door if you want no part of this."

I wanted no part. But then why didn't I go? Why wasn't I running back to Tombore? I'd put this man on the throne. I made him, and now his rule was being undermined by enemies within and without. Despite my long absence, I had a daughter that looked up to me and a father that expected much. And what the hell happened to Magus Agneya?

I stood and looked my shah in the eye. "My first memory was as a slave arriving in this land. I'm told that I came from a country far to the north in Yuna, beyond even the Crucian Imperium."

"We all know that. You're fairer than a clean piss." The Shah laughed at his own joke.

I didn't laugh. "I have no ties to any house but yours. My father taught me to be loyal to the Seat and the Seat alone. Know that I don't plan to stay forever, but while I'm here, use me as you see fit."

The Shah pulled the pipe off the hookah and blew the ash out. "Oh, I will."

2

MICAH

It was said the waters of the High Holy Sea flowed through the Archangel and fell upon the world from heaven. It was said that baptism in the water rebirthed a soul, cleansing it of sin and darkness. The priests never said how cold the water was or how it tasted like rust. It was "heavy water" born of angels' blood and should not be ingested, but when being drowned, it was hard not to swallow mouthfuls.

"In the name of Imperator Heraclius — the Breath of the Archangel and Custodian of the High Holy Sea — lift your head," the Ethos priest said. "And be reborn as Micah the Metal."

That was my name now. I was born just Micah, the son of an innkeeper, who I'd watched cough bile as a lord's hireling stabbed him six times in the belly. Why? Because that was the world. And now I was reborn in the name of the Archangel, into the same broken world, but this time I held the knife and aimed only for the deserving.

I didn't even have to lift my head; the priest pulled my hair.

"I baptize you with heavy water and cleanse you of all sins, before the Archangel and the Twelve Holies."

At the lakeshore, my army covered the horizon. Fifty thousand armored paladins watched the rebirth of their grandmaster.

The old priest grabbed my shoulders. "Do you believe in the Archangel and the Twelve he has appointed to guard the believers?"

"I do."

"Do you reject the Fallen Angels and all their temptations?"

"I reject them."

"Will you follow the will of your imperator, no matter where it leads?"

I hesitated, then said, "No matter where."

Once the rite was over, I waded out of the water. Berrin, my second-in-command, handed me a loincloth, and I proceeded to the fire he'd prepared. I plucked a fig from a tree, sat at the fire, and enjoyed some warmth. Ah, how light it was to be a newborn — a blank parchment upon which holy script could be written.

"What's it like to be Micah the Metal?" Berrin asked. He looked like a baby with those fat cheeks. But he was the first of my paladins and wore the black armor of our battalion as if it were molded onto him at birth. The red accents of the breastplate complemented the stray, ruddy hairs of his eyebrows, which now pointed downward in trepidation.

"Before I stepped into that water, my soul was covered in tar. And now, it's sinless, shimmering like a star." I spat a fig seed into the fire. "I don't want it to darken ever again." I raised my hands, palms up. "Berrin, will you help me be a good man?"

"My liege, you're the best of us. That's why you were given this honor."

"No...I am no more deserving than any of you." I pressed my eyes to shut out tears. "When the priest pushed me down, and the water surrounded me, I saw all that my hands had wrought." Another image flashed of Miriam in the windowless room, screaming shrill from birthing pangs, surrounded by hateful one-eyed priests. How could I have left her there? "The things I've done...I should be flung into the deepest pit."

"That heavy water washed it all away. This is your great day, my liege. Don't sully it with melancholy."

Berrin fidgeted and hid his hands behind his back. How unbearably standoffish. Yes, by being consecrated in the High Holy Sea, I was now equal to any lord, even the Imperator. But the last thing I wanted was for my men to think me superior. To see me like the villainous lords that had trodden upon them.

"It's a great day for us all," I said. "Any honor I'm given, I share with each of you. And Berrin...please don't call me 'liege.' I'm not whipping you for wheat."

"As you say, Grandmaster."

"Much better."

I devoured my fig, shrugged off the melancholy, and looked upon my men. They knelt as I passed: my holy swordsman, their longswords pounded from the metals of Mount Damav; my gunners, their matchlocks forged with dark steel melted from the Colossus of Dycondi; my alchemists and sappers, their faces burned and blackened by firebombs. The sailors I'd taken from the isles of Ejaz were not versed in our customs, but they too knelt with their heads high.

I climbed a rock on the shore. What a perfect place and day: pure blue sky, craggy green hills surrounding us, and the High Holy Sea's turquoise water shimmering in the sunlight. I gazed upon my men, proud as ever. Every honor I'd earned was due to their steadfastness, piety, and loyalty. No commander could ask for a braver bunch; so how could I keep these blessings for myself? "At attention, one and all!"

They did as commanded and became a wall of black metal that stretched across the shore.

"The priest asked me three questions. I have three questions for you."

A chill breeze blew through.

"Will you pledge your swords, your guns, and your fire to defend the true faith and all who follow it?"

Fifty thousand men shouted, "Yes, Grandmaster!"

"Will you follow me to the shores of our holy lands to take them back from the infidel?"

"Yes, Grandmaster!"

"Look to your left and your right. Look upon your brothers. Look at the fire of the Archangel burning in their eyes."

My men did as commanded.

"Do you pledge to die before you turn your back on your brothers?"

"Yes, Grandmaster!"

"As I am Micah the Metal, so shall you all be reborn. You are my house, you are my kin, and each of you shall carry my honor." I gazed at the Ethos priests standing beneath an olive tree in the distance. They were not going to like this. "Go, every one of you, and bathe in the waters of the High Holy Sea. Be reborn, warriors of the Faith, one and all!"

Fifty thousand men shed their armor and became naked as pealed pears. While my army swarmed the lake and bathed in its strange waters, I sat by the fire and endured protestations from the Ethos priests:

"They have not been permitted to enter the High Holy Sea!"

"Baptism is only for those chosen by the Imperator!"

"We honored you, and this is how you repay us? Bishop Yohannes will hear of this!"

I hated priests. I hated holy men who claimed to speak for the Archangel. When I wanted to talk to the Archangel, I opened my heart and prayed. I needed no intercessors. But I kept silent and let the priests protest. My fifty thousand could not be stopped.

One man who did not bathe in the water was my engineer, Jauz. Bald and bristled, he was from the Empire of Silk far in the northeast, where the ice melts and turns again into grassland. Though he and his engineers had taken to dressing in the paladin black and red, it seemed as foreign on him as armor on a pig. Jauz spent his nights burning incense and meditating before a jade idol. Because of his knowledge and skill, I tolerated it. At least he was not a worshipper of Lat, the wretched Fallen Angel and temptress.

"Compliments, Grandmaster." Jauz stuck a knife into an apple and plucked out the seeds. Even how they ate fruit was strange. "I share the holy feeling of this day."

"Are you not interested in the heavy water, Jauz?"

"It's just water."

"No, there's something odd about it. It tastes like steel."

"We had a lake like that back home. Dive deep enough, and you'll find an underwater mountain full of iron and copper. You definitely shouldn't drink it."

"If that's true, I wish we could mine it all."

"Our emperor felt the same." Jauz crunched a piece of apple. "He drained the entire lake."

I couldn't imagine the words he'd just said. "You can't drain a lake. Where would the water go?"

"When you have a million men and the knowledge to mold the earth," he tapped on his own head, "you can do anything. The Silk Emperor is, no doubt, the most powerful man alive."

"Good thing the Empire of Silk is so far away."

Jauz tossed the apple pit into a pile of ants. They swarmed it. "Good thing for you I'm not."

Once I'd dressed, Jauz and I traveled by horseback to the docks. By the Archangel, Nixos was a paradise in an emerald sea. Were I a man who sought pleasantry, I'd settle here. But something more beautiful waited offshore: my five hundred ships. They filled the horizon.

"How much more time do you need?" I asked Jauz as we climbed off our horses.

My paladins had donned their work clothes. Some readied their carts to haul wood. Others took measurements of ship dimensions. Burly men heaved planks on their backs like oxen. Even on a holy day of rebirth, my men didn't cease their righteous labors. I had to succeed, for them as much as myself. In the new world we would build, I pledged that each paladin would have his own fief and never endure a lord's whip again. But for that we needed land, and the only land I'd not conquered lay east, defended by the sea walls of the holiest city on earth: Kostany.

Jauz brushed his bald head. "Modifying all the ships will take a moon."

"Too long. The Shah's spies must've sent word that we're massing for an invasion. If we wait a whole moon, he'll have double the men at his walls."

We stopped at one of the ships on the dock. Work had completed on it, but all I noticed was the flatter angle of the hull. Jauz had explained how rebuilding the hull would increase upward pressure. This would allow a ship of a hundred men and thirty cannons to speed through the shallow strait that led to Kostany.

"Your men are not shipbuilders, and work like this takes time," he said. "With the men we have to spare, we can do ten to fifteen ships a day. If you want the ships done faster, then we won't have enough men to make guns and ammunition and armor and artillery and all the other things we need."

"Finish in a fortnight."

Jauz twirled his mustache, as if it were a crank by which he processed his thoughts. Were all engineers from the Silk Empire bald mustachios? "You know, I've studied the sea defenses of Kostany. Even with ships that can travel in shallow water, you won't get through the seven sea walls. The Shrunken Strait is rather narrow. You can only confront each wall with seven or eight ships at a time, and they will endure fire from a few hundred cannons."

"We have five hundred ships and the best sailors in the world.

A shock attack on the sea walls would be unexpected." Though the specifics still had to be drawn up, I had a gut ache the Sirmians would be unprepared. That if we got through the sea walls, we could easily scale the embankments that led to the Seat.

"You'd need a miracle to survive those walls," Jauz said. "The Silk Emperor has a navy of two thousand and engineers more knowledgeable than me. Even he wouldn't succeed. Our best course is to land at Demoskar, march inland, and put Kostany to siege from land."

I'd imagined that scenario. The march from Demoskar to Kostany, dragging artillery, would take days. How many raids would we endure during that march? Though it was Crucian land, stolen by the infidels, we'd forgotten its secrets. The Sirmian horse archers would whittle us down without ever engaging in a real battle. By the time we reached the walls of Kostany, the zeal we'd gained from this holy day would be snuffed out by the realities of war. A siege could take years. To feed my army, we'd have to pillage the villages around the city, many of which still practiced the Ethos faith. That would turn the people against us and swell the Shah's army. A protracted siege was not winnable.

"All five hundred ships should be ready to sail the Shrunken Strait," I said, "in a fortnight."

"Grandmaster, did those holy waters turn one man into two?"

"There are five thriving towns on this island, filled with the best shipbuilders on this side of the world. I will bring them to you."

"How? With all the metal and ships we bought, we have no gold to pay them."

"We won't be paying them."

Jauz grinned, turned his head sideways, and nodded. Did these heathens have to nod strangely, too? "And they say you have a kind soul."

"Who says that?"

"Your men. You know, they would follow you off the edge of the earth."

I shook my head. "We're not going to the edge of the earth." I pointed toward the ship-covered eastern horizon. "We're going to Kostany."

I ordered five legions to the seaside towns to bring back ten thousand shipbuilders by dawn's light. We promised the guilds repayment, but the unwilling leaders wouldn't press their own into my service. And time was too short for deliberation.

As the shipbuilders marched to my ships in chains, I cursed myself as assuredly as they must've cursed me. Dozens had died resisting, preferring death to working without pay. Instead of watching them herded like cattle, I returned to my flagship the Watersteel and begged the Archangel to forgive me for spilling Crucian blood. I'd just been cleansed of my sins and had now amassed many more. The weight of it crushed me, and I could scarcely lift my head off the moldy floorboards of my office. I trembled at the thought of the Archangel's rage for each innocent Ethosian I'd hurt. How could I do this? How could I be like the lords we were trying to escape?

As birds chirped to welcome the morning, ten thousand men — including all the shipbuilding guilds of Nixos — were toiling to modify my ships.

Zosi, the youngest brother of my deceased wife, came to me as I watched the workers from a rocky hill. He'd led one of the five legions that I'd sent to round up the shipbuilders. Though barely a man, he had the valor of a veteran. His soft features betrayed his soft heart, which, from his sulking expression, seemed to be bleeding like mine.

"Is this truly right, brother?" he asked. It seemed he was growing a beard, probably to look older, but his almond-colored hairs were hardly noticeable on such fair skin. "The streets are filled with weeping children and wives praying for their husbands' safe return. Can we bear this sin upon our backs and still expect the Archangel's favor?" He couldn't look in their direction, so heavy was his shame.

I too could scarcely watch. They were believers, and I forced them to labor ceaselessly. The noon sun blazed. It was a windless day, and the toil must have been crushing. The crack of whips striking flesh echoed through the hillside. I myself had suffered at the hands of more powerful men and could only empathize.

"Once Kostany is ours, I will reward them a thousand times over. I will open the vaults of the Shah and rain his treasures upon all who toiled for us."

Zosi nodded and smiled. "I've never known you to be false with your words. But it's not me you'll have to convince." His shoulders tensed up again. "An Ethos knight came to your flagship. You've been summoned."

"By whom?"

"Bishop Yohannes."

Of course. The people of Nixos were his flock, and I'd stolen them. I couldn't refuse a summons from the second-highest bishop of the Ethos Church, so I made my way up the island's second-tallest hill to the cathedral. The white brick structure had two purple spires, and stained-glass windows adorned every wall.

Inside stood a solid gold, towering likeness of the Archangel. Melted down, it could pay for five hundred more ships. Not that I would go that far. Perhaps I could be forgiven for acts against my fellow man, but to act against god himself? There's only so much a man should do against his own soul, though it all be for the greater good.

The Bishop had me wait. That's what pompous men do — waste the time of those they think are beneath them. He had me sitting in the pew for thirty minutes before he showed his gray face.

"Micah the Metal," Bishop Yohannes said. His robe was gray too, as were his whiskers. "Welcome to the Holy Sepulcher of Benth the Apostle." Even his voice lacked color. What was he hiding behind his plainness?

He led me to his office, a small room attached to the cathedral's library. It was devoid of luxuries, with only a plate of figs on a stone desk and a well-stocked bookshelf.

"Have you heard the story of the angel Micah?" he said. "Your namesake."

"Only a thousand times."

"It is said that Micah's wings—"

"Destroyed a star and burned the earth, then covered the sun for a hundred years until the earth froze. It did not warm again until all sinning ceased. While I love the scripture dearly, I didn't come here to hymn with you."

"Your time is precious to you. You want to be somewhere so fast that you can't spare a moment to remember the Holies." The Bishop grabbed a book from a nearby shelf and opened it: Angelsong, the chapter of Micah. "Recite it to me, from the first verse."

I laughed so hard, the spot in my ribs that the Alanyan pirate had slammed with a hammer hurt. "I'm not one of your choir boys. And you're right, my time is precious. Goodbye, Bishop."

Before I could step out, the Bishop said, "Cross that threshold and I'll declare you a heretic."

That wiped off my smile. "You wouldn't dare. Imperator Heraclius sent me here to receive your blessings."

"You may be Imperator Heraclius' favorite pet, but it would take several days for him to hear about my declaration. And in that time, well, what would happen to you?"

"Nothing at all. I have fifty thousand men on this island. How many do you have?"

The Bishop must have stared down dozens of upstarts with his beady eyes and thought I was another. "There are only two who hold a higher position than me in the Ethos Church — the

Patriarch and the Imperator. As holy paladins, your men are devoted to the Archangel. You have willed them to commit acts against their own souls and the souls of fellow Crucians. How many already doubt you? And how many would refuse your orders once I proclaim you a heretic?"

"My men would never take your side."

"We'll see," the Bishop said. "One thing I'm sure of — the work on your fleet will take far longer without the total loyalty of your men."

I walked to his side of the desk. Bishop Yohannes stood and faced me, a filthy grin on his face.

"This is a holy land," he said, "one of the few not defiled by infidels. And you came here and treated it like it was yours, and not the Archangel's. You will answer for your crimes."

I refused to blink and stared him down. "I've sent more men to hell than there are on your placid little island. Choose your words carefully, Bishop."

"You are valued by Heraclius and thus beyond reproach." He stopped grinning and looked away, his tone losing its sharpness. "But your soldiers are not. I must show my flock that I can administer the angels' justice to those who have wronged them. I want the five commanders of the five legions you sent to our towns. They will face justice in your place."

"You will never sit in judgment over my men. They will die on the battlefield, not in your noose."

The Bishop closed the book of hymns and dusted it. "Well said. A true commander never forsakes his men." He cleared his throat. "But true men forsake their commanders all the time. Loyalty is easy when you're winning, but you cannot win against the Church. I will give you a recourse…"

I sat again and grabbed a fig. Rolled it in my hand. "Go on."

"You've just returned from the isles of Ejaz, where they worship the accursed Lat."

"Indeed. We sent many infidels to hell to be with her."

37

"Ah, and you also took many infidels prisoner, didn't you?"

He was referring to my shipmen, the Ejazi sailors. They stuck out with their eastern dress and manner, so of course the Bishop took notice.

"The Ejazi are the best sailors in the world," I said. "Still, I executed thousands I'd captured. The two hundred I spared proclaimed their faith in the Archangel and now are our brothers. You can't have them."

The Bishop fingered the spine of the book. "I'm not talking about the sailors. I'm talking about your *other* prisoner."

He couldn't mean…I'd been careful to hide her from everyone other than my closest lieutenants. Though the Ejazi knew…but still…

I swallowed my dread and disappointment. "What other prisoner?" How bitter to think I'd been betrayed. Not just me, but every paladin who dreamed of freeing Kostany, who dreamed of being free.

The Bishop's smile was so smug, I would have bashed it off his face were he not a holy man. "You thought I wouldn't find out? To climb high in the Church, one must know where the limits of loyalty lie."

"Who told you?"

"Just a lowly Ejazi — his limit was his large toe. I barely got a squeal from the small one."

A righteous fire flared through me. "There's nothing softer than the heart of a new believer. Are you so cruel?"

"Oh Micah, men don't forsake their gods so easily. He screamed out for Lat when my inquisitor brought the knife to his throat." The Bishop's chuckle was as dirty as his grin. "Now give me the prisoner, and you and I will be as one." He clasped his hands. "Of and for the Ethos."

. . .

I DIDN'T GIVE Bishop Yohannes an answer. He gave me one night. I had to know if this prisoner was of use or better on the Bishop's pyre.

We kept the prisoner on my flagship, the Watersteel. I'd seized it from Alanyan pirates. Unlike Crucian galleons, it had a second deeper hold, which could only be accessed by a trap door and was meant for hiding gold from tax collectors. That's where I kept the prisoner.

Save for my lantern, it was utterly dark. The mold-stench was stronger here than anywhere on the ship. The prisoner sat in the corner, chained by the ankle to an iron ball. She looked at me with eyes as green as the water surrounding the ship. Her face showed no fear, anger, or sadness, only an utter calm.

"How've you been passing the time?" I asked from across the room.

"In truth."

Strange answer, perhaps she didn't know our language well.

"I could make things better for you. A lot better. Would you like that?"

She stared in silence.

"Here's my proposal," I said. "Renounce your false goddess, proclaim faith in the Archangel, and join my crew. You'd be the only girl, but I'll guarantee your safety and honor. The alternative is much worse. I give you to the Bishop and he burns you."

"I will not renounce my goddess."

"I am pledged to destroy her faith, as she is the enemy of my angel. You can't worship Lat in my crew."

I held up my lantern to see her better. There wasn't a wrinkle on her face or a hair that wasn't lustrous. She couldn't be any older than eighteen — too innocent to be what the Ejazi insisted. I'd fallen for a few girls like her in my hometown, forever ago. The baker's daughter. The butcher's niece. The moneylender's suspiciously young wife. They weren't stunners — a bit pasty and narrow — but plenty for an innkeeper's son.

39

"Understand this," I said. "I will burn your shrines. Any who refuse the true faith, I will put to the sword."

"Yes, you will do all that and more." Her broad eyes stared straight ahead, as if looking at an invisible man behind me.

"We're enemies unless you change your faith."

"We are not enemies, who serve the Dreamer."

Another language fumble? But she seemed to speak Crucian well enough.

"The Bishop will be pleased to have you," I said. "Burning witches is his special joy."

I grabbed the metal rung of the ladder.

"The seven sea walls of Kostany have never been breached in the history of the world. How will you cross with a thousand cannons raining death upon you?" Now it was obvious she spoke our language better than most foreigners. "Below Kostany, there are tunnels. I know the way through."

"Tunnels? What tunnels?"

"Labyrinthos."

"Impossible," I scoffed. "Labyrinthos is the gate to hell. There's no way through."

She stood and walked toward me until her body recoiled from the weight of the iron ball. "Where did you find me?"

"In the titan mines of Ejaz," I said. "You just appeared, as if a ghost."

"Do you know where I was a day before?"

She pushed closer. The iron ball gave way. She lifted her legs and pulled it, as if it was air. I stopped myself from gaping in awe.

And then I could smell her breath. Like mint and ice and honey. She'd been locked in this dungeon for days and had little water for bathing. How did she smell so tempting?

"I was in Kostany, six hundred miles away," she said. "In Labyrinthos."

I sniggered. "I ought to spank you for fibbing like that."

40

"I can lead you through the tunnels in hours. You'd appear beneath the Sublime Seat while the Shah and his armies sleep. You'll butcher them and capture the sea walls. Once you sail your ships through the Shrunken Strait, Kostany will be yours."

The Crucian flag flying over the city. Divine hymns bursting from our holiest chapel. It sounded too good to be true. But her words made the image of conquering Kostany so real.

"There is a cost," she said. "One that heavy water cannot cleanse. Those who enter Labyrinthos don't leave quite the same. Ahriyya touches them."

Ahriyya was another false god, believed by Lat worshippers to be the embodiment of evil. As if sin wasn't bad enough. As if you needed something evil to embody it. Yes, the Fallen Angels were evil too, but their sins were their own.

I laughed in her face. "Here's how I know that my religion is true and yours false. You people take slaves. You believe a man can be owned. If anything is evil, it's enslavement. It's the sins we commit against each other that are evil, not some dark god who rules over hell."

I swear she smirked, but it was so slight I might have imagined it. "And what is it you're doing? How many men toil to modify your ships without a speck of silver?"

I winced in surprise. "Who told you about that?"

"I know a great many things, just as I know you're not as unyielding as you pretend."

"I am a man of faith. The first thing I'll do when I sack Kostany is bring all its gold and silver back to this island to pay everyone who even so much as lifted a plank for me. And to the widows of those who fell in the heat, I'll give a shipload of the Shah's precious jewels."

"You'll have to conquer Kostany first. You won't without me."

The girl walked away, pulled the iron ball across the room as if it weighed nothing, and sat in the corner.

· · ·

41

TWO CHOICES LAY before me that night: give the Bishop the witch or my five lieutenants. I stayed huddled in the nook where I slept, in the office onboard my flagship, and covered my head with a sheet to drown out the world around me. I begged for guidance and deliverance from the one who heard all prayers. How could I ever entertain giving up my men? And yet, the girl's promise of Kostany lingered in my heart. She had shown me a sign of her power by moving the iron ball, and I could not hand over such a promise to the Bishop and his inquisitors. By dawn, I was writhing on the floor, still covered in a sheet and crying for the Archangel's forgiveness, because I knew what I had to do.

I called the five lieutenants who'd overseen the conscription of the workers to my office. I explained how the Bishop wanted them to face justice in my place but omitted mention of his offer to hand over the witch.

"We're ready to die for you," Berrin said at the head of the five. "Don't hesitate because of your love for us. We know it's the same love the Archangel has for mankind."

I could only say, "I'm sorry."

"Don't be sorry, brother," said cleareyed Zosi. The thought of him swinging at the noose made me tremble. "We've all just been baptized in waters that cleansed our sins. We'll die with so few, and perhaps our books of good deeds will be weightier than our books of sin."

"May the Archangel put all your sins in my book," I said. "Let me carry them, as you have carried our holy cause."

Orwo, my chief alchemist and sapper, put his burnt hand on my shoulder. "I don't want to die. I've too many recipes to try. But I'd be honored to see the angels with this bunch." The man had no eyebrows, yet his raw face was more beloved to me than that of the fairest maiden.

Edmar, who had as many scars as he had hairs, nodded in agreement. "You can name a bridge after me in Kostany. Nah, make it a bombard. The biggest bombard." Each scar on his face was holier than a sacred hymn, for they were rent in service to the Archangel.

Only Aicard remained silent. Not just silent, but dismissive. He tugged at his blond goatee, a vain fashion that I hated. My chief spy changed his facial hair every week, and it seemed he was pondering what to grow next, as if he knew he would live.

"I will pray with my last words for your victory in Kostany." Berrin smashed his fist on my desk, almost crushing my brass compass. "Crush the Shah beneath your boot and tell him my name!"

Just thinking about what the Bishop would do to him turned my blood to fire. I could not accept it. I was Micah the Metal — reborn in the heavy water of the High Holy Sea, servant of the Archangel and the Twelve Holies, conqueror of Pasgard, Sargosa, Pendurum, Dycondi, and Ejaz. In a decade of blood, I'd tripled the size of the Imperium. What had Bishop Yohannes achieved to presume authority over me?

I unsheathed my sword, threw it on the table, and looked into the unyielding eyes of my five loyal lieutenants. Men so brave that death was but a trifle. Nay, men so faithful they welcomed death.

"Today, it begins," I said, "our war for a pure place, outside the grip of rotten priests and cruel lords. A land ruled by the Archangel and only for those faithful in word and heart." I grabbed my sword and raised it in the air. "Onward!"

THE SIX OF us killed or maimed every Ethos knight guarding the Holy Sepulcher of Benth the Apostle, though Edmar did most of it. His throwing knives always found flesh, whether the underarm gap in the plate or the back of the knee. I was a big man with a big sword, so cutting down the knights was like rending armored children — not that I'd ever done such a thing.

Bishop Yohannes was counting tithes in his office when I burst in. I dragged him by the hair out of the cathedral, bound him with rope, and pulled him up the tallest hill. He'd built a pyre there — of all ways to deal death, burning was the most painful. Did he presume I'd give him the witch and so prepared a pyre? Or was he going to torch my men?

Either way, his fate was decided.

"You are lost, Micah the Metal," he said as I tied him to the pyre. "I speak for the Archangel. Have you no sense?"

"Then seek his forgiveness. You're about to be judged."

Paladins gathered. My five lieutenants stayed close. Baby-faced Berrin, soft Zosi, Orwo, Edmar, unflinching Aicard — I would never again think to forsake them.

But there was another that I didn't expect. My prisoner — the witch.

"Who freed you?" I asked as she strolled toward me, her expression plain as the clear sky.

She removed her yellow headscarf. Her pupils reflected sunshine as emeralds would.

The Bishop's eyes bulged when he saw her. "This is the cursed woman! This is whom you are willing to kill for, Micah? Do you not know who she is? Do you not know what she is?"

"Whatever she is, she's mine."

"She's a magus!" the Bishop shouted. "A sorceress with powers you cannot comprehend! You must kill her before she brings ruin to us all!"

Berrin whispered in my ear, "Grandmaster, this man is a bishop, consecrated in the name of the Archangel by both the Patriarch and Imperator Heraclius. He baptized the Imperator's sons in the High Holy Sea with his own hands. Are you sure you want to do this?"

A good argument. Though I desired to see Bishop Yohannes burn and was furious toward his cruelty, he was still an Ethosian. I tempered my fury with mercy, as all good Ethosians should.

"I'll give you a chance to save yourself, Bishop," I said. "If you're truly a believer, then answer me — in the story of Micah the angel, when he covers the sun with his wings, why does he let the righteous freeze along with the sinners?"

The Bishop spat in my face. "I will not debate theology with you, nor will I be judged by you!"

I wiped the slime off my eyebrow. "Because we're all sinners." I grabbed the flint from Berrin. "We all deserve a painful death. Ice cleansed the believers of sin in the time of the angel Micah. Now fire will cleanse yours."

"You are a curse upon this land." The Bishop began his final lamentations. "Imperator Heraclius will excommunicate you. He will declare you an enemy of the Faith, and all that you've done will be for naught!"

I struck the flint. It took a few tries to create fire with this wind.

"You're right, Heraclius probably will," I said. "I've committed grievous sins and will continue to. But all will be forgiven."

The Bishop laughed for the last time. "How can you be so filled to the brim with hubris!? The Imperator will never forgive this! The Archangel will cast you into the deepest hell!"

I lit the pyre. Fire crackled up the wood. "I will be forgiven because I will give Imperator Heraclius what he wants the most. What he has wanted since he ascended the throne. I will give every Ethosian what they yearn for with raging hearts."

The Bishop bleated like a dying goat as fire charred his feet. The stench of burnt flesh assaulted my nose.

"For the Archangel and all his worshippers," I said, "I will cleanse the holiest land upon this earth. I will open Kostany. I will defeat the unbelievers and take the east back for the Ethos."

I hoped the Bishop's screams were heard through the island. I enjoyed each one. When it was over, I turned to the witch, who'd been watching without emotion.

"Who freed you?" I asked again.

"I was a prisoner because I wanted to be," she said, her ashen hair messy in the breeze. "Now I'm free because I want to be."

She gazed upon the Bishop's charred remains. Her blemish-free, almost child-like face betrayed no feeling. Was death even a curiosity to her? More importantly, was it a curiosity to me?

I stared at my hands. What the hell had I done?

"He's only the first," the girl said.

"The first of what?"

She whispered in my ear, "The first of many you'll kill for me."

What a strange thing to say. No matter how pretty, a girl was not worth killing for, though she wasn't just another girl from town.

My men began marching down the hill — silent, as if in mourning. Most of them admired priests, so they'd be shaken. I'd have to work hard to reaffirm the justice of our purpose.

The witch looked upon Nixos, her eyes shimmering like its emerald waters.

"You haven't even told me your name."

She came close and said, "You can call me Aschere." And then she walked away.

3

KEVAH

CHARRED BODIES AND ASH LITTERED THE STONE CHAPEL, WHICH WAS once home to an Ethosian apostle. Blood-fat flies buzzed above the pews as janissaries pulled the cooked men out on litters. I coughed into a handkerchief; roasted human flesh overwhelmed even veterans. I stepped outside, amid the sultry sun and smoky air on the narrow, brick-lined street of Kostany's ancient Ethosian quarter. According to their scripture, angels had descended and hymned at this site almost a thousand years ago. But I couldn't imagine an angel looking upon the death that covered it today.

In response to this sudden massacre of Ethosian pilgrims, the Shah convened a council in the great hall. Grand Vizier Ebra sat to the left of the Shah, and other viziers gathered around alongside the local Ethosian bishop. We sat on the floor — excepting the Shah, who sat high upon his golden divan. A few of the Shah's older children also sat with us, looking pretty. But the man who stole everyone's attention was Grand Mufti Taymah, the leader of the Fount of Sublime Scholars. Being seated to the right of the Shah was an honor only for him. And of all present who were not Shah Murad, he was the only one who possessed official power. If the Shah wished to execute anyone from the royal Seluqal House, for any reason, he needed permission from the Grand Mufti.

I'd watched ten years ago when the Shah cut off his own brother's head at the Blue Domes, the highest point in Kostany. Selim, the secret heir to the throne, died with a smile. He'd lost the war of succession — mostly because I slew the magus keeping Murad's cohort from the capital. Once Grand Mufti Taymah proclaimed Selim guilty of tyranny, the Shah's broadsword did the rest.

Mufti Taymah was not so different today from then. He wore a white caftan and a cream-colored pantaloon. His thick yet trim brown beard and golden spectacles portrayed a scholarly man, whose esteem was the essence of his power. He was the kind of man I'd feared in my youth; his judging eyes could pierce through you like a spear through a flour sack.

The local Ethosian bishop, who had burns and bandages up his neck and cheek, was recounting what happened with a quavering. "Soon, fire erupted around the altar. When we tried to escape through the back hallway, there he was…a man covered in flames. At first, I thought he was suffering, and so rushed to help him. But the way he walked…with such ease…he raised up his hand and fire engulfed the hallway too. I had inhaled too much smoke and collapsed. That's the last thing I remember before waking up in the hospital."

The other witnesses had reported seeing the same burning man. All were Ethosians, and I'd never met an Ethosian who wasn't given to flights of fancy, especially when it came to faith, war, and death.

"Let me make plain," Mufti Taymah said, "it is not permitted in our religion to kill anyone — whether a believer in Lat, a believer in the Archangel, or a believer in an idol made of mud — without due course." He spoke with the fluidity of a gushing stream. "Whoever has done this has profaned the saintly recitals and must face justice."

No one wanted to say it. We looked at each other like school children afraid to name their tormentor.

"The witnesses were clear in their descriptions." Ebra gulped. Sweaty eyebrows showed the fear in him. "'A man covered in flames.' A sorcerer did this."

"A magus!" The Shah slammed his side table, rattling gold goblets and fruit plates.

Was I wrong about Magus Vaya? He didn't seem bloodthirsty and was more interested in serving strange teas.

"Half the city worships the Archangel!" It seemed the Shah wanted to draw his sword and lop someone's head onto the floor. "When fifty thousand Crucian paladins put Kostany to siege, this is perfect reason for Ethosians to rally to them!"

"The only recourse is to bring the responsible to justice," the Grand Mufti said, "and show those who worship the Archangel that we will protect them as we would our own. Summon Magus Vaya to answer."

"Kevah, go now," the Shah said. "Tell the magus to present himself no later than tomorrow, or I will brand him an enemy of Lat and a traitor."

My only thought was *fuck*. History was littered with headless messengers. "Would it be wise to antagonize him, my Shah?"

"Ebra, assemble a hundred of the best janissaries," the Shah said, ignoring me. "Once Magus Vaya enters the Sublime Seat, he will not be leaving until the Mufti passes judgment."

"And what makes you think he'll obey?" I had to press the matter, lest we suffer the fate of those Ethosian pilgrims. "If he can wield fire, could a hundred janissaries contain him?"

Stunned silence. But I knew it was on everyone's mind.

The Grand Mufti's smile was like that of an old friend. "You were the first man to kill a magus since Temur the Wrathful. Wouldn't you be an expert in the matter?"

I often wondered if I'd really killed that magus. We were fighting amid the hailstorm he'd conjured, and then he looked to the sky, eyes wide with wonder, as if an angel had appeared on the horizon the way it supposedly had in that burnt and flesh-soaked chapel. The distracted magus didn't flinch as my sword sliced his neck.

I was hungry for glory in my youth. There was no better trophy than a magus' wooden mask, which was the source of their powers, though it turned invisible when they put it on.

"A magus is flesh and blood," I said. "Take his head off, it doesn't grow back. But doing that is another matter entirely. And truthfully, I don't know how I managed to."

"Regardless, laws must be followed and justice carried out." The Mufti peered down at me through his golden spectacles. "The magi have laws too. They pledged to protect the Faith of Lat. Sometimes, a stray magus misinterprets this pledge. To them, defending the Latian faith could mean killing those who follow different religions or even killing rival claimants to the throne — as happened ten years ago."

"Ah, don't we love to remember my sweet, wonderful brother." The Shah sat back in his divan. "Magus Vaya and his ilk wanted my brother on the throne. He's always been a weed in my garden." He sighed and groaned. "We shouldn't have spared him the fate of his master. It was a mistake...one you advised me to make, Ebra!"

Ebra winced as if his tutor slapped him. "Apologies, Your Glory." He bent his neck. "As always, you should follow your own wisdom. It is a thousand leagues deeper than mine." It seemed he knew how to placate.

"Then what fucking good are you!?" The Shah rose, kicked his golden divan, and stormed toward the verandah. Then he turned and shouted, "Fix this! Fix this fucking mess, all of you who claim to serve the Shah! Because if you don't, I will show those who bow to the Archangel the Shah's justice — by holding you all responsible for those the magus killed!"

ANOTHER MISERABLE CARRIAGE ride to Balah awaited. I borrowed a sword from the janissary armory and was tempted to grab a matchlock, but couldn't forget how I'd almost blown off my fingers the first time I tried one. *"In the Silklands, they don't even use swords anymore!"* Tengis would say. I guess I would never have become a famed warrior in the Silklands. I should've moved there.

Today, my carriage resembled a miniature palace on wheels. At least I would be comfortable, riding to my death. Janissaries on horseback would guard me on the journey. How awkward, to be the guarded rather than the guard. I opened the door and plopped in. Someone was sitting there, in ambush.

"Melodi? What in Lat's name are you doing here?"

She wore chainmail over a yellow caftan and rose-colored pantaloon — colorful enough to be a janissary. A sword and dagger hung from her belt. She was more prepared than me.

"You're slow and fat and can't protect yourself," she said. "I'm going with you."

"No, you're not. I may not come back from where I'm going."

"I'll make sure you come back."

"Get out, Melodi." I pushed open the carriage door. "How'd you even hear of this?"

"Some of the slaves Grandpa trained grew up to be palace guards. I have friends in high places."

"Tengis will boil my liver in a bath of virgin blood if I take you."

Melodi shut the carriage door. "I'm not getting out. You're my responsibility."

"By Lat, you're fifteen!" I opened it again. "Get out or we're not going."

"What were you doing at fifteen?" She closed it and scowled.

At fifteen I was a palace guard and had already washed blood off my spear. Though it was a horse's blood — I stabbed the beast and it flung the bandit off. He crashed head-first into a ditch and broke his neck.

I opened the door again. "There's no way I'm taking you to what could be a bloodbath."

She closed it. "If you die, I won't forgive myself."

"You won't forgive yourself? How do you think I'll feel if you die?" I kicked the door open and pointed outside.

"You won't feel anything because you'll probably die first." Melodi pouted, slid off the seat, and got out.

I slammed the door and yelled, "Get me to Balah!" The driver whipped the horses and I was off.

I AWOKE from a bumpy nap to a mob outside my carriage. Those sweaty fanatics from Balah were blocking the road. Flanked by the stony Zari Zar Mountains, there was nowhere to run. I slapped myself alert and jumped out of my carriage to parley.

Magus Vaya stood at the head of the mob — never smiling, never frowning, never an emotion on his forever-young face. The air here was dry enough to catch fire — which is what I feared.

"Thank you for saving me the trip," I said. "I wasn't looking forward to climbing the steep slopes of Balah."

Five janissaries stood with me and four remained on horseback. Surely one janissary could kill ten of this mob, but the magus could kill us all.

"You've come to take me to the Shah," the magus said.

"That I have." I fake-laughed. "You've even saved me breaths, thank you." To say I was nervous would've belied the tremors in my bones.

"As a faithful servant," Vaya said, "I've come to answer the Shah's call for justice."

I hadn't realized I was gripping my sword until I let go. "How'd you know he called for you?"

"When I heard of the awful massacre, I knew the Shah would blame me. May I ride with you?"

I couldn't refuse. I assumed Vaya wanted to talk on the ride, but he spent most of it in prayer. His prayer beads *clack-clacked* worse than the uneven road. He didn't reek of weeks old sweat, like his followers. Didn't have a smell, in fact.

"After the war of succession, I took an oath to obey Shah Murad," he finally said as we rode along the cobbled Kostany streets. A rider had gone ahead to inform the Shah we were coming. Not long now for the palace. "We magi are bound by our oaths, even if our followers are not. I'll admit, I turned a blind eye to the ransacking, so long as no one was being killed. But I would never break my oath and murder people in the streets."

"Oaths. Every janissary takes one. Hasn't stopped them from rebelling."

"I was in Balah when the tragedy occurred. A hundred and one witnesses will testify to that."

"All who, conveniently, follow you."

"A hundred men would not tell the same lie." Vaya peered into me, as if reading my soul. "I can feel your hesitation...and fear. But behind even that, I sense a sadness that drinks deep."

"I'm not as good as you at hiding emotions."

"I would never harm you. I've seen your *ruh*, your true nature. You are good."

"Good or not, fire scorches everyone."

The unaging magus looked at me with trying eyes. "Do you know what I fear? I fear Lat. I fear her wrath, the day her mercy runs out the way a spring dries in the desert sand."

"We all do."

"And I fear Labyrinthos." Was the magus trembling? "Labyrinthos is the end of all. Faith does not survive the touch of Ahriyya. Will the Shah send me there if I'm proclaimed guilty?"

I hunched my shoulders. "Maybe. But if you're so afraid of his judgment, why not run?"

"And leave my followers at the mercy of the janissaries?"

The *clop-clop* of the carriage horses stopped. We'd arrived at the Sublime Seat.

Vaya asked, "Do you believe that I'm innocent?"

"What I believe won't save you."

"It may save us all." The magus grabbed my hand. "Something terrible has happened to Sheikha Agneya. I saw her in a vision, marching through icy tunnels to the tune of a maddening song. I won't follow her into those depths." He tightened his grip. "You've known the Shah a long time. Help me...or you'll all have to help yourselves."

Unsure of what to do and terrified by the threat, I could only nod.

The janissaries surrounding our carriage left a path for the magus and me to walk into the Seat. Inside, a crowd of courtiers and viziers jostled for standing position at the back of the great hall, instead of the front. Did the Shah want the whole kingdom to burn with him? As we waded through and brushed against their silks, they made way.

Above, the gold Seluqal peacock gazed upon all with its piercing ruby eyes. Incense burners spread an amber wood aroma through the room. A line of janissaries, their matchlocks drawn and aimed, separated the Shah and his entourage from the rest of us. The Shah sat forward upon his golden divan, with Grand Vizier Ebra to the left and Grand Mufti Taymah to the right.

Once we reached the front of the crowd, Magus Vaya bent his neck, as did I.

"I have brought whom you asked, Your Glory," I said.

"I sent you to deliver a message," the Shah said, "not to bring me a magus."

"You're right. Forgive me if I presumed to do too much."

Shah Murad laughed while slapping his leg. His father would laugh the same way. The courtiers and viziers imitated, and it became a room of laughter. Then the Shah shouted, "Silence!" and it became a room of silence. "Gaze upon this man!" the Shah boomed. "Kevah the Blacksmith, once a slave from Ruthenia, who killed a magus, and with only forty men — and one exceptional woman — defended the Valley of Saints from my brother, who had four hundred. Gaze upon him, all who claim to serve me!"

I rubbed my face and smoothed my shirt. Were my pants pulled up? Did my belly bulge? I hadn't even washed the crusts from my eyes.

"Gaze at him, long and hard," the Shah said. "This is a man you all would do well to imitate. I sent him to deliver a message, and he brought me a magus. This is service!" The Shah clapped, so everyone clapped.

I smiled and bent my neck. "You honor me, Your Glory."

"Aye, I do. Now stand aside."

I waded through the crowd and stood among the janissaries guarding the exit. I figured I could escape first, should things turn sour. All eyes were on Magus Vaya's bowed head. A foreboding swept through the room.

"Raise your head, magus," the Shah said. He sat so forward in his seat I feared he'd fall off.

Vaya did as commanded. Silence seized the great hall as the trial began.

Ebra stepped forward and unrolled a scroll. He cleared his throat. "In the name of Shah Murad, the Glorious Star, Shah of Shahs, Khagan of Khagans, Shadow of Lat and Her Vice-Regent upon the Earth, Sword of the Faith and Shah of Sirm, you, Magus Vaya, are hereby charged with the crime of waging war against Lat, committing acts of violence against the people, and showing enmity to the Seat." He cleared his throat again. It sounded drier than a rat dying of thirst in the desert. "What do you say to these charges?"

"They are all quite vague," Vaya said. "But I know what they refer to, and I can only say the truth. I could not have done what you claim."

Ebra whispered to a young, beardless courtier who handed him a different scroll.

"Then let's establish the facts," Ebra said. "When were you born, Magus Vaya?"

"I was born on the third day of the Pilgrimage month, during the fifth year of the reign of Shah Bayzid."

"So you're...seventy-three years old," Ebra said.

"Seventy-seven," Vaya corrected.

The crowd stirred. It didn't surprise me. The magus I killed had looked young too, but the moment his head flew, and the invisible mask that covered his face fell, wrinkles and gray skin revealed his true age.

Ebra continued, "And how old were you when Shah Bayzid sent you to Holy Zelthuriya to learn the magi way?"

Honestly, by now I was leaning against an ornate pillar. With the summer heat lulling me, I paid little attention for the next half hour as Ebra went through Vaya's life, training, and service. I gleaned that he'd fought against the Crucians, helping push them out of the continent of Lidya, though he had never stepped foot on the continent of Yuna — just across the Shrunken Strait. The magus reiterated that he was forbidden from fighting other Latians and so refused to participate when Shah Jalal, who was Shah Murad's father, called for the conquest of Alanyan lands.

I perked up when Ebra asked Vaya about the war of succession ten years ago.

"You supported the Shah's brother, Selim. Why?"

"Because Shah Jalal named Selim as his secret heir. Selim took the throne and the janissaries and army pledged fealty to him.

Grand Magus Agneya decided that, for the sake of unity, we would 'go with the wind.'"

"You paint a very one-sided picture of the succession," Grand Mufti Taymah interjected, the first time he'd spoken at this trial. He adjusted his golden spectacles off his nose and up onto discerning eyes. "The Fount did not back Selim. The people, especially, did not back Selim. We all knew well his cruelty."

"What can I say?" Vaya said. "We were wrong. A magus died because of it. When the wind blew the other way, we retreated to Balah until the conflict was over. But Magus Agneya was found guilty of treason...by you, Mufti Taymah."

"And I do not regret that judgment."

"But who will defend this city, if we magi are lost in Labyrinthos?"

The crowd stirred.

"Quiet!" the Shah commanded. "Go on, magus. Make your case."

"A magus hasn't been trained in Zelthuriya for thirty years. Unless you can pull Magus Agneya out of the depths of Labyrinthos, I am the last one in this country. Consider who will defend the border we share with Crucis — an empire that has tripled in size during your reign, while we haven't expanded an inch."

Stunned silence. Even the birds on the roof must've gaped their beaks at Vaya's open criticism of the Shah. It was the first thing I'd enjoyed all day.

"You're not wrong," the Shah said. "I will not hold those words against you, and I will not blame you for the rest of my days for supporting my brother. But I cannot accept bloodshed in my streets. We all heard the witnesses speak of a 'man covered in flames.' You are the last magus in our country. Could it be any other?"

"I was in Balah when this tragedy occurred," Vaya said. "A hundred from the shrine are waiting outside the Seat. Each will attest to this fact. They are true believers, who night and day struggle to rid themselves of pride, avarice, and anger. They would never tell a lie to save me."

While I doubted a hundred fools could tell the same lie, I had little doubt they would try. I'd never known fanatics to weigh the means more than the ends.

The Shah, Ebra, and Mufti Taymah conferred. Magus Vaya looked around, studying the crowd. He paused when his gaze met mine. Was that fear in his eyes?

"I have come to a decision," the Shah said. "I hereby ask my appointed judge, Grand Mufti Taymah of the Fount, to relinquish judgment to me."

Mufti Taymah bowed his head. "You are the source of all earthly judgment. I could never refuse."

The Shah stood. Janissaries around the room raised their heads at attention. The crowd seemed to be bating their breaths. Vaya had said he wouldn't go quietly into Labyrinthos. But he didn't seem a vicious man; though the first time I'd met Selim the Cruel, he stuck a portion of halwa in my mouth and slapped my back as if we were bosom friends. And then he went on to slay hundreds.

"I don't care if you burned those Ethosians or a few houses of vice," the Shah said. "Days away on the isle of Nixos, a Crucian armada of five hundred ships and fifty thousand men waits for us to be at each other's throats so they can sack our cities and force us to bow to the Archangel. They are led by the conqueror Micah, who, my spies tell me, has been baptized in the High Holy Sea and consecrated as Micah the Metal. He has expanded the realm of Imperator Heraclius north, west, and south. The only way left is east. Tell me, Magus Vaya, do you pledge with your eternal soul to fight him?"

For some reason, Vaya turned to look at me, his face as placid as ever. I raised my eyebrows and held up my hands in surprise.

What kind of trick was this? Or was this the Shah's intention all along?

Vaya gazed up at the Shah and bent his neck. "Of course, my Shah. I am alive only for that purpose."

The Shah stepped off his dais. Face to face with Magus Vaya, he held out his hand. The magus stared at it, then looked back at me again. What did he hope to glean from my shocked face? I nodded as rapidly as I could to express my approval. Finally, Vaya took the Shah's hand. They raised their clasped hands above their heads.

I joined in the cheering and clapping of the crowd. This was better than burning, for sure, and I think everyone felt the same. Nothing united like a common enemy.

"From this day forward," the Shah said, "all magi are free in the Kingdom of Sirm. I decree a holy army be raised, led by Magus Vaya, for the purpose of defending the one true faith from Crucian invaders." The Shah's eyes met mine. "There he is! Kevah! Come here!"

I joined the Shah and the magus just below the dais.

"Kevah, you will be first among them."

I bowed my head. Being a commander didn't sound bad. "As you like, Your Glory."

More cheers.

The three of us walked to the gate of the Sublime Seat, where Vaya's followers waited. For the first time, they would see their magus' and their shah's hands clasped in unity. They cheered and sang praises to Lat and chanted "Glorious Star" in praise of the Shah. In an instant, he transformed a rabble that had mistrusted him into an army of his own. It seemed the Shah was as shrewd as any.

As for the mourners: the bishop and worshippers of the Archangel — even if the Shah had avenged them, would they support him over an army of their brethren? Were I a calculating man, I'd think not. But I wasn't a calculating man, and as the cheers climbed in intensity, I couldn't help feeling for those who'd burned and suffered.

I STARED at the barely familiar ceiling of Tengis' guest room, moonlight and a breeze streaming through the open window. I turned on my side and imagined Lunara holding me at her bosom. She smelled like home. The warmth of her body flowed into me as she hummed a poem by Taqi:

Lovers find secret places,
Inside this painful world,
Where they make a deal,
With the lord of time.

I hoped to dream of her. I hoped the world would disappear, and that I'd wake from this nightmare, and she'd be tossing eggs by the fire as I pounded my anvil and smiled at the sight of her. Then someone burst into my room and jolted me from my fantasy.

"Sorry!" There Melodi stood in a dress patterned with lilies. "You sleep earlier than the birds."

"I've had a long day." I sat up on my mattress.

"I heard. You're a holy warrior now."

"I don't think I'll be doing much fighting. There's no shortage of young men for that."

"And young women." Melodi sat at the base of my mattress and smirked.

"Oh no, Melodi, you can't be in our army."

"Why not?"

"You know why. You're too young, and your grandfather will invent a new way to snap my spine."

Melodi pouted. "Temur swept through Lidya with an army of a million at my age."

"You'd compare yourself to the greatest conqueror known?"

"When the Crucians come, you think I'll run and hide? I trained to be a janissary, like Lunara. It'd be treason not to fight."

She spoke truly. The Crucians were coming. Who knew how they would attack, what weapons they would use, what subterfuge they'd planned? If it came to life or death, no one could stop Melodi from using her training, and I'd rather she be fighting under my nose.

"I'll think about it."

"That's all I want." She kissed my forehead and left. It was good to have a daughter again. How vast was her forgiveness that, despite my ten-year absence, she could be so kind? At some point, the sadness of absence turns into anger, and anger to bitterness. And yet, aside from her welcoming slap, my daughter had only shown me tender care.

I tossed and turned, anxious by thoughts of facing a siege. I wanted to grab Melodi and ride to Tombore or an even more distant land. If only it were that simple.

I went to the pantry for coffee. Tengis was sitting at his floor table, reading a scroll an inch from his face and already drinking some. He poured me a cup.

"What are you doing with all these books and scrolls and astrolabes?" I asked.

"Measuring moon phases. Nothing your dull mind would understand."

"Try me, old man."

Tengis sighed as if already bored with my feigned interest. "There's going to be an eclipse in the next few months. I'm trying to figure out when."

"Whatever keeps you from death's shore, I'm all for." I sipped coffee. So much for sleeping. "Speaking of dying, you know what your granddaughter wants?"

He closed the scroll, then rubbed his tired eyes. "It's time she did something with her training. It's a damn good fortune you'll be there to keep her safe."

"She'll be keeping me safe."

Tengis shook his head. "I told you that you had no right to be weak at your age."

"It's not age that makes me weak."

A lizard ran across the kitchen floor and chirped. Even it had a lover to sing to.

"Let go, Kevah." Tengis covered my hand with his wrinkled and spotted one. "Let go of Lunara. You've suffered enough."

"You say it like I have a choice. You say it like I haven't tried, like I haven't been trying for ten years."

"You are my son," Tengis said, "and as long as I'm alive, you will always have a home — a family. Melodi and I are here for you. You are not alone, do you understand?"

This ancient man, whose care and concern were my first memories, who was as hard with me as he was kind, hugged me like I was four years old again.

Shamefully, a forty-year-old cried in his father's arms that night.

4

MICAH

WHAT COULD HAPPEN BETWEEN NOW AND ETERNITY? THE DEATH OF humanity, the resurrection at the Fountain, and the angels' judgment. What was I, but a speck amid that? No, not a speck. A flash. A flash of holy fire upon this sinful world.

There were those who wanted to snuff out that fire, to douse it before it engulfed them. You'd think them unbelievers, but among them were many who called themselves Ethosians.

The Bishop was one and he'd burned. Another of them boarded the Watersteel and entered my office. He was a messenger from the court in Hyperion, the imperial capital of Crucis.

"Imperator Adronikos Heraclius Saturnus is dead," he said. "His son Alexios has been crowned imperator and taken the name Josias, in honor of the apostle. He orders you to return to the capital."

Heraclius…dead? When? Where? How? I didn't ask any of these questions and remained stoic. Better to stay armored with those you don't know. "You saw my fleet and men. Why would I go back?"

"I am only a messenger from the imperial court. I was not told 'why', just 'what.'"

The messenger wore a velvet tunic with a fresh sword in his sheath. The son of some exarch judging by how high he kept his nose. Did the court not care to send someone I knew or at least a man with some scuffs on his scabbard?

"Tell me, how did the court react when I burned alive one of the high bishops of the Ethos Church?"

He gulped and stared at me with anxious eyes. "There was a great debate."

"So there were those on my side?"

"There are some at court who see you as blameless."

"And is our new imperator among them?"

The boy trembled and hunched his shoulders. I'm sure he wanted to run back to court. After much thought, he said, "Imperator Josias was not pleased with what you did to the Bishop."

"So if I go back, I'll be tried. Doesn't sound very appealing." I let out a thoughtful sigh. "Did the succession go smoothly?"

"The court is unified behind Josias. As the eldest, he is the natural successor."

"Good to know. Tell Alexi...Josias I'll see him soon."

I dismissed the messenger and relaxed in the velvet and iron chair I'd plundered from the Doge of Dycondi's treasure vault. The Watersteel rocked on a slight tide, lulling me. I pushed a bundle of maps off my desk and put my feet up. What a day to be alive — to have witnessed the end of an era, the end of Imperator Heraclius. Some called him "hero," others "hated." I poured honeyed lemon juice in my mug and sipped — it tasted sweeter with him gone. That pompous pissant could no longer wear the glory of my victories. My taste soured on the realization that his son would likely be worse.

My office door creaked open. Jauz, my chief engineer, walked in, sweat dripping off his brow. "Work is done, Grandmaster. Your fleet is ready to sail the Shrunken Strait."

I rose from my chair in awe of those words. "I demanded a fortnight, and you gave me ten days. You'll be first to choose from the Shah's treasures."

"Thank you, Grandmaster." As he beamed with delight, his mustache reached his ears. "I might ask from among his harem. I hear he has collected vixens from every country on earth."

The thought of a palace full of slave women, whom the licentious shah mounted as he pleased, disgusted me. "They are slaves. I'll set free whoever proclaims faith in the Archangel... those remaining will be judged accordingly. They will not be yours or mine for the taking."

Jauz smoothed his fine mustache. "Would it not be more merciful to let me care for those who don't take your faith?"

"I don't do it to be merciful. I do it to be just." I clapped at a fat fly buzzing around the room. The Watersteel was full of them. Missed. "But Jauz, as you are an unbeliever and have excelled in your service, I'll let you choose one. But you'll have to marry her. We do not take slaves in the Imperium."

"Sadly, I don't think I'd make a good husband."

"Why is that?"

"I'm already married to you!" His belly shook as he laughed. I smiled too.

It was time to inspect my fleet, ready my men, and ensure we were stocked to conquer Kostany. But first, I had to see Aschere.

I grabbed my lantern. I'd been planning through the night, so the wick stuck up above the wax. I trimmed it, then lit the wick with a bit of flint and steel.

Aschere stayed in the deep hold of my ship by choice and stopped pretending to eat the food I'd send her. The water I'd given her for drinking and bathing remained full in their buckets. Did she even sleep?

Since I'd reinforced my hulls with metal, no daylight shone into the deep hold. What was she doing in darkness, aside from praying to her god?

The throbbing light of my lantern showed her sitting in the corner and whispering prayers in a silky tongue that sounded like Paramic — the language of the Latian religion, mainly spoken in the Kingdom of Alanya. The Ejazi sailors spoke the language too. But it didn't matter what she prayed for; false gods cannot answer prayers.

"Micah the Metal," she said. "Are you ready?"

"I'm ready to extinguish your country and reclaim our holy land." I chuckled, unafraid of a sorceress whose only ability so far was pulling an iron ball across the floor. I shined the light up close in her face. "You know, half my men say I should burn you alive. The other half say I should drown you."

She didn't flinch or blink and nudged the lantern away. "What do you say?"

"I say you're too interesting for that."

"Falling in love with me already?" She didn't smile when she said it.

But I couldn't hold my laughter. "Maybe I would, if once in a while, you smiled."

"What's there to smile about?"

"Everything! The wind, the sea, the squawking of seagulls, the quacking of ducks — it's all the garden of the Archangel. Should we not marvel at it? Should it not make us happy?"

"If that's all it takes to make you happy, then what matter is Kostany?"

She may have liked this dark place, but I despised it. The Fallen Angels loved darkness. They drank dark waters from dark fountains. To bathe in darkness, as this woman did, invited their whispers.

"You're pastier than an albino mouse." I gestured for her to follow me. "Let's get you some sun."

We climbed the ladder to the deck. From here, one could marvel at green hills bathed by sunshine or the armada that prepared at the shoreline. My fifty thousand were busy stocking supplies. Using pulley ropes, they loaded wooden crates filled with food, cannon-fodder, and gunpowder onto the ships. My strongest men hauled barrels of water on their backs.

A group of Ejazi sailors whispered as Aschere and I walked by. They'd said she was a magus when we found her in the titan mines of Ejaz. Her face was *"youthful, radiant as the full moon, and without feeling — like all magi,"* they'd told me. What my fellow Crucians said was different: *"Dark drinker. Infidel. Accursed."*

The salt air cleansed me of such thoughts. Seagulls squawked and wind whipped through my hair.

Aschere still wore the gray rags and yellow scarf we'd found her in; earlier I'd ordered our tailor to make dresses and hoped to see her looking better when they were ready. I joined her at the bow as we gazed eastward, where the three infidel kingdoms of the Latians waited — all ruled by descendants of Seluq the Ruinous. They were cousins: Sirm, Alanya, and Kashan. I yearned to conquer the family, for what they'd done to mine.

Aschere had asked, *"What matter is Kostany?"* It was the bridge between the continents of Yuna and Lidya and gate to the east. It hadn't fallen for three hundred years, since the conqueror Utay moved his ships over mountains, with the help of the Fallen Angels, to avoid the seven sea walls that made the Shrunken Strait impossible to cross. That's why most conquerors sieged it by land...but was that any better?

Sieges tested the soul. We'd camped outside the iron walls of Pendurum for six moons, during which I lost half my men. I remembered the shriveled bodies encased in ice, agony forever frozen on their faces. I could never forget the thousands we had to burn in a pit because wormrot struck their bellies and how limbs scattered with each cannon blast. Day and night, we breathed sulfur and smoke and were lucky to pile fish paste on bread hard as stone.

There was a crimson moon the night Orwo's bomb brought down the iron walls. Our faith taught that eclipses brought miracles, and Orwo made his miracle manifest. His sappers tunneled to the wall and detonated his cocktail, collapsing the foundation with a blast that melted metal and turned night into day. But this miracle wouldn't work in Kostany. Its walls burrowed into the ground like an iceberg, so there was no way to collapse them with sapping unless you could pierce earth's hardest layers.

My men called Aschere a dark drinker. I hoped they were right. Only the Fallen Angels knew the way through Labyrinthos. If in the pitch black of the deep hold they whispered it to her, then I needed to know, because sometimes unholy methods can be used for a holy purpose.

"Mind if I tell you a story?" I said to her.

Strands of ashen hair blew over her face as she struggled to tie a knot with her yellow headscarf. The most human I'd seen her.

I began, "There was a man named Len who owned an inn. One day, a hungry traveler came to him in need of food and shelter. But the traveler had no gold, so Len sent him away. The next night, another traveler came in the same state, and Len refused him again. For nine more nights the same thing happened, and Len refused them all. Until on the twelfth night, when a weary traveler arrived and told Len that he was the angel Servantium sent to test him. He revealed to Len that on each night, a different angel had tested him and that he had failed each time. They were the Twelve Holies.

"But Len didn't believe Servantium. He demanded proof — a sign. So Servantium and the Twelve Holies appeared on the horizon in their true forms. Between the twelve angels were a thousand eyes and a hundred wings of gold and white feathers. Servantium alone had fifty wings, each the size of a mountain, and twenty eyes, each as bright as the moon. It was not clear where one angel ended and the other began, such were their heavenly forms. They hymned in a language incomprehensible, but that somehow Len's soul could understand. He repented and, from that day until his death, devoted himself to Angelsong."

Aschere gazed at me, unblinking. Her green eyes were deep enough to drown in. "You want me to show you a sign...that I am whom I claim."

"Even an apostle needed proof, so shouldn't I?"

"Hold still." Aschere came close. Honey lingered on her breath. She touched my forehead. I backed away.

"What are you doing?" I protested.

"Showing you."

I held still as she pricked my forehead with her fingernail.

Then she smiled and her cheeks reddened. "You have a daughter."

How could she know? I'd kept that secret close to my heart. I'd not told my most trusted lieutenants, preferring their respect to their sympathy.

Aschere closed her eyes, but her eyeballs moved as if dreaming. "There was thunder and rain the morning their ship docked at your town. They ransacked your inn and found Elaria as she slept. You ran through the marshes after them, but you didn't even own a sword. They laughed as they kicked you into the sea and rowed away."

My armor of stoicism fell away as I gaped, awed by the detail in her words. Someone clever could figure out I had a daughter, but how did she know so much? About the weather of that day? And the laughter of the slavers?

"It's not possible. You can't know these things. Not with a human's knowledge."

Her eyeballs moved as rapidly as her breaths. "Your father... the inn...burned — dagger — Black Legion —Sempurian — Heraclius — Sargosa — Pasgard — Pendurum — Dycondi —

Ejaz—" Aschere's cheeks paled. She opened her eyes, then closed them and clutched her forehead. I caught her before she hit the floor.

I TUCKED ASCHERE into my bed, which was just a nook in my office. It might as well have been the floor, hard as it was, but there were blankets to comfort her. A blurry-looking sea stared back through the porthole. The same sea the slavers had sailed when they took my daughter Elly, all those years ago.

Berrin poked his baby face through the door as I sat by Aschere's side.

"How is morale?" I asked him.

He entered, shut the door, and said in a hushed tone, "Messengers from court are spreading word that Imperator Heraclius is dead. The men are devastated. There is talk you will be declared a traitor by his heir, Josias."

"Not if we take Kostany."

"We all believe we can win, but a siege will take months — years, even. And without supplies and reinforcements from the Imperium…"

"What do the men say?" I gestured for him to sit in my iron chair while I rose and leaned against my desk.

"That we ought to go back to Hyperion, win the favor of Josias, and then proceed with his blessing." Berrin sat, his back straight and stance regal like a shah. With its broad, velvet cushioning, the chair seemed meant for a man of his noble stature. Its comfort was wasted on a peasant like me.

"No…the advantage will be lost." I grunted in disagreement. "The Shah would have a hundred thousand men at his walls. The odds of victory would go from slim to none. We strike now or never."

"The death of Heraclius is an ill tiding." Whenever Berrin pleaded, he would scrunch his face and his eyebrows would

almost bend below his eyes. "I want Kostany as much as you —
more than you, even — but we'll have one chance at it, and I'd
not waste it now. We can take our fleet to conquer other shores.
The Ejazi tell me that several Alanyan cities have neglected to
rebuild their walls. Treacherous Rastergan is ripe for the taking,
too."

I thought of my daughter Elly and her pinchable cheeks. I
thought of the slavers who grabbed her in the night, who cursed
in Sirmian as they kicked me into the sea. After so many years,
she was beyond saving. I wouldn't know what she looked like,
and she wouldn't know where she came from. All I could do was
punish those who stole her and eradicate the vile way of life that
taught souls could be bought and sold.

"There is only one city," I said. "And its name is Kostany."

"If that's your will, Grandmaster, then I'm with you." Berrin
gestured his eyebrows at sleeping Aschere. "What happened to
her?"

"She smiled."

A quizzical look seized Berrin's round face. His bushy
eyebrows pointed at the ceiling, which hadn't been painted in
years and was now peeling. "I'd seen a few magi when I lived in
Sirm, but her I don't recognize. The men say that she's bad luck.
That it was her prayers that killed Imperator Heraclius...and her
witchcraft that made you burn the Bishop."

"Such superstitious talk is heresy. An infidel's prayers have no
power. And I burned the Bishop because he was a cunt." I tried to
pour lemon juice from the pitcher into the mug, but only drops
came out. I had nothing to offer my second-in-command. Such
poor hospitality was unbecoming of the Grandmaster of the Black
Legion.

"Since when is 'cunt' reason enough to burn a priest?"

"Priest or peasant, lowborn or high — anyone who stands
against our dream, I will strike down."

Berrin inhaled deeply, like he always did when preparing

heavy words. He exhaled a gust. "We can set sail anytime. Go anywhere. Whether Kostany, Hyperion, Alanya, you know I will follow you. But you commanded me to be true, and it pains to say that the door to Kostany is closing. Can we move our ships over a mountain, as Utay did?"

I didn't have an answer.

Berrin rose and approached the door. "I'll stick my ear among the men and bring you their thoughts. Whatever you decide, I am with you till the last." He closed the door behind him, leaving me with the slumbering sorceress.

Aschere's pale face betrayed no feeling. Nothing moved under her eyelids, so her sleep must've been dreamless and peaceful.

But then why did she awake gasping? She flung up her hands, as if she'd been drowning and had only just pulled above water.

I got a clean handkerchief from my clothes chest and dabbed sweat off her forehead. "What did you see?"

"A rain that drowns the world, each drop dark as pitch."

I'd dreamed of drowning more times than I could count. Among the most frightening ways to die, surely.

"You smiled, you know?"

She brought my hand to her cheek — cold as steel frozen beneath an icy sea.

"We must go soon," she said. "To Labyrinthos."

I pulled my hand away, lest it freeze. "Let's say we go to Labyrinthos with a hundred of my best men. Let's say we come out the other side, as you claim, beneath the Sublime Seat. We take the sea walls and clear the way. Will my armada be there, waiting? Or will they have mutinied to save themselves from the Imperator's wrath and sailed to Hyperion instead?"

"You don't need five hundred ships and fifty thousand men to take Kostany. You can do it with a hundred ships and ten thousand. Take only your most loyal. Send the rest back."

I shook my head. "As we speak, messengers from court are

sowing descension in my ranks. Most of my men have families. They come from every province of the Imperium, each ruled by a lord or exarch. While the men are mine, the lords are the Imperator's, and that means their families belong to him. None of them want to desert me, but none want to forsake their families either. When forced to make that choice, even the most loyal can't be counted on."

Aschere stared at the porthole behind me. "Kostany will fall in a day."

"Do my men know that?" I got up and paced back and forth. "To them, capturing Kostany will take months or years. They are all veterans of siege. We broke many walls with cannon fire, with bravery, with steadfastness and sacrifice. Never with sorcery. Why should they believe? Why should they follow?"

Her ashen hair fell on her face as she pushed to sit up. "So you want me to fill the horizon, like the angels did for Len the apostle?"

"Not for me. For them."

"I have no power except what she gives."

"Are you so weak?"

"Weak?" A hint of indignation shone in her eyes. "You know nothing of sorcery."

"My father used to scare me with tales of the magi in the east." I sat on the bed next to her. Even the blanket was cold. "Magus Ghafar commanded his demons to bring him the thrones of all the kings of the world. But the angel Principus guarded the throne of the Imperator, enraging the magus and his demon horde. They invaded to take it, but with the help of the angels, the believers banished the magus and his demons to hell."

"Those magi of legend could command the jinn. I cannot."

"Then we go back to Hyperion."

"If you return to Hyperion, Crucis will never reclaim Kostany. Not until the moon splits and the world turns to ash."

"Give us a reason to follow you." I grabbed her shoulders,

then pulled away from the burning cold. "Give us a reason to believe. To defy our imperator and do the impossible. Because without it, this won't work."

"Faith, Micah."

"If faith wasn't enough for an apostle, then it's not enough for my army."

I think I was finally sensing the utterly subtle emotions on her face. Her cheeks would raise when stressed, so slightly, and her irises would sink a hair's breadth.

"And what of your daughter?" Aschere said. "Are you going to let her captors go unpunished?"

"You think I'm doing this for her?"

"Why do it then?"

"For the Archangel." That was what I'd told everyone and hoped to be true. But in my heart, love for the angels competed with hatred for the Sirmians and their wretched beliefs. I hoped a righteous hatred could be holy, too.

As Aschere shook her head, her ashen hair got in her eyes again. "No one does anything for god, not truly."

"And what about you? Why would you help me conqueror your people?"

"I'm the exception. I do it only for god."

"Which god?"

She got up to my ear and whispered, "The only one I've ever seen."

I RETURNED to the deck of my great galleon: the metal-plated sea monster that had sunk countless galleys, including those of the Doge of Dycondi and the emerald pirates of Ejaz. I walked beneath the fluttering, black and red sails and past the cannons toward the bow, upon which stood a statue of the angel Cessiel, her four eyes arrayed in the shape of a diamond. The captains of the ships and my lieutenants waited on the dock. Berrin argued with them as they demanded to see me. I looked out from the bow, and seeing me, all were silent. Even the seagulls.

Zosi, my brother by law, was at the head of the group. If I'd lost him, I'd lost them all. He charged at me once with a spear, the day I took his father's castle. I broke that spear, smashed my shield on his face, and threw him in the dungeon. I kept him there for two moons. When I came to see him, he was praying. Lice nibbled on his scalp, and his feet bulged out of his shackles like ripe melons. But he didn't lose faith in the Archangel's mercy.

I became that mercy when I convinced Imperator Heraclius to pardon his house, though he did take Zosi's sisters to court in case Pasgard rebelled, marrying them to minor lords. Save for Alma, the one I married. Even after she died of pox, Zosi never broke faith with me. But there he was, at the head of a rabble meant to challenge me, his eyes laden with doubt.

I licked my finger and stuck it in the air. An eastward wind cooled it.

"I lied to all of you!" I shouted.

The group stirred. Everyone mumbled to each other.

"You think me a holy warrior, a gun of the Archangel, but it is not so."

Heckles sounded from the crowd. Must've been the Imperator's messengers.

"I killed men because I wanted to, either out of hatred, or because I enjoyed it. I didn't do a thing for the Archangel."

They quieted and stilled, probably from shock.

"And I want to kill more, for many reasons, but one reason above all. Pain."

Zosi looked at me the way I looked at my father after he'd been stabbed: eyes laden with sadness and fear.

"Pain, because of a truth I kept from you. Many years before I'd learned to hold a sword, I fathered a beautiful girl born in the month of the angel Cessiel."

Even Berrin's round face was red with expectation.

"Her name was Elaria, but I called her Elly. Born out of wedlock, to a woman from a nearby convent who was sworn to celibacy in service to the Archangel."

It was not like my men locked their cocks away. They'd all had their fill but saw me above it.

"I heaped sin upon sin, yet was blessed with a girl that was more angel than human."

Many more gathered. My army was a sea on the docks.

"But my sins would not go unpunished. One night while I slept, she was taken. The slavers who stole her wore the scimitar under the sun on their turbans — the sigil of Hayrad the Redbeard who, to this day, is still admiral of Sirm's largest fleet."

Brother whispered to brother, all the way to the back of the crowd, spreading the story to those too far to hear.

"Redbeard sails to defend Kostany with three hundred ships. We'll draw him into the open sea and destroy him. We'll put an end to slaving on these waters. I know you don't want to siege Kostany. The Imperator has called us back, and I intend to go. But let's fight one more battle on the seas."

Cheers erupted. I raised my hand to silence them.

"I will repent for my sins until the day I die. But not with words." I looked upon my people, their eyes sparkling with zeal. They ate my words. They believed in me. "I've always asked you to fight for the Archangel. To fight for the Imperium. To fight as a Crucian and Ethosian. Today, I ask you to fight for all those reasons — and one more. This will be my last battle. Will you fight for me?"

I didn't wait to enjoy the cheers, disgusted by how I'd used my lost daughter to rally the men. Elly was no prop, and yet what choice did I have? The same old speech about fighting for faith and country wouldn't have roused them to attempt the impossible. But fighting for a leader who took nothing but a metal chair from the treasure vaults of Dycondi, who'd been biting down on the shame and pain of a lost bastard daughter for as long as they'd known him — now that had a winning ring to it.

I returned to my room.

"Rousing speech." Aschere had thrown the blankets on the floor and now sat on the bed, cross-legged.

"It was a lie." I poured myself some water. Offered her some, but she shook her head. "The slavers didn't wear his sigil," I said, "and Redbeard's too sly to fight us on the open sea."

"And yet, it was as truthful as you've ever been. When I pricked your forehead, I saw your life from birth to now. You truly loved her, didn't you?"

"Any man would love his child."

"And you loved her mother, and your father, and all your neighbors. There was nothing in you but love, until it all turned to hate."

"Enough. Gather your strength, Aschere. We'll take my fastest vessel, fill it with a hundred of my best, and sail for Ejaz."

"We need not go to Ejaz." Aschere lay on her stomach, then rested her head on her fists and peered at me with eyes of emerald fire. "Labyrinthos burrows through the earth. Like a kraken, its tentacles reach all countries. There's an entrance a few miles away."

"Then that means…"

"We can be in Kostany tomorrow."

"The fleet won't get there for a few days. We'll have to plan it so we reach at the same time." I gulped water and wiped my mouth. "Why not just march my entire army through?"

"Because only the strongest can survive the Deep." Aschere got off the bed and came close. Her honeyed breaths perked me up. Did she enjoy this? I would've pushed her away if I didn't like it or freeze at the touch. "Now picture yourself," she whispered in my ear, "high upon the throne of Kostany."

5

KEVAH

Hayrad the Redbeard rode at the head of the procession on an elephant with glossy tusks. Each thump of the elephant's feet cracked cobblestone. Melodi gawked and gushed with glee, almost ambling into the parade; I pulled her off the street lest she be trampled. After the elephants came the Kashanese horses, with lean bodies and silky tails, the swiftest steeds in the world. The onlookers gasped as treasures emerged on wagons.

I admired the iron coffin covered in magic runes. It was said to contain the body of Saint Askarli, who would awaken upon the Great Terror. More shocking was the hourglass that sent sand back upward so it never depleted — if only life were the same. But my favorite treasures were the Abistran mangoes all piled up, which with vinegar created a dance of sweet and sour on your taste buds.

Then came the slaves. Red-colored men stood in iron cages, as if forever blushing. The fair-skinned women of the Thames iceland had hair bright as fresh snow. There were steely dark people from the Himyar lands, their skin shimmering like gunmetal. The slave markets would be busy.

So would the Seat. Hayrad the Redbeard climbed off his elephant and entered the Sublime Seat with his head bowed. The man wore his legend: jewelry and trinkets from the farthest reaches of the world hung off him. And when he smiled, his teeth reflected light in five colors. But Shah Murad was in no mood for pomp. His war council had assembled by the time Hayrad's chronicler had finished.

"I will not throw my fleet at Micah the Metal," Hayrad said, sitting on the floor before the Shah in the great hall. "A fool's task."

"Your avoiding him for years is why he's grown so strong. Why did you even come?" The Shah was the only one not impressed by the spectacle and legend of Redbeard. "To parade your vanity through my streets?"

"Let him siege Kostany," Hayrad said. "Let him surround it. I'll pick him off with my speedy fustas. Have your zabadar horse archers waiting behind the Zari Zar Mountains. I've brought you five hundred more of the best horses known to heaven and earth."

Sublime disgust spread across the Shah's face. "The Imperator will refill his stocks as we deplete them."

"Haven't you heard?" Hayrad smiled. He guffawed, deep from his belly. "Imperator Heraclius is with his angels."

The entire congregation gasped, as did I. If true, Crucis had lost one of its greatest kings. A man I felt I knew, if only from across a blood-soaked, cratered battlefield.

"Praise Lat," the Shah said. "How did that ancient shit finally die?"

"Officially, in bed. Though I've heard whispers of hemlock."

The Shah frowned and nodded slowly, as if captured by a bittersweet memory. "My father always cursed the man. No matter how many Crucian armies he put down, Heraclius the Hated would raise another. And another. And another. 'How do his people not revolt?' my father would say. 'How are there any men left to sow the fields?' What he didn't realize is just how fanatical these Crucians are. Faith fills their bellies when food runs out. Would that we were the same. Would that a Sirmian's faith in Lat be nourishment enough."

"His eldest Josias has claimed the throne," Hayrad said while polishing one of his many rings, "and Micah is not in his good graces. Josias took offense when Micah burned the priest who had baptized him in the High Holy Sea. We can use this divide to our advantage. Sign a peace treaty with Josias, in exchange for pilgrimage rights and holy relics."

The Shah sniggered. "Peace? Would Temur have made peace? Would my father? There can be no true peace between Sirmian and Crucian. Peace is just cover to prepare for the next war. And after ten years of peace, that war is here. You think the Imperator will forsake his own for pilgrimage rights, which we already grant them? He'll have every right when the city is his!"

And yet, aside from having Redbeard raid Crucian towns, the Shah had never led a war against the Crucians. And Redbeard's raiding was done under his own flag, not Sirm's or the Shah's. I began to see the cracks in the Shah's facade: was that tough talk from the heart or merely for the onlookers?

"It's a good idea," Ebra said in his raspy voice. "Don't write to Josias directly. Write instead to Patriarch Lazar, offering control over some holy sites and a return of relics. Whatever it takes to have Micah declared a heretic. There's no better way to end a siege than by cutting the umbilical cord."

The Shah nodded but kept his head high. "All right, it's good statecraft."

"What of the food?" I interjected. I could never forget how we starved in Rastergan. We used to suck on rat bones to quell the gnawing hunger.

Ebra replied, "Whereas the fisheries remain dire, we have grain stockpiled underground to feed the entire city for two years. Maintenance is being performed on the mills as we speak."

Good enough. I listened to them discuss battleplans. The army would dig up the streets so that cannonballs would sink into dirt instead of exploding into stone. Micah would not be at the gates for a fortnight, enough time to fill the weapon stocks and cannon batteries. If necessary, the army would evacuate and burn the port city of Demoskar and the surrounding farmland, ensuring Micah couldn't use it as a base.

Micah's paladins were heavily armored and wielded guns; it was best to fight at range and wear them down, so only mounted gunmen and archers, riding the fastest Kashanese horses, would engage his army from outside the walls.

On the water, Redbeard would keep some small and agile fustas near the sea walls. His main fleet of galleys and mighty, three-masted barques would wait off the coast. If Micah got too close, the fleet would encircle him. Even a thousand warships couldn't get through the sea walls. He'd have to repeat the miracle of Utay and move his ships over the mountains.

I FOUND Melodi drilling under the midday sun with Vaya's followers, who had joined our holy army. I sat on a bench in the training yard, sucked the juice out of a canister of Abistran mangoes in vinegar, and watched as Melodi took the men down with a flurry of kicks and stabs with her blunt sword. It wasn't fair. She was trained by Tengis and they were devout supplicants who drank strange teas. I was a better match for them but didn't feel like training. What good was one more warrior in a siege of a hundred thousand?

"Papa!"

Steel clattered at my feet: a blunt sword. Melodi grinned as she stood over some poor fool.

"You should train them with spears." I left the sword and picked a wooden stick from a weapon rack. "A swordsman has to be three times as skilled to win against a spear."

I twirled the spear and impaled the air. My movements were slow, but the skills hadn't left me.

"Wouldn't a gun be best?" The poor fool on the ground got up and slapped dust off his trousers. "An accurate shot will kill anyone in an instant."

This young man with brown hair and yellow teeth was more muscular than the others.

"An accurate shot, yes," I said. "But guns take time to reload. In a close fight, miss and you're dead. I've never been disadvantaged by not carrying a gun. Why, during the reign of Shah Jalal the Thunder, I helped defend Rastergan's crumbling walls with nothing but a spear, though it was a big one..."

Imperator Heraclius was in the field during that battle. We'd pushed deep into Crucian territory and sacked city after city. But within a year, Heraclius assembled the largest army we'd ever faced and reclaimed what he'd lost. Except Rastergan.

The people there followed the Church of Ethos. In the center of town, a steel statue of the Archangel stared at the city. It had eleven wings — five on the right side and six on the left — and eleven arms in the opposite composition. I'd always thought the Ethos religion played with twelve, the way ours played with eight, so where were the twelfth wing and arm?

Bombards pounded Rastergan. It took a week for Heraclius to destroy a chunk of wall large enough to march through. There was nothing between us and forty thousand paladins but our spears. And if they broke through, not only were we dead but so was Shah Jalal.

The stench of men piled high as a tower never leaves your nose. Shit and blood and bone marrow stews together, spiced by the sulfur of gunpowder. Death screams and the *clop-clop* of horses raging at you are only terrifying when you haven't already been deafened by the cannon blasts. Heraclius charged the breach in our wall with ten thousand heavy cavaliers, but with shields an inch thick and pikes the length of two men, we repulsed them for six moons until blessed rains forced them to abandon the siege.

Experience taught every weapon's purpose. A gun could down the fastest horse. An arrow shot at the perfect angle could rain fire on an encamped enemy. Swords were best in close quarters, but keep to the right distance, and a spear was hard to overcome.

After enchanting them with my tale of blood and bravery, I gave them spears. I let Melodi keep her sword in hope they'd challenge her.

"Both hands on the spear!" I commanded. "Feet spread and forward!"

They had odd grips at their heads or bellies. "Hold the spear to the chest, at the angle of attack. Thrust with your whole self but never overcommit."

Melodi and I drilled them under the midday sun. I thought on the Shah's words: *Peace is a disease.* How had they avoided learning how to fight? You could attack a pleasure house wildly swinging a mace, but face a Crucian paladin without discipline and you were dead.

Training them was the first time I felt useful in Kostany. It moved me to purpose. If I couldn't be a warrior, I could be a commander.

Afterward, Melodi and I were drenched in sweat and seeking relief from the heat.

"There's this vendor at the overlook who mixes honey with ice and apples." Melodi loosened her chainmail and wrapped a towel around her shoulders. "It's like god peeing in your mouth!"

"By Lat, from what twisted mind did you learn that phrase?"

"Uh, Grandpa, I think?" She flushed. "Let's go!"

I'd never tasted god's pee so didn't protest as she dragged me along.

We sat on a stone embankment facing the Shrunken Strait and shared a bowl of the sweet ice. The seven sea walls stood over the strait — a floating fortress with countless cannons. Each sea wall connected to the wall that covered the shore, and that wall connected to the Sublime Palace. To take the city, you would have to sail through the sea walls, land on the embankment, scale the strait-facing wall, then fight to the Seat. But cannon fire would shred ships trying to sail through the pillars that held up the sea walls. If the ships destroyed the walls, debris would block the way. Overcoming the sea defenses was unthinkable.

On the continent of Yuna beyond the strait, the Nocpla Mountains tasted the clouds. How had Utay moved his ships over them to the other end of the strait? That was even more unthinkable, and Utay took the secret to his grave.

Melodi devoured the sweet ice, but I just sipped. I never liked purely sweet things. Even poetry should mix sweet with sour. After sweet love comes a bitter separation and sour loneliness. Even the love of Lat, sweet like divine nectar, mixed with the bitter winds of life. Food ought to be the same. That's why I liked Abistran mangoes with vinegar. But a fifteen-year-old girl, who'd grown up in peacetime, wouldn't know bitter. This honey-apple-ice treat must've tasted like her fondest memories.

"Melodi, what was the happiest day of your life?"

She licked honey off her spoon. "This is the happiest day of my life." She chuckled.

"Come on, don't joke."

The sun set beneath the Nocpla Mountains, casting a ruddy light through the sky.

"What kind of question is that?" she said. "Do you know yours?"

The day Lunara and I married. Even the Shah had attended that solemn ceremony at the Blue Domes. For our achievements, he'd freed us from the janissary vows and permitted us to marry.

By Lat, Lunara was radiant as a summer sky. She wore a blue dress patterned with gold flowers that must've been cut from heaven. When she walked upon the dais and took my outstretched hand, I almost fainted with happiness.

But it was time for new memories.

"Sorry, Melodi." I thought of all I'd missed — the times I wasn't there to laugh with my daughter or hold her when she cried. "I wish I'd been here. I've missed so much of your life. That's why I ask stupid questions."

"Just don't miss anymore, all right?" Melodi said. "You, me, and the old man are family. I'll never abandon you if you promise the same."

That's when I knew I could never leave Kostany. I had to make up for the lost time. I yearned to be a loving father and devoted son to the only two people who genuinely cared for me. Lunara may have been gone, but there was something to live for.

I hugged Melodi. Once the lamplighters went about illuminating the streets, I took her home.

I NEEDED to speak with Magus Vaya about the progress of our holy army, so I climbed the steep stairs to the Seat. Grand Mufti Taymah waved to me once I passed through the gate.

It seemed he'd just given a sermon and was relaxing by a fountain, his turban spread over his shoulders like a towel and spectacles hanging from his neck on a gold chain. Some of his congregation were buzzing about, but the Mufti excused himself to talk to me.

"You trained them well earlier," he said. "Turned a rabble into a band of brothers."

"You were watching?"

The Mufti smirked. "The Fount is always watching. It's our job to know what goes on."

"I thought it was your job to tend the souls of the people."

Mufti Taymah and I walked through the night garden. Aside from moonlight, it was only lit by faint musk candles. Evening dew softened the grass and glistened on the flowers lining our gravel path.

"Faith is not just about the soul," he said. "Body, mind, and soul are all paramount. What is a believer if he wastes away at a shrine? Is it not the greatest worship to fight and die for Lat? Are the shrines her house? Or is it the body of a holy warrior, muscled from discipline and training?"

"What about the bodies of fat men like myself?" I laughed.

The Mufti smiled, though I doubted he found it funny. "Kevah, it is your mind that is the holiest of shrines. A mind that can turn weakness into strength, that can point an arrow at its target and guide men to holy purpose. What is better worship than leading men to victory?"

Fireflies buzzed near my head, throbbing with a somber glow.

"Thank you, Grand Mufti. Your words fill me with hope. I see why you are such an inspiration to the people."

His warm smile made me smile too. He seemed good-natured, but could someone genuine rise so high? In this kingdom?

"Can I ask you something personal?" he said.

"I prefer to answer personal questions with a hookah pipe in my mouth, but as there are none here, go ahead."

"That young, spritely girl who seems to adore you — is she of age?"

What kind of question was that? Melodi was obviously of age. Did he want to marry her off already? She'd not taken the janissary vow, so it was possible, and with the Fount around, probably her only way up in life.

"I'd assume so. I mean, obviously."

"A thousand and one apologies for asking, it's just the two of you seem so familiar. So affectionate. And yet, you are not family." The warmth had gone from his face. Staring at me were judging eyes.

"She's my adopted daughter. What's it to you?"

The Grand Mufti took my hands. "If you are to be a holy

warrior in the sight of Lat, you must not break her laws. Nothing is worse for morale than a leader who flouts the law of god. There's much blessing in raising a slave girl, but only until she has bled. You're not her captor, nor her father by blood. If you like the girl, take her as your wife. Otherwise, do not be so familiar."

I pulled my hands away. "Melodi is my daughter! How dare you suggest something so vile!?"

"It's well known what janissaries do with their *daughters.* What you do in private is between you and Lat. But in the streets, she can only be as a stranger to you. That is the law as decreed by the Fount." He pointed to himself. "By me."

I'd heard stories of janissaries adopting orphaned girls and boys, only to be found doing unmentionable things with them. But I didn't realize the Fount had outlawed adoption entirely.

"She is my daughter. I'll not have you dictate how I treat her, whether in my home or on any street." I shook my head and walked away. Never had my opinion of someone fallen so low in seconds.

Once in the Seat, I grabbed a torch and lit it with flint. The gold Paramic calligraphy that covered the walls shimmered in the firelight.

I asked a janissary, who stood stern like a colorful statue, "Where's Magus Vaya?"

"Down."

I descended a flight of stairs and asked the same question to the guard at the canteen.

"Down."

I went down another flight and asked the guard of the dungeon. Same answer. So I went farther down the spiral stone staircase until I was at a place as dark as a crypt.

Two janissaries guarded a threshold at the end of the hallway. Beyond that threshold was black, as if torn from a starless sky.

"So this is Labyrinthos," I said. "I've heard so much about it."

I peeked through the threshold. Iron bars covered the entrance to a cave. A door made of the same iron bars was creaking open in the wind.

The janissaries stood with the blankest faces. I snapped my fingers in front of their eyes. They were tranced, their backs straight, heads high, and eyes wide open.

Could this be Vaya's sorcery? What was he doing in Labyrinthos? Did I dare enter?

The darkness groaned. A deep croak. Or was that wind? Did I imagine it?

I stepped through the door.

"Vaya!" I called.

"Vaya!" echoed back. "Vaya! Vaya! VAYA! VAYA!" rang in my ears.

Wind blew through. But how? Wind meant there was an exit not far off. Its icy wisp chilled my bones and made my eyes water. Or maybe they were tears of fear?

I touched the black cave wall: cold. My hand came away with tar stains. What was this place?

I shined my torch ahead and stepped forward. The light barely illuminated my way, as if suffocated by darkness. And then I heard it: *patter-patter. Patter-patter.* Bouncing off the walls. Behind me. Above me. *Patter-patter.*

I turned left. I turned right. I turned around. But I saw nothing but the tar walls and the iron bars from where I'd entered, which now seemed distant. Surely, I hadn't walked that far!

Patter-patter. Closer. Closer. *Patter-PATTER.*

I stumbled and dropped my torch. Darkness doused its fire. I couldn't see. Someone pulled me to my feet. I shouted. Light lit the world again. The young face of Magus Vaya. He shook my shoulders until I came to sense.

Behind him was Redbeard, lantern in hand.

"The fuck are you two doing?" I wanted to punch them.

. . .

WE SAT at a floor table in the royal canteen, a pitcher of fermented barley water between us. Viziers and courtiers crowded the other tables with their pink drinks, amid dim and soothing candlelight. I demanded the serving boy bring a hookah with cherry hashish. After five minutes, I was smoking and relaxed.

"I've been to the edge of the world," Redbeard said, flashing his colorful teeth. Even his eyebrows had red hairs. He was toughly built, and though getting on in years, not a man you'd want to wrestle. "I've seen wonders like the Colossus of Dycondi before Micah melted it to make ten thousand guns. Its longsword pointed at heaven." He pretended his cup was a sword and held it high. "It stood taller than a mountain, and its iron eyes told a story of bravery that built a city of a thousand and one years. I've also sailed the islands of Pilimay, where there are statues as old as time, said to have been chiseled by warlocks…"

Redbeard went on and on. He loved to talk. I loved to smoke, so didn't mind listening, as long as cherry-flavored hashish filled my lungs.

"…but despite sailing the world, I'd never been in Labyrinthos. Curiously, the Shah was glad to let me enter. Giddy, even. Vaya protested, but since the Shah had made his decision, graciously joined to keep me safe. I wanted to feel it — the wind coming from hellfire. It's a cold wind. Strange, that hellfire would be cold. Can fire be colder than ice? What say you, Kevah?"

Finally, he stopped speaking. Even on the finest hashish, I could only endure so much thinly veiled boasting.

"Ahriyya rules over hellfire," I said. Redbeard gestured for the pipe, so I let him have a few puffs. "He froze the world with his breath, according to the saintly recitals. It wasn't until Saint Chisti founded Holy Zelthuriya in a valley of stone that the world warmed again. Point being, cold can burn."

"This one is a great storyteller!" Redbeard blew out a ring of smoke. All show-offs liked to make rings with the smoke. "I'd listen to you all day if I didn't like to listen to myself more!" He laughed — gruff and deep.

At least he was honest, so I laughed too.

"Well, I'm glad we didn't go any deeper into Labyrinthos." Redbeard clanked his cup on mine. "I don't want to die until the life is squeezed out of me. Or until I've squeezed the life out of time."

Squeezed the life out of time...a verse from the warrior-poet Taqi.

"How much Taqi do you know?" I asked.

"Would I be a cultured man if I hadn't memorized at least three of nine volumes?"

I clanked my cup on his, spilling barley water on the table. He had brought me the best mangoes in heaven and earth and knew his Taqi. Though a blowhard, I couldn't deny that Redbeard was endearing.

Magus Vaya recited a blunt poem of Taqi's dying lamentations:

There is no place on my body,
That hasn't been cut by a sword,
Or pierced by an arrow,
But here I am,
Dying in bed like a camel.

Redbeard clapped. "Even this one knows his Taqi!"

"If it weren't for Taqi," Vaya said, his face plain as stone, "my sycophants would have turned me from a whirling dervish to a churling oarfish." I had no idea what that meant. Hayrad and I laughed anyway, boisterously enough to shake the table.

Hayrad poured me more barley water. "Now tell me, Kevah, is the Shah your friend? What is he really like? Which of his harem delights him most?"

I took a deep puff of cherry hashish and let it settle, then blew it out. "Would a friend call upon you only in his time of need?

Would he risk your life instead of his own? We are not friends. But we don't need to be for me to serve. I admire the man for what he is, the true heir of Shah Jalal the Thunder, whom I did call friend."

Hayrad must've noticed my somber tone and so changed the subject. "Let me tell you, if I could build a harem, I'd make one entirely of Alanyan women. The red-haired ones from the Karmaz Mountains. They are fierce women, in the street and the bed! Let me tell you…"

We drank and smoked and joked. Even the magus had a sense of humor: dry as a dead rat in the desert. The moon beamed an invigorating light through the palace windows. And yet, as my bones ached from laughing, something the Shah had said bounced inside my head until my skull ached too:

Ten years of peace does not go unpunished.

6

MICAH

THE HIGH HOLY SEA GLISTENED SAPPHIRE IN THE MOONLIGHT. MY hundred best, led by Edmar and Orwo, stood in ten rows of ten at the seaside. As the waves hit the shore, I recalled the moment I was made Micah the Metal, my soul purified by heavy water. How holy I'd been, and how sinful was I now?

Aschere recited Paramic words under her breath. I could've brought an Ejazi to translate but instead ordered the best sailors in the world to sail for Kostany. The fleet had departed days ago and would be ready to strike in hours. But where would we be? Was the witch really taking us to Kostany through some miraculous tunnel?

Aschere finished her recitations and stared at the water. Did she think me a fool?

"We've been standing here an hour," I said. "Where's the entrance?"

"It's in there," she said. "I can feel the cold wind of the Deep."

"Do you see gills on our cheeks?"

"I didn't know the entrance was in the water. I just followed the wind."

Even the full moon couldn't illuminate the sea's innards. The water seemed as oil.

"So what do we do!?"

I wanted to strike Aschere and drown her. She turned to me, lips quivering just enough for me to notice. She feared something; I had a strong sense it wasn't me.

"I'll light the way and you follow," she said. "In the meantime, ease your loads."

"Light the way? Fire doesn't burn in water!"

"Hers will."

She waded into the water, drenching the green dress I'd given her, then submerged her head and disappeared. I commanded my men to drop everything save for chainmail, rations, guns, swords, and incendiaries. Piles of black plate, helmets, and spears littered the seaside, along with various knickknacks: paring knives, wooden bowls, spoons, coins, beads, dice. Now we waited.

And waited. Had she drowned? I was ready to sail to Hyperion and throw myself at Imperator Josias' feet.

A firefly buzzed near my head — so strange that its light was green. I swatted it, but more appeared. They came from the water and twinkled in the night. Their emerald light blazed through the sea and made clear the way. And they glowed together as if one mind. I waded into the water to follow, almost forgetting about the hundred men behind me.

I could expect my best to hold their breaths. "With me, one and all! To Kostany!"

I filled my lungs and dived. The twinkle of emerald light led me deeper and forward. Metallic water burned my eyes, but I kept going until I reached a hole in the seafloor. My lungs half empty, I pushed inside. The passage narrowed, but the emerald glow of the fireflies continued. My eyes flared and my lungs yearned to breathe. I swam and swam until my head hit air and I gasped for breath.

I pulled onto a rocky floor, where the fireflies illuminated a cave with tar walls. Aschere stood at its mouth, surrounded by the pulsating green bugs. She was panting and, had I not caught her, would have fallen in a heap.

"Can you go on?" I asked.

Her skin stung me with its sharp cold. I could barely hold her as I helped her stand.

"I have to. I have to get you to Kostany."

"Sorry I doubted you."

"I doubted myself too, but I never doubted her."

My men climbed out of the water, their black and red chain-mail dripping in the throbbing green glow. Soon the cave would be full of paladins.

The fireflies whizzed into a black tunnel. The darkness was all-encompassing, as if not the absence of light but part of the air. And the wind...it chilled my wet body and whispered words I couldn't understand. But one thing I knew: that wind led to Kostany.

7

KEVAH

My encounter with Labyrinthos had scared me so much, of course I went there in my sleep. Something whispered from that darkness. And as I went deeper through the caves with a torch, a woman hummed. She sang a song so familiar that I knew it in my soul, though I didn't know why.

I hurried through the cave, eager to find the singing woman. Then hands of black smoke grew out of the walls and extinguished my torch. I gasped in terror, stumbling through the darkness until fireflies throbbed to illuminate a way forward.

They guided me closer to the song, to the woman. I reached a cavern lit by glowing sapphire water that stretched across the black cave. And there she was.

The woman sat on an ice throne that floated on the water. She was naked. Slender thighs gave way to slight hips, then a thin abdomen and small breasts. Now she reclined sideways on the seat and put a leg on an armrest, her back resting against the other armrest. She dipped her leg in the water and made tiny, circular ripples. The strangest thing was her azure hair, so long it fell in the water. She looked like one of the slave women from Thames that Redbeard had carted through the streets.

I stepped on the water to reach her, but my foot slipped through the liquid and burned cold. I could only watch as her tender humming pulled my heartstrings.

She stopped singing when she noticed me. Her smile wasn't tender; it was as frigid as the icy water. I didn't run as she walked on the water toward me. She came close and glared with eyes of green fire, her breath smelling of ice and honey. Then she pricked my forehead with her fingernail and I woke up in a sweat.

Outside my window that looked upon the Sublime Seat, a firework exploded in the sky and the world flashed red. The Shah used fireworks to signal the army. Red meant war, and red bursts filled the sky with a cacophony of explosions.

I grabbed my sword and ran out of the room. Downstairs, Melodi was putting on her chainmail with Tengis' help.

"What happened?" I asked.

"The hell if I know." Tengis strapped on Melodi's sheath. "Are they here already?"

"Melodi should stay," I said, almost out the door.

But then I saw the desire in her dark eyes and knew that no matter how much I loved her, I couldn't keep her from this. She was a warrior and had a duty to her shah and country.

Outside was dim and humid. The air stank of stillness. Wide-eyed people filled the streets. Melodi and I pushed through them toward the Seat, where the fireworks had been launched from. Whatever was happening, it was happening at the Palace on the Shores of Time.

Janissaries marched through the royal gate and up the steps. We ran past them. I was breathless at the top, but Melodi stormed through the second gate.

"Wait!" I panted and squatted to catch my breath. "Melodi!" She hurried on, so I forced myself up and ran after her.

Dead men littered the palace entrance. Gun-toting janissaries ran by toward the western part of the Seat, where bridges led to the seven sea walls.

Melodi knelt over an injured janissary. "Tell us what happened," she said.

"They came from the palace." Blood lined the injured man's lips. "A whole army."

"Where'd they go?"

"West." He pushed against a wound in his abdomen that gushed blood. "The sea walls."

We followed the janissaries to the sea walls. Gunshots and shouts pierced the air. Healers dragged the screaming wounded on litters in the opposite direction. How long had this battle been raging? Judging by the bodies, at least an hour.

As we neared the sea walls, a roar came from the sea. Cannon fire. Explosions sounded as light and fire flashed. The Crucians did not go to Demoskar. They were here. In the distance, ships streamed through the strait and fired on the city. But the cannons on the sea walls did not fire back. That meant the enemy had captured the battlements. How could this be? Was I still dreaming?

The battlements were ahead, and I was heaving with every breath, my legs stiff and strained. The littering of dead bodies thickened. Blood trailed along the gravel and streamed between the cobblestone. The stench of burnt flesh — like sulfur mixed with blood and sweet meat — filled the air.

A soldier dragged himself across the plaza, clutching burnt flesh on his belly, his intestines poking out like coiled snakes. Another one had been shot in the knees and the flare turned his leg black. No one to help them.

Melodi and I ducked for cover beneath a stone fountain. We couldn't catch our breaths; a bomb exploded in a nearby bush, where a janissary huddled. He ran on fire and fell off the battlement onto the embankment below, screaming with burning lungs.

This wasn't war as I remembered. Too much gunfire. Too many bombs. How could we close the distance to use our swords and spears?

A young man clutching a spear ducked next to me. It was the aspiring holy warrior we'd trained this afternoon. His yellow teeth chattered.

"Get out of here," I said to him. "You're not ready."

"I'm ready to die for Lat." He quavered. Tears filled eyes that reflected an explosion above us. I pulled him and Melodi down and shielded them as my ears went numb.

When we pulled our heads up, the battle raged in silence.

"Listen," I shouted, my hair still simmering. "Below Kostany is a food stock enough to last years. Go burn it."

"No," the young man cried. I could barely hear him over the ringing in my ears. He'd regressed to a child, the way many do in war. "I have to stay," he said. "I have to fight."

"The city is lost!" I put Melodi's hand and his hand together. "The ships have entered the strait. Burn what you can!"

Melodi trembled, her breaths violent and shallow. "I just got you back." She cried as she spoke. "I won't let you fight alone."

"I'm your commanding officer, you'll do as I order." I clutched her cheeks and kissed her forehead. "Go, Melodi. Carry out my command. And then get out of the city."

She nodded, her eyes red and gushing tears, and kissed my cheek. She and the young warrior crept away.

Once they'd gone, I felt ready. The bombs hadn't ceased. Neither had the cannon fire that turned night into day. I wished I had barley water to calm my nerves or a puff of cherry-flavored hashish. But all I had were prayers. I said a quick one and unsheathed my sword.

The janissaries around me were dying or dead. I peeked above the fountain. Scores of enemy soldiers were dug-in behind sand-bags on each sea wall.

Several ducked on the seventh wall. There was a woman, too.

Her dress glimmered green in the moonlight, and her hair was long and light. The yellow scarf around her neck dangled in the still air. Though I couldn't discern more, she seemed familiar — dreamlike.

A hand touched my shoulder. I almost stabbed Magus Vaya, who'd crept next to me. If anyone could save us, it was him.

"What do we do?" I asked.

I could barely hear myself, ears ringing with a hundred bells. I put my ear against his face.

"That woman," he said. "I have to kill her."

"Who is she?"

"A servant of Ahriyya. A magus gone astray. See the man next to her?"

I squinted to see him. Though he crouched behind sandbags, I could tell he was big. Every minute, he threw bombs that exploded stone and made janissaries scream.

"That's Micah the Metal." Vaya didn't show fear. He spoke as if we were still drinking in the canteen. "We kill him and maybe we can save the city."

"So we attack the seventh wall."

Five janissaries ran to our cover and huddled with us. They set their smoking matchlocks on the ground, apparently out of ammo. Soot already stained their chainmail, which covered their rose-colored cottons to the thighs. The plumes on their helmets seemed plucked from bloodied doves.

Any second, bombs could hit our position. We had to act.

"I'll kill the woman," Vaya said. "The rest of you go for Micah."

The five janissaries and I nodded. A bomb exploded a few feet away. A chunk of the midsection of a janissary painted the fountain red. Blood splattered on my face and over Vaya. We were bubbles, ready to be popped.

An unfazed Vaya rose and walked toward the seventh wall. Gunfire pierced the air. He didn't flinch as bullets arced around him. Incredible — but not unlike the magus I'd faced ten years ago. I rushed forward, keeping low. I dove beneath rubble to avoid gunfire. A janissary fell with a scream. Vaya reached the seventh wall's battlement and drew most of the fire. I ran forward.

My raging heart heightened my reactions and brought to the fore skills I'd learned years ago. I was young again as I charged the battlement with the janissaries. We slid behind the sandbag wall, which was about waist high and thick, and kept low; Micah the Metal crouched on the other side.

"Fuck you!" I shouted.

He shouted something in Crucian, so distant sounding as if he were on a mountain.

Beneath us, the strait-facing walls crumbled from the ships' ceaseless cannon fire. Men bellowed war cries as they jumped off the ships and onto the embankment, ready to scale the walls and claim the city. Even if we killed Micah, we would lose this battle. But maybe without his leadership, we could win the next one.

I had to kill him. The three janissaries with me waited for my command. Vaya stood ahead in the middle of the battlement. The Crucians had stopped firing at him, realizing the futility. Nothing had hit him.

Vaya said something to the woman. Then he raised his hand and pointed at her.

Wind! It hit the wall like a cannon, hurled several paladins into the water, and sent the woman flying. Was this Vaya's power? She landed on her feet at the edge of the battlement, the wind carrying her yellow scarf into the mountains. Vaya ran toward her. I took the chance. Signaled to the janissaries with me, and together we climbed over the sandbags.

Micah was staring at the spectacle of the magi. I swiped at his neck, but he blocked with his sword at the last moment. He towered over me and minded my movements. The janissaries killed some of his men; I barely heard their screams.

His lips moved with nonsense words. I lunged, but he was baiting me and dodged. Then he swung at my neck and cut my shoulder. Blood dripped down my arm. I didn't feel a thing.

Big men don't know their feet, so I ducked and swiped at them. I'd never seen a big man jump as he did. His foot smashed into my face. I crashed against the sandbags and spat bloody teeth.

"Fuck you!" I rose and lunged at his midsection; he side-stepped. His sword threaded the air a thimble's breadth from my cheek as I slid away.

The man grinned — he took pleasure in our fight, in living in the valley between life and death. Ten years younger, I would have wiped that grin off his face.

Green fire reflected in his eyes and a blast pushed me forward, into the man. We both fell over. My clothes were so hot, they scalded my back. The blast had destroyed part of the battlement behind me and dropped debris onto one of Micah's ships. The sailors screamed as it capsized.

Where had the magi gone? I didn't have time to look. Back on my feet, I stared Micah down. The janissaries had finished his men, and the three of us surrounded him. Nowhere to go.

We lunged at him. Micah elbowed me as he impaled the throat of a janissary and kicked him off the wall. The other janissary charged and Micah sliced his chest like hot wax.

I recovered and swung wildly — steel singing as my sword knocked his onto the stone ground. I wound up to slice his neck, but he grabbed my throat before I could swing. Choked and picked me off my feet. How strong could a man be? He dangled me over the edge where the green fire had blown up the battlement. Light faded from my eyes. Nothing in my lungs but a squeeze that shook my soul with death pangs. The end had come, and I was too terrified to pray.

And then Micah's hand tore off and flew in the air. I fell and grabbed onto the edge of the crumbling battlement. Dangling, I breathed deeply and alerted to a girl's whimpering. I could only pull up just enough to see.

Micah held Melodi by the neck. Her blade was red with his blood. It clanked on the ground as she flailed against his suffocating grip. The stump of his right arm oozed.

"Melodi!" I tried to climb. I pulled on the crumbling wall, grabbing whatever broken stone I could. Even though I heaved with twice the power I'd ever possessed, my arms were too weak to lift my decadent body.

In the final seconds as I struggled, Micah crushed my daughter's neck. He dropped her on the ground, picked up her sword that was red with his blood, and plunged it in her throat. Blood shot from her mouth. And then my hand slipped.

8

MICAH

I HAD TO HAND IT TO THE JANISSARIES. THEY FOUGHT ZEALOUSLY AND died with prayers on their tongues. Of the hundred paladins I brought through Labyrinthos, only thirty survived intact. One janissary cut through my men with a shamshir that glistened silver and red in the moonlight. But trained as the janissaries were with swords, guns won the night.

I bit down on the stick and reminisced as Jauz cauterized my stump. Even the little girls in Sirm could fight. How many big fuckers had I killed who couldn't cut a hair off me? And then some skinny girl sneaks up and slices my hand like a juicy ham.

I wished I'd let her live and shown her the true faith. What she could've been in my army. I wished I had one janissary for ten of the enemy — I'd never lose a battle. Or a hand.

But what matter was a hand? Its sacrifice brought me Kostany, the holiest city on earth. The infidels had turned our holiest chapel into a shrine for one of their accursed saints and called it the Blue Domes. I dreamed of restoring it as a place to hear the hymns of the angels.

Too bad for the janissaries that they had no leadership. Berrin told me the Shah was worn from mounting the dogs in his harem and so slept through the battle. Without direction, the janissaries ran at us as we shot them.

I couldn't blame the Shah. In his darkest nightmare, a hundred holy paladins wouldn't have appeared beneath his palace. For that, I had to thank Aschere. But I hadn't had the chance because...where was she?

Berrin hunched his shoulders and shook his head when I asked him. He'd commanded my fleet and with the help of the Ejazi squeezed enough ships through the strait and unloaded enough men on the shores to breach the weakest wall. I hadn't seen Aschere since she blew up half the wall I was fighting on. Now we couldn't access the inland Siyah Sea. Backbreaking labor could clear that debris, but no one wanted to work on this day of holy celebration.

Though not everyone could celebrate because the city below the Seat was on fire. We let it burn. What good were these Sirmian hovels? And if fellow Ethosians burned too? The thought pained me, but the Archangel would know his own.

Thank the Archangel the girl sliced my hand clean. Jauz wrapped my stump and tied it to my shoulder with a cotton strap. The hand that I didn't have burned. The herb tea helped a little.

So much to do. I assembled my lieutenants in the great hall. We dragged a long marble table and fancy metal chairs from storage so we wouldn't have to sit on the floor like beggars. The Shah must have used them when entertaining his Rastergani allies. To make this room proper, I'd have to tear down the Paramic nonsense that glistened on the walls and melt the gold peacock with the ruby eyes. But these were matters for later. Justice mattered now.

"The prison beneath the Seat overflows with those we captured," Zosi said. He nursed a wound too. While taking the walls, a militiaman bashed his nose with a shield and now he spoke as if his nose was pinched. "Even with this sad nose, the place smells ungodly. Reminded me of my long days in the hole."

"From now on, no more prisoners." I sat back and put my feet on the table. Kostany air tasted of sweet blood and smoke. "Where do the Sirmians do their beheadings?"

"Up in Angelfall," Berrin said. That was the true name of the hilltop where the Blue Domes sat. "The only place in the city we don't control." His cheeks reddened with righteous fury. "They've bloodied our holiest chapel with their injustice for too long."

"How many are holed up there?" I asked.

"No more than forty," Zosi answered.

"I'll deal with them myself."

"And what of the Shah?" Berrin asked, his voice dripping with loathing.

Fuck. I wished someone had done me the favor of killing the Shah. You'd think it simple to kill a king — lop off the head. But killing a king was more politics than war. If the Imperator heard I'd beheaded the Shah without permission, I'd be in deeper heavy water.

"I'll write to the Imperator regarding the Shah. For now, keep him locked in his chambers. Let him have a few more nights of the good life."

Aside from the Shah, there were no safe worshippers of Lat in Kostany. Only one thing would cleanse this holy place: the eradication of disbelievers.

The fire did some of that. We hadn't started it, but it purified the streets all the same.

"One more thing." Berrin hesitated to speak his facts, clearly not wanting to ruin the holy mood. "The larders are bare."

"Have you checked underground?" Zosi asked. "Our spies mentioned they'd stockpiled two years of grain."

"Burned," Berrin said. "All of it. Once the food on our ships finishes, we'll have to find more. Outside the walls."

"Two years of grain would've secured our conquest," I said. "Whoever gave the order to burn it was a quick thinker. Curse him."

I could purify Kostany, but the land outside the wall? The Sirmians had held this city and the surrounding lands for three hundred years. The Ethosian farming villages could help us, but getting to them while being hunted by zabadar horse archers would be difficult.

"It's zabadar country outside the walls," I said. "I promised each paladin a fief. We'll have to fight for every blade of grass."

Unlike the janissaries and professional armies of Sirm, the zabadar lived in the yurt villages of the plains. It was said that zabadar children learn to ride horses before learning to walk. Both boys and girls served as warriors, so there was no shortage of them, and each owned five foals from birth. Their recurve bows were said to be made from the sinew of ice mammoths, but that sounded fanciful. The truth though: put a zabadar on a Kashanese horse and even the best gunner would be challenged to down the rider before an arrow found his head.

"We haven't achieved our dream of a free land," Zosi pinched the bandage on his nose, "until we force the zabadar back into the Waste from whence they came."

The shahs made it policy to settle scores of zabadar tribes around Kostany. This was why worshipers of Lat now outnumbered worshippers of the Archangel in these lands.

As I pondered what to do, the gold peacock stared at me. Its malevolent ruby eyes sent shudders through my body. With its wings outstretched and head tilted down, it looked ready to attack. These Seluqals were not merely heathens; they were garish too.

"Zosi," I said, "take a contingent of heavy riders with matchlocks and attack the zabadar villages within a day's ride."

"As you command, Grandmaster." Zosi walked away to do his job, still clutching his nose.

Berrin and I discussed rudimentary matters. Where would the army be housed? In the janissary barracks. What could they claim? Anything in the city, but they were not to plunder the Seat, as its treasures belonged to the Imperator. Who would man the walls? Edmar's men. What would we do with our dead? Bury them. And the enemy's dead? Throw them in the Shrunken Strait, where they would flow down to the shores of the Siyah Sea and fatten the birds.

I found Aicard smoking a hookah pipe in the palace garden. He'd let his blond hair grow longer than was fitting. All an act. He always played a new part wherever we went, whatever direction his fancies took. I didn't claim to understand it.

"Is this what it means to free a city?" He blew out smoke. I never liked the hookah. It led to sin. For Aicard, sin was a tool by which he served the Archangel.

"We didn't massacre disbelievers in Ejaz," he said.

"The Ejazi didn't profane our holy sites and relics. Enough. I have a task for you."

Colorful birds fluttered overhead, oblivious to the death. Their vulture cousins knew well and picked at the dead throughout the palace grounds.

"I've been waiting for you to task me." Aicard was on something, his eyes red and gazing nowhere.

"Sober up, then go into the city. Go outside the walls and into the plains if you must. Make your connections with the people — your eyes and ears — and find Aschere. Her part in our war is not over." I grabbed his shoulder. "You understand?"

"And what of your part in her war?" Aicard's complexion cleared. The red in his eyes turned white, and he stared at me straight-faced. A trick. Somehow, he'd appeared intoxicated when he was perfectly sober. He played his parts so well. "I'll find out what I can. Not just about her, but the other magi and all who would plot against us."

A good man and among the five I trusted most. His faults were between him and the Archangel.

I RESTED and ate and drank. I prayed and gave thanks to the Archangel. Then I cleaned my sword of bloodstains to make space for more.

At the top of the steep stairs to Angelfall, I looked upon the city. It would've been beautiful if smoke didn't smother the air. But the purifying fire was its own divine beauty.

The Seat seemed peaceful. Its green dome shimmered under the sun, not unlike Aschere's eyes. Where had she gone? Strange, to be yearning for the presence of a disbeliever. But the way she fought that magus upon the wall, flinging green fireballs from the sky…better that power be for our cause than against it.

Gold Paramic calligraphy profaned the outer walls of our holiest chapel. The Archangel revealed himself to mankind here. And within Angelfall, buried deep, was our holiest relic: the Tear of the Archangel, who wept at the sins of the Fallen Angels and those that followed them. It was said that the Tear was a shard of clear crystal, and those who touched it died with a smile of divine ecstasy. That's why the apostle Josias, namesake of our new imperator, encased the Tear in glass and hid it below Angelfall.

Was the Tear still intact, or had the Sirmians profaned it like everything else? I shook off such thoughts. Today was not for ruminating.

"I am Micah the Metal," I shouted at the double door of the chapel. "Profess faith in the Archangel and I will let you live. Cling to your false god, and I will bloody this place."

I gestured to my warriors, who stood with guns drawn, to go down a few steps so they couldn't be seen. Now I was alone with the forty unbelievers inside the chapel.

The door creaked open. A man with a tidy hazel beard limped out, covered in sweat. He wrapped his turban like a scarf around his shoulders. Distant eyes lay behind his golden spectacles — a look of defeat, not defiance.

"Peace, Micah the Metal." He spoke Crucian with a thick accent. "I shepherd the flock within these walls."

"I was told you numbered forty."

"Forty ready to die." The man rubbed at a burn wound on his leg. "But far more innocents who would rather live."

"Who are you? How do you know our language?"

"I am Grand Mufti Taymah. I know your language because I minister to your people too."

"Too bad you minister for a false god."

"I am not here to argue theology. I am only here to safeguard the lives of the innocents within these walls. Dozens of mothers, clutching their babes and praying for succor. And children. Who can help them but you? Are you a man of mercy?"

"That wound in your leg..." Bloody pus festered over the hole in his trousers. "You'll be dead if you don't treat it."

"I'll gladly die for what I believe. But enough blood has been split. You are the victor. Show them the mercy of the Archangel and let them go."

I looked up at the blue-colored domes and imagined the Archangel standing above, his form stretching to the sun. What glory it was to the faithful who witnessed him, a thousand years ago. Eleven wings and a single eye stared down at them, a form that drove all but the true believers to madness. Would that I could see him too.

And then I saw a little girl standing on a dome. At her height, she couldn't have been older than three. She wore a gray rag and had long dark hair. Her eyes were black — only black, no whites — and she smiled widely with black teeth. I squinted, but the only other detail I could discern was the straw doll she clutched.

I closed my eyes. Could it be the lack of sleep? When I opened them, she was gone. Ah, and then I realized: Jauz had mixed some strange herbs into my tea to numb the pain in my phantom hand.

"I will show mercy to all who profess the true faith," I said. "Tell your flock to bow to the Archangel and they can go."

"Our faith is dear to us, as is yours to you."

"There is no other way. If you are their shepherd, guide them to the truth. The next time you come out, my sword will be drawn to slay any who do not submit to the one true god."

Once the Mufti had gone back inside, I whistled to my paladins waiting on the stairs. They returned and drew their guns. Angelsong taught us to be merciful, even to a stray cur. Though the Sirmians had never shown us mercy — raiding our towns, bloodying our streets, stealing our wives and children — I pledged to be better than them. And yet, how many Ethosians wailed for justice? To choose between vengeance's sword and mercy's shield…

We waited an hour under the sun, and then the door opened. Out came mothers, children, and old men, all haggard from a night of terror. They must've numbered a hundred. And behind them were forty youths who, upon exiting the chapel, dropped their guns and spears and swords on the ground. Some wore the gaudy colors of the janissaries, others a black frock, and yet more were in rags.

In the meantime, I'd summoned Berrin to translate. He spoke perfect Sirmian since he was once one.

He asked them to bow before the Archangel and be saved. To say the words "I testify that my ally is the Archangel alone, and my enemy the Fallen, and to bow only before the Archangel till my dying breath" then get on their knees and kiss the holy ground.

The mothers and children and old men did just that. They testified to the Faith, got on their knees, and even the mothers pushed their foreheads to the ground while clutching their babes.

But the Mufti and the youths did not follow. Their lips

remained closed to our holy words. Their knees did not bend, and their foreheads were not dusty with the sacred soil of Angelfall.

Nothing was worse than false faith. Professing true words that you don't believe only to save your life. But I couldn't judge the hearts of those who knelt — that was the angels' duty. I could judge only words and actions, and those refusing to bow made their hard hearts known.

The Mufti limped through the throng of new believers to ask, "Will you let them go, now?"

"I made you a promise on sacred soil. And I am a man of mercy, as the Archangel compels. They are free." I stuck two fingers in my mouth and whistled. "Make way!"

My paladins stood to the side. The mothers and children and old men rushed down the steps as if running from a raging bull. That left us with the forty or so youths who'd refused to bow.

"Your heart is hard." I unsheathed my sword and plunged it in the Mufti's heart. He croaked and recited dying words. Blood gushed from his mouth and onto holy ground.

"But not hard enough." I wiped my blade on his robe. Red stained white.

The forty did not resist as my paladins painted Angelfall red.

HOURS LATER, I was eating a sour fig beneath the ugly gold peacock when Berrin burst in, breathless.

"Forgive me, Grandmaster." He dropped to his knees.

"What happened?"

He closed his eyes and shook his head in that strange, diagonal Sirmian way, as if swaying to slow music. "We just let the heir go."

I sat up on the golden couch. "What heir?"

"The Shah's heir was among those we let go at Angelfall!"

"But we only let mothers and old men and children go at Angelfall. We have all the older sons in the dungeon."

Berrin covered his face with his elbow. "It's my fault. I foolishly assumed the secret heir was one of the older sons, but for some reason, it seems the Shah chose a small boy. We let him and his mother go."

"Are you certain?"

"One of the high viziers we captured spat out the secret as the torturer twisted his nails off. The chief harem eunuch confirmed. The governors of the lands, the khagans of the zabadar, the janissary commanders — they'll all flock to wherever the boy and his mother make court."

I unsheathed my sword. Berrin trembled as if my blade was for him.

"Oh Berrin, only the angels are perfect." I beckoned him to follow as I headed outside. "Send our fastest horses after them. It's their country so we may already be too late."

Sunset dyed the world red. Fire still raged below in the city and smoke obscured the waning light. A garden stroll sounded like a pleasant respite.

Once there, I climbed the dais of the garden's sitting area, leaned my sword against a wooden chair, and sat upon a wide cushioned bed. "I'm going to relax here." The garden was more garish than the great hall. Gold, purple, and white flowers surrounded us, clustered in star shapes. Manicured bushes took the form of birds. A stream even ran through it. The whole place smelled of musk roses, congesting my nose. "But I could do with some company. Bring me the Seluqal House. The harem. The boys and girls. The babies. All of them."

Berrin nodded. Before he left earshot, I called to him again. He turned to face me, thick eyebrows pointed to heaven.

"One more thing. Bring me the Shah."

A delighted grin seized his face. There was no one Berrin hated more than Shah Murad. Ten years ago, Murad ordered the massacre of Berrin's noble house because they supported the chosen heir Selim. The zabadar who attacked Berrin's fief left the bodies of his brothers to rot in a ditch. They raped his mother before impaling her to the door of the manor. His sisters escaped in the night, though he never heard from them again. Berrin had wanted to die that day too, but not before vengeance. Unfortunately, I couldn't kill a king without the Imperator's blessing, but I planned to give Berrin some comfort.

Jauz, his bald head glistening, walked into the garden holding a hookah pipe. What was with these sinful pleasures?

He sat beside me, smelling of olive oil, which it seemed he'd rubbed on his scalp. "I know you don't like it, so I won't smoke in front of you." He rested the hookah behind him.

"Jauz, you can do anything you want, and I won't begrudge you. You know that."

"It was a long night. We all need to unwind. Find some pleasure amid this fire."

"And what pleasures delight you? Aside from that pipe."

"All pleasures, Grandmaster. There aren't any I deny myself."

Colorful birds fluttered and danced in the cedar at the center of the garden.

"Then you're no different from those birds," I said, "except that you know better."

He laughed from his belly, as if I were joking. "My religion believes that each soul has only one life before it returns to the one, indivisible soul, which we call the Wheel. Best to make the most of life before we return."

His nonsense religion did not interest me. But Jauz was a man I always suffered. I nodded and pretended to care. "And why do you call it the Wheel?"

"Because a wheel never stops turning, like birth and death. We are just spokes on that wheel, distinct yet a part of it."

"If we're all the same, then our actions, good or evil, don't matter."

"A thousand years ago, a meteor landed in the Silklands and killed nearly everyone. Did that meteor care who was good or evil?"

"Obviously not, a meteor is just rock." *The one who sent it did.*

"The thousand-mile crater — that is our holy land. And the jade we mined from it — our idols." Jauz took out the jade idol from his pocket. It was fire green, like Aschere's eyes. But where was *she*? "To remind us that we are just spokes on the Wheel."

I'd never heard a greater absurdity. Even the Latian goddess made more sense. At least they bowed before something with form. This jade idol was just a lump.

Berrin walked into the garden. And behind him were men, women, children, babies — all wearing silks and brocade and jewels. I'd never seen such finery in one family, and I'd conquered several kingdoms.

The Seluqal House assembled before me. My paladins stood as a black wall around them. Then they brought him out.

The Shah was in his nightclothes, which for Sirmians was a baggy shirt. I didn't think Berrin's story about the Shah sleeping through the battle to be true, but it seemed it was. Disappointing to see a great king unkempt and stinking like a street dweller.

"Bring him here." I seated the Shah on the chair next to me, where I'd leaned my sword. His dark and rage-filled eyes would not leave mine.

"Unbind his hands."

I hoped the Shah would grab my sword and go for my throat, giving me a reason to kill him that the Imperator couldn't fault. But he dropped his arms and glared at me.

His harem and children, standing in the grass, bowed their heads. They still revered their captive shah. I suppressed a chuckle.

"You have a wonderful family, Shah Murad," I said. He, of

course, understood Crucian. "Beautiful women, with hair and eyes shades of the world's prettiest jewels."

I smiled at one of the dozen children. She was Elly's age when I'd last seen her and had chubby cheeks. "Look at this one." I waved at her and she puffed her cheeks and smiled back so sweetly. "A treasure from god. All your children look to me as treasures divine."

I stared at one of the older girls, who hid her dazzling face under a red scarf. "And the girls, they are ripe pearls. But I'm sure your poets have more colorful words to describe them."

The Shah did not cease glaring at me, rage coursing through his iron-red face.

The older boys wore white vests with pearls and rubies glistening from the seams.

"The princes are like from the stories. Tall and muscular, with straight jaws and chiseled noses." I dipped my head toward the Shah's fuming face. "You surely are the son of Seluq. I see a family that would make even our imperator jealous. Imagine how I feel, a man who has none?"

The Shah sat forward in his chair and looked upon his family, his breaths rapid.

"I'll give you a chance to save them. Proclaim your faith in the Archangel and I will let them go, just as I did those in the chapel."

The Shah did not break silence. His eyes moved across his family, to each of them.

I gestured to Edmar. He unsheathed his dagger and stabbed one of the older princes in the throat. Blood sprayed into the grass and reddened the garden's stream. The rest of them gasped and screamed. A woman in a blue dress — probably the prince's mother — wouldn't stop wailing until a paladin smashed his hilt into her teeth.

The Shah gaped, eyes bulging. He clung to the armrests and trembled. But he did not break silence.

"You make me do terrible things, Shah. I don't want to hurt them. Proclaim the true faith!"

Berrin's baby cheeks rose; he bit his lip to keep from smiling. Jauz tugged at his mustache, mouth tight.

One of the older princes ran, but he hit the wall of paladins, bounced off a shield, and fell on the gravel. Edmar stabbed him in the stomach and kicked his body into the flower bed. Blood pooled. A concubine fainted with slobber on her chin. Another mother down.

The Shah's eyes were so wide, I feared they'd fall out. But he did not break silence.

I gestured to a paladin to start on the girls. Surely that would break the Shah.

While Edmar killed the next mature prince, the paladin stabbed one of the older girls in the back. Her death scream was shrill as an animal. And as more of the Shah's family ran into the wall of shields, more of my paladins joined in, poking their spears at whatever flesh they could find. One of them impaled the lovely girl with the red scarf. The screams of terror and despair could haunt a demon.

Tears welled in the Shah's eyes. His hands shook, banging against the armrests. He eyed my sword but did not break silence.

I gestured for my men to stop. Seven bodies lay on the ground. The stream was bloody, and blood-stench filled the air.

"Shah, this will end the moment you profess your faith in the one true god. Save your family."

He turned to me, his quivering lips heavy with slobber. But he did not break silence.

I nodded for my men to continue. A concubine with the deep eyes of the Silklanders tried to jump over the wall of paladins, but only found the edge of a blade. That paladin then thrust forward and stabbed the heart of a woman with dark Kashanese features who was cowering on the ground with her little prince.

The paladin had a good streak going, his sword dripping with flesh bits, and so turned toward a concubine with cinnamon skin and red hair. But she ducked under his slash, and from her white dress, pulled out a dagger and uppercut it in his throat.

He fell to the ground and joined the bodies. Another paladin swung down on her with an axe, but she sidestepped, yelled a war cry, and jammed her dagger through his cheek.

The women of Sirm had impressed me again. Ten paladins aimed their spears at her.

"Wait!" Jauz shouted and stood. "Don't hurt her!"

A paladin knocked the dagger out of her hand with the back of his spear, and more jumped to restrain her. She wrestled until they pushed her to the ground. It took four paladins to keep her there.

"You promised me one of the treasures of the Shah." Jauz pointed at the red-haired woman, who screamed and flailed as paladins restrained each of her limbs. "I choose her."

I laughed. "She'll murder you while you meditate."

"Maybe, but is she not the most beautiful woman you've ever seen?"

Her light brown skin glistened. Her nose was slender and her large eyes a warm amber. Not to mention her deep red hair, which was exotic enough. But she was not beautiful. True beauty comes from faith, and I did not see the light of the Archangel in her face.

"I can't let you have this one. She's already killed two of my men."

Jauz stared me down. "You promised that if I chose one to marry, she would be mine."

"Not this one!"

"Who made it so your ships could sail the shallow strait, just in time to ensure victory? Who designed the fast-firing guns that left the weapons of the janissaries as useless as sticks and stones?"

I did not like his tone, but Jauz wouldn't have defied me unless he really wanted her. And I needed him...for all the reasons he'd just mentioned.

"Don't blame me when she sends you back to the Wheel."

My paladins dragged the woman away, to wherever Jauz intended to keep her. He left with them.

The worst thing was the defiance in the Shah's face. He raised his head with pride, tears streaming into his ferocious beard. That woman must've been dear to him, and now Jauz had taken her away.

I gestured to Edmar and the paladins to continue.

Minutes later, concubines and mature children of the Shah littered the garden. He stared at the dead with vacant eyes, head swaying as if dizzy.

But the little ones remained, and babies cried in their mothers' arms. I commanded my paladins to slay the mothers and seize the babies. The cries of mothers and children filled the garden as steel rent flesh. The final song of his family.

"Shah Murad, it's not too late to spare the little ones. Profess the true faith!"

But the Shah did not break silence.

I brought forward the little girl with chubby cheeks. I scratched her head and caressed her cheek. Dried her tears a little. Then I forced her head into the bloody stream. She choked and shook and her legs pounded the ground. I pushed harder until her body filled with water. Life left her and she lay still.

The Shah retched his soupy dinner onto his bare legs. Then, as if he'd had enough, he sat back and shut his eyes. But it was hardly over. I stood behind him, put my fingers around his shivering head, and pulled his eyes open. He had to see what was coming.

I'd chosen vengeance's sword. And I did not regret it. Every Ethosian who'd ever been wronged by these curs would be made right. Our dead would not be forgotten, and our living would know that by my hand justice was wrought.

My paladins drowned each child. Then we put the babies in the grass. Covered them with dirt. We trampled them until their crying ceased. In one hour, I'd extinguished the Seluqal House of Sirm.

Still, the Shah did not break silence.

9

KEVAH

THE BODY IS THE SHRINE OF LAT. TO BRING IT BACK TO EARTH, ONE must wash it. Wipe away blood and cut loose flesh. Sew wounds and cover what can't be sewn with cloth. The shroud must be pure. The grave should be dug deep so that no animal could unearth the holy shrine. When placing the body to rest, the holy words must be recited: *To Lat we belong and to her we return.*

When the bodies pile up, this holy work never stops. But no matter how large the pile, the work must be flawless. To hurry a step or set her shrine to earth crudely is to offend Lat.

Every morning, bodies washed ashore. And every morning, I buried them. All were bloated, but I imagined them at their best. I built my hut at the shore so I could watch them float in. And they continued to.

I buried men without arms. Men without legs. Men cut in half and men without heads. Women too. Some with burnt faces that smelled of moist charcoal, and others serene as if only asleep.

I buried girls and boys. I buried babies. But I did not bury Melodi.

She never showed. I waited. I prayed for her — my only

daughter. Of the hundreds of shrines I planted, I could not plant hers.

At first, I was sure she wasn't dead. I looked for her among the bodies, knowing that she would only be asleep. The Crucian hadn't stabbed her throat…he couldn't have. She would float to me on the Siyah Sea, and I would mend her wounds and hold her until she was well.

When she did not come, I beat the earth. I covered my face in dirt and cursed Lat. I screamed that I would never believe in her, that I would spend my days profaning her name.

And then I prayed for her to send Melodi to me. Send me sweet Melodi, so I could plant her shrine. But even that, Lat would not give. What kind of god was she? What kind of god takes and takes from those who give and give?

And so I gave. I cleaned bodies. I planted shrines, and though I had no cloth to make shrouds, I wrapped each body with leaves from the forest. And I waited for Lat to give me one, small thing: Melodi's lifeless body.

Why was I alive when she was dead? Why did Ahriyya curse me with life? Why did he put that cloth sail beneath me to break my fall and make me land softly in the sea? Surely a life such as this was his dark doing.

Every morning, more bodies floated to shore. I was sure I'd buried the whole of Kostany, but Melodi was not among them. Just to see her face, even decayed and half-eaten, would've been more succor than Lat had ever shown me. But even that was too much for her.

In my hut by the night fire, I saw Melodi's eyes dim a thousand and one times. Micah the Metal stabbed her throat a thousand and one times. So even while jackals and foxes prowled, I buried bodies. If I slept, it was in the minutes after I'd dug a deep hole with my hands, which were so swollen I could barely feel them. Whenever I rested longer, I'd see Melodi's eyes grow cold.

I'd see blood spew from her mouth and Micah the Metal's insane smile.

No one bothered me because no one was here. Until a horseman rode to shore. He wore a thick blue caftan beneath a maroon leather vest and pants, a turban wrapped around the sheepskin and fur of his zabadar cap. He watched me bury the bodies and rode away.

The next day, more came. Three horsemen and three horse-women. They watched me, straight-backed and high on their horses. I prayed that they would kill me, but that was not their purpose. I had nothing of value, and the zabadar didn't kill for sport.

Then the next day, a horde rode to shore. Men and women on horseback covered the seaside. I protested as they dragged the bodies, washed them, and dug graves. These were my holy tasks, not theirs. I shouted and cursed, but they did not heed and continued burying the bodies. If they made a mistake, I waved my fist and corrected them. They always listened, and in the end, did it right. We planted hundreds of shrines that day, but not Melodi's.

After, I returned to my hut of sticks and leaves and kindled a fire. There were no more bodies to distract from Melodi's dead eyes. I wept so loudly that the zabadar must have laughed at the aged, mad, weeping man. A man too weak to protect those he loved. A man who did not deserve the breaths he stole from life.

I saw her watching me: a young woman with dark red hair and kind eyes. I'd seen her earlier directing the zabadar. She approached the fire and knelt at my feet.

"The work is done now," she said. "You should not stay here. It isn't safe."

I rubbed my eyes to dry my tears. I didn't want her kindness. I wanted Lat's. "I cannot leave."

She took my swollen hands. "Are you waiting for someone?"

I must have seemed mad. Waiting for the dead.

"I'll keep some men here to bury the bodies that wash ashore," she said. "They will be honored and buried properly. I promise."

I shook my head. "No, I must do it. It is the last thing I must do before I die."

"And why would you die?"

She truly had the kindest eyes. The softest voice. Like a mother calming a child.

I gazed into the fire and saw Micah the Metal laughing with Melodi's throat on his sword.

"I will kill that man!" I said.

The young woman sat next to me. How bad I must've smelled. I'd washed so many bodies yet neglected to wash myself. I was still wearing my bedclothes from Kostany. And yet, she didn't seem to mind.

"What's your name?" she asked.

"Kev...ah." I hated the sound of it.

"I knew of someone with your name. My father used to talk about him. A great warrior."

"I'm nothing of the sort. I don't deserve to share a name with him."

She shook her head. Tears welled in her eyes. "I disagree. My zabadar told me of a man dragging bodies out of the sea and burying them in the holy way. I scarcely believed it. But then more of them told me of you, and I had to see for myself. Whether or not you realize it, what you have done here is great." She wiped her tears. "You deserve better than this."

"No, I let the city fall. I let my daughter die. Had I only been stronger. Had I only been as strong as I once was, I would have sent that man to hell!"

The woman hugged me as I wept. How could she bear the smell?

She touched my shoulder wound. Bloody puss dirtied her fingers. "You must have this treated. I'm bringing you to camp."

I protested while two muscled zabadar doused my fire and broke my hut. Then they grabbed me and plopped me on a horse. When I tried to jump off, they bound me with rope.

An hour later, I was sipping soup in a colorful yurt while a healer cleaned my wound. Still, I wanted to run back to shore.

I slept through the night on a warm mattress and awoke to chirping birds and croaking cicadas. My wound was sewn and bandaged, someone had scrubbed the gunk off my skin, and I was wearing fresh clothes. Maybe the soup contained a sleeping herb? Or maybe I'd blacked out from all the nights I hadn't slept.

Though I wanted to go back to shore, I didn't want to get out of bed. Melodi was dead. To obsess on finding her body was lunacy. So I stayed in bed.

Nothing could stop those moments from repeating. I'd lost. I wanted to cry and rage, but I felt numb. My tear ducts were dry like the fire in my heart. All I could do was stay still. But it hurt to pass time.

I sat up when the young woman entered my yurt. She held a composite bow half her size and set it against the wall. Her red hair had the shine of a dying fire's embers, and her amber eyes were mellow and comforting. She took a chug from a waterskin as if putting out a flame inside her, then wiped sweat beads off her tanned forehead.

"How's your wound?" she asked.

"Feels better."

"And what about you?"

I sighed. "I'm sure you know I've seen better days."

"Tell me." She knelt over me, her knees touching my mattress. A long, leaf-patterned vest hung off her lithe form, beneath which were a leather shirt and pants. When she came close, it became plain she was sweating through her leathers, and it all smelled warm. "Do you feel sad or angry?"

"A lot of both. And a lot of nothing."

"Last night, you screamed 'I'll kill that man!' Who is he?"

"It doesn't matter. I'll never kill him. I'm not good enough."

"Micah the Metal." Her eyes were not kind anymore. Those amber pupils burned.

I looked away and nodded. The bells on the ceiling chimed as a breeze blew through the flaps. This yurt seemed finer than how I imagined a zabadar to live. The walls were a tapestry of blue, orange, and purple in diamond patterns. Aside from my bed, the floor was covered in similarly patterned carpets. An unlit stove in the center could provide fire, with a pipe that vented smoke rising out the ceiling flaps.

"I want him dead too," she said.

"So what?" I slouched into the sheepskin blanket. "Think Lat cares?"

"I don't need her help. Rely on god and you'll never know your own strength."

She removed her sheepskin cap and dabbed sweat off her hair, which curled upward at her shoulders.

"So you command the zabadar here?" I asked. "You seem far too young."

She smiled, revealing a chipped tooth. "I'm not what I seem."

A man wearing the vibrant cottons of the janissaries burst into the yurt. "Princess! I come with news." He bowed his head.

"What is it?" the young woman said. "You may speak freely."

"The heir is alive! Your brother Alir fled Kostany and rides for Lyskar. The janissaries now flock to his banner!"

Her eyes twinkled. "Thank Lat." She breathed a sigh of relief. "Then we ride to Lyskar too."

The janissary bowed his head and walked backward to exit the yurt.

"I can't believe I let a princess hug my unwashed body," I said. "I thought you were a zabadar."

"I am a zabadar."

"I can't imagine the Shah let one of his daughters become a zabadar." I bit my tongue. "Meaning no offense. I love the zabadar. I'd spend my time with a horse warrior over some well-fed ninny any day. But I saw the Shah's children in Kostany. They were not like you."

"I am more my mother's daughter than I am his." She winced as if she'd swallowed something bitter. "I don't expect either of them are alive."

"I'm sorry, Your Highness," I said. "I threw my sadness on you and neglected to realize you carried your own."

"We've no use for formalities. All zabadar sit high upon their horses."

"What shall I call you, then?"

"My name is Sadie." She looked me over. "And you're Kevah. *The* Kevah."

"Disappointed?"

She shook her head and smiled. It was the warmest thing I'd seen in days. "Not even a little."

THE NEXT DAY, I awoke at dawn and walked into the forest. The birds here were unlike any I'd known. Some had narrow beaks that stuck out like horns, which they used to bang against tree bark. I loved the knock-knock-knock sound they made.

I came upon a pond where a family of turtles nestled. The pond must've been the world to them, small as they were. Would that I could be so oblivious of the wider world too.

And then I came upon a clearing. Blue flowers bloomed amid yellow grass. The petals blew into the wind and smelled of spring water. A stream bubbled through that led back into the forest.

I found an empty patch amid the field of flowers and dug. I dug and dug, just as I'd done for days, until the hole was deep enough for a body to stay safe.

I cupped water from the stream. Though there wasn't a body, I washed her anyway. I washed her hair, face, arms, and legs. I gathered the blue petals and wrapped her body in them, then put her in the hole.

"To Lat we belong and to her we return."

I filled the hole with blue petals and dirt. I would never forget this place. It was Melodi's shrine.

I turned to see Sadie standing over me. She didn't look like a zabadar today. She wore Seluqal clothes of white and yellow silk, embroidered with rubies that, while sharp, couldn't compare to the sheen of her auburn hair.

"You look different," I said.

"Just trying on some old clothes. I'll need them in Lyskar." She knelt in the grass, kohl evoking her amber eyes. "Whose shrine did you plant?"

"My daughter's." The words were hard to swallow. "You would have liked her. She was a zabadar in spirit...and kind of stupid."

Sadie chuckled, then covered her mouth. "Sorry."

"No, she loved to laugh. Laughter is better than tears."

"What was her name?"

"Melodi. A strange name."

"A beautiful name." Mud soiled Sadie's royal dress. She didn't seem to care.

"I'll kill the man who did this." My hands shook. "No matter what it takes. I'll descend into hellfire. I'll make a pact with Ahriyya if I must. Even if it costs me my soul, I will kill him."

Sadie took my hands. Her touch calmed the shaking. "Come with us, and we'll do it together."

"Lyskar is the wrong way."

"Are you going to storm the walls of Kostany by yourself?"

"If that's what it takes."

"My brother is in Lyskar. He'll be declared Shah, and the janissaries and zabadar will flock to him. Gholam from Alanya and khazis from Kashan will range through deserts and jungles to answer the call. Together, we can take Kostany as Utay did."

It sounded like a fairytale. Did she think it would be so easy? When Utay took Kostany, our people held it for three hundred years. I'm sure there were a bunch of sorry Crucians who thought they would take it back within a lifetime.

"You do that." I pulled my hands away and stuck them in the dirt. The ground was warm. I imagined Melodi's body inside, soothing the earth with its light and fire. "But I'm not a zabadar, and your father retired me from the janissaries. I'm a free man. Free to make his own foolish decisions. Free to die trying to kill a man twice his strength."

Sadie's amber eyes flared. "Do you want to kill Micah the Metal or die trying? Because there's a difference between avenging your daughter and failing at it."

I laughed and shook my head. "Throw all your horses and armies against him. We'll fail anyway. Better to fail quickly than slow."

She grabbed my shoulders and shook me. "My father told me about you, Kevah. A hundred armored Crucian cavalry broke through the ranks of the janissaries and thundered toward my grandfather's camp. On foot and with only a spear, you jousted a dozen riders off their horses and my grandfather lived to keep on fighting."

"It was only six. I embellished." It was actually four.

"As all great men do. You think Utay really moved ships over a mountain?"

I fell backward into a bed of flowers, laughing. "Don't compare me to Utay, all right? I was a boaster in my youth and could make rings with the smoke. And now I'm even less than that. I'm useless. I'm too fat and slow to fight, my reflexes too dull. I've got nothing to offer but a hopeless attempt at revenge — one that cannot wait."

Sadie knelt over me. What had she done to her dress? Mud seeped into the white silk.

"As my Alanyan mother would say, you have *ruh*, Kevah. A

spirit that could move a ship over a mountain. And we need that. You may not need our help to die — that's easy enough. But we need men like you to fight this war."

At that, she left me. I lay in the blue flowers and drifted to sleep. I wished to dream of Melodi and Lunara, the three of us making breakfast at my cottage in Tombore. I bought lamb and gutted and cut it while Lunara stirred the stew. Melodi chopped onions. But a fantasy isn't real and your mind knows. A dream though feels as real as life.

I should have known that even the jinn that whisper to us our dreams didn't care what I wanted. I woke from a dreamless sleep and returned to camp.

The zabadar went about their business around the yurts. Some fed chow buckets to horses while others cooked meat in pits. A zabadar blacksmith banged at an anvil to forge a spear tip. He should have been making a gun. Even the zabadar, swift as they were on horses, would struggle against Micah's fast-firing guns.

I found Sadie crying in her yurt. She clutched a scroll to her breast and punched the ground. I picked her up. She wailed against my chest and beat her hands against me.

"He killed them all!" she screamed.

I unrolled the scroll as she sobbed. Over thirty names were written, all of House Seluqal — her brothers and sisters and the Shah's concubines.

"He killed them all!"

The Shah was not on the list. Was he dead or not? Did it even matter?

I left Sadie to her sorrow. Sometimes you need to cry out grief, other times you need to hammer it out. No matter how strong you are, sometimes tears are the only comfort.

A blacksmith was banging at an anvil.

"Know how to make a gun?" I asked him.

The burly man squinted and looked at me like I was speaking another language.

"Guns, you fucker! Make guns!"

Other zabadar heard me, stopped what they were doing, and crowded around.

"Do you all want to die?" I shouted. "The fucker who seized Kostany has ten thousand guns that breathe fire and metal. Think your horses and arrows and spears will be enough?"

Sadie's wail punctured the air.

"Hear your princess crying!? Know why?"

"You!" I gestured to a tall, dark-haired zabadar clutching a spear. "Do you know why?"

He looked away.

"And what about you?" I glared at a wavy-haired zabadar girl kneeling by a fire. "You know why?"

I pointed at the bulky blacksmith, now smoothing his mustache. "Blacksmith, have you any answer?"

The entire clan crowded around me while their leader wailed in her yurt.

"Because we are weak. And you know what made us weak? Peace. For the last ten years, Micah the Metal has been spilling blood and conquering countries. And what were we doing? Raiding fishing villages."

I pointed to the blacksmith again. "Make some fucking guns!"

That was all I had to say. I returned to my yurt. I hated the look of my mattress. I hated the embroidery on the walls. I hated everything. So I went back outside.

The blacksmith was not happy to see me. He stood up straight and furrowed his lip.

"Give me a sword," I said. "I know I said to make guns, but just give me a sword."

He gestured with his head to a shamshir on the back table. I wiped the dust off the blade. Good enough.

The stable smelled like horse shit. Flies buzzed about. The stable master was a homely woman with too many missing teeth.

"I need a horse," I said.

"To go where?"

"With you lot."

The stable master smirked and patted the horse behind her: a brown beast with white spots and a silky tail.

Sadie emerged from her yurt. Tears had dried on her cheeks and trailed kohl across her face. A fierce look. I liked it. She still wore her muddy royal dress. She stumbled over it as she walked toward me. Fuming, she ripped off the part that hung on the ground, revealing tights underneath. I didn't mind.

10

MICAH

THE MATCHLOCK IS METAL PERFECTED. STUFF AN IRON BALL IN THE barrel on a bed of gunpowder and pull the trigger. Then, faster than the eye can see, your enemy is dead or screaming. It is a weapon unmatched, and when they write the history of Micah the Metal, it will be said I conquered the east with the matchlock.

But it took time to put more gunpowder in the barrel and stuff in another ball with a steel rod. A spearman could impale your throat as you fiddled with balls and sticks.

So Jauz made an ingenious modification: a revolving cylinder that fed the barrel with ammunition. It didn't always work. I'd seen it jam and explode and inflame the hands of my men. That was why I didn't use guns myself and wouldn't start considering I had only one hand.

Life with one hand was trifling, especially since I still had my dominant hand. Perhaps the creator gave us two hands as an excess. If it meant Kostany stayed free from unbelievers, I'd lop my other hand off.

Jauz had told me that in the Silklands, clever men devised metal arms that could take the place of flesh. His expertise, however, was limited to medicine, guns, and statues, and his fast-firing guns worked the night we took Kostany. So did the ships he'd modified. I didn't like relying on one man, especially when that man wasn't me. Especially when he wasn't a believer in the Archangel and had openly defied me.

While the rest of us were purifying Kostany of disbelief, Jauz had stolen one of the most ostentatious rooms in the Sublime Seat. The roof could open to the blue sky with the pull of a lever. A fountain bubbled in the center, adorned by marble busts of peacocks. He modified the room in one way: added an iron cage next to the royal bed to house his murderous new wife.

As I climbed the spiral staircase to his room, I wondered how their relationship had progressed. Before I knocked, I put my ear to the wooden door. By the Archangel, I had to cover my mouth to keep from laughing.

The woman was teaching Jauz what sounded like Paramic, and he was teaching her Crucian. And they were giggling! It had only been a week since we'd dragged her screaming from the bloody garden. I never knew Jauz could be so charming.

I decided not to disturb them. The love between a husband and wife is one of the three divinities that man can experience, the others being the love for your children and for the Archangel. I would deter none of those, lest I be working for the Fallen.

Back in the great hall, I ate bread with plum jam. I'd never liked sweets but craved them since losing my hand. Jauz had said my body needed nourishment to heal. But as I licked plum jam off my fingers, I felt guilty enjoying delights that my paladins couldn't.

Food was running out. I'd sent Zosi with five thousand paladins to raid the zabadar tribes, only to learn that the horse warriors had scorched their own fields and villages to deny us farmland and remain mobile.

They were ghosts. The riders would thunder at our flanks, launch arrows, and escape into the endless plain before we could fire back. They knew our weaknesses — our slowness and igno-rance of the land — and ruthlessly exploited them. According to Zosi, the zabadar clans were divided — ruled by khagans and khatuns — though nothing united like a common foe.

Every day, more city folk professed faith in the Archangel. Many slaves, grateful to be free, climbed the steps to Angelfall and kissed the holy soil. Once the fires had burnt out, my paladins started rebuilding the city. It would be holy again, and I pledged that under my custodianship, no vice or profanity would be tolerated.

I was first to break this rule when I cursed upon hearing the news from Berrin.

"Patriarch Lazar has arrived by ship with a hundred priests and choristers."

"Fuck!" I threw my plate at the gold peacock. It shattered against the ruby eyes. "What in the Archangel's holy name could he want?"

"Perhaps he's come with the Imperator's decision regarding the Shah's fate."

I'd kept the Shah in the dungeon, where his bed was a piss-smelling pile of hay. Berrin would visit to laugh at and taunt him. Since I didn't speak Sirmian, I didn't know the meaning of his insults. But they were not clever enough for the Shah to break his silence.

"You're too obsessed with that lecher." I snickered. "We've already given him a punishment a thousand times worse than death."

Berrin bowed his head. "Apologies, Grandmaster." We do not bow in the Ethos faith except to the angels, but he'd forgotten and reverted to his Sirmian ways. "But he yet lives. How is that justice?"

"Straighten your fucking neck." I wished I had another plate to throw at him. "As far as you're concerned, the Shah is dead, you understand?"

"As you say, Grandmaster. But does a dead man need a head?"

"Focus, Berrin! We are running out of food. The zabadar have made a fool of us. Go and do something about it."

"By your command, Grandmaster." He bowed his head again. Old habits always surface under duress.

"I swear if you bend your neck one more time, I'll take your head clean off it. Bring me the Patriarch, and then don't come back until you've done something about the zabadar."

It didn't feel good to scold Berrin. I trusted him more than anyone. He loved the Archangel earnestly. But the question was, did his hatred of the Shah burn fiercer than his love for the Archangel? That too was a kind of blasphemy.

I headed to the baths. After scrubbing myself raw of a week's worth of dead skin and dirt, I wore clothes my late wife had bought me: a black tunic with golden trim and soft blue pants, all beneath a blue and gold robe studded with a sapphire bauble. I'd been raised to believe that mankind was a flock and the Patriarch of the Ethos Church our shepherd. We'd never met; he was elected Patriarch after the last one died of the death sweat, shortly before my campaign in Ejaz. But my experience with priests had never been positive. And as he was the highest priest in the land, I imagined him the biggest cunt.

Would he chide me for burning Bishop Yohannes? Probably. Would he commend me for retaking our holy city? I hoped so. Already I wanted his approval, as if he were my father. I guess that was why they called him the Patriarch. And I loathed myself for it: the only approval one ought to seek is the Archangel's — all else was an impurity on the heart. Though I'd be lying if I said I didn't miss my father...

Angelsong hymned by angelic voices is the godliest sound. The choir men marched into the great hall on the left and the choir women on the right, wearing pure white gowns. The Patriarch's choir filled the Sublime Seat, and it became a holy place.

They hymned in unison, and the melody of their voices brought me to tears.

I didn't have time to dry my eyes. The Patriarch stood in front of me, beaming. He would not shake my hand. Instead, he embraced me and didn't let go until I'd stopped crying.

Had I prejudged the father of our faith? Was he a goodly man?

"It is a sin that it took us this long to meet," the Patriarch said. His hair was gray, and he even looked like my father. Just a simple, lanky old man. "I say that in jest, of course. The Archangel has willed our meeting at just the right time."

"Patriarch Lazar." I kissed his hand, as a good son should. "You honor me with Angelsong. Apologies, but I cannot contain myself."

"What is more beloved to the Archangel than the soft, bleeding heart of a believer? Did the Archangel not weep at the condition of man?"

I eyed the profane gold peacock with the ruby eyes. How I wished I'd melted it already. Though the hymns of the choir were holy, the Paramic verses on the walls were anything but. "Forgive me for the state of this room. I have not had time to purify it of falsehoods and idols."

"You should not ask forgiveness of me, Micah the Metal." The Patriarch grimaced as he bent his knees, yet stopped me when I tried to help him. On one knee, he looked up and said, "In the sight of angels and men, I beg forgiveness of you."

I shook my head, eyes still teary. "How can a shepherd beg forgiveness from a lamb?"

"Because I doubted you." Now the Patriarch cried. "I did not believe you would take this city back and cleanse it of unfaith."

I helped him back to his feet. "It was the angels who did that. I was but their instrument."

His tears were already dry. The Patriarch smiled. "As are we all."

Hand in hand as the apostles had done a thousand years ago,

we climbed the steps to Angelfall. I'd recently ordered my paladins to expunge the profanities and falsehoods from the chapel. I opened the double doors, and the Patriarch and I entered the holiest place of the Ethos faith.

The Paramic calligraphy had been painted over in Crucian purple. Beams of red, green, and gold shimmered through the stained-glass windows. The Latians worshipped on the floor, so we'd have to install pews. Angelfall today was a hollow hall ready to be filled with holy relics and hymns. But I'd leave that task to the Patriarch.

I helped him drop to his knees. He pushed his head to the floor and bowed. I did the same. We kissed the cool stone and prayed.

Though I said different words with my tongue, I prayed for Aschere in my heart. I begged the Archangel to bring her back. Together, we'd achieved a great good by reclaiming Kostany, and together we could do more good, but I'd heard nothing from Aicard since I'd tasked him to find her.

"Take me to the crypts," the Patriarch said, his voice trembling with fervor. His eyes were that of a boy bearing witness to the Archangel's glory. "I must see our holy relics."

"The crypts are empty. The relics gone. We don't know where they were taken."

"Then our test is not over." The Patriarch's lips quivered. His voice grew hoarse. "We have not reclaimed the whole of this place until the relics are back where they belong."

"Even if I must rend that godless mountain city they call Zelthuriya, I will bring all our relics back."

The Patriarch took my hand. "You truly are a warrior baptized in the heavy water of the High Holy Sea. With you leading our armies, I believe I will witness the Tear of the Archangel before I die."

Seven hundred miles of Latian-infested country separated us from Zelthuriya, and the Patriarch was old. Still, I believed that one day I would conquer that land, find the Tear of the Archangel, and make him and all Ethosians proud. My father used to tell me of the Tear's miracles at bedtime, and I'd dream of holding it. My hope when we reconquered Kostany was that it would be waiting for me in the crypt, throbbing with white light. But it seemed my dream lay farther east.

"I will sit and pray in silence for a while," the Patriarch said. "If you don't mind."

While he prayed at the bare altar, I descended into the crypts. Books and scrolls littered the floor and shelves. Most were written in the strange Paramic lettering, with its swirls and flourishes. Why hadn't my paladins burned this profanity?

Maybe it was good they hadn't. Berrin could sift for clues about the whereabouts of the Tear of the Archangel. There could be other useful information too. It was worth wading through this unholy muck to gain knowledge of the enemy. I'd learned long ago that knowledge wins wars as much as steel.

The ruffling of paper. Behind me. I shone my lantern and saw a leg move behind a shelf.

"Patriarch Lazar?"

No response. Only footsteps. I didn't have a weapon and shined the lantern with my only hand.

I crept to where I saw the leg. Nothing there. Perhaps I'd imagined it, but I wasn't drinking Jauz's herb teas anymore.

Laughter. A child's sweet chuckle. I knew that laugh. I rushed toward the shelf where it came from. Nothing. Just books and scrolls.

"Are you all right?"

I gasped at the Patriarch's voice and almost dropped my lantern. "I'm...all right. Just a little...jumpy."

He looked upon the books and scrolls. "Quite a library." He picked a dusty book and opened it, then read some words in Paramic.

"You can read that unholy language?" I asked.

"No language is unholy, Micah. All can spread Angelsong. One day men will hymn praises to the Archangel in Paramic, too. Perhaps it will be you who sees to that."

The Patriarch was halfway up the stairs when I asked him, "Could...could a demon profane a holy place such as this?"

Patriarch Lazar scratched his chin, then nodded with a glint in his eyes. "Didn't they for three hundred years?"

WE RETURNED to the Sublime Seat. I took the Patriarch by the hand into the dungeon.

"I must warn you," I said as we descended the spiral staircase, "the smell is unbearable for the uninitiated."

"My father was an undertaker. I've tolerated all manner of smells."

My lantern light revealed prisoners cowering in their own piss and shit while cockroaches nibbled on their shins and lice coursed through their hair. They called to us as we passed, begging in the Sirmian language. One or two of them even shouted "Help!" with their thick accents. I hated that the Patriarch had to walk through this mess, but we'd placed the Shah in an isolated cell at the end.

The Shah was standing. He looked better than the others because we gave him more food and bathing water to keep him sickness free. It was the least I could do for the Imperator, who had the right to decide his fate.

Patriarch Lazar said some words to the Shah in Sirmian. A man of many talents, clearly. How many languages did he speak?

My eyes almost flew out of their sockets when the Shah muttered a response. It was the first time he'd said a word since I'd taken Kostany from him.

"What did you say? What did he say back?"

The Patriarch ignored me and continued conversing with the

Shah. Was I so small? The Shah kept stoic as he spoke, not a hint of emotion in his eyes.

Finally, Patriarch Lazar said, "Don't be taken aback, Micah. He only spoke to me because we've met before."

"When was this?"

"More than a decade ago during a negotiation in Rastergan. I simply asked him if he remembered me, and he affirmed. We talked a little about that day, beautiful as it was, to refresh our memories. Nothing else was said."

I waved the lantern in the Shah's face. He blinked, jaw loose and gaze placid.

"I cut down his family like chattel, and he didn't say a word. But now suddenly he talks to you for the sake of reminiscence?"

The Patriarch took my hand and led me away. "About that… Micah, you must temper your holy metal. You may conquer many more countries in the east, but you cannot again do what you did with his family."

Now he really was acting like my father.

"Have you ever conquered a city? Ruled a country? None of it can be done without blood and fear."

The Patriarch put his hands on my arms as rotting dungeon stench filled my nose. "I am not here to school you. You are no doubt the expert in those matters. But what would happen if our imperator's family were to fall into their hands, angels forbid? Do you think history will forget what you did? The Seluqal House rules three great kingdoms, and you have made a mortal enemy of them all — till the end of time."

"I promised each paladin a fief in the east, and the Seluqals claim all the land from here to the Waste. They called themselves conquerors — until they met me."

I parted ways with the Patriarch and stormed out of the dungeon. How many Ethosians had been murdered or enslaved by the dogs of the Seluqal House? How many widows had wailed and orphans shed tears? Instead of praising me, I faced a chiding? I would slaughter that family a thousand times to avenge each fallen Ethosian. Just because they were of king's blood, I should have spared them? Holding some higher than others, for blood or wealth or rank, was the root of injustice.

Back in the great hall, I ate a semi-ripe fig, sour as it was. The fig was known to calm the blood, and it did much to ease the simmering within. The Patriarch's scolding had upset me, and I was reacting like a child. He had disarmed me with angelic hymns and treated me as an underling, as any lamb ought to be of their shepherd. But I preferred butchering lambs to being one.

I visited the Patriarch in the chambers I'd assigned him: a simple, though large room in the Sublime Seat. Some choristers were there, hymning as he ate his meal. He stood when he saw me and wiped his mouth with cloth.

"Forgive me, Micah. I did not know you were coming."

"Oh, please don't trouble yourself," I said. "I just wanted to see how you were faring."

The choir numbered six — three young men and three young women. The woman in the middle was short, barely five feet, but her fairness transfixed me. The light of the angels beamed through her skin. I darted my eyes away when she noticed me looking.

"You must think me vain," Patriarch Lazar said as I sat at his table, "eating while these little angels sing. Truth be told, I am not just the Patriarch but a choirmaster. We are practicing."

"How can holy words ever be vain?"

"They can be when spoken insincerely. Many holy men have hearts as hard as gunmetal. You burned one, remember?"

I knew this topic was coming.

"Are you saying Bishop Yohannes was not a true believer?"

The Patriarch stripped the bone out of a fish. "I cannot judge his heart, but his actions were of a hypocrite. He was pilfering the tithes. Imagine that, a holy man enriching himself. It has happened throughout history, but I'd hoped it would never happen under my nose. And to think Yohannes believed he would be named Patriarch in my place when Imperator Josias came to power." He chewed the fish and swallowed. "You rid me of a terrible problem…another reason to thank you."

As the Patriarch spoke, I peeked at the girl again. She was no older than sixteen, which would've been Elly's age about now. The glow of her face made me flush.

The Patriarch smiled when he noticed me looking, fish bits in his teeth. "Micah, I must tell you truly why I am here. Imperator Josias sent me for many reasons, but primary among them is his answer regarding the Shah's fate."

Now the Patriarch had my full attention. "Which is?"

"The Imperator orders you to send the Shah to him without delay."

"And what will the Imperator do with the Shah?"

"Whatever he wants. Parade him through the streets of Hyperion. Hang him. Keep him as a bargaining piece. We all know he is no longer the Shah. His heir has already claimed authority in Lyskar, though a young boy he may be. When the city fell with the Shah still in it, he was dead to those he ruled."

Though I didn't want to see the Shah sail away, I couldn't refuse the Imperator. It was true that the Shah's life was but a vanity. I hoped agreeing would repair my relationship with Imperator Josias and set things right.

"There's more," Lazar said. "The Imperator wants half of your ships, the treasures of the Shah, and the services of the Ejazi sailors as his share of tribute."

"The Ejazi sailors are my men. I'll need them and those ships to go east."

"You burned the bishop who baptized the Imperator in the High Holy Sea. And then you disobeyed his order to return home. Though you've done much good — in both respects — his slight is not unimagined. And unlike the angels, imperators are not so forgiving."

A mellow sun gazed at us through the open window, which brought in a calm sea breeze. I didn't want to give up my men and ships, but an Imperator's favor was priceless. I needed arms, grain, and fresh troops to keep Kostany — all which Hyperion alone could give.

"My Ejazi are believers. You must promise they'll be treated as nothing less. And I would ask that my ships transport a portion of the Shah's treasures to Nixos first, to pay the men whose labor I borrowed."

The Patriarch sighed in relief and nodded. "Of course, as long as it's your share."

Truthfully, I hadn't even considered my share of the spoils. We shook hands.

I gave the order. My paladins dragged the Shah from his cell and put him on my fastest galley. I hoped Imperator Josias would be pleased with how I bent.

THAT NIGHT, before I slept, I thought about the crypt. I thought about the laughter of the little girl who was nowhere to be seen. No question, that was Elly's laughter. Was it all in my mind? Or was there a ghost haunting Angelfall?

A knock sounded on the door. I sat up in bed. It must've been important because no one dared disturb me this late for a trifle. "Enter!"

Patriarch Lazar did so, warmth beaming from his cheeks and eyes. Behind him was the choir girl with the angelic face. I blushed at the sight of her.

"What is this, Patriarch?" I said.

He laughed with my father's dismissive tone. "Do not be alarmed, Micah. Please relax."

The girl glanced at me, then looked away, as if too bashful to stare.

"I bring you a gift," the Patriarch said.

I shook my head. "No man or woman can be a gift to another."

"Oh, this one surely can. A dove, isn't she? Her face is radiant with faith. I know you noticed it too."

The Patriarch brought the girl forward. She stood in front of me, still wearing her white choir gown. She gazed at the floor, pink leaking from her fair cheeks.

Was this a test? Or was this the true nature of the Patriarch of the Church of Ethos?

"Do not think I mean anything vile," he said. "This is a pure girl, sworn to chastity. She has touched no man and has vowed that she never will."

I rose from my sheets and stood face to face with the Patriarch. "Why did you bring her here?"

"Because this girl is the key to your future, Micah." He stroked her hair as if she were his pet cat. "Her name is Celene, the only child of Imperator Josias. Princess Celene of the Holy Imperium of Crucis. And though her father will not like it, she will be your bride."

11

KEVAH

THE TRIBE RODE TO LYSKAR ON HORSEBACK: YURTS AND EVERYTHING packed on hundreds of horses and mules in a procession that stretched to the horizon.

My horse was temperamental. Earlier a deer leaped over a bush while she was drinking, and she panicked and galloped off. It took me hours to find her. I rode plenty of horses in my youth, so knew that the moody ones were better in battle. Yes, they could be jumpy, but they also reacted faster than a calm horse, though you don't want a horse that panics from gunfire.

Sadie busied herself during the journey by riding through the procession and assigning tasks to her people. She organized foraging parties. She sent rangers to scout ahead and at our flanks and back. She checked on the sick and elderly and ensured they had seats within the few carriages.

Each night, darkness ate the waning moon, leaving more of the world in shadow. We always camped by fresh water and made plenty of crackling fires, with whole lambs or rabbits roasting over them, but the nights kept me on edge. On the plains, enemies could come from anywhere. My heart thumped when I stared into the darkness. I feared that from those shadows, Crucian paladins would attack with their fast-firing guns and hand bombs, and we'd all be dead by dawn.

Each night, we got farther from Kostany. It was madness to expect the Crucians to be this far inland. But wasn't it also madness that Crucian paladins appeared in the night and seized our walls? No one in Kostany had gone to sleep thinking the city could fall before light broke. And yet…

Sadie came to my fire during the last of those anxious nights. The next day, we would arrive in Lyskar. The thought put me on edge. A part of me wanted to wander forever. There was simplicity in the journey, whereas destinations revealed their complexities. Even now, even with the rage that drove me — with desire fueled from fire so hot it could only be that of hell itself — I thought of Tombore and the simple life I'd lived. I thought of banging a horseshoe with my hammer and reading Taqi before bed. Once I cut the life out of Micah, could I ever go back?

"You haven't spoken much this whole trip." Sadie sat at my fire and handed me a waterskin.

I sniffed the liquid in it…the thick stench of kumis. I'd noticed the zabadar fermenting the mare's milk in horse-hide sacks strapped to their saddles as they rode. Then they would hang the sacks on their yurts and punch them whenever entering. I had no idea how that worked.

"Maybe I'm just quiet." I chugged. The cool, milky intoxicant soothed my throat. I wiped my beard and handed the waterskin back. "Maybe I have nothing to say."

"The quiet ones have the most to say."

"You want to know what I think? You have four hundred warriors in your clan, but I counted only twenty guns and barely any ammunition. That'll get you all killed."

Sadie's auburn hair glistened in the firelight. "I have more than four hundred." She took a swig of kumis. "I command two thousand."

I looked around to find them. "They invisible? Because that would help."

"They're with the other zabadar tribes, harassing the paladins Micah sends from the city. He's looking for food and can't find any because the tribes have scorched the earth around Kostany."

"I'm sure he knows how to fish."

"The fisheries around Kostany are bare. My father even banned fishing for a time to help them replenish. He won't be able to feed his army on fish alone. Kostany will be easier to take if Micah's men are starving."

An owl's hoot and the flutter of wings turned my attention to my back. Footsteps and ruffling noises sounded from a bush in the distance. I grabbed the hilt of my sword. A jackal leaped out of the bush, howled, and ran off.

Sadie glared at me. "There's no one out there but the jinn."

"Maybe we should ask them for help."

She grinned. I didn't see the Shah in her; she didn't look Seluqal. Her eyes betrayed a kindness all found comfort in. But when she gave commands to her zabadar and talked of scorched earth, that's when the Shah Murad in her came out.

"You know, your father was the wisest of us," I said. "And I don't say that because I liked him. I still resent how he forced me from my peaceful life. But he knew this was coming. Everyone else was sure that Kostany couldn't fall, but he knew that we were too weak to stop it."

"And you think guns will make us strong?"

"They don't call him Micah the Metal because he shoots steel-tipped arrows. He conquered the west with guns, and now he'll do the same to the east."

"I assume they call him that because he uses a lot of metal weapons. You know where metal comes from?" Sadie stretched her arms wide, palms to the sky. "See any mountains here in the plains? With the metal it takes to make one gun, we can make five spears or twenty arrows. For us, it's scarce."

"And now Micah has the Zari Zar and Nocpla Mountains."

"We'll have to ride all the way to Alanya to find mountains as big."

"I'm not willing to go that far." I shook my head. "Lyskar is as far as I'll go from Micah."

Sadie giggled, teeth apart and tongue almost sticking out. "You talk as if you're in love with him." Her chipped front tooth was endearing. Strange words, though. Was the kumis starting to speak?

"What did Taqi say? 'Love and hate have the same mother but different fathers.'"

"Who's Taqi?"

"Oh Lat." She had failed the Taqi test. I covered my face with my palm. "Do you know Ravoes, Kindi, or any of the warrior-poets who rode west with Temur?"

She just stared at me. "Wasn't Kindi a saint?"

"You're thinking of Kali. Not the same."

She raised her wavy eyebrows, as if I were speaking an unknown language. And then she cracked a smile and laughed soundlessly. "Of course I know who Taqi and Kali are. You're just like those stodgy eunuchs. Forget the name of the fourth son of the seventh sultan of some lost kingdom a thousand miles away, and they would puff their cheeks, ready to burst." She puffed her cheeks in imitation. "I had to find some way to entertain myself." Now the kumis really was talking.

I sighed. "So you did grow up in the harem."

"I lived in Kostany until I was eighteen. But…well…things were complicated in the Sublime Palace."

Her irises sank. Seeing her like that made me sad too.

"I'm sorry," I said, "for all you lost. You're a lot stronger than me."

"I can't lead my zabadar if I'm writhing in the dirt and smashing my knuckles. But truth be told, that's all I want to do."

I tossed a stick in the fire to keep it going. Its warmth did little to calm my nerves and nothing to soothe the pain. "You're not alone in that, Princess."

I SLEPT a few hours and awoke at dawn. The clouds were laden and black and smothered the light of the sun. Except they weren't clouds.

Smoke. The fire that fueled it must've been far, as I couldn't see flames beyond the tall grass of the plains.

"Bushfires," Sadie explained later as we trotted toward Lyskar. "Not uncommon in summer."

A line of smoke fed the cloud, as if its umbilical cord. It spread through our sky.

"That's some bushfire," I said. "Pray for rain."

Sadie snickered. "The clouds couldn't care less for your prayers. And it's behind us, anyway." She trotted on ahead.

It did rain. It looked to be the first day of summer rains, in fact, but they didn't start until we reached the farming villages outside Lyskar.

Shirtless boys danced in the rain amid a wheat field. Muscled men wrestled in the mud as onlookers cheered around them. Young girls chased each other, lifting their country dresses to avoid puddles. Lyskar was a different world. Why wouldn't it be? Why would the common people of Lyskar care about a war hundreds of miles away?

The gates of Lyskar were red like its walls: the color of rusted iron. The red clay wept in the rain like kohl trailing down a cheek. When Temur the Wrathful took the city from its Crucian-speaking inhabitants, he drowned them all in the Syr Darya, leveled every brick, then built upon its corpse. The streets were cobbled and the buildings of the city ordered, by his design. Red clay wept from them as well. Here too, children played in the rain as mothers raised their heads in thanks.

Most of Sadie's zabadar did not enter the city; they camped

outside the walls instead. She chose ten warriors and me to accompany her to the palace. While she rode in a carriage, the rest of us remained on horseback. She had to keep dry because she dressed not as a zabadar, but as a Seluqal princess. Kohl outlined her eyes, and she wore a gold tiara that shimmered with rubies and sapphires. Her airy, rose-colored dress was embroidered with blue and gold peacocks. I didn't mind however she dressed. The dark red leather and faded vest she wore during the journey looked equally good. But if you only knew one side of her, you'd struggle to recognize the other.

We reached the moat that surrounded the palace. Once we passed the drawbridge, we entered what seemed like a forest but was really a manicured garden filled with cedars and olive trees. Amid them were stone paths for walking, streams filled with white stones, and peacocks. They strutted around the garden, their wings spread as if they were peacock shahs.

Finally, we reached the palace. A fountain of sapphire water bubbled in front of it. A troop of janissaries stood at the entrance, matchlocks and swords at their sides.

Inside, janissaries in colorful cottons lined the great hall. A boy of no more than eleven years sat on the golden divan. He wore a golden turban with peacock plumes. A jade caftan covered him, with Paramic verses embroidered in gold thread. As Sadie approached the dais, he looked upon his sister as if she were a stranger. From what I knew of the Seluqal House, she probably was.

The rest of us brought puddles. Rainwater dripped off our clothes and onto the marble floor. The musk incense burning in the corners did nothing to weaken the wet cold, but none of us showed discomfort.

Sadie bowed her head; we followed. "I'm relieved to see you safe, Your Glory."

The boy remained silent. Footsteps sounded from behind the golden seat. A man and woman emerged and stood next to the boy shah. The woman had an imperious nose and curly brown hair. She covered herself in gold brocade and jewels, and around her neck was a sapphire the size of my palm.

I'd gazed too much at her and forgotten the man. It took a second to recognize his thin face, slender eyebrows, and narrow beard — the ever-lofty countenance of Grand Vizier Ebra.

"Shah Alir is overjoyed to see his sister in good health," he said. "To have her by his side is a great comfort amid trying times."

Sadie raised her head; we followed. "It is I who is comforted to be in the presence of the Shah."

Ebra walked down the dais. He wore a dark green cape with glittering trim, draped over his shoulders in the manner of a prince. Imprinted on it were shimmering suns in gold thread. Brocade fit for a shah.

Sadie gazed at the floor again. Ebra examined her as if at the horse market.

"A ruby should be on a crown, not in the dirt," he said. "The plains are no place for you, Your Highness."

He looked upon me. His eyes narrowed. Then he nodded as a smile stretched across his face. "You've brought with you a man of great renown. We'd all feared your demise, Kevah."

"Lat has blessed me with a bit more life," I said.

"We'll certainly make the most of it." Ebra walked with a higher chin and straighter back than in Kostany.

The woman spread out her arms, palms open, as if they held treasures. "A feast has been prepared, in honor of my son and his sisters who survived. Pearls and emeralds and rubies — they will adorn the greatest crown." She walked down the steps and looked at Sadie head to toe, like Ebra had. "You resemble your mother." Her glare turned serious — deadly, even. "All the kohl and silk in the kingdom won't change that."

Sadie kept her gaze low and tongue still.

· · ·

AT THE FEAST, a Kashanese man with a curly mustache plucked on a sitar amid a trio of flute players. Dancing girls with bare midriffs swayed to the rhythm, sometimes fast and sometimes slower than time. Strange the Fount were not here to stop it.

The food smelled better than anything I'd eaten in a while. Lamb spiced in cumin sauce shared the floor table with seared eggplants doused in a cooling yogurt. But I didn't eat much. I had no appetite since Kostany, and even the best food couldn't change that.

Sadie sat with the other princesses. I sat with the zabadar and watched her.

"You just gonna stare at her the entire time? Oy!"

The wild-eyed zabadar girl wrinkled her nose. Her name was Nesrin, and she had twin braids that reached her waist. Considering how young she was, she must've been growing them in the womb. And she must've come out of that womb angry and miserable because I'd never seen her in a good mood.

"One of us should be with her," I said, "protecting her."

"You daft? There are a thousand janissaries in this city." She glanced at my bare plate in disgust. "I've never seen a fat man who eats less than a bird."

"Maybe I don't want to be a fat man anymore."

"Whatever you want to be," Nesrin chugged her mug of fermented barley water, then wiped her mouth, "it'll never be good enough for her."

I laughed in disdain. "I'd accomplished a whole lot more than you by the time I was your age. Knew how to respect my betters, too."

She leaned onto the table and pushed toward me, almost dragging her braids into the yogurt. "I've heard the stories. A magus killer. Shah Jalal's favorite janissary. And the man who put Shah Murad on the throne." She spat a bone onto the table. "But you're just a fat old man."

The zabadar man next to her pulled one of her braids.

"Ow!" Nesrin winced.

"Sorry about her." He had the same wild eyes but the opposite disposition. His name was Yamin, and he was Nesrin's better-natured twin brother. "This one is protective of our khatun."

She slapped his hand and bit down on her lamb shank.

"Guns are my weapon of choice," he said. "Wish we had more. I know how easy it is to down a horse with a gun."

I studied the janissaries guarding the banquet hall. Etched metal and dark green wood encased the short barrels of their calligraphy-covered matchlocks. "Ebra has a lot."

"He must get them from the Alanyans," Yamin said while dipping some eggplant in yogurt. "I hear they trade much in Lyskar."

"Well, I'd like to talk to him."

Yamin nodded. Nesrin glared at me with a mouth full of lamb.

I asked a janissary where Ebra was. He escorted me to a private dining hall where Ebra, the Shah Mother, and other guests laughed and feasted on a floor table surrounded by serving girls and beardless boys. I supposed this was where the dignitaries dined — so why wasn't Sadie invited? The food here smelled even better. The hot aroma of skewered kababs spiced with onions and peppers filled my nose. But even a stack of the puffiest white bread and a salad with twelve different colors didn't move my appetite.

"Kevah!" Ebra said when he noticed me. "Do join us!"

There was an empty seat a few spots from him. A serving girl fluffed and dusted the floor cushion for me. The girl took my plate and filled it, despite my protestations. I could only stare at the mound of kabab and soft bread as my stomach twisted without appetite.

"Already full?" Ebra asked. "Truly Kevah, you can't waste delights such as these!"

"If you'd seen what I'd seen, you'd be full too. You'd be full of sorrow till the end of your days."

The conversation around the floor table hushed. Ebra wiped his mouth with a golden cloth.

"Today we do not dwell on grief," he said. "Today we celebrate the reunification of the Seluqal House of Sirm. We celebrate heroes like Grand Mufti Taymah, who gave his life to save our young shah and his mother."

Everyone thumped on the table and cheered.

"And what of all those we lost?" I said. "Have you spared a thought for them?"

Serving girls went around the room and filled cups with rose water.

"We celebrate them too," Ebra said. "The purpose being, we celebrate!"

More thumps and cheers.

The Shah Mother watched me. Everything about her flowed — flowing brown hair, flowing bright gown. Even her kohl flowed. And yet, she seemed the most serious person in the room. Until she smiled when our eyes met.

Despite the horrors of Kostany, her son's station had lifted. And Ebra's too. He no longer advised a shah who would overrule his advice. Now he was the shrewdest and perhaps most powerful man in the kingdom.

The Shah Mother held her glass of rose water as if it were floating above her palm and glided across the room with a queen's grace, then ordered the man next to me to sit somewhere else and took his place.

Now she stared at the golden tablecloth, as if lost for words.

"Forgive me," she said. "When I was a young woman in Shah Jalal's court, I heard stories about you. The girls would gossip that you were fairer and stronger than the wolves that howled from the Nocpla peaks. And then one day — oh it was so long ago — I actually saw you." She licked her lip. "At your wedding. I was so envious of the gorgeous woman at your arm, and by then I was already married to the Shah."

I didn't have the stomach for this conversation. It used to be bittersweet to remember the hopeful days of youth...now it was just bitter.

"I appreciate your kindness," I said.

"Where is she? Your wife?"

"She..." My tongue stalled in my mouth.

"I'm so sorry." The Shah Mother took my hand. "You will always be welcome at my son's court, as you were for his father and grandfather. Whatever you need, we will provide."

"I'm afraid, Your Highness, what I need you can't provide."

She smiled, pity in her stare. "You're a janissary. What you need and what the Shah needs are one and the same. Isn't that so?" Strong words said so tenderly.

"Janissaries can't marry, and yet I did. What does that tell you?"

"It tells me you're special. But we all have a place, and the Shah's is only below god." Her expression turned cold, imperious. "A janissary need not be galivanting with an insignificant zabadar tribe when his shah needs him." She came close to my ear. "Don't let her fool you. She's the daughter of a goat herder. If you seek real power, look around."

All I saw were laughing men with kebab bits in their beards. I excused myself and walked outside.

Out in the garden, the clamor of the feast competed with the rain's hard patter. I stayed on the verandah to keep dry. Lightning lit the sky as thunder roared. The summer rains were not known to be so harsh. They were usually just enough to refresh the fields and those who worked them. Strange.

Footsteps sounded behind me: Grand Vizier Ebra had followed me from the dining room. We watched the rain for a few silent moments.

"We need this to bring the people together," he said. "I'm sure you remember the last time a shah died and how difficult it was to stay united."

"Do you have a plan to retake Kostany?"

Ebra sneered and shook his head. "You're no fool, Kevah. You know we won't be taking Kostany back any time soon. What's important is that we consolidate power under the new shah, gain allies, and assemble our armies."

"And you're the man to do that?"

"Who else? The Shah is just a boy, and his mother is not versed in statecraft. I don't want to rule, but I must. It falls on me to keep this country together and ensure we don't lose another inch of land."

Lightning split the sky. For a moment, it was morning again.

"You don't know Micah the Metal," I said. "He will take everything from us if you fail."

"Help me, then." His eyes grew large and serious. "I will listen to you."

Would he? Shah Murad had made plain his distrust of the Grand Vizier when we spoke at the coffee house in Kostany. He'd painted the picture of a shrewd man who abhorred conflict, unless there was a gain to his power or position. But shahs, blinded by their own obsessions, were often poor judges of character.

"I hope you don't mind," Ebra said, "but I overheard your conversation with Rudabeh. The Shah Mother." He pulled his ear. "Lat blessed me with a good pair." His throaty laugh was hardly endearing. "I bet a hundred gold pieces that you didn't know this, but I too was at your wedding."

I preferred to drown in mud than endure more false admiration. I groaned, but not loud enough to stop Ebra.

"Watching you in your glittering groom garb, I'd never been more jealous of anyone. Even when we were children under Tengis' roof, the girls would surround you, pinching your cheeks and ears. The cute boy became the handsome man became the hero. A legend, even. That was the story of your life. But I didn't have your blessings, so I had to—"

"We need more guns!" I shouted, attempting to put this conversation right. "Arm the janissaries, zabadar, and the regulars with guns."

Ebra nodded with a satisfied grin. "I'm doing just that. The Alanyan crown prince is in that dining hall. A thoroughly debauched fellow. I don't believe a woman moving her body to be entertainment, but he does. And for this positive reception, he's agreed to supply us with two thousand guns."

"Micah has more. And his are better. We need our engineers to figure out what he's done to make them fire so fast and far."

The rain got heavier. Water flooded the garden. The smell of moist dirt and wet flowers filled the air.

"We'll do that. I promise," Ebra said. "Your story isn't over, Kevah. Mine, too, is just beginning." He straightened his back and raised his chin. "Two legends among the janissaries — one a hero with the sword, the other the hero behind the throne. Here we stand, holding a kingdom together."

"Here we stand," I repeated, "two legendary janissaries. Our shah captured or dead. Our city and throne seized by the infidel. Our families put to the sword."

"Look at yourself." Ebra shook his head. "Drowning in grief."

I put forward my hands, palms up. "Look at them." The puffiness had gone, but blisters and blotched skin surrounded my fingers. The wrinkles and scabs were of a hundred-year-old man. "I buried hundreds of bodies. Some of them surely men and women you knew…maybe even cared for." I stuck my hands in the rain. Almost soothing. "Aye, I drown in grief. Yet you refuse to even sip it."

"I said my prayers and let them go. We're janissaries. At the end of the day, no matter what words we use, we don't have families." He sighed, colder than the rain. "It's better that way. It allows us to focus on what really matters — winning. We can't beat Micah the Metal with anger and sadness. You understand?"

Ebra left me to my anger and sadness. The rain was the perfect music for it and the night the best canvas.

I SLEPT in a guest room and awoke at dawn. I looked for Sadie in the great hall, where the boy shah, Shah Mother, and Ebra were entreating with the Alanyan delegation. The Alanyan prince wore a bright turban with a cream-colored caftan. Metal pins were fastened across his shirt, a style I'd never seen. His shoes were a memorable oddity: the toe-end curled upward.

But Sadie was not there. When I asked the janissaries, they shook their heads and said they didn't know. So I took my horse and returned to the zabadar camp at the city gate.

Nesrin lay on a hammock beneath a tree, her twin braids hanging in the dirt. She was peeling a pear.

"You seen Sadie?" I asked.

She crunched into the pear and said while chewing, "Still obsessed?"

I jumped off my horse and stood over the girl. "Is she here?"

"She didn't come back last night." Nesrin threw the pear into the nearby chicken coop. A hen clucked and plucked at it. "Maybe she met a dazzling prince," Nesrin stretched and moaned, "and lay with him. I hear the Alanyan crown prince is quite tall and handsome."

She grinned. I glared at her with disdain.

Her brother Yamin chopped wood nearby. He cleaved logs bigger than me with each swing. In my youth, whenever I pictured what a typical zabadar looked like, the image was strikingly him: tall, muscled, and sporting a ferocious black beard. But he was far more likable than the zabadar in my mind, and spoke in an even-handed tone, as if a scholar rather than a warrior.

"Know where Sadie is?" I asked.

"Sadie's a Seluqal princess." Yamin wiped sweat from his forehead. "She's with her family."

"I've seen that when a crown passes, the Seluqal House is anything but a family."

"You've known her, what, a few weeks? I've known Sadie for years. She's not a pleading maiden, she's a zabadar khatun. She doesn't need our protection."

Lightning flared. Summer rain poured again. Wind blew through the trees and sent leaves scurrying past my face.

"Odd weather," Yamin said. "Let's go inside and make a fire."

I spent the rest of the day inside by the fire, reciting Taqi and a bit of Ravoes to distract from the worry. Fierce winds almost blew my yurt away.

The next day, I returned to the palace and found Ebra scribbling at a scroll in his office — a gaudy room with busts of golden owls above the incense burners in the corners. He burned sandalwood, a scent too floral and mellow for my taste.

"I have urgent business with Princess Sadie," I said. "Where is she?"

He stopped scribbling and looked up at me. "Do you like the owls?" He feigned a smile. "They were gifted to me by the Shah of Alanya when I became governor here, around the time you were off with Shah Jalal in Rastergan. I was trying to tell you about it the other night. I expanded this city through trade with Alanya and Kashan. Some of our merchants even went as far as the Silklands, seeking the world's treasures. And then I became only the third janissary to attain the position of Grand Vizier. Do you know why?"

"You're a shrewd man, Ebra. I need not be reminded."

"Because I wanted to prove I was worth more than the pouch of silver my mother and father sold me for. To think, the most powerful man in the land was once traded for less than a night with a pleasure girl. Behind your...oafishness — apologies, but I can't think of a better word — I see that same yearning to prove yourself. A yearning that knows no bounds."

"I care about your opinion as much as I do a rotting fig. Where is Sadie?"

"Is that so? And I thought we had quite the heart-to-heart the other night." Ebra smirked like a lust-filled drunk. "Sadie is indisposed. I'm afraid you can't see her."

"You think me a fool, Ebra!?" I banged at his desk and sent his scroll flying into an incense burner. "I was there ten years ago when Selim threw his baby brothers off the city walls. I saw with my own eyes when he gutted his older brothers and then put his sisters in chains, all because he feared their claims to the throne."

Ebra stood, fire flaring in his eyes. "You're unhinged! You've let sorrow take the place of sense."

"And you use the kingdom's sorrow as a ladder. Now let me see Sadie!"

Two janissaries entered the room, hands on the hilts of their swords. Ebra gestured for them to stand down.

"Sadie is a subject of the Shah," he said, "as are you. She will do what she is told and so will you."

"A subject of yours, you mean."

"I'm doing what I must to keep the country united. I can't have a princess, who happens to be a zabadar khatun, running around out there during a succession. You, most of all, know what can happen."

"What did you do with the brothers?" I asked. "Where are the princes?"

Ebra shook his head in disgust. "You think I...it was Micah the Metal who saw to that!"

"Convenient for you."

"The Grand Mufti would forbid it all. We cannot kill a member of the Seluqal House without his permission."

"The Grand Mufti died." I spread my hands. "And I don't see the Fount here, or you wouldn't have had half-naked girls gyrating at your feast."

"I told you the dancing girls were for the Alanyan prince. I'm a man who follows the laws of the Shah and the Fount. Shah Murad himself chose Alir, and so that is the law."

"Selim was chosen too," I said. "That didn't stop Murad from pressing his claim, and you know that very well."

Ebra raised his fist and fumed. "I've seen the way you look at the Princess. You covet her, don't you? You would take her as your wife and rule. It is you who takes me for a fool."

"And you call me unhinged?" I sniggered. "Where were you, Ebra, when the city fell?" I grabbed the hilt of my sword. "Coward—"

"Kevah." A sweet voice from behind me. I turned to see Sadie. Her golden tiara was all rubies. She smiled weakly and took my hands. "Listen to him. Do as he commands."

"Your zabadar are waiting for you." I knelt and stared up at the Princess. "We all want you to come back, to lead us. We need your strength to win this war."

She shook her head, sullen as I'd ever seen her. "I won't go against my brother's wishes."

Ebra glared at me with smug, satisfied eyes. "The Princess knows her place. She would do anything for her family, for the Shah."

"We cannot be divided, Kevah." Sadie knelt, her eyes wet. "If we want to win, there can only be one leader, and we must obey him."

I wanted to rip her tiara off and throw it at Ebra's smug face. "This is not you speaking," I said. "This is not you. You belong out there on the plains at the head of your zabadar."

"It doesn't matter." Her hands shook as she held mine. "Most of my family are dead, and I cannot go against those who are left. I'm a princess of the Seluqal House, and I will do what is best for my family, for my country, even at the cost of my life and all that I love. That is the sacrifice we make."

I stood. Sadie continued kneeling and stared at the floor, her breaths heavy.

"Seize him," Ebra commanded.

Two janissaries grabbed me. I was no match for their strength. One punched me in the gut. The air in my stomach rolled around. I almost retched.

"Don't hurt him!" Sadie cried.

Another covered my head with a sack. I could only flail and push. The janissaries dragged me outside the palace wall and threw me in a puddle of muddy water. I removed the sack to see Ebra standing atop the wall.

"Return and I'll behead you for treason. Go back to Tombore and waste away. You outlived your usefulness long ago."

The gates to the palace shut. Wind and thunder raged throughout the world. And in my heart.

12

MICAH

AROUND US IN THE GREAT HALL, THE PATRIARCH'S CRAFTSMEN painted and chiseled to turn this seat of vanity and disbelief into one befitting the Ethos. Holy hymns in Crucian script replaced the falsehoods in Paramic calligraphy. And we'd melted the gold peacock, though nothing looked upon us in its place.

As we enjoyed the last catch of fish in the city, Patriarch Lazar framed his argument tactfully.

"The Imperator has no heir." He pulled the meat from his fish with such ease. "If he dies as suddenly as his father, it will throw the Imperium into chaos."

Beneath the clever words and twists of phrase lay one root: ambition. Like gunpowder, it could launch you into the stars as a firework...or blow up in your hands, burn your face, and leave you for dead. I'd burned ambitious men myself, as Bishop Yohannes would attest. But if it weren't for ambition, I'd be an innkeeper. Faith called to me, but if it were only faith, I'd be a priest. Faith found ambition in my heart and transformed me into a weapon of the Archangel. I was a steel ball fired from the Archangel's gun, but who would I destroy?

I never thought the Imperator of Holy Crucis could be among them.

I struggled to pull fish meat off the bone with one hand and chewed everything instead, then spat what remained. "I will not steal his chaste daughter."

The Patriarch poured some of his clean fish meat onto my plate, as if I needed his help to eat.

"Do you know the history of Patriarch Theodorus?" Patriarch Lazar chewed and swallowed. "He preached during the reign of Imperator Maximilian the Third, who also had a daughter sworn to celibacy before the Archangel. When the Imperator struggled to produce a male heir, he declared that the Patriarch could rescind pledges of celibacy if in the Imperium's interest. And because of that, power transferred peacefully when the Imperator passed. A war that would have killed thousands was avoided. We find ourselves at the same impasse."

"The difference being that Imperator Maximilian consented. Imperator Josias does not, as you've made plain."

"Sometimes, Micah, what is best for the Imperium and what the Imperator wishes do not overlap. But a true servant of the Archangel always knows which to choose."

I refused to eat any of the fish meat the Patriarch had pulled. I spat a bone as sharp as a needle. "If Josias never accepts it, then what you are asking will start a war. It will be the very thing you want to avoid. I'll not war with Ethosians when so many disbelievers walk the earth."

That was the final word, for now. I was sick of fish and left my plate of bones to do more important tasks — like visit the crypt of Angelfall.

I didn't tell Patriarch Lazar about what I saw there. He thought my daily visits to Angelfall were out of piety. It only furthered his belief that I was the right man to marry Princess Celene. But what I was looking for was far from holy.

Being in the crypt reminded me of the cold, dark hours we

spent in the belly of Labyrinthos. And that reminded me of Aschere, who guided me through it with the throbbing lights of green fireflies. But I wanted to see or hear *it* again. Whatever took the form of my daughter atop a blue dome the day I cleansed Angelfall of disbelief. Whatever laughed with her voice and ran across the room the day I'd first come here with the Patriarch.

But today, like every day since, *it* did not show. I left without answers, wondering if it had all been in my head.

Berrin, hymning on his knees, waved to me in the prayer hall.

"You spend more time down there than up here," he said.

The knocking and banging of hammers and chisels filled Angelfall. I looked forward to the day the prayer hall would glow with the Archangel's glory.

"I can't stand all this banging," I said. "The crypt is peaceful."

"Peaceful, but dark. Didn't the Fallen Angels drink from darkness' cup?"

In the hymn of the Fall in Angelsong, the angels passed around a cup of darkness. Those who drank from it gained arcane knowledge of the stars. What they learned corrupted them, and they rebelled against the order of the Archangel. Thus, the Fallen came to be. To drink from that cup was something we all had to avoid, lest we follow them to hell.

"The fisheries are empty, Berrin," I said to change the topic. "You need to find more food."

Berrin's eyebrows pointed downward. "Is it not Zosi whom you tasked with fighting the zabadar?"

"His failure doesn't excuse yours."

I had to take this problem on. Zosi had failed to handle the zabadar because they'd attack his flanks and flee. Without quelling those horse brutes, we could never farm the land.

"Get me Edmar and Orwo," I said. "We'll teach the zabadar the perils of playing with fire."

· · ·

I TOOK MY THIRTY BEST — the men who had been through Labyrinthos and survived the assault on the sea walls — and seventy others. A hundred didn't sound like much against hundreds of zabadar, but I never relied on numbers for victory.

We rode along the coast of the Yunan Sea to the villages south of Kostany. Though they paid taxes to the Shah, the people of the coast never left the true religion. Vibrant trade with Crucis kept their faith strong, and no one longed for a reconquest of these lands more than them. I hoped to fulfill their longing.

The sea air was pure. You could taste salt when you stuck your tongue out. We took a break after hours of riding and foraged for blackberries. They melted in the mouth. Edmar led a hunting party and caught several horned boars. Sitting by the spits and laughing as they roasted, we almost forgot our purpose.

We were reminded upon reaching the coastal villages, where smoke trailed toward the sky and merged into an encompassing gray cloud.

The zabadar had burned all the homes. The chapel was a ruin and the stone figure of the Archangel defaced. Dead men with spear wounds in their bellies littered the streets. The village stank of char and blood. Outside it, a field of wheat burned. The smoke ascended to heaven and ash rained.

I entered the ruined chapel. Though small and stone-built, it was as holy as any of the marble and glass chapels in Hyperion. I cleaned the defaced Archangel and set it on the altar. With Orwo and Edmar, I knelt and prayed for the Archangel's vengeance. I prayed he would use me as his gun, so I could light a fire that would burn the unbelievers as they'd burned our own.

"Grandmaster!" The call of a paladin interrupted my prayer. He took us behind the chapel.

A man wearing the gray robes of a priest writhed in pain against the broken wall. The spear had pierced his back but not his stomach. Still, he would die within the hour.

I fed him from my waterskin. He coughed and spat the water,

then reached out and touched my nose. His rough fingers coursed my face and hair. He stared at nothing because he was blind.

"I don't hear anything," he said. "Where are the children?"

There were no children. No women either, except for the elderly, who were killed like the men. The younger women and children had surely been enslaved.

I took his hand and prayed, "They will enter the land of light and joy, in the fellowship of the angels, whose reign will light up the earth."

The man coughed blood onto my armor. "When we heard our hero had taken Kostany, we were so overjoyed." He shuddered with death chills. "The children made kites in the forms of the Twelve and laughed and played on the beach. But our hero never came. He forgot us."

"He did not forget," I said. "He will avenge you all, a thousand times for each."

"And then what? We will still be dead."

It was not long until his breaths stilled.

We spent the afternoon burying the dead on the grass near the beachside. The kites were still there, held down by heavy stones and blowing in the wind. We put out the fires with seawater. We prayed for those we'd neglected to save.

We'd forgotten so many, for so long. Kneeling at the beachside, a breeze blowing sand in my hair, I resolved that no Ethosian would ever have to live in the shadows of the unbelievers' swords. I would be their savior. I need not marry Celene — it would interfere with my holy purpose. Though I had only one hand, it was my best hand, and with faith fueling my body, I resolved to cut down ten thousand unbelievers.

I rose, patted the sand off me, and grabbed my sword. Vengeance would not be delayed.

We tied our horses to whatever still stood in the broken village. Orwo couldn't hide his smile as he brought out a box of his latest concoction. He popped the box open and inhaled deeply. The man had been a cook most of his life and had the red skin for it. His eyebrows barely existed, and his face constantly scabbed. But for Orwo, it was a small price to enjoy a successful recipe.

Orwo took a red rocket from the box and smelled it. His nose twitched, as if he were inhaling the aroma of a sumptuous spiced lamb. It looked like any other firework. He called it "Fallen Scream." I gestured for everyone to stuff cotton bits into their ears. I didn't because I wanted to hear its full power.

Orwo was a little boy playing with a new toy, such was the grin across his cheeks. He lit the string and it rocketed into the air. The rocket exploded with a whimper of light. And then came the scream.

It was as if my dead wife's mouth burrowed in my ear and shrieked with the force of a hundred iron lungs. I clutched my ears and almost retched the horned boar I'd eaten. Men mostly regret their bravado, as I did in that moment. It was the most terrifying thing I'd ever heard, but it was over in a second.

A horse jumped so hard its rope broke off the tie. It galloped away as if running from the angel Marot. Other horses fell on their sides and kicked dirt into the air. Most were in the distance by now.

Orwo didn't care. He looked as satisfied as the day he'd brought down the iron wall of Pendurum with a cocktail that lit up the sky. The same crazed grin seemed stuck on his face. Gunfire would not spook a zabadar's horse, but his rocket would.

MY PALADINS REARRANGED the burnt village. They piled stone together to make cover and dug trenches. I huddled behind a mound of stone, a sword in my only hand, with Orwo and Edmar at my side. By now, the zabadar would have tracked us by our earlier foraging and hunting. Their attack would come, in time. Nothing to do while we waited but chatter.

"Labyrinthos wasn't as shite as the sorceress pretended," Edmar said. "She kept saying spooky things that you say to scare children, but it was just a cavernous cave."

"A cavernous cave by which we crossed hundreds of miles in hours," Orwo said. "You think the Fallen Angels don't toll their roads?"

While they argued, I listened for the rumble of horses. But all was silent, save for the seagulls squawking above.

"Still, that don't explain what I saw," Edmar said.

"What did you see?" I interjected.

Edmar was the hardest of men. A bandit in his former life, before faith found him. He concealed his daggers so well, I wondered if he hid them in his skin, which was scarred from the tortures he'd endured while captive in Sargosa. Since then, I'd never seen fear alive in his eyes. Even now, he sat there with his legs spread, staring at the seaside as if at a picnic.

"War makes you see the dead," he said. "I saw my sister, same as she looked the day our lord strangled her because she didn't suck his cock right."

"I saw my mama." Orwo shuddered as if a cold wind blew through him. "She passed in her bed at sixty, but there she was, watching me as I slept. You seen anything, Grandmaster?"

"No," I lied.

"I've talked to the men who went through the cave," Orwo said. "They all say they've seen things."

Edmar scoffed. "Half those fools say that, Labyrinthos or not. The Fallen Angels play tricks on us all."

"Shh." I raised my hand to quiet everyone.

Footsteps. One person. Walking in the grass toward us.

I peeked out of cover, but the grass was too high. Something black stood in the distance. I craned my neck to see better.

A figure stood afield, his body covered by a black robe and

head by a hood. Darkness obscured his face. It reminded me of the darkness of Labyrinthos that seemed thicker than smoke.

My men pointed their guns at the hooded figure.

"Who comes to us?" I shouted.

He stood still beneath the setting sun.

With Orwo and Edmar at my side, I left cover to approach the figure. He didn't react as we neared, our guns on him. His face remained dark and obscure, no matter how close we got. We were steps away when we heard it.

Rumbling. Horses galloping in the distance.

They thundered toward us from behind the hooded figure. Orwo, Edmar, and I looked at each other, eyes wide. We needed cover.

"Go!" I ordered Orwo.

He ran back toward his fireworks box. Edmar grabbed me and dived, flat against the ground in the tall grass.

An arrow cried through the air. Orwo screamed and thudded onto the ground. Scores of arrows flew over me as the riders closed in.

Gunshots sounded and men shrieked and fell. Horses thumped into earth as their riders flew off and landed with a crack on the grass. I pressed my body against the ground. The horses were so close, I could taste the dust they kicked up. One would trample me any second.

Edmar jumped to his feet, fired his gun, and a horse crashed into the earth. It slid forward as dirt filled the air. The rider flew over me. Edmar threw a knife and cut his throat before he landed.

Arrows rained toward Edmar. He ducked and slid but one pierced his side. Still, he fired more shots and screams rang.

I crawled toward the fireworks box. Someone had to set it off, or we were dead. I rolled away as a horse almost galloped through me. I slithered through the tall grass, keeping away from the horses, as arrow shots and gunfire raged.

I passed Orwo's still body. An arrow jutted through his left eye. The horses charged in the other direction now, retreating from their first attack. I hid in a bush until they passed, then sprang to my feet and ran toward my cover.

I threw open the fireworks box and reached for the red firework. The riders charged toward us again. Arrows hit my cover and flew by. Gunshots sounded and more horses died, but so did my men. Their bodies laid against the fortifications we'd built. I had to focus and light the rocket.

I ducked at the sound of an explosion. One of my men had thrown a bomb into the field, exploding a horse and rider to pieces.

How to light a rocket with one hand? I bit down on a piece of flint and struck the firesteel against it, unconcerned that it would set my mouth on fire. But the flint slipped out of my jaw.

"Over here!" I called to one of my men. He ran out of his cover toward mine. An arrow pierced his neck and he fell onto the grass. I hoped to see him in paradise.

The zabadar attacked and retreated, attacked and retreated. From the sound of the horses, they must've numbered two hundred. We were down to less than eighty. Without the rocket, we would all die.

The bomb thrown earlier had set the grass on fire. I clutched the rocket, took a deep breath, and ran out of cover toward it. I kept low as arrows arced over my head. A rider thundered at me with his spear. A shot rang and flung him off his horse just before he could get me.

An arrow pierced my stump arm. Pain burst through my upper body. I ignored it and ran for the fire. It was getting bigger, and the smoke gave me cover. But the zabadar charged. One angry rider was coming for me. Holding the rocket, I pushed my only hand into the fire. The rocket flew off and soared into the sky.

The shriek of a Fallen Angel engulfed the world. Zabadar howled as their horses kicked them off and panicked. A horse slid into the fire ahead of me. I backed away and covered my hand with dirt to douse the flames.

My men ran out of cover and executed the zabadar on the ground. They fired on the zabadar running away, though I couldn't hear the screams. I backed up as much as I could, then collapsed and stared into the flames that now engulfed the grass. I must've inhaled too much smoke.

I saw him there: the hooded man. I clutched my stump arm with my burned hand as blood trickled. A horse ran through the hooded man as if he were a ghost...but he was no longer a hooded man; he was a three-year-old girl with eyes of all black, clutching a straw doll of the angel Cessiel — the one I'd bought Elly on her birthday.

Pangs of pain and exhaustion filled my throat. Was this the end? I wanted to pray, but the figure of little Elly transfixed me.

Elly changed as the flames flickered behind her. Another horse ran by, and she was bigger — five or six years old, but still my Elly. I laughed and smiled at the sight of her straight, dark hair and pinchable cheeks. Was this the Archangel's reward? Was this a portent of paradise?

Another horse ran through her, and now she was taller. Her hair dropped to her shoulders and her slender nose resembled her mother's. I blinked, and she was tall enough to be eleven. The shades of a woman were on her face, and she wore a white dress that evoked the purity of her soul. It helped me ignore her black-on-black eyes.

A paladin ran over and held my burnt hand while another attended to the arrow in my stump arm. They poured water on both wounds. I didn't care. Elly was almost here. She looked thirteen, barely a woman, and smiled at me with pink lips.

Something else about her was familiar. I knew this girl, but not as my daughter. I'd seen her...very recently. The thought sent a painful shudder through my soul.

Elly stood over me and watched as my men cleaned my

wounds. My hearing returned. The gunshots and cries of battle hadn't ceased. She crouched, close enough to kiss. I knew that face — the face of Elly, now a young woman, mature enough to be married. I'd watched that face cough blood and grow cold, not long ago. There was no mistaking it.

The girl kissed my forehead. As she did, I stared at the gash scar in her neck — the scar I'd carved with her sword when I cut her throat on the sea wall. The hand the girl had cut off flared with phantom pain as she took me in her arms, and the paladins who mended my wounds didn't give it a care. She whispered in my ear, as tender as the kiss:

"I missed you, Papa."

13

KEVAH

EVEN THE TREES MUST'VE FEARED THEY'D FLY AWAY, SUCH WAS THE raging wind. The streets were empty of people. They watched me from their windows as I hurried to the city gate, the wind pushing me on. The children laughed and must've thought I would blow away, but I was firmly on the ground and wasn't going anywhere while Sadie remained a prisoner.

By the time I got through the gate, I was doused with rainwater and my teeth were chattering. The zabadar outside the city struggled to keep their yurts pitched on the ground. Some yurts already floated away like ghosts. I entered the largest yurt, dripping water. Zabadar stood and sat around a life-breathing stove fire.

The wind beat so loud against the cloth walls that the zabadar had to shout. It didn't sound like a rainstorm, rather an earthquake.

Yamin clutched a scroll. "We will obey our orders."

"What orders?" I shouted.

Everyone turned to look at my shivering form.

"Sadie ordered us north to join the raiders." Yamin handed

174

me the scroll. "That's her handwriting and signature." The penmanship was beautiful but simple, with only mild flourishes. It said as Yamin described, undersigned with Sadie's name in calligraphy.

I crumpled the scroll and tossed it in the stove fire. It burned with a satisfying crackle. Yamin looked on, mouth agape.

"Sadie is a prisoner," I said. "They forced her to write it."

Yamin's face glowed red. He brought his hulking form over me. "You have proof?"

"I was just at the palace. Ebra said he wouldn't let her go and threw me out when I insisted he free her."

Yamin shook his head. "She did not look like a prisoner. Sadie would never give orders against her will."

"I swear it. She's a prisoner. And if we don't free her, she'll be one till death."

Wind blew the door flap open and shrieked against the cloth walls. The stove fire flared and sent shadows dancing.

"This wind...it is unnatural," Yamin said. "The jinn howl along with it."

"Something's not right." Nesrin spoke up. She rose from her kneeling position, twin braids falling to her waist. "Let me at least ask her. To hear the words from her mouth."

Yamin nodded. "Don't waste a moment. Go now."

Minutes later, the girl returned, her leathers soaked and hair doused.

"They closed the gates," she said. "They say the zabadar are not allowed in the city and must leave by order of the Shah."

"Sadie took an oath to obey the new shah," Yamin said. "And as her zabadar, that oath binds us. If she ordered it and the Shah ordered it, how can I disobey? It would be treason!"

Nesrin's eyes grew wide. "There is something very wrong here, Yamin. We should not leave our khatun."

"Even if you're right, I can't let our tribe be outlawed," Yamin said. "We'd be hunted to extinction."

"If you leave her, you'll regret it for the rest of your days." I did my best to stand face to face with Yamin, who was a head taller. "You'll be deserting her when she needs you the most. How can zabadar ride away when their khatun wastes away in a dungeon?"

"He's right, Yamin." Nesrin tugged at her brother's bulging bicep. "Whatever his flaws, he cares about her as much as you or me and wouldn't lie."

"All right...you've made your case." Yamin paced around the fire, dragging his shadow against the walls. "We'll ride north for three days and make camp outside the range of Lyskar's scouts. Ten zabadar will remain with Kevah to learn their intentions. If they're holding our khatun against her will, then it won't just be us riding back. We'll call the raiders from the front and descend on Lyskar with the fury of the whole tribe."

Now he spoke with the fearlessness the zabadar were known for. It was a decent compromise, and I respected Yamin for it.

"I'll not leave Sadie," Nesrin said. "I'm staying."

Nesrin and a few zabadar remained with me. At the zenith hour, they formed a line. In unison, they swayed their heads and chanted Lat's praises in an unfamiliar, yet fierce style. They begged for intercession from a saint I didn't know, named Aban.

Afterward, I asked Nesrin about what surprised me most: "Didn't the Fount teach you that men and women shouldn't share a prayer line?"

Nesrin shrugged. "See any muftis here?"

"No, and I didn't see any in Lyskar either. I wonder what else goes on when the Fount isn't around."

"Don't get any funny ideas. We zabadar are this way because everyone, man and woman, must work for the tribe to survive. We can't separate ourselves like you city folk do."

"Speaking of the city, they won't keep the gates closed much longer. When they see that most of the zabadar have gone, they'll open them. But the palace gates are another matter."

She sat next to me, her braids in her lap. "Tell me truly, everything that happened with Sadie."

I told her truly.

"So she wants us to leave." Nesrin summarized what I'd told her. "She agreed to stay here."

"Many shahs did this when they feared that a brother or sister could ever rival them for the throne — put them in a golden cage, so to speak. Sadie is only going along with it because she doesn't want a war of succession like the one her father started."

"Is she wrong?"

"Let me ask you a question," I said. "Who would be a better leader — Ebra or your khatun? Who could take Kostany back? Who could bring us the head of Micah the Metal? Some scheming upstart or a rider with the blood of conquerors?"

"But she doesn't want to."

"I don't care what she wants. She has to lead us, because Ebra will sit here and gather his armies and fortify his position and make alliances and then do nothing with them except bask in his status. The Shah warned me about Ebra. He's a climber and a coward. We'll never win with him holding the reins."

"You're not doing this for her. You're doing it for yourself. To sate your vengeance."

I laughed and shook my head. "You're young. She's young. I'm not. I once lived in a cage I'd constructed for myself, one made of grief, not gold. It made me numb inside, and I lived numb and dead for ten years. And now look at me. Look at me!" Nesrin looked at me, sympathy in her glare. "Sadie may be fine with it today, but how will she feel after a month? After a year? After ten years? She belongs on the plains on the back of a horse, the wind coursing through her hair. What would a cage do to someone like that? After ten years, what would be left of her, of who she really is?"

Nesrin fidgeted and bit her nails. "So what are we going to do?"

"The Fount aren't around…that matters for certain men. I have an idea, but we'll have to wait till the gates open."

"All this talk of the Fount reminds me of a story Sadie once told me, of when she was a child. Her mother was despised by those who ran the harem, and so Sadie often found herself scorned and alone. One boy was kind and would play with her despite this. They'd adventure around the palace, pretending to be holy warriors." Nesrin giggled, as if it were her own memory. That was how close it seemed she and Sadie were. "Even when they grew up, when the Fount demanded that boys and girls separate, they would sneak out together to do who-knows-what. And then one day that boy disappeared."

"A servant boy fooling around with a princess? I suspect the Fount got rid of him."

Nesrin shook her head. "You're right about the Fount. It's why Sadie hates them. But he was no servant boy. He was executed after the war between her father and her uncle… because he was her uncle's son. That's why Sadie doesn't want to fight back. She fears hurting her brother, the way her father hurt his."

What would Vaya say about a *ruh* like that? Sadie had a good soul, I was sure.

"We all fear hurting those we care about," I said. "But how many more will be hurt because Micah occupies the Seat? We fight the first battle to retake it, here and now. We will free our leader, whether or not she likes it."

"You have a way with words, Kevah," Nesrin said. "I'm sorry for the cruel things I said to you."

"Don't be. Every one of them was true."

· · ·

THE STORM RAGED JUST AS FIERCELY when the gates opened the next day. Nesrin and I headed for the largest pleasure house in the city. Like the other buildings, it was a slab of red clay that bled in the rain. We found the entrance at the end of a grimy alleyway. Absent the Fount, it was sure to be lively and full of all types, especially those influential within the palace.

The clamor of a good time could be heard over the violent wind. Peace had made Lyskar rich, and the rich craved vices. Inside was a sea of people enclosed by colorful walls with murals of coiling snakes. The raucous hum of laughter and shouts drowned out the oud player in the corner. Amid the sea were islands where barely-dressed dancing girls swayed their hips to a slow rhythm. A dark-skinned girl from Kashan wearing a sapphire-studded undergarment eyed me. To her left, a Silk-lander with braids longer than Nesrin's flashed her breasts as a silver coin landed beneath her. There was also a slender girl from Rastergan, and one that resembled the vixens of Himyar, and—

Pain flared in my ear. "Ow!" I yelled.

Nesrin tightened her pinch. Were her nails made of steel?

"We're here to get information!" she growled. "You can live here, for all I care, after we free Sadie."

I slapped her hand away. "I was observing my surroundings."

"Whatever you want to call it. Now let's get to work."

Where to start? The upper floor. The dignitaries wouldn't dally with the rabble. Nesrin and I waded through the sea toward the stairs. A serving girl banged against me and almost spilled wine on my shirt. Brawny men to my left tossed cards on a low table, while girls dandled on their laps. A scant man in a turban blew smoke rings bigger than my head as a beardless boy caressed his cheek.

Finally, we made it across the room and up the stairs, only to be stopped by a helmeted man with a sword.

He shouted something in a language I didn't understand. It was musical despite him trying to be rough, typical of Paramic.

"You speak Paramic?" I asked Nesrin.

She shook her head.

The man grabbed the hilt of his sword and shouted again, gesturing with his hands for us to go away. I did my best to see past him. It seemed much quieter upstairs.

A familiar face peeked out from behind the guard. He wore a brilliant cream turban. One orange plume stuck out from the top, with the seal of a simurgh emblazoned at the center: the sigil of the Seluqal House of Alanya. It was the Alanyan crown prince whom I'd seen meeting with Ebra and the boy shah.

He studied me, then whispered to the guard. The guard stood to the side, making way for Nesrin and me.

Up here, the strings of the sitar player — the same fellow from the feast — sounded sweet and clear. Two other men lounged on a wide turquoise sofa that covered the entire wall. All around were bare-breasted girls, dancing to the slow sitar. One with light hair and fair skin, who looked as if she hailed from my native Ruthenia, licked her lips at me.

"Sit!" The Alanyan prince plopped himself in the middle of six girls. I wondered what it would smell like if it weren't for the cinnamon incense burning in the corners. Taqi did say that cinnamon-scent increases lust.

Nesrin and I sat at the end of the turquoise sofa.

"I remember you," the prince said. "You were at the dinner, but not in the best of moods. You did catch the Shah Mother's attention, though. Anyone who could make her smitten must be a lion among men. Do my paramours make you uncomfortable?"

The Alanyan prince barked some orders in Paramic and the guards led the girls out the room. One of the other men followed, and now there were four of us.

"Forgive me for not introducing myself," he continued, "a bad habit in my family. My name is Kyars, crown prince of Alanya."

The other man who remained sat on the far side of the turquoise sofa. He had short yellow hair, a barely budding beard, and fair skin. The apple flavor he blew out of his hookah filled the room with apple-cinnamon air.

I told Crown Prince Kyars our names. He didn't seem to care. Rarely did I meet important people who didn't know me by reputation. Tales of my renown must not have spread outside Sirm.

"So tell me, Kevah, what did you do to make the Shah Mother gush? Did you know that she ordered the governor out of his seat just to sit with you?"

"I killed a few people a long time ago."

The prince's laugh built up with a throaty hum before turning into chuckles. "Women love warriors. It pains me so. I haven't sharpened my sword in years. Alanya has become far too peaceful since your shahs stopped invading us. Now and then the Kashanese and Himyarites cause a bit of trouble, but we send them a few elephants and they quiet down."

The prince's eyes kept slipping onto Nesrin. He grinned at her. "Ah, this one looks wild. I love the braids."

Nesrin's face glowed pink.

"Oh, I forgot to introduce my friend! This is—" The prince gestured to the man smoking apple flavor at the other end of the sofa. But he wasn't there. When had he left? The prince shimmied over and picked up the hookah pipe.

"Not worth wasting a full bowl." He inhaled. The water in the pipe gurgled and he blew out apple scent.

Nesrin elbowed me and whispered, "Ask about Sadie."

"Prince," I said. "Did you meet the princesses?"

His eyes glowed as if I'd asked him his favorite question. "Oh they were all so…so elegant and so…oh I don't want to be rude. But were I a bit drunker, I'd have a few more *colorful* words. Speaking of being drunker!"

The prince snapped his fingers and a topless girl brought goblets of wine. It bubbled the color of sunshine and smelled fruity and crisp, like Tombore summers. We all raised a toast.

"Who was the best of them?" I sipped the wine and appreciated its bubbly texture and hints of peach.

Nesrin took several swallows as the prince thought about my question. He slurped his wine and finished it faster than I thought possible. Then he mumbled and nodded to himself, as if arguing with imaginary people in his mind.

"Well, there was this…" he said. "This…ohhh…she had red hair…like the mountain women. But she looked so sad. It made me want to make her so happy."

"Her name is Sadie," Nesrin said. "And if you want to make her happy, you'll help her."

The prince sank in his seat. "I wish I could. I wish I could take them all back to my palace in Qandbajar and make them so happy. But, alas, Ebra would never allow it."

"What will he do with them?" Nesrin leaned forward.

"Just keep them out of trouble." The prince belched. It had an apple aroma too. "So they can exchange their silks for frocks and bow before Lat while their hair turns gray and their buttocks sag and—"

"What does that mean?" Nesrin interrupted.

Crown Prince Kyars removed his turban. Raven hair fell to the middle of his neck. "Ebra is such a…such a stodgy, serious man. Nay, *all* you Sirmians are dour and unimaginative. Even your language lacks color — Paramic has fourteen words for love, one for every tantalizing stage. See, in Alanya, we stopped sending —" He sat up, alert. "Wait…you're trying to ply me for information. I'm not drunk enough. What is it you intend?" He snapped his fingers and yelled, "Kichak!"

A dark, steely man in gold and bronze armor entered the room, hand on the hilt of his scimitar. Behind him came more armed men.

"It's been a pleasure meeting you," I said to the Crown Prince. "But we must go."

The soldier named Kichak blocked the stairs as Nesrin and I tried to slip by.

"You can't just leave," the prince said.

"What shall we do with them?" Slowly, Kichak pulled his scimitar from its sheath.

Crown Prince Kyars tossed a gold coin at me. I caught it as it rebounded off my chest. The same majestic simurgh on his turban glistened on the coin's front, its wings and feet outstretched as if ready to carry a man to a faraway land.

"Fighting in a house of pleasure brings ill fortune for the year," he said, "but so does leaving without sampling its delights. Have the Ruthenian one with the silky tongue." He winked. "I know backed up when I see it."

We left the pleasure house. Back to the angry, wet winds. The man who smoked apple flavor approached us in the alley. I couldn't place where he was from, except to say west. He wore a striped red and black cloak and black scarf. Neither a rich nor poor look, but warm enough for this weather. His yellow beard was barely sprouting.

"The Princess will be exiled," he said.

"Exiled?" Nesrin gasped. "To where?"

"Zelthuriya."

The holy city...it made sense. Exiles would take the oath of a holy order, wear only carded wool, and renounce all claims and titles.

"Who are you?" I asked, "and how do you know this?"

"I'm an earnest friend of anyone interested in retaking Kostany. And I've got another friend — a powerful friend — interested too."

Only a fool would trust a man on word alone. And yet, his assertion about exile rung true.

"You'll help us free her?" Nesrin asked.

"Certainly," the man said. "A zabadar khatun and a princess...

she's the leader we seek." The more he spoke, the clearer it became that his lofty accent didn't match his middling appearance. If he was smoking hookah with the prince, he must've been a palace insider, though I hadn't noticed him at the feast.

"You could be leading us into a trap," I said. "Or maybe you're deranged. Or just having a laugh. Why should we believe a thing you've said?"

"Believe whatever you want." His expression untensed, and he smiled as if we were old friends. It was at once disarming and potent. "We'll free Sadie...when the time is right."

"Ugh! Stop dancing around your words!" Nesrin grabbed one of her braids as if she were about to whip him. "*When* will the time be right?"

"That's up to my powerful friend. Now if you'll excuse me, I'm off to see him. I advise you not to do anything until we return." The man turned his back and scurried away.

"Wait!" I shouted.

He disappeared into the rain and wind of the street beyond. Nesrin and I rushed after him, but turning onto the street, he was nowhere.

Truth be told, I didn't care for his commitments. But I did believe that Sadie would be exiled, which meant that they would transport her from the city. We could free her then.

NESRIN and I sat in silence in the yurt, digesting our experience. I rekindled the fire as she rested her head on a pillow.

"You can only get to Zelthuriya from the southern road," I said. "Let's move camp."

"Is that what a prince is like?" She stared at the ceiling, as if lost in thought. "I thought princes were noble."

"Princes are just men with gold, name, and power. Those don't make anyone noble."

"Then why is Sadie the way she is? Where did she get it from?"

"I don't know where virtues come from." I fingered the gold coin with the simurgh and flipped it in my hand. Like in the poems, the fabled creature had the claws of a lion, the wings of a falcon, and the head of a wolf. "Certainly not from gold, name, and power."

And yet, those three things were exactly what we needed. Sadie was the key to them all. With her Seluqal name and status as a khatun, she could rally the zabadar tribes, regardless of what Ebra plotted from faraway Lyskar. Gold wins wars, and with Sadie's clout, we could secure loans from the jewel-dripping Dycondian merchant-kings. Gold would get us guns, and guns would gain us power, and only with overwhelming power could we crush Micah. Without Sadie, it was all but smoke.

I pondered a thousand opportunities, Sadie the bedrock upon which they stood. I could guide her toward them. As I fantasized about hiring Rastergani engineers to construct monstrous bombards, something dawned on me: was I so different from Ebra, now? Was I turning into the plotters and planners that I'd despised?

The truth: plotters and planners ruled the world, and to win, I'd have to do things I hated. Until now, I'd been living wrong. I'd been clinging to peace, when war was eternal. It was the inevitable, and you either won or watched everyone you love choke on blood.

Later that day, we moved our camp to the southern road. The storm made it tough to pack up our yurts. But the ten zabadar with us were capable.

The gutters lining the southern road filled with rainwater that flowed into a nearby lake. But when we arrived at the lake, it was empty: a crater made of cracks, covered in fish bones. I'd heard of small lakes being drained, but one this large?

"An odd sight," Nesrin said as she trotted next to me. "You'd think these rains would have refilled it."

"We're not lacking in oddities these days," I replied. The fish bones were…charred, as if they'd been boiled. "I'm not fond of fish anyway."

We camped in a clearing between the dried lake and the road — close enough that our scouts could alert us if a procession were coming, yet far enough not to spook any travelers. And we waited.

The next day was the fiercest yet. But the day after was calmer. Still, we had to hammer the nails that tied our yurts down every few hours to keep them from flying off. It was while hammering nails that one of our scouts galloped toward us.

"Carriages just left the city," he said while pulling the reins of his horse. "I counted twenty."

Twenty carriages for a bunch of princesses and their janissary captors. We gathered our men and rode to meet the procession.

On horseback, the ten zabadar led by Nesrin and me blocked the road. The first carriage rolled toward us, pulled by two white horses. The driver recoiled. Two janissaries wearing heavy coats jumped out of the carriage and drew their matchlocks with the carriage door as cover.

"Off the road!" one of them yelled. "Or we'll blow you off!"

Nesrin cantered forward. "Give us Princess Sadie and the road is yours."

Out of almost every carriage, janissaries sprang forward with matchlocks. There were at least fifteen, about what I expected.

The wind howled with a renewed fierceness. Lightning lit the world and thunder called out.

Another carriage door opened. A janissary jumped out and opened a canopy. A man stepped out and walked toward us, careful to stay dry under the canopy. It was Grand Vizier Ebra, trepidation in his stare.

I cantered forward as Ebra approached. We met in the middle of the road as the storm raged.

"Didn't know you would be here," I said.

"I have business in the south."

"That's how I know you're a coward. Kostany's the other way."

"This will be bloody, Kevah." Ebra's eyes were hardened rocks. He shook his head. "Many will die. Don't you care?"

"If you cared, you'd let Sadie go. Or I'll do what I've done many times. I'll win."

"You were a lot stronger back then."

"I have eleven hardy warriors with quivers full of steel-tipped arrows. I'm not relying on my strength."

Nesrin galloped to her men to prepare the assault. They rode off the road and out of range of the janissary guns, ready to attack from both sides with their bows as soon as ordered.

"This is madness!" Ebra said. "What's worse than fighting your own?"

I was as drenched as I wanted to be. But I barely felt it in anticipation of battle.

Another carriage door opened. A princess fell out. Her red dress splashed in the mud as she kicked the janissary who lunged after her. Then she got to her feet and stepped on the gold tiara that had fallen off her head. Sadie held her dress and walked toward us, rain dampening her hair.

"I forbid you from doing this, Kevah," she said. "Order the zabadar to retreat!"

I smiled at the sight of her and shook my head. "If Lat ordered us not to worship her, wouldn't we still?"

"Fucking fool!" Sadie said. "I don't want to fight my brother. Ask yourself — do you really think they could cage me in Zelthuriya forever?"

"Even if you could escape, by then snow will have covered these grasslands. Let Micah the Metal winter in Kostany, and come spring he'll be marching east, a hundred thousand zealots behind him. Holy Zelthuriya itself won't be safe. I won't waste months waiting."

"And how many lives will your gambit here waste? Are you so impatient to die?"

"Micah is impatient. He didn't wait to slaughter our city, and I won't wait to fight back. Live or die, it starts here."

The janissaries aimed at me. I refused to cower. I prayed under my breath: *To Lat we belong and to her we return.*

I galloped away and raised my sword to signal the attack. Then I sheathed it and took out my bow. We would do what zabadar did best: attack with our arrows and retreat until we'd whittled down their numbers.

The zabadar thundered as the janissaries repositioned to face them. Some of them surrounded Sadie like a wall, ensuring we couldn't snatch her. Ebra darted away and locked himself in a carriage. Horse hooves shook the world. The zabadar hollered cries of war. Rain raged against my face as I galloped forward.

I dug my feet into the stirrups. I kept low, knowing that a gunshot could send me tumbling. While most of the zabadar would hit the janissaries from the sides with their arrows, I and two other riders would attack head-on. I picked my target, a lanky red-faced janissary, and charged with my arrow nocked and drawn.

I was about to loose on the poor fool when my horse whinnied and almost tossed me off. But not because of gunfire.

The wind had stopped. The air pressure changed, each inhale suddenly requiring more force. The rain ceased. The world stilled. Every blade of grass stood as if stuck in time. The janissaries fidgeted with their guns and looked around. The astonished horsemen stopped their charge, and the horses whinnied in wonderment. The air turned dry, as if all the wet had been sucked out.

What the hell was happening? It was as if Lat forbade brother killing brother, stilling the world to show her displeasure.

The janissaries and the zabadar, remembering we were in battle, aimed their bows and guns. I sat on my horse amid the standoff, dizzy by the sudden change of temperature and humidity.

I wasn't the only one. Ebra stepped out of his carriage. He squinted at the heavens and coughed. Sun dazzled the world while a blue sky smiled on us. Sadie, who was surrounded by janissaries, bent down to feel the dry grass while clutching her forehead. Nesrin brushed the fur of her horse and came up with dry hands. Then she fingered her braids, which were also without wetness.

"Praise Lat!" one of the janissaries shouted. Soon the rest followed.

"Praise Lat!" a zabadar joined in, and soon everyone was praising Lat with their weapons drawn on each other. Perhaps we could find a way out of this?

As we were praising Lat and deciding whether to fight or pray, a horse galloped toward us from the southern road. I recognized the man upon it: the yellow-haired, barely-bearded fellow who smoked apple-flavored hookah with the crown prince of Alanya.

"I hope I'm not too late," he said as he trotted past the zabadar. "I recall advising you not to do anything until we returned."

"Did you cause this?" I asked him. "Are you a—"

"My name is Aicard, by the way. And no, I didn't do this. He did." He stared at the empty road behind him and sighed, then pointed up.

In the now clear sky, a dot descended. That dot became a man as it neared. He glided downward, as if invisible birds carried him. No one could withdraw their eyes, nor close their mouths, as he hovered toward the ground and landed with the softness of a feather. A man with the sweet face of eternal youth. As good-natured, wrinkle-free, and virtuous a face as you'll ever see.

Magus Vaya, freshly descended from the heavens, stood before us.

"Good to see you alive, Kevah."

"Likewise," I said, blinking to make sure I was seeing right.

"I've not the patience to resolve this mess." Though Vaya didn't smile, the glimmer in his eyes betrayed some joy at seeing us. "Your Royal Highness, come here."

Sadie looked around and noticed everyone staring at her, then pointed at herself, eyebrows raised in disbelief.

Vaya nodded. Sadie scurried over and stood behind him, the janissaries seemingly frightened to stop her.

Grand Vizier Ebra glared at the magus, his nostrils flaring at the sudden turn of events. "That princess is the subject of Shah Alir. On his authority, which you have sworn to obey, return her to me!"

"I never swore allegiance to Shah Alir." Vaya motioned for Ebra to step aside, as if swatting a fly. "You've won a lot of battles, Grand Vizier. Take a loss. We'll be going."

"Going where?" Rage filled Ebra's defeated face.

"Where a coward doesn't go. To face his enemies."

"I'll order my janissaries to fire!"

"Go ahead. None of your bullets would hit." Vaya stuck his finger in the air, just as a westward breeze disturbed the stillness. "You'll also learn what else the wind can do."

He gestured for me to go and pointed north. I pulled Sadie up on my horse. We slipped by the caravan and rode north before Ebra could act.

14

MICAH

I LOST ORWO AND THIRTY PALADINS IN THE BATTLE. EDMAR breathed but seven arrows stuck out of his body. His trampled leg had looked like lumpy bread, but Jauz ensured he would survive by sawing it off. At the end of a bloody day, we'd killed scores of zabadar, avenged dead Ethosians, and proved that the Fallen Scream worked. But I'd trade it all to have Orwo back and Edmar whole.

The Patriarch himself cleaned Orwo's body and rubbed heavy water on his head, arms, and legs. He chose the angel Marot for Orwo's casket because hundreds of years ago, Marot tempted men by offering them fire magic. It was said that the order of the magi descended from those who failed that test, but the Patriarch insisted this interpretation wasn't canon. A stone likeness of Marot went with Orwo in his casket.

We prayed for Orwo at Angelfall. He died an avenger for innocent Ethosians, so surely his soul rested on a silk bed in the care of the angels. Orwo and all my men who died would be at peace in Baladict, the chapel in heaven where souls awaited the

Reckoning. I prayed his promised fief would be waiting in paradise.

Would that I'd died and joined them. But here I sat, in a hot bath, as Jauz treated the new hole in my stump with ointments and alcohol.

"You don't want to hear it, Grandmaster," he said as he rubbed my stump. A boil grew over the arrow wound above my elbow. "But best we take off the whole arm."

"I look ridiculous as is."

I rested my only hand in a jar of iced milk. It was the best way to treat the burns, which though disfiguring, would not hinder its use.

"You're lucky the arrow hit a part of you that was already useless."

"There's no such thing as luck. The Archangel decreed it. And my arm isn't useless. I'm planning to attach a gold hand."

Jauz rubbed the boil with ointment. It flared and burned to the bone. My phantom hand felt squeezed by a steel fist. I did my best not to holler.

"I'll give it another day," Jauz said. "But if that doesn't improve, I'm taking your arm. Or your Archangel will take your life."

He put his scissors and other instruments in a green satchel.

"How's that wife of yours, Jauz?"

Jauz blushed like a little mustachioed boy. "She's quite the charmer. Tells me all kinds of stories. She was brought here as a slave from Alanya. A bit cold towards the Shah but loves their daughter dearly."

"I guess she's your daughter now. Imagine that. You're the stepfather of a princess. They'll soon be calling you Shah!" Jauz and I shared a good laugh. Nothing distracted from pain like laughter. "You let her out of that cage yet?"

His expression turned grim. "I'm no fool. A captive comes around, but it takes time. The Patriarch visited her, you know.

Has been ministering to her — since she's the only Latian remaining in the city — and even had the choir sing for her. She tells me he speaks perfect Paramic."

"He's a man of many obvious talents. And I'm sure many more I'm not aware of."

"You don't trust him?"

"Imperator Heraclius once said 'never trust a low born man in a high station. He did something wrong to get there.'"

"Such wisdom. I bet he was talking about you!"

Jauz and I shared another good laugh.

"Actually, he was talking about himself." Remembering Heraclius soured my mood. How much glory he'd heaped upon himself when it was the Archangel who'd brought us victories — by the steel and blood of my paladins.

"Get some rest, Grandmaster," Jauz said. "An order from your shah!"

One more good laugh cheered me up.

I slept through the day. Jauz gave me herbs that would help me sleep through the night. But I didn't take them. I waited in the darkness, without a candle. Waited for her.

Fifteen-year-old Elly stood in the light of the waning crescent that shone through my window. Her black-on-black eyes didn't bother me. She wore a pure white dress patterned with lilies. Her raven hair was straight, like mine, but fell to her shoulders. An angel in the darkness. She watched me from across the room.

I beamed at the sight of her. "Come here."

She walked toward me but cast no shadow on the wall.

Elly knelt at my bedside. "Papa, are you feeling better? Will you be all right?"

"I'll be fine, Elly." I held out my hand to touch her cheek, then stopped, not wanting to disturb her purity with my burnt skin.

But she grabbed my hand and placed it there. I missed her soft cheeks. Now she was a woman, and her cheekbones had stretched and made her face lean. Still, I could feel my Elly again and couldn't stop crying.

And then I saw the gash scar in her neck. What made that?

The image of me choking a girl on the sea walls shot through my mind. I'd dropped her and stabbed her neck with her own sword. No, that couldn't have been Elly. Only the Fallen could do something so horrific, and I was no disciple of the Fallen.

Elly noticed me staring at the scar and chuckled. She brought her hand to her neck and slid it across. When she lifted her hand, only smooth skin remained. I let out a breath of relief. My Elly was safe and unharmed, and as her father, nothing mattered more.

"I want to see you happy, Papa."

"I am happy. Just seeing you again has made me happier than I've ever been."

"You know what would make me happy?" She slid my hand across her face and hair.

"Tell me. I'll give you anything."

"I want a mother and a brother. So we can be a big, happy family."

She kissed my burnt palm.

"That's all I want too. To be a family again, with you."

I reached out to kiss her hair. But my lips landed on air. She was gone.

I LAY in bed all morning, sniffing my palm where Elly had kissed. Her saliva smelled of lilies. When Jauz came to wash and check my wounds, I shouted at him to come back tomorrow. Didn't even let him treat the boil on my stump, which was now a mush of blood and pus.

Zosi visited, his nose still bandaged. I'd always admired that long and proud nose. His red and black chainmail hung loose on his bones. He'd not been eating.

"I pray for your health day and night, brother, just as I pray for Orwo's soul." He stood at attention and looked at me as a dog would after a scolding. Perhaps he blamed himself.

I sat up in bed. "Life and death, sickness and health, are decrees of the Archangel on high. They are tests of our will, of our temperament, of our faith."

"I told myself the same when my sister passed away."

"A precious soul, Alma was. And a good wife. I didn't eat for six days after. But the Archangel's tests always restore us to faith. Every hardship carries a blessing."

Zosi sulked. He swallowed hard, then said, "What blessing did her death bring you?"

I reflected on the question. Zosi was a deep thinker, and to match him I had to speak my heart. "Strangely, her death taught me about my anger. I used to blame evil for the disasters that befell me. The evil unbelievers. The evil of sin. But is sickness evil? Did the pox that claimed her life do it with evil intent? Disasters are not born of evil but rather of the Archangel's deep mercy. For by enduring them, we earn our places in paradise."

"All I learned when she died was that it hurt too much to lose her."

Berrin stuck his round head in the room and intruded on our conversation.

"Sorry to interrupt," he said. "But our scouts say the zabadar are massing in the plains to the south. How should we respond?"

"Take as many Fallen Screams and men as you need," I said. "Set fire to every zabadar yurt. No prisoners. Kill every man, woman, and child that wears their leathers."

I wasn't sure Berrin heard what I said. He looked at my arm with a pity-filled pout, his baby cheeks dangling.

"Berrin!" I shouted.

"We'll do as you command," he said, now focused. "And what of the Ethosian refugees?"

"Resettle them on the coast. Send a hundred paladins to guard each village. And Berrin, stop gawking at me as if I were dying."

"Dying?" Berrin laughed and grunted. "I'm just upset I wasn't there." His chuckles turned to rage as his eyes bulged. "I would have taken a hundred arrows for Orwo. I'll miss his spiced lamb stew."

"We all will. Both of you can make amends by carrying out my orders. But I forbid either of you to leave the city."

Zosi blinked as if puzzled. "Why, Grandmaster?"

"I don't want to lose any more of my lieutenants. Besides, I need you both here...for something very special." I grinned at the thought of how shocked they'd be for what I had planned. "You'll see."

I dismissed them. But my business wasn't done. The Patriarch was my next appointment.

The old priest entered holding a potted plant that looked like a porcupine with white bulbs growing off the ends.

"What's this?" I asked.

"It grows in Piro, my hometown. Angelflower, the botanists call it. Not the most creative name, but its fragrance speeds up healing. It used to grow over the graves where my father worked." He brought it close to my nose. "I bring the seeds wherever I go. You'll see them bloom around Angelfall by summer's end. I'm a bit of a green thumb, I'm afraid."

I sniffed it. A syrupy smell made a home in my nose and relaxed me. "I've never heard of Piro."

"An obscure village that borders the iceland of Thames. I miss everything about it, save the backbreaking cold."

"May you see it again."

"And may the Archangel hasten your healing," Patriarch Lazar said. "Alas, I will not be here to see it. I leave on the morrow."

"So soon? I thought you would minister here. Kostany is our ancient capital and holiest city, after all." Words not from my heart. I wanted to keep Kostany pure — from the priests most of all.

"I would, but Imperator Josias bids me to return." As the Patriarch patted my windowsill, puffs of dust erupted into the air. He placed the angelflower there. "It'll do well with some light. As would you."

"Has Josias sent a messenger?"

"No, but he did not permit me to stay longer than I have."

"A loss for us, then."

Patriarch Lazar did not have the glow of days before. He seemed at a loss. "I'll be back…with the Imperator, when he takes the throne and declares this city our holy capital."

Worse than priests were the Imperator and his court of lords. We hadn't sacrificed blood and limbs so they could spread their corruption and decadence to this holy land, like they'd done elsewhere I'd conquered.

"And what place do you think I'll have in the holy capital?"

"Oh, I imagine you'll be sent to conquer the rest of the country. Invade Alanya. Bring back our relics from Zelthuriya. You're a gun, are you not?"

I stared at my burnt palm with Elly's kiss. I looked to my stump with its blood-filled boils. This was what it meant to be a gun of the Imperator. If I died on the battlefield, then what would I leave for Elly? Had she returned only for me to die so far from home? How would that make her happy?

Patriarch Lazar was almost out the door when I asked, "How is Princess Celene?"

He paused at the threshold. "Eager to return to the convent."

"What if she didn't?"

Now a sparkle glistened in the Patriarch's eyes. "Care to tell me what you mean?"

"You know what I mean."

"Micah, you don't look like you're in good enough shape."

"I may not look it, but I'm better than ever."

The Patriarch shook his head like a disappointed father. "I think the time for that has passed. Look to regaining your health, so you can fight on."

He was almost out the door again, when I said, "Wait."

The Patriarch halted but kept his back to me.

"You don't want to cross that threshold," I said.

"And why is that?"

"Because then you're going to find someone else for your scheme. Perhaps someone with two hands and a name. And then I'm going to burn you like Yohannes for slighting me."

"Burning a bishop is one thing...but the Vicar of the Archangel on Earth...really, Micah?" My father had scolded me in the same tone when I told him I'd bedded a girl from a convent.

"Don't hide behind holiness. Nowhere in Angelsong does it say anything about priests and patriarchs. You're nothing but squatters in the houses of god. I know whom I serve...do you, Lazar?"

Patriarch Lazar turned to face me. "It doesn't have to be like this." His eyes were alive again with whatever schemes filled them. "You have been consecrated in the High Holy Sea, that makes you equal with anyone. And what is a hand when you have an army to fight in your name?"

"I will marry Princess Celene."

"I see now how determined you are. No man can stop Micah the Metal when he wants something. Fool of me to get in the way."

I sat up in bed, careful not to wipe Elly's saliva from my hand. "You need to tell me how this will work. No lies, tricks, or games. Tell me truly, because I know that when I marry her, I will become the enemy of the Imperator."

"No, Micah. You will become the Imperator."

I'd never seen the Patriarch laugh. His teeth seemed polished to a shimmer.

"The poison I gave Heraclius was untraceable," he said. "It will be just as easy with Josias."

The depths holy men will go...

"Why did you poison Heraclius?"

"Heraclius was a disaster for our imperium. He blinded himself to the corruption of Rone of Sempuris and others who stole from the treasury while pillaging the peasantry. Without your conquests, Heraclius' rule would have collapsed years ago. He needed to go for our country to turn to its next great chapter."

"You're not wrong," I said. "The common folk have suffered unbearable indignities. I bore some of them myself when our wretched lord burned down my father's inn. Almost every paladin has suffered the same. Truthfully, I would have killed Heraclius were it not a sin." I couldn't believe the treachery that spewed from my mouth. "But Patriarch, I'm not one of your choir boys. Don't expect me to obey."

"Oh no, I don't want you to. You are the farthest thing from pliant." Patriarch Lazar stroked his bare chin, then took my hand by the wrist. I sighed in relief that he didn't touch my palm, where Elly's scent lingered. "We're in this together. I will be the right hand you lost, and we will rule the greatest empire in history."

"How do I know you won't poison me too?"

"Because I don't want the throne. I want to be its shadow, cast across the world by the light of the Archangel. You are that light, Micah. You are the Opener. And together, we will fill the world with faith."

I'd been taught about the Opener as a child. It was a sign of the End of Epochs, that the faith of the Archangel would spread to the easternmost edge of the earth — by the sword of the Opener.

"How can you call me the Opener? That's presuming much."

"You fit the description. A man low born, ascended to kingship. Who wields a sword in his left hand and faith in his right. Who—"

"Enough. Do not fill my head. Let's see to making me a king first."

"I heard you promised each paladin a fief. Become Imperator, and you can give each a province." Patriarch Lazar beamed with delight for his clever hyperbole. "I will prepare your wedding, then."

I'd told Zosi that hardships brought blessings. After this hardship, I hoped to be blessed with a crown.

15

KEVAH

FIRE ENGULFED THE PLAINS. SMOKE WAS ALL THAT REMAINED OF these zabadar villages, and it billowed and blackened the sky. Horses lay dead with the bodies of zabadar men, women, and children. It was as I'd feared.

There were dead paladins too. Their black plate with red accents couldn't be more out of place on the verdant plains, along with the earless horses that died with them. But it was their weapons I noticed most — axes, spears, swords, and guns — the last of which I was very interested in.

I took guns off the bodies of dead paladins, then retreated to the camp that Sadie's two thousand zabadar had set up on an open plain. Most of the zabadar tribes had pledged to Shah Alir and were preparing to migrate toward Lyskar and Tagkalay. We were losing.

Our warriors barely left their yurts. No amount of feigned strength could hide the defeat and fear on their faces. They had ruled the plains until Micah the Metal and his strange guns.

This place wasn't all fire and ash, though. Push over one of the boulders scattered about the grass, and you'd likely find a family of hamsters, chittering about with their red stripes and beady eyes. Unlike Kostany, the summer air couldn't choke a man with its thickness, so breathing deeply was a pleasure. Though they called it the plains, craggy hills, hazel forests, and sun-reaching grasses made it anything but plain. A general with knowledge of the land could exploit its hiding spots, choke points, and high ground, so I remained astute and surveyed what I could.

That evening, I showed one of Micah's guns to Sadie. We sat at the lakeside as the sun set toward Kostany. Frogs croaked and crickets chirped and the world sang with life.

Though the gun was about an arm span, the barrel was longer and narrower than anything we used in Sirm. That meant that the bullet ball was smaller. Inside the barrel were wavy grooves; when staring down the barrel, they resembled a whirlpool. Somehow, they increased the speed of the bullet ball as it shot through.

The rotating cylinder next to the trigger was the cleverest addition. Four holes contained bullets that fired as it rotated, rearming the serpentine being the only limitation. While the best janissary matchlock took five seconds between shots, this gun took one second.

"So you see," I concluded, "they can sustain fire on charging cavalry with one line of soldiers. Once they use up their four shots, the next line continues. The losses we'd take trying to charge them with that fire rate would be enormous. We'll need guns just as good...and allies to wield them. We need to be as strong as Micah to win."

Though Sadie listened, her eyes were distant and melancholy. "The zabadar tell me it wasn't just guns...it was a rocket that screamed like Ahriyya and sent our horses fleeing."

"They told me the same." I fingered the grooves in the gun barrel. "We'll have to cut the ears off the horses."

"Will we cut their eyes out too when Micah learns to spook them with lights?"

"Whatever advantage he gains, we have to match it. He's cut the ears off his horses already."

"Then where do you draw the line?" Sadie shivered as wind blew strands of red hair onto her face. "Clearly not at my wishes, which you disobeyed when you freed me."

"I'm not trying to fulfill your wishes. I'm trying to kill the man that killed my daughter and free Kostany."

"And why do you need me for that?"

"You're a princess of the Seluqal House and a khatun of the zabadar. Your position will bring many to our cause."

"So you'd use me just like Ebra uses my brother Alir."

"Use you? You have as much reason to fight as I do!"

"I do, but I have the sense to know we can't fight an empire many times our size if we're fighting each other! I would've escaped from Zelthuriya, eventually, and returned to the tribe. But now we are outlaws."

I shook my head, almost laughing at her overconfidence. "Zelthuriya is hundreds of miles away, and there's no guarantee you would've escaped, considering your jailers — the Disciples of Chisti. I heard they tattoo runes onto every exile, and if one attempts to flee the holy city, the runes burn the flesh until the bearer returns."

Sadie snickered. "I think I can outfox a dervish or two."

"Regardless, aren't you burning to avenge your family?"

"That's what this is about — my family!" She looked at me with hardened, unyielding eyes. "The ones alive matter more than the ones who are dead. If I rebel, then power-hungry factions will use me to fight my brother and that means I'll have to kill him or be killed. What's the purpose of avenging my family then?"

Even her father had refused when we wanted him to be Shah...until his brother Selim threatened to kill his children. Sometimes you've no choice but to kill your own brother before he kills you.

"You know, I didn't like your father, but I respected him because he was willing to shed blood when needed."

"My father didn't want to be Shah! He was used by the Fount and a faction of the janissaries who mistrusted my uncle Selim. And when they forced my father to power, the Grand Mufti ordered not only Selim's execution but all Selim's sons. Even the babies. Even..."

I was part of that faction, though merely a foot soldier. I hadn't known the fate of Selim's children until Nesrin brought it up earlier. It reminded me of the children and babies I'd pulled out of the Siyah Sea, whose shrines I planted in the earth with my bare hands. I shuddered.

"And they say Selim was cruel," Sadie said, "but my father let the Fount execute Selim's children. How was he any better?"

An orange frog jumped out of the water and croaked at my feet. I recalled Tengis saying the orange ones were poisonous. I'd been so overcome with rage for my daughter's murder, I hadn't spared a thought for my father. I hoped he was alive, somewhere.

I slid away from the frog. Sadie didn't flinch as it bounced over her leg.

"I knew both brothers," I said as the frog jumped back in the water. "While besieged at Rastergan, Selim was tasked with rooting out spies. He crucified hundreds on mere accusations, left them to bake till their skins sloughed off. To Selim, bloodshed was the first course, not the last. He killed for terror rather than justice. That's why he's remembered as cruel.

"Your father was nothing like that," I continued. "He let the Fount execute Selim's sons because one day some of them would have grown into hardened men and come for his head. The Fount's primary objective is to ensure the public good, and that means avoiding succession conflicts at all costs."

"Fuck the Fount and all they teach." Sadie punched her palm. "There has to be a better way. Otherwise, we're worse than

Micah. Every time a shah dies, we do to each other what he did to us."

If we lived in a just world, Sadie would be right. Perhaps she was too young to realize that we had to protect what mattered with strength alone.

I said, "If I've learned one thing, it's this — in war, you're either the butcher or meat. I hope one day you find a better way, but right now, my only concern is defeating Micah."

"At what cost? My father once told me that 'a king sets the character of his kingdom.' When I became the head of the tribe, I told my zabadar that no matter what they pillaged, that they were to avoid hurting innocent men and women."

"That's like telling fire not to burn a forest. How did you come to lead a tribe of ravagers while clinging to such ideals?"

"By being the butcher." Sadie looked away, forlorn.

Like her father and grandfather, it seemed Sadie was full of contradictions.

"I'd like to hear the story of how you were the butcher," I said.

"Why should I tell you?"

"Because despite what you think, I care about you and want to know your struggles."

Now Sadie looked at me with a stinging pity, as if I'd just given her a piece of my heart that she didn't want. But I was simply being honest.

"Believe it or not, I grew up in Kostany. In the harem." She cleared her throat. "My father's wife — Alir's mother — didn't like the affection the Shah showed my mother. She schemed with the eunuchs to drive them apart. After all, a wife is more deserving than a concubine."

The Shah Mother did seem like a schemer. But from what I'd heard of the harem, you had to be to thrive.

Sadie continued, "One of those schemes was to send me as far away as possible, out of spite for my mother. It was six years ago." Sadie threw a stone in the lake and ripples whirled. "I was eighteen when I left Kostany. I was supposed to travel to Tagkalay, to be tutored at the great university. But one day I woke up and all the wagons in our caravan were on fire."

"On fire? Just like that?"

"We never caught whoever started the fire." She threw another stone. It skipped on the water twice and splashed. "Anyway, a tribe of zabadar sheltered us. We were far from both Kostany and Tagkalay and winter was near, so I lived with them. They taught me the zabadar way, but I especially loved the composite bow." Sadie smiled as if dreaming happy memories. "I became so good, I started winning all the archery competitions. So the leader of our tribe put me at the head of a hunting pack. I knew then that I never wanted to leave." Her smile faded. "Then one day, years later, the tribe across the river attacked."

"A battle?"

"No, a slaughter. They were much more numerous, and we couldn't resist. They seized our land and killed Nesrin and Yamin's father. In anger, I challenged their khagan to a duel.

"He thought me weak and made a joke of it, filling himself with kumis before the bout. He didn't even wipe the milk from his beard and was so drunk he could barely climb his horse. In an open field, we charged toward each other, bows nocked and drawn." Sadie threw a third stone at the water. It skipped so many times, I could scarcely see where it splashed. "It was too easy."

"You killed a cruel fool. So what?"

"When a khagan is slain, his khatun must avenge him. She was younger than me and barely strong enough to draw her bowstring." She poked a spot just below her neck. "My arrow went through here. I watched her choke on blood as her mother and father screamed." Sadie sulked and looked away. "It was like watching myself die."

It was difficult to reconcile the girl in her story with the one throwing stones at the water.

"You defended your tribe. I see no wickedness in that."

"They say we Seluqals have the blood of conquerors." Sadie held back tears, her voice trembling. "That day, I felt my blood boil. I felt I could drown the world in my rage. When I saw what I'd done, I realized I never wanted to feel that way again. There must be another way. A way to avoid such slaughter."

"Sometimes there is. Most times, it's us or them." I took Sadie's hand and placed it between mine. "I've known many leaders. Cruel men like Selim. Cowards like Ebra. Men like your father, who don't follow their instincts and bend to advice. Do you know whom you remind me of?"

"It could be said that Selim was strong, Ebra measured, and my father prudent. Yet you see the worst in them."

I sighed. It had been a long day filled with fire and ash. "These are hard times. The worst in us will be our downfall."

"So whom do I remind you of?"

"Your grandfather." Thinking about Jallu made me smile. "Shah Jalal was kind and just. He never killed unless he had to. And he was humble. He'd tell me his doubts as we sat by a hearth drinking barley water. He'd compare himself to Utay and Temur and think he was the worst man to ever sit the throne. He was also strong. Imperator Heraclius had four times as many men, but Jallu did not surrender, and to this day Rastergan pays us tribute."

"I didn't know Grandfather well. I'd only met him a few times. Do you think he could defeat Micah the Metal?"

I took a deep breath and wished I'd exhaled cherry smoke. These were questions better answered with a hookah. "With honesty, I don't know. Like I said, you are either the butcher or meat. And judging by all the shrines we planted, Micah understands that better than anyone."

· · ·

HORSES WAITED OUTSIDE EVERY YURT, lazily eating from their chow buckets. After our meeting, Sadie held a gathering with the tribe and decided, despite pleading from Yamin and others, that we'd have to cut the horses' ears. Adjustments would be made to the bridles and both rider and horse would have to retrain. To the zabadar, cutting the horses' ears might as well be cutting their own, but it had to be done. War begets unthinkable cruelties.

Magus Vaya waited on the path to my yurt. He wore a light blue robe and hood that seemed jolly on him, though would be dour on anyone else.

"Did a jinn really tell you to free Sadie?" I asked as we walked. "Or was that your special brand of ill-humor?"

"You don't like my humor?" He said it with such a plain face.

"It could use a bit less subtlety."

Once inside, I lit a fire in the stove. Almost poured two mugs of barley water, then remembered Vaya didn't eat or drink.

"Like I said, I don't know why they asked me to free Sadie."

"My guess is they want us to win." I gulped the water, cooling my throat.

"The jinn care about our war as much as we'd care about one between ants."

"Well, I don't care what they think. I can't see them." I chugged the water again, then wiped my beard. "You know who I *can* see, going about his business? Your yellow-haired sap. Days of traveling and you still haven't told me who he really is. We've reached the front of this war now, so I think it's time you did."

"He's a Crucian."

"That's not very reassuring. They're the ones we're fighting."

"He's one of Micah's five lieutenants."

I stared at him with my mouth open, then laughed. "There. There's that humor. Very good."

"I'm not joking."

"Why would you consort with one of Micah's lieutenants?"

"His name is Aicard. His *ruh* is good. I have seen it."

"Another thing you see that I can't."

I dashed out of my yurt to find this lieutenant of Micah's. Aicard was conversing with a blacksmith in the light of a fire. He waved to me and smiled as I approached.

"Give us a moment," I said to the blacksmith. The mustachioed man left us.

"I hear cherry is your favorite," the Crucian said. His grin reminded me of a childhood friend's. From a bag behind his back, he took out a hookah. "I'm an apple man myself."

"You're a spy."

He gathered embers from the fire with a stick and dropped them in the hookah's burn plate. They made a satisfying clank. "Not a very good spy who reveals his identity."

I remained standing even as he bid me to the pipe. "Why turn tail on your master?"

He inhaled. Water gurgled. Then he blew out cherry-apple smoke. "Sure you don't want any? It's beyond sublime."

I sat at the fire and tried it. The apple added a tartness to the cherry that I could appreciate.

"Micah sent me to find the witch," he said. "The one who led him through Labyrinthos."

I almost choked. Had to stop during my inhale and cough out smoke. "Wait. What do mean 'through Labyrinthos?'"

Aicard explained how the witch, a woman named Aschere, had led Micah and a hundred paladins through Labyrinthos. Vaya stood near and listened too.

"How could this be?" I asked him. "How could no one have known?"

Vaya sat at the fire. "The jinn above say they know nothing about the jinn below. Labyrinthos' secrets are obscure to me, I'm afraid."

"If he used it to get in," I said, "then we can too."

"No," Aicard interjected. "That's exactly what you mustn't do. That's why I can no longer serve Micah. Something changed him ever since we found that witch in the mines of Ejaz. He's under a dark spell, one that could destroy what we all hold dear."

"How do you figure?" I asked.

Aicard gestured for the pipe. He took a long hit and let out a cloud of cherry-apple smoke. "Knowing that Aschere likes dark places, I sent trackers to explore all the caves around Kostany. We found her in one. She was…" Aicard shivered. "She was covered head-to-toe in green fireflies. They seemed to be talking to her."

I turned to Vaya. "This make any sense to you?"

He shrugged.

"When she saw me," Aicard continued, "she told me to tell Micah that if he wanted to see her again, to 'drink from darkness' cup.' That she would be back only once Micah was ready to open himself to her god, whom she called Hawwa."

"It translates to the Dreamer," Vaya said. "It's Old Paramic. But I've never heard it used as a name."

I took the gun off my belt. Turning the cylinder made a satisfying click. "Sounds like something meant to scare children. I've never seen witches win a war." For all we knew, Aicard was fibbing. I shoved the gun in his lap. "I've seen these win a few. Tell me how it works."

Aicard picked it up and brought it to his chin. "Micah's Silklander engineer designed it."

"Where did he get a Silklander engineer?"

"The Silk Emperor sent Jauz to study the Colossus of Dycondi so he could build one in his likeness. And then Micah melted it." Aicard chuckled. "Jauz was so thrilled to be saved from that laborious task, he went into Micah's service openly."

"Do you know how to make guns like this?"

"I know nothing about Jauz's toys." Aicard returned the gun by the hilt. "But I can tell you, he is the cleverest of men. You've not seen the half of it."

I stared into the yellow-haired man's eyes. They sunk as he darted his gaze away.

"Even after all that, why join us?" I asked. "Why not run?"

"I've seen Micah kill thousands of men — each one guilty of heaping suffering on others, each deserving. He was never cruel and always let the Archangel guide his hands. It all changed after we found the witch. In Nixos, he enslaved thousands and burned a bishop. And then in Kostany, I saw him drown a little girl and trample babies as if they were weeds." Aicard closed and opened his eyes rapidly, as if to release the image from his mind. "I must do my part to see him fall."

I wasn't convinced. But if Vaya — a man who saw the unseen — trusted Aicard, then I'd at least give him a chance. I resolved to watch him.

Yamin and Nesrin watched us from their fire. I went to sit with them.

Yamin swallowed a spoon-full of lamb stew. Nesrin reclined and stared at the stars.

"I don't trust either of them," Yamin said between a swallow and a gulp. "They are a danger to us all."

Nesrin sneered. "And where were you when Sadie needed us? Turned tail!"

"Obeying orders!" Yamin growled. "Sadie said I did the right thing."

"Well the magus was there," the girl said. "He saved us. If he were a danger, he could have flung us into the sky with a little blow of wind. As for the patchy-bearded one...there's something off-putting about him."

"She's right," I said, ignoring her comment about Aicard. "I trust Magus Vaya with my life. He's saved it more than once."

"That's because you haven't seen what I have." Yamin was frightened of something in his mind. He stared at it as he ate his stew.

"Tell me," I said.

Yamin began, "I didn't believe the stories at first. Of a man covered in fire scorching everything. Turning a field of flowers black in seconds. Sending fireballs from the heavens crashing down. Fire that would chase men as they rode away, as if alive." The bowl of stew shook as the muscled man trembled. "I didn't believe it, and then…"

Nesrin put her hands around her brother's shaking bicep.

"Last night I was out alone, scouting," Yamin continued. "I saw him. I saw him boil a pond and turn it to steam in an instant. I only survived by the grace of Lat and the speed of my Kashanese horse."

Every hair on my body stood and chills seized me. A man covered in fire had massacred Ethosian pilgrims back in Kostany. I recalled the bushfires that blackened the sky on our way to Lyskar and the dried lake full of charred fish bones. Could this burning man have been responsible? Could he be a magus?

"I'll bring this to Vaya's attention," I said. "Trust me, he's with us."

Perhaps Vaya had noticed something. Back in my yurt, he was weaving a sheepskin cap with fine red and yellow string.

I stood over his shoulder to admire his work and said, "You're a man of profuse talents."

"We all had lives before we became magi. I was a carpet weaver's son when the jinn sent for me."

"Speaking of magi, Yamin tells me he saw one burning fields and boiling a pond." I brushed my straw-strung mattress. "And he was covered in fire. Sound familiar?"

"I overheard. Let me state the obvious — it's not me. Tomorrow at dawn, I'll leave to investigate."

"I won't wrongly accuse you twice." I dusted off my sheep-skin pillow. "And I have no problem waking up at dawn."

"No. If what I think is true, then I can't protect you." Vaya breathed so slowly, as if each breath took the length of a lifetime. It seemed at odds with his speedy weaving. "You must stay with Sadie, where you are at your best."

"Nothing feels worse than sitting among these depressed horsemen."

"Sometimes the best thing is to do nothing. During my training in Holy Zelthuriya, I once waited four years for my master to task me."

"Must've been some task." I gathered my sheepskin blanket.

"It wasn't. She had me travel to Kostany, pick up a few relics and oddities they'd stored in the crypts of the Blue Domes, and return to Zelthuriya. That part of my life was nothing but patience, I tell you."

"It's good to know you feel impatience. I thought the invisible mask you wear quelled all feelings."

"My mask doesn't make me unfeeling — it merely keeps me looking young. It was the training that taught me to quell my emotions...and how to command the jinn."

"'Merely!?'" I settled into my bed and blanketed myself. I kicked at a prickly spider scurrying by. "Tell me, what is it you suspect?"

"Remember my trial...we were all so distracted by my exoneration that we forgot someone burned people alive."

"My thought, too."

I recalled the charred bodies of the Ethosian pilgrims. I didn't want that to be my last image before bed, so I thought of my wife. But it was hard to picture her, and whenever I tried, Sadie's sullen face popped into my mind.

"Tomorrow I'll visit a tribe of jinn nearby," Vaya said, "to find out more. Afterward, we'll have a talk — just you and me. We've much to discuss. About the past...and the future."

Thinking about Sadie reminded me of how close we were to losing her in Lyskar, which reminded me of the Alanyan crown prince, which reminded me of the yellow-haired man who smoked apple scent. "The Crucian seems sincere. How did you meet him?"

"Make use of him, Kevah." Vaya dusted off. How would

someone who doesn't sleep pass the night? "He sought me out and found me when no other could. He is as resourceful as can be."

"I hope you're right. We could use someone who knows Micah. There's no greater weapon than knowledge."

"Fire is a close second." Vaya continued weaving as he walked out my yurt.

IN THE MORNING, I shaved some bullet balls so they could fit in the matchlock's cylinder. I put a bit of gunpowder in each hole, then stuck the bullet balls inside. Pressing the trigger was a gamble I wouldn't take as I aimed at a tree. I was lucky to have a nose, given how the first gun I'd fired exploded. Though I wanted to learn the secrets of Micah's matchlock, I couldn't get over the trauma of my hands on fire.

Afterward, I approached Sadie's yurt. Voices sounded from inside.

"Why do the ends always curl upward!?" Sadie's. "I look like I'm about to fly away!"

"Let me braid them, that will solve it." Nesrin's

"No way. That's the one thing I'll never do. The eunuchs loved to braid each other."

"There's no one here to look pretty for anyway." Nesrin sneered. "The magus though…he's got a…stern sort of charm."

"Ugh, I smiled at him earlier, and he just stared back at me. Not what I consider charming. Anyway, if we're going to maim our horses, the least we can do is not look like shit when we do it." Sadie's voice hoarsened. "Is this really what it's all come to? I'm not made for any of this." She sniffled. "I wish I'd been stillborn."

Eavesdropping was not my vice, so I returned to my yurt.

A few hours later, the zabadar were strapping down the horses and heating blades at their fires. Each would have to maim his horse. I found Yamin patting his horse and sulking. She was a pure, white-haired Kashanese steed. A rare sight. Kashanese horses were uncommon west of Holy Zelthuriya.

Yamin sang from his belly a slow dirge in a Rubadi language, which the zabadar spoke hundreds of years before they settled in Sirm. I didn't understand it, and most likely he didn't either. Still, it saddened me.

"Where'd you get this one?" I asked.

"On a raid across the sea. The lord of the town had kept her as a racing steed." Yamin's eyes were drained of spirit. "I heard this was your idea."

"It's the right thing to do. The only thing to do."

"I used to sleep with the horses as a child. You see a horse, and they're all the same to you, except one might be white, the other black. One may be Kashanese, the other Rubadi. Tell me, would you cut the ears off your children?"

"If it would save their lives."

"But it's not their lives we're saving. It's ours."

I didn't have a response. "Tell me about her."

Yamin's eyes lit up. "Faster than the clouds. Yet a soft ride, like floating on a cloud. Only a bit temperamental."

"Tell me what you would know that I wouldn't."

"She enjoys being in the sun but hates the smell of the ocean. Most of all, she likes it when you sing to her."

She wouldn't be hearing any more songs.

Yamin handed me a small wooden box. "Take this."

I slid it open. Four red rockets with their wicks intact lay inside. "What'll I do with these? Micah's horses are earless."

"Whatever you want. I hate them and don't want them."

I nodded and thanked him.

I left the box in my yurt, then walked far so I wouldn't have to hear the maiming. Eventually, I'd have to maim my horse too.

I'd eaten my horse during the siege of Rastergan. We ate the horses first since their meat was like beef. If there was a bird in the air, we shot it down, and then we caught all the dogs, cats, and rats. Finally, we boiled all the leather off our shoes and chewed that too. Just remembering those days left my stomach in knots. Somehow, eating a horse seemed less harsh than cutting its ears.

A field of blue lilies lay before me. The buds glowed a ghostly hue and reminded me of Melodi and the shrine I'd planted for her. Even now, nothing beat in my heart but a desire to avenge her. And yet, here I was, smelling flowers. I should've been seeking out allies to march on Kostany, but where to start? We couldn't even defend our own land — the screaming rocket made sure of that, so there was nothing to do until we'd cut the horses' ears.

I lay in the field for an hour, reciting Taqi's poems about flowers. *It is rain that grows flowers, not thunder.* One of my favorite verses...yet now it sounded so distant, as if it were describing a different world. Perhaps Taqi, who lived with a sword in one hand and a pen in the other, dreamed of that world, too. A place of peace, a garden where we could grow flowers...and not have to bury our daughters among them.

I must have drifted to sleep. When I awoke, Magus Vaya stood beneath a tree, several paces in the distance.

He turned to me and said, "He is following you."

"Who?"

"An Efreet — fire jinn. But why is he here? Could it be..."

Vaya looked up, as if staring at an invisible giant. Something was there. Though the sun shone behind it, it was as if it were shining through a distorting lens big enough to cover a chunk of sky.

"I'd tell you to run," he said, "but it wouldn't help."

"I hope this is your humor on show." I lay there, too scared to move.

"I'm not that clever."

Fire! It erupted from the ground and burned the blue lilies. I rolled to my feet. Too slow. Fire raged toward me.

A zealous wind lifted the flowers, blew the fire out, flung me onto my stomach.

I pushed up. Coughed smoke and dirt.

Vaya stood ahead. There was someone else. A man on fire. No, a man *made* of fire. Not a speck of skin showed beneath the coursing flames.

From the sky, a fireball crashed onto Vaya. Wind whirled him away just before it hit. He slid to his feet and another wind screamed toward the burning man. A dark smoke shielded the burning man and sent the wind whirling toward me.

I crashed on my back with a painful bang as my matchlock flew off my belt and landed yards away. I got to my feet and grabbed at it. It blew into the grass beyond.

I ran after it as fire flared around me. But every time fire erupted, wind screamed. Fire and wind pounded and sundered the earth as cracks appeared and the earth opened and shook as if quaking. I searched for my matchlock while Vaya and the burning man battled.

A sword of flame appeared above the burning man, larger than a cypress tree. It thrust toward Vaya as a vortex slowed it. The flaming sword and the vortex pushed against each other.

Wind blew the matchlock to my feet. I picked it up and dashed toward them.

I used a flaming bush to light the serpentine, then aimed at the burning man's head.

My first bullet missed. He snapped around and sent a fireball in my direction. A gust of wind blew it off course. It screamed by me.

My second shot curved off him. This time three fireballs raged my way, as large as elephants. A windblast flung me past them and put out my slow match.

Bones bruised, covered in dirt, and stunned by the speed of

wind, I kept my head down and watched the battle. The sword of flame tried to cut through the vortex, as the vortex tried to dissolve the sword of flame. As fireballs raged toward Vaya, winds deflected them.

And then a wet gale put out the flaming sword and the burning man's fire. He stood, naked and pale — so thin his veins bulged blue. And strangely…familiar. The body curves, the lips, the soft features — that wasn't a man.

I remembered her in a bright scarf and rough wool robe. She'd given me the tastiest bread I'd ever eaten, in the great hall of Shah Jalal, twenty-five years ago. No doubt, she was Grand Magus Agneya — survivor of Labyrinthos.

Before the vortex could swallow her, a flaming spear appeared in the sky and raged toward the earth. It smashed the vortex with its scathing light. Still, the vortex did not break. It seemed to be growing and churning faster.

I rubbed dirt off my face and slapped myself to focus. I lit the slow match on burning grass. I aimed at the woman's head and fired my third bullet.

It turned to ash. Vaya's vortex grew fiercer and almost engulfed his sheikha's flaming spear. Were my shots helping? I pulled the serpentine to ready my fourth shot. The flaming spear burned green. It pierced the vortex. Vaya split in half and blood rained.

A gust of wind blew through my hand. I fired. Blood splattered from the woman's skull. She fell to her knees and collapsed on ruined earth.

16

MICAH

THE DAY OF MY WEDDING, I AWOKE IN DARKNESS, A THIN CRESCENT casting a pale glow through my window. I watched the spot where Elly had appeared the night before, but it remained empty. The scent she'd left on my palm was gone. I'd almost given up that she would come.

"Papa."

I turned to see Elly lying next to me in bed. Her black-on-black eyes met mine, and her breath smelled like the lily flower.

"I'm so happy, Papa. We're going to be a family. I'll have a mother and a brother."

"Yes Elly, today you'll have a mother. Then in nine moons, your brother will be born."

She giggled. It was sweeter than plum jam. "I can't wait to be a sister. I'm going to teach my little brother so much."

I wanted to hug her but didn't want to scare her off. So I lay there, paralyzed with a longing to feel my daughter.

And then she climbed on top of me. She kissed my cheek and nestled her face on my neck. All of her smelled like lilies. Even the sweat under her arm and the hair on her scalp. It wasn't a human smell, but I loved it because it came from her.

I put my arms around her and pressed her close. I'd never felt anything better than the warmth of her body. I closed my eyes and prayed to the Archangel that we could stay like this forever. But when I opened my eyes, there was no one on top of me.

I cried for forgiveness until dawn. But I wasn't going to stop. Whatever darkness brought Elly back, I would drink from it. I'd never felt more whole than the minutes when we hugged. I was going to keep her, no matter what. I prayed the Archangel spare me the fires of hell. No one was perfect, and all were saved by the Archangel's mercy. I hoped the good deeds I'd done would balance this cup of darkness.

Holy hymns from blessed voices filled the city on my wedding day. No heart, no matter how hard, wouldn't melt upon hearing them. They bounced off the walls of the Sublime Palace. The choir even walked the streets, hymning to the commoners.

Zosi brought me the clothes I'd worn when I wed his sister. He'd kept them, such was the honor he felt. The top was a Pasgardian tunic with silver buttons and a red rim. Tiny crystals adorned the collar, which was tight around the neck. The trousers were the softest cotton but clung to my legs like a layer of skin. I was more muscular than the day I married his sister, so my thighs stuck out. Finally, a cape of light blue, the color of the Pasgardian flag, hung over my shoulders.

Zosi held me as I dressed. I could barely lift my muscles, so harsh was the fever that toyed with me. I felt like a princess being attended to by her handmaiden. Afterward, once I looked as dazzling as a Pasgardian prince, Zosi asked, "Would you honor me by letting me escort you to Angelfall?"

"You think I'm too weak to go myself?"

"No...it's just...why have you refused to have that stump cut?"

I tapped my nose. "They never taught you about Goldnose in Pasgard?"

Zosi shook his head.

"His enemies cut off his nose so he'd be too hideous to ascend the throne. It's said he traveled the earth in search of a miracle. Twenty years later, he returned to the capital, a gleaming golden nose high upon his countenance. He expunged his enemies and became Imperator. At least with a stump, I can wear a gold hand and the masses will think I'm whole. But without even an elbow—"

"You won't be Imperator if you're dead!" Zosi seethed. "I need you to...we all need you to succeed. Once you're crowned, I can bring my sisters here to your capital. They'll be hostages no more."

I didn't want to swallow bitterness on my wedding day. I hymned Angelsong in my mind to assuage my anger. "I won't die. I have much to live for. More than you could ever know."

He looked me over with a solemn gaze, the barest hope in his smile. "Thank you for honoring my sister by wearing these clothes."

"Alma died with more honor than I could ever give her. Now go."

At the steps to Angelfall, sweat dripped from my forehead; my body felt like lead. Jauz had warned that the rot in my stump would sicken me whole. Two steps were all I could climb before stumbling. Berrin caught me and held my back as two paladins held my legs. They carried me up the steep steps as holy hymns rang.

Patriarch Lazar waited at the door to the chapel, dismay on his face. "This is no shape for your wedding."

Berrin and the paladins helped me to my feet. Standing nauseated me.

"We could do the ceremony in your room," the Patriarch said. "You cannot gain it all, only to die from a sweat."

"Let me get married while I still look somewhat whole," I said, "then I'll cut this arm off and all will be well."

"Not if the rot has spread." The Patriarch glowered like he'd just been robbed. "You cannot die, Micah. We've come so far."

"Dying is the last thing I'll do," I slurred as delirium crept through my mind. "You can be sure of that."

Berrin bowed his head to the Patriarch, forgetting that we don't bow. "I implore you, Your Holiness, proceed with haste. We don't know how much longer he'll stay standing."

I entered the chapel. Dizziness blurred my sight. People sat in the newly installed pews to the left and right, but I couldn't tell their faces. An angel waited at the altar. Her dress was dove feathers. She stared at the floor, not bothering to look at me.

The Patriarch stood on the dais and gestured for everyone to sit. The holy hymns ceased.

"By the infinite mercy of the Archangel, we congregate to join two souls. The soul of a man pure of faith, and the soul of a woman pure of faith. Let us—"

I almost retched as something twisted in my stomach. A man put his arms around me. Jauz's mustachioed face peered over me. Berrin's baby face too.

They held me up.

"Your Holiness, please hurry," Berrin said.

I straightened my back to keep what little composure I had.

"In the sight of the Archangel and for the good of the Imperium, I break the holy vow of chastity that Princess Celene swore. In the sight of the Archangel and for the good of the Imperium, I join these two pure souls."

I retched something hot and soupy. Vomit spewed onto the floor. I hoped none got on Celene's angel dress. The crowd gasped.

Berrin and Jauz pulled me up. The Patriarch joined my and Celene's hands. Hers was soft as silk.

"Micah the Metal, do you accept Princess Celene into your soul to become one with you till the end of time?"

"I do," I croaked.

"Princess Celene Saturnus, do you accept to join your soul with Micah the Metal till you meet the angels at the Fountain on the Day of Resurrection?"

No answer. My eyes flickered and my limbs shivered.

The Patriarch said it more forcefully, "Princess Celene Saturnus, do you accept to join your soul with Micah the Metal till you meet the angels at the Fountain on the Day of Resurrection?"

No answer.

"Lovely, dearest Celene," I whispered with all I could muster. "You may fear the Archangel. You may fear your father the Imperator. But that's because you don't know me yet."

She shuddered. I squeezed her silky hand with my last ounce of strength.

The Patriarch repeated the words for a third time.

"Y-yes," she whimpered.

The Patriarch doused our handhold in heavy water and recited Angelsong. Everyone cheered and hymned. My ears rang as if I were swallowing bells. I collapsed and blacked out.

In my dream, the earth was on fire. Char and flame covered every inch of land. Flames that reached heaven engulfed cities, and dead fish floated on a boiling ocean.

A star burned. Red and purple fire surrounded it in concentric circles, as if the star were smeared over a patch of sky. It was the Blood Star, whose death reset the world according to Angelsong.

A shadow covered the earth. The angel Micah soared and filled the horizon. One massive black wing stuck out of his back, larger than Mount Damav. As the angel flew toward the sun, it plunged the world in darkness. Micah's ten eyes glowed in a straight line down his face, each eye staring in a different direction. Only the eye at the top looked upon me.

The angel Micah hymned in an incomprehensible language — as if a hundred shapes with a hundred sides, all in different configurations, turned into sound. But I knew the meaning of the words in my soul.

Opener.

Drink from the darkness.

Let it enter you as you enter it.

Then remake the world.

With the demons on your sword.

An icy wind blew from the west and put out the fires and froze the ashfall. The boiling sea turned solid. But no matter how cold the world became, it could not extinguish the fire inside me. Nothing remained in the world but darkness and ash.

I AWOKE days later to the sound of Berrin's prayers. I would have preferred the sight of my daughter, or even Aschere, but it was good to see life. The crushing pain that seized my phantom arm was better than death.

"Elly...where's Elly," I groaned.

"Jauz!" Berrin stared with wide, reddened eyes. "Get Jauz!"

Jauz burst into the room. He fed me drips of water. My throat was drier than the ash in my dream, and I could only move my tongue and eyes, as if I were stuck between life and death. As if my body was a coffin that trapped my soul. For a few hours, I drifted, unable to grip the waking world.

Later, Berrin fed me dried fig soup and praised the Archangel each time I swallowed. Apparently, this was how they'd kept me alive while I slept. Zosi got on his knees and kissed the floor at the sight of me alive. I wondered if my new wife would be as joyous.

I resolved not to ask for her until I was strong enough. My

throat pain eased the next morning, but my phantom arm still felt like it was being squeezed by a snake. I talked little and prayed much as I bathed in an alternating tide of agony and numbness.

After a few days, I regained movement in my toes and fingers and was finally lucid. Good signs, according to Jauz.

"When will I be myself again?" I asked as he rubbed ointment on my now shorter stump. He'd cut it right below the shoulder.

He paused and gazed away. "Grandmaster, it will take months, if at all."

"But I'm feeling better."

"A good thing, for sure, but we don't know the toll the fever took."

I wished the fire in my soul were enough to move my arms and legs. I wished my will were iron and could speed my healing. But we are, after all, mere men bent on the will of the Archangel.

"A man who can't lead his armies from the front can never inspire loyalty," I said. "You're the cleverest man I know…is there not something you can do?"

"I'll do everything to see you lead us again." The hope of Jauz's words didn't match the despair in his tone. "But I'm not like your angels. I can't make a miracle."

The Patriarch visited the next day. My father once returned home from chapel only to find his tavern ransacked. He'd been robbed while hymning praises to the Archangel. The Patriarch had the same puzzled and rueful look on his face.

"Archangel hasten your healing," he said. "This is but a test."

I didn't waste time with niceties. "What news of Imperator Josias?"

Patriarch Lazar stood with his hands behind his back, eyes steely as the day I'd met him. "Spies travel fast. Surely, he will have heard of the marriage by now. As for his response, I cannot say."

"Response? Did you not say he would die like his father?"

"Then who would rule, Micah?" Lazar sniggered. "A man who cannot defecate without two others holding him?"

If I could, I would hit him bloody for that slight.

"You planted these seeds, Patriarch. Now you must reap the harvest."

"Not necessarily." A smug smile took the place of false concern. "I've been sending the Imperator letters. I told him how you forced me to dissolve his daughter's vow and marry the two of you. He will believe my word over yours. You burned a bishop, after all, and I fulfilled my mission when I sent him the Shah, your ships, and the treasures of the city."

Outmaneuvered by a priest. Not for the first time. "Heraclius once told me that 'a clever man always hedges.' Seems you're the cleverest among us."

"Most importantly, the marriage has not been consummated. Celene is still as pure as an angel feather. She can go back to her convent, and all will be as before."

"Patriarch," I called as he turned his back, "you better pray I never leave this bed."

"On the contrary, I pray you leave it a better man." The Patriarch left me to my dark thoughts.

DAYS LATER, I awoke to the best present: my cock stood like a cypress tree. I could barely move my hands, but my erect cock throbbed with desire. I pointed to my cock with my tongue and commanded Berrin to get my wife.

Princess Celene wore the white-gray garb of a choir girl. Her hazel hair fell to her plump breasts. She was short and shapely, and her face glowed with the light of faith.

"Take off your clothes," I said.

Berrin blocked the door and averted his gaze. Celene twirled her hazel hair and stared at the floor.

"Please do not do this," she said. "I am pledged to touch no man."

"Right, no *man*. But we all know what goes on in those convents. Shall I have Berrin pluck out the eyes of the choir girls until we find the one you're fond of?"

She shuddered but did not disrobe.

"Fine, I'll go first."

Berrin pulled up my gown. My erect cock was clear for all to see.

"Wife," I said. "Do your duty."

Celene shut her eyes and looked away.

"The hard way then."

"No!" Celene cried. She ran for the door. Berrin caught her. He tugged at her gown as she screamed and pushed against him.

"Archangel help me!" she cried. "Do not do this!"

Berrin pulled her robe off, then the smock she wore beneath. Celene covered her bare breasts with her hands and fell to her knees in tears.

"Archangel forgive me!" The girl cried, as if this were her fault. That could've been my daughter, whimpering as some vile Sirmian forced himself upon her.

"Berrin, is this how the Shah broke his slaves?"

Berrin gulped. "No, Grandmaster. Murad is a vile, wretched—"

"Cover her up!" I shouted. "Cover her up now!"

Berrin helped her back in her robe as tears streamed down her pure cheeks.

"Take her to her room."

I couldn't do it. I couldn't do what they must've done to Elly and countless Crucian girls whom they stole. I couldn't be the people I despised, even if it meant my demise. I resolved to die without an heir, a traitor to my country.

I ordered that no one enter my room. I didn't even have the courage to pray. Surely the Imperator was coming to reclaim his daughter and sit upon the throne of Kostany. I'd still be lying here, so slow was my recovery. Would Berrin leave my side? Would Zosi? Would Jauz now serve the Imperator? Had my prayers, my victories, led to this?

Night came. Crickets chirped in rhythm outside my window. No moonlight, as the new moon couldn't yet be seen.

But a greater light came. Elly. She lay next to me.

"I'm so sorry, Papa."

"I'm the one who's sorry, Elly." At least my tear ducts worked. "I couldn't protect you when they took you. I was too weak."

"No, Papa. You're strong." Her stroking my hair was the best feeling in my entire wretched life.

"I killed all these people and came all this way just to find you. And now that I have, I can't make you happy."

"You make me happier than you can know." She touched her head to mine.

"I can't give you a mother. I can't give you a brother. I can't do what I promised."

"You can, Papa. Let me show you how."

She left me. Alone. In darkness.

"Elly? Don't go!"

"I'm here, Papa."

Elly stood in the dark, a wide smile beneath her black-on-black eyes. She raised her arms, then pulled out of the sleeves of her white dress. It dropped to the floor. I wanted to look away, but I couldn't help but compare her to Celene. Her breasts were much smaller and her body leaner. I shut my eyes before more vile thoughts seized me.

My daughter climbed on top of me.

"Elly, what are you doing?"

"Will you let me, Papa? Will you let me give you strength, more than you could ever dream?"

"H-How?"

"And in return, you must give me something too." She

grabbed my cock and stroked it. Stroked it until it was hard as stone.

"No, this is the worst sin. Elly, stop it!"

She nibbled my ear and whispered, "Let it enter you as you enter it."

Elly stuck her tongue in my mouth. Her saliva mixed with mine and tasted like lilies. My cock was enveloped by warmth and wetness, as she pushed on top of me and did what she did.

17

KEVAH

Vaya's body was ash, as was his mask. But the mask of Grand Magus Agneya lay in her blood on the ground. She was bones and skin — every hair had burned away. Wrinkles lay within wrinkles on her face, as if she were hundreds of years old. The hole my bullet made under her right eye wept blood.

It all smelled of burnt sinew. The wind had lifted dirt into mounds taller than me, and charred grass and flowers rained as ash. It seemed the two magi had wrought the destruction of armies.

I grabbed the mask and trundled toward camp. The bones and muscles in my back and chest ached with all the times I'd been slammed on the ground. Only then did I realize Vaya was dead. A man I trusted and admired had been incinerated — a loss to our cause that I couldn't count. More than that...he was a friend, and I didn't have many.

I stopped when I heard the whispers: Paramic words... echoing in my ears. I didn't understand the language, but they sounded like saintly recitals. And yet, the meaning of the whispers appeared in my mind.

"Do you want power over us?" sounded in my right ear.

"Do you want eternal life?" sounded in my left.

I held the mask with both hands. It called. I wanted to put it on. I'd never felt this desire with the mask of the magus I'd killed ten years ago.

This mask overpowered my senses. When I sniffed, I smelled its earthy wood. Its sheen and veneer transfixed my eyes, and the smooth texture seduced every finger. I could even taste a sweet amber when I swallowed. In my thoughts, the mask hovered in darkness.

I closed my eyes. Micah the Metal stood on the sea wall in black and red armor. He aimed his longsword at me; it was so sharp I couldn't see the edge. But as he lunged, his face ignited. He howled and fell to my feet, then burned so hot it left only charred bone.

"Do you want power over life and death?" The words rang in my ears.

"Papa." Melodi's voice silenced the ringing. She wore a dress so bright and yellow it must've been a piece of the sun. I ran my hands through her dark hair and rested my nose on her head.

"Do you want the power to save me?" Melodi whispered. Then she exploded into yellow fireflies. They buzzed around me. The fireflies turned red and reformed into someone else: an old man, hunched over a fire and knitting a turban. I knew him when he was youthful. His radiant skin was now loose and rough, but there was no doubt: Vaya stood before me.

"Do you want to be me?" he asked.

I was back on the grass field, holding the mask. There was no question of what to do next. I lifted the mask to my head and pushed it into my face.

It stayed there. I blinked and looked around, but nothing changed. I touched my face and felt only soft skin. I felt my nose, ears, cheeks. The mask had disappeared. I looked for it on the ground and dug into the grass and dirt. It was gone.

I made it back to camp, where Sadie sat with her horse's head in her lap. She stroked it as it lay on the ground, bloody bandages covering its ears. Poor beast.

"Vaya was killed," I said as I dropped to my knees. "I couldn't save him."

She turned her head sideways and glared. "Umm...who are you?"

Zabadar with swords and spears gathered around, as if I were a threat to their khatun. I backed away as they closed in. I darted toward the lakeside. I almost stumbled in the water but stalled and looked upon my face.

I gaped at a face and body I hadn't seen in twenty years. The fat in my abdomen was replaced by lean muscle. My face was cleanshaven and without blemish, and my skin didn't sag. I was young.

Sadie approached, wide eyed. The longer she stared, the greater the shock that seized her. "Kevah?"

SADIE LIT a fire on the stove and handed me a mug of kumis. She wrapped a blanket around me. Wind blew through the flaps of her yurt. She closed them and knelt.

I told her everything.

"It's known that a magus draws his power from a mask," she said, "and you put one on?"

"I didn't want to." I sniffed the kumis. Sour — almost acrid. "But..."

"But?"

I shook my head and hunched my shoulders. My shirt was too loose. My belt didn't have enough notches to tighten on my slimmer body. I squeezed my chest and arms — toned and muscled, as if I were at a peak I'd never reached.

Sadie held her hand out, flushed, then retracted it.

I grabbed her hand and placed it on my chest. "See?"

She pushed on my muscles, then clutched my bicep.

"The mask did all this?" she said while poking my abdomen. "I can't believe it. I can't believe you're the same man."

I took a swig of kumis. It went milky smooth down my throat with only the slightest burn. "Vaya sacrificed himself so I could kill the fire magus."

"Who was that magus?"

"Before Kostany fell, we investigated a massacre of Ethosian pilgrims at one of their holy sites. She was the culprit. Her name was Grand Magus Agneya, Vaya's sheikha."

Sadie's jaw dropped. "Magus Agneya!? But my father threw her in Labyrinthos."

"Labyrinthos has entrances all over the earth. Aicard said as much. That's how Micah snuck into the city unnoticed. Perhaps we could do the same."

Sadie reflected in silence for a moment. The fire of the stove danced in her amber eyes.

"I've heard that a magus needs to train to attain their full abilities," she said. "And that this training can only be done in Zelthuriya."

"Well, I'm not going there. Not until Micah is dead and Kostany freed."

"About that." Sadie bit her lip. "Tell me, what do you know of Hayrad the Redbeard?"

It felt like a lifetime since I'd heard that name.

"He's a skilled commander with hundreds of ships."

"And what of his character? Have you ever met the man?"

I nodded. "He seemed...as you would expect of a corsair. Brazen...though affable. Why do you ask?"

"One of our scouts discovered that Redbeard is at Demoskar."

"Then we should go there. Seek his aid. He would hear us out."

Sadie chuckled. I wrinkled my nose, wondering what was so funny.

"Sorry, it's just that you look like one of my younger brothers. His mother was from your part of the world. And your voice isn't as deep as before."

"Ugh, don't say that." I tried speaking from my belly. "I'll have to regrow my beard, lest someone get the wrong idea."

Sadie smirked as if she'd caught me stealing bread. "Are you trying to deepen your voice? It makes you sound like a eunuch."

"Fuck. But at least I'm handsome now, right?"

"Who says you weren't handsome before?"

"I'd gained too much weight in Tombore."

"So? You had a rugged charm. But now—"

"Never mind that." I made a fist, then cracked my knuckles. "What matters is that I feel faster. Stronger. I wonder if I could defeat my daughter in a duel."

"You dueled your daughter?"

"When I arrived in Kostany, I was slow and weak. She crushed me."

Sadie laughed, tongue sticking out beneath her chipped tooth. "She sounds like someone I would've liked."

"You know, sometimes I think it would be nice to join her in Barzakh, with all the other souls. I think that's why I'm brave now. I've looked upon death, and it seemed no worse than living. I wish it'd been me, not Vaya, that burned."

"I'm so sorry you lost a friend." Sadie's gaze turned sullen. "He seemed...well...he never smiled. I wish I'd gotten to know him better than that." She looked at me with the kindest amber eyes. "Now you'll take his place. You'll live forever. You'll watch those you love grow old and die, as you remain young."

"So what?" I looked back at her, unshaken. "Everyone I love is already dead."

AICARD STOOD in silence in the yurt he'd shared with Vaya. The usually bright wall weavings seemed so dull, as if the colors had bled out. The ceiling bells chimed as a withering wind blew through the flaps and my bones.

We sat together on a wolf fur carpet. A forlorn hookah sat across from us, sooty from the other night.

"So...he's dead," Aicard said. His yellow beard was still patchy. At least he had one. "Another good man gone from the world."

"A good man with a lot of power."

Aicard's dim eyes showed sadness and stress. If it was an act, it was an impressive one.

"And now you inherit that power," he said. "Can you command the jinn?"

"Command the jinn? I've never even seen one."

"Vaya said that the jinn he commanded despised humans. That it was the power of the mask and the Old Paramic recitals that bound them to his will."

It seemed Vaya had said much to Aicard. Why would he reveal such things to a Crucian unless he was confident in the man's character? But all I saw was a puzzle.

"I know nothing about it," I said. "But I saw the jinn fight. I mean, I couldn't see them, but I saw what they did. If we had those jinn with us, retaking Kostany would be a trifle."

"No...if Aschere fights for Micah, it would only make the odds even."

"You said they'd found a way through Labyrinthos, and that it has many entrances. Where are these entrances?"

"I also said that Labyrinthos is evil. That it curses those who pass through it." Aicard spoke with an iron tone, his expression grim.

"Micah didn't fear it, and it bought him Kostany."

"But at a cost we don't yet know." Aicard sighed. "We have to find another way."

"I still find it strange...the way you say 'we.' I'm not convinced, Aicard, of you. Men don't turn for no gain."

"I haven't turned. I never pledged my fealty to Micah or the Imperator."

"Seems like a tall tale you're spinning." I sneered. "Why'd he let you serve, then?"

"Because I helped him. The Black Legion was a mercenary company, once. The Grandmaster, the bastard son of some Sempurian noble, was a cruel man. When we'd sack a town, he would herd all the married women into pens and force their husbands to pay a gold coin for their release. The ones who couldn't pay, he'd sell for the night to a soldier. I helped Micah kill this man and take his place as Grandmaster because he swore to uphold the goodly teachings of the Ethos faith. But even men of faith find ways to justify faithless cruelties."

"If he was such a saintly man, what changed him?"

Aicard stared up at the yurt's ceiling as the bells chimed with the wind. "I could say it started with Aschere...but even before that...with every success, his ambition would swell, until it grew past the bounds of our religion. Men are complicated, and leaders even more so. But the witch was a turning point."

"I see now why he found value in you, Aicard. You're not what one expects of a spy. You're not a fast talker. You're not a seller or a swindler. You're sincere. It's as if you're such a good actor, you've convinced yourself you aren't acting."

"Or maybe I'm not acting."

"We'll see. When the time comes, you'll help us. Or I'll open your throat."

Aicard looked at me with an incredulous smile. Then he laughed — deep and absurd. "You're the actor. I don't buy the heartless facade. When the ear cutting started, you ran away so you wouldn't have to hear the horses cry. You're just a talker, Kevah. And more than that, I believe you're a good man, who will do the right thing when the time comes."

"We're all good men until we're pushed to the edge. Then you either die a good man, or the good man in you dies."

"The good man can be brought back."

Another conversation that would've gone better with a hookah. A gust blew through the flaps and pushed soot off the empty hookah's top.

"So that's what you believe," I said, "that Micah can be redeemed. Maybe. Our religion is full of saints who were once less than good. Saint Kali buried her own son in the sand because she couldn't provide him sustenance, then she went on to feed ten thousand orphans. Lat accepts penitence, no matter the sin." I nodded, as if it all made sense. I looked Aicard in the eyes, so he wouldn't forget. "But I do not, Aicard. I won't give Micah the chance. He will die by my hand and be remembered for what he truly was — a monster."

18

MICAH

IT WAS SAID THE CREATOR MADE THE WORLD IN SEVEN DAYS BUT WAS frightened of her creation. It was a place of total chaos, with no rules to guide it. So the creator made the angels to tame the world and bring it under law. Then, as if ashamed, the creator unmade herself and ceased to be.

In the absence of their creator, the angels despaired. Those who decided to fight against chaos became the Twelve Holies and appointed the Archangel as their supreme. And those who declared that chaos was their master, that it was the inevitable end, drank from a cup of darkness and became the Fallen.

My father told me this story on those nights I couldn't sleep. He'd stir me a mug of honey milk, put on a fire, and recite stories of the angels and their trials. From the beginning, good and evil, order and chaos, were clear, and we all had to choose. He loved me dearly and wanted me to choose right.

But the world was chaos. I learned that the day mercenaries hired by our local lord set our inn on fire, stabbed my father with a jagged-edge dagger, and stole the gold he'd saved his entire life because they believed he was skimping on his taxes. I'd already lost Elly the year before and now had nothing but anger in my heart.

But anger is only chaos if you let it choose. Guided by the angels, anger can be turned to holy purpose. That is what I believed this to be about. All the conquests, killing, and victories in the name of the Archangel: rage transmuted to worship.

But what can the darkness transmute? What can the mother of chaos create?

Birds chirped outside my window. A big drongo sat on the windowsill as if we were old friends. Its black feathers matched the gunmetal sheen of my new right arm — an arm as black as the darkness of Labyrinthos. And within the arm was heat. Not the heat of life but the heat of death, of annihilation, of a chaos that engulfs.

The angelflower the Patriarch had given me lay withered on the windowsill. Its white bulbs were as ash. The sweet fragrance gone.

I had no difficulty getting out of bed. I stretched dormant muscles and bones and repeated the fitness routine I'd learned when I joined the Black Legion months after my father's murder. Stretch up and to the side. Stretch to your toes. Jump and spread your arms and legs twenty times. Drop to your stomach and push your body up with your arms.

Arms. It felt good to have arms and hands again. Everything worked. I moved my body swifter and stronger than ever. If this was the power of darkness, the power of chaos, then perhaps my father was wrong all this time.

Someone banged on my door. "Get it open!" Berrin burst in, sweat dripping off his bushy eyebrows. "We have to get him to the—"

The sight of me standing with two full arms silenced him. The paladins behind him held a litter. And yet more paladins waited in the hallway, their guns and swords drawn. They all stared at me as if I were a Fallen Angel. A smile spread across Berrin's face and he erupted with laughter.

I laughed too, then put my arm around my most loyal lieutenant. My new, black metal arm. "How does it feel?" I asked.

"Hot." He recoiled as if my arm were a stove. "Is this…Jauz's work?"

"No, Berrin. This is nothing less than a miracle of the Archangel."

Berrin hymned praises to the Archangel. Then he puffed his cheeks and became serious. "Imperator Josias is coming with an army. He's declared you a heretic and enemy of the Imperium, and proclaimed that all Ethosians and loyal Crucians must do their part to bring you to justice and open the city to him."

"So who betrayed me?"

"The Patriarch has been preaching unceasingly that it is the duty of all to obey the Imperator."

"Who else?"

Berrin's lips quivered. "It seems Zosi has taken his side."

"No, he would never—"

"His sisters, Micah. You saw to it yourself that they be married to lords in the Imperator's court. The Imperator singled them out in his proclamation, to remind Zosi of his power over his sisters. He cannot oppose the Imperator without jeopardizing his family."

"You think that excuses treachery?"

"Not at all. Either way, we must go. The Imperator is only a day from the walls. I did my best to keep the men loyal, but it wasn't enough."

"How could all this happen overnight?"

"Grandmaster…" Berrin shook his head, pity glistening in his round eyes. "You've been asleep for twelve nights. And not one night too late."

I laughed. Twelve nights in peaceful slumber — surely a gift from whoever gave me this arm. "This is my city. I earned it with blood and souls. Let's go to the great hall and see who would face me."

I threw off my gown and walked naked. Vibrant skin clung to the muscles of my legs, arms, and chest. My body looked more like stone than flesh, hard and chiseled as it was. Let them see that their grandmaster was whole and strong.

The great hall lay empty. The work of remodeling it to suit a holy purpose was only partly finished. Pure white and purple replaced gaudy gold, and the artisans had painted the likenesses of the angels on the walls. The seat was still gold and remained how the Shah left it. I got comfortable on the silky couch.

"Open the palace gates," I said. "Let whoever wants to submit or challenge me come freely through the golden arches."

Concern and confusion seized Berrin's baby face. His eyebrows didn't know where to point. "Grandmaster, if we do as you say, paladins loyal to the imperator will storm this hall."

"I welcome it. Send a messenger to the Imperator. Demand that he accept my solemn marriage to his daughter, declare me his heir, and return to Hyperion."

I reclined on the seat. My naked behind so enjoyed the golden silk. "Where is my wife?"

"Holed up at Angelfall, with the Patriarch."

"And Jauz?"

"I believe he meant to take a ship and sail to the Silklands."

"Make sure they all know that I am alive and whole and seated on the throne. And surround Angelfall. I will let each decide his own fate."

An hour later, Jauz arrived with his Silklander engineers. The mustachioed man fell to his knees.

"Your arm," he said. "How?"

"By the mercy of the angel you disbelieve in," I lied. "Come feel it."

Jauz approached slowly, as if I were a sleeping lion. He brushed the black gunmetal of my arm, then darted his fingers away. "It's hot to the touch. You can move it?"

I swung it around, reached up, and wriggled my fingers. This hand felt no different from the one Elly had chopped off. I supposed she'd owed me a new one.

That thought hit like a lightning strike. I'd killed the girl who cut off my hand, and if that was Elly, then I'd killed Elly. That could not be true. I would never snuff out the most precious light to ever grace my life. Amid the horrors I'd experienced, I must've misremembered.

"We in the east used to think you all barbarians," Jauz said, breaking my train of thought at the most welcome time. "And yet, I've never seen a mechanical arm that was...alive like this. Your angels truly are great."

"Don't give up on the Wheel so fast. Let's first deal with those who betrayed me."

I then realized Jauz's red-haired hothead wife was not with him. "Where's that woman of yours?" I asked.

He winced as if my words hurt. "In the chaos as we ran to the dock, we were separated. I've sent men to look for her."

"Won't be too hard to spot a creature like her. Don't be down, I'm sure you'll be reunited."

"Down?" Jauz roared and let out a raucous laugh. "Micah the Metal, the only man with ambition to put my talents to use, is seated on the throne once more. I haven't been this happy since you melted that fucking statue!"

Jauz and I shared a hearty laugh. He took his place to the left of my golden seat.

Paladins came and went. They knelt with their heads straight and hands on their hearts. I told them, "You are either with me or with the Imperator." Many trembled at the thought, others fell sullen. Yet more looked upon me with doubtless gazes. I'd drawn a line, and all men in the city would choose sides before the day ended.

Edmar limped into the great hall. Jauz had replaced his trampled leg with a peg and his sword with a cane — my best fighter, reduced to this.

Before he could speak, I said, "What miracle the angels worked on me, I pray they do to you."

"I don't need a leg to kneel, Grandmaster. Know that my heart is with you. Even on wood, I can still throw knives better than any."

"Take your seat at my side," I said. "You are among the saved."

The midday bell rang. The march of troops climbing the stairs vibrated under my seat. Zosi entered wearing resplendent gold and blue Pasgardian armor. Behind him followed fifty paladins in the black and red. He took off his helmet and knelt.

"Grandmaster, forgive me! You are clearly no less than a chosen of the Archangel, for he has blessed you with miracles I cannot comprehend."

"Comprehend them." I approached my lieutenant, my black arm in a fist. "You are either with me or with the Imperator. Choose, Zosi of Pasgard."

"There must be some accord we can come to." Agony stirred in his eyes and choked his voice. "Brother cannot fight brother. There are few worse sins than fratricide."

"Of course." I returned to my golden seat. "The Imperator can accept my marriage to Princess Celene, declare me his heir, and return to Hyperion." I spread my arms as if to embrace everything. "All will be well with the world."

"Grandmaster, everything you have said is as you deserve." Zosi stared up at me with the dismal gaze of a despairing child. "Allow me to relay your terms to him."

"I've already done that. We'll know his answer by tomorrow." No one had it harder than Zosi. If forced to choose between Elly and the Archangel, I scarcely knew what I would do. And here knelt Zosi, forced to choose between his sisters by blood and his brother by law. If I could find a rope to save him from that pit, I would tie it around my own back and haul him out. But this day was not for kindness.

"Today, each and every one of you must choose," I said. "Micah the Metal or Imperator Josias. Who will you stand with?"

"You are my brother, from now until the end of time." Zosi put his hand to his heart. "I stand with you, always."

"I have heard otherwise, Zosi. But I'll give you a chance to prove your loyalty." I pointed my new, black metal forefinger to the ceiling. "Go to Angelfall. Bring me my sweet wife and our treacherous patriarch."

"It will be done, brother, as you command." Zosi walked out of the palace. He cradled his Pasgardian helmet as his troops marched behind him.

MANY PALADINS KNELT and declared fealty. But many were absent, too. It appeared an untold fraction had deserted, which Berrin estimated at ten thousand, taking the remaining ships and sailing back to Crucis whilst I was in slumber.

Berrin ran into the great hall, breathless.

"Zosi went to Angelfall as commanded," he said as he panted, "parleyed with the Patriarch, and then…" Berrin choked on his hesitation. Coughed a few times.

"And then what!?"

He cleared his throat with a wet gargle. "He marched to the sea walls."

"So…Zosi has made his treachery plain." I stood and was reminded that I was naked. "You will all find out what is born of such treachery."

Berrin fetched my battle clothes and armor. I put them on while staring at the likenesses of the angels on the walls. Cessiel stood near a window, nine wings on each side and four eyes in the shape of a diamond. Malak stood behind the throne, his six legs like an insect's. He was the fount of power and watched kings with his spider eye. Principus was only partly finished; the angel of fire and judgment looked like a jellyfish without tentacles.

With my longsword on my belt, I felt once more like a leader of men. I chose twenty paladins whose faces were stern as granite, who looked upon me with doubtless eyes. Berrin would sit on the golden couch and take fealty in my place. Faith in me would be asked of all.

It saddened me that Angelfall was now the refuge of the faithless, as it had been when I took Kostany. Charlatans hide behind the shield of holiness, thinking it strong enough to stop a just sword. But false piety is an illusion. Justice cuts through it as a sword through cloth.

I stepped outside. What a beautiful day for fighting. The sun presided over a cloudless sky. I ascended the steps to Angelfall with twenty paladins, feeling brighter than ever. At the top, I gazed down on the city. The streets lay empty, the common people huddling in their hovels. The walls were empty too. If the Sirmians knew the divide that choked us, I was sure they'd seize the city. But I resolved it would be mine again before long.

A gunshot whizzed by me as I entered the plaza around the chapel — a warning fired by one of the ten paladin gunners who guarded the door. I continued toward them, undeterred.

"Your choice, brothers," I said. "If you back me, pledge your fealty now and step aside. Or you can be among the dead and lost."

They stared at each other, waiting for someone to act. The loyal men behind me on the stairs drew their guns, and I stood amid the standoff. Tense seconds passed in trepidation. Then the first paladin dropped to his knees and put his right hand on his heart. "I am with you, Micah the Metal!"

The next did the same. And another one. As more paladins dropped to their knees, the ones that didn't ran through the doors of the chapel.

I handed my sword to the man behind me. "Stay outside," I said. "I will not profane our holiest site with Crucian blood."

I walked through the double doors, armed only with the knowledge that I'd already won.

The Patriarch sat on a chair upon the dais, flanked by his paladins. On the second level, paladins drew their guns at me as I walked the same hall where I'd been married a fortnight ago. Before I could get too close, the paladins formed a wall, their black shields forward, to block my path.

"I come with no weapon," I said, "save the conviction that I've been wronged. By you, Patriarch Lazar."

His paladins moved to the side. The Patriarch did not stir in his seat. He'd turned this holy chapel into his great hall, but instead of a throne of golden thread, his was of twine.

"I did not wrong you, Micah. You wronged our Imperator and his daughter by compelling me to perform a marriage that has no validity in our law."

The Patriarch rose from his chair, squinted, and pointed at my arm. "The Fallen have blessed you, I see. You have consumed their darkness and turned it to form."

"No." I stretched my arm forward. I spread out my fingers, then made a fist. "This is a sign from the Archangel that my purpose is true. And all of you are witness to this sign. I am the Opener. I gave Kostany back to the faithful and cleansed it of disbelief. Do you think the Archangel would forsake me? It was only a test, one that presents itself to each of you now."

"Do not profane this holy place with your lies!"

"Your position is the lie," I said. "In the world I'll build, there'll be no need for intercessors. For priests and patriarchs. The Archangel and the Twelve shall dwell among us."

"You are but a deceiver, guiding men toward the fire!"

The paladins on the second level whispered among each other, as did the paladins surrounding me in the pews.

I spread my arms, as if to embrace everyone. "Join me! We will go east and conquer every city until we reach the waterfall at the edge of the world. Each of you will be a lord unto his own with lands and castles aplenty." I pointed to the Patriarch. "Or I'll bury you in the same ditch as him. Choice is yours, my paladins!"

At that, I left the chapel. Shouts erupted and gunshots exploded. Steel clanged as the Patriarch's paladins fought each other. The blood of Crucians spilled onto the soil of Angelfall. But not by my hand.

I waited at the steps as a troop of paladins, their black armor stained red, dragged the Patriarch outside.

"Where's my wife?" I asked my new prisoner.

Lazar glared at me, his eyes erupting with anger.

"He doesn't want to use his tongue?" I unsheathed my sword. "Let's make sure he never hymns again."

"Not here!" Patriarch Lazar cried. "I swear on the Twelve — she is not with me."

I gestured to my paladins. "Search Angelfall! Search the crypts! Find her!"

Zosi and the cadre loyal to the Imperator controlled the sea walls. When I'd handed over the Shah, I'd also sent most of my ships to Hyperion. If I didn't retake the sea walls, the Imperator's navy could use the ships Jauz had modified to sail through the Shrunken Strait, climb the embankments, and take the city as we'd done.

I'd not visited the sea walls since I conquered the city. We'd cleared the debris from the seventh wall, which was halved by Aschere's fire. It was where I stood when we won the city. It was where I killed...that girl. And today, it was where I had to go to keep the city.

Thousands of paladins had joined Zosi. When we took the city, we held the walls for hours with only a hundred. Though I had more men, I couldn't reclaim the walls in time to prevent the Imperator's fleet from landing. Zosi had laid sandbags across the battlements and turned his guns in our direction.

We agreed to meet next to a fountain that a bomb had destroyed on the night we took the walls. It was just a pile of stone and char now. Most importantly, it was open space under the clear sky.

Zosi came with the afternoon sun. A breeze provided relief from a hot day. His blue and gold Pasgardian armor clashed with the black and red of the paladins surrounding us.

"Of all things," I said, "you wear the armor of the day I defeated you."

He didn't look different from that day, the same doleful scowl on his face.

"It's the armor of my country, of my house, and has been so for hundreds of years." Hope glimmered in his deadpan eyes.

"You hope the Imperator will grant you independence because of your service to him on this day?"

"Nothing of the sort. I wear it to remind myself that I am not you. That I have a duty to my house, or what you left of it."

"What I left of it? Heraclius would have ended it, if not for my intervention. I saved your sisters. I even married one of them! I am your brother. And this is how you repay me?"

"Yes, you did save them." Zosi stared far into the strait, toward the lands of Crucis, as if hoping to see the sails of his savior the Imperator. "But it is the Imperator who has them now. And if I am loyal to anything, it is my family." His lips quivered. "But when forced to choose between my brother and my sisters, when forced to choose between family, what would you have me do?"

"You still hope the Imperator and I can come to some peace?"

"It's the only way out for me."

I let the squawking of seagulls provide Zosi some respite for his thoughts. Truth be told, I was honored to have him in my army. He was the only one among us born in a castle, although Berrin was of noble Sirmian blood. They both proved that ours was an army of faith, not of lineage or language or anything that divides men.

"When I first joined the Black Legion, they put me in ugly, brown armor," I said. "The color of mud. Didn't let me wear the black and red for at least a year."

"It was a mercenary company back then. Different values."

"Not as big a difference as you think, worshipping gold and worshipping the Archangel."

"How so?"

"Faith runs out as gold does. And nothing replenishes both like victory."

Zosi looked at me, as forlorn as I'd ever seen him. But behind his sorrowful gaze, I could sense the stern brood of determination. "And what did this victory do to your faith, Micah? Is that arm a gift of the Twelve or of whatever Fallen Angel brought you through those tunnels?"

"Stand down, Zosi. I'll let you leave the city. Go to your imperator and be with your sisters."

"And now you want me to leave?" Zosi sneered and shook his head. "Do you think I'm not a faithful Ethosian? A loyal Crucian? I will hold the sea walls, for our imperator. If this city is more important to you than your faith — if you're truly willing to slaughter your brothers — then fight us. Do the deeds of the Fallen. Show us all who you really are, Micah the Metal."

It seemed we couldn't avoid battle. The Imperator would be here by midday tomorrow, at the head of three hundred ships and thirty thousand men. Combined with the men under Zosi's command, it made the odds very even. We had to take the sea walls, or tomorrow would be a day where Crucian slaughtered Crucian. And if the Sirmians attacked us thereafter, it could be a quick end to the Crucian reconquest.

At sunset, I sat at the garden's wide glass table with Berrin and Edmar. We'd not manicured the place, so the trees and bushes bulged unevenly. Too many birds had made their homes in the trees, and their chirping was endless and grating. I shook a tree and most of them fluttered away. It was the first satisfying thing I'd done with my new hand. Berrin lit the fire lamps, and we chattered under the swelling moon until the topic turned to the battle at hand.

"Blow up the sea walls." Edmar's small face and gait now seemed sickly rather than a mark of fitness. "Block the strait from the mouth. The Imperator will never make landfall."

"No-no-no." Berrin sighed in disgust. "What happens next time? What happens when Redbeard returns with three hundred ships?"

"The strait will still be blocked!"

"The debris will have eroded," Berrin said. "And unless we can build another seven sea walls, we'll be defenseless."

Edmar sank back in his chair, defeated.

On the request of Berrin, a paladin brought us rose water from the palace kitchen. It shimmered pink in its silver mug.

"Smells sweet." Edmar sniffed his cup. "I don't like sweet."

"You all said you would try it," Berrin chided. "Don't back out now because it's something different. If you're going to conquer my country, learn its ways."

I swallowed a mouthful. It was not unlike sweet summer wine but without the sharpness of alcohol. Despite their vileness, these Sirmians could make a drink.

Edmar nodded. "It's not the worst thing I've ever had. But if this is my last night on earth, I'd rather be full of wine than pink water."

"Drinking the night before battle," Berrin scoffed. "Is there anything more foolish?"

"Have you seen my leg? I won't be fighting much."

Jauz strolled in, bald head glistening with sweat.

"Here comes the man who cut it off with a surgeon's blade!" Edmar exclaimed.

Jauz sat to my left. "Did a count of all the guns in the armory. Zosi plundered our stocks. He may have one gun to a man."

"We'll die like the janissaries if we charge the walls." I took another sip of the sweet water. "We don't stand a chance."

Jauz snapped his fingers at a paladin on guard. He pointed at my cup. "Get me some of that." He turned to me. "Princess Celene is nowhere to be found, either."

"Without her, this is all for naught," I said. "My claim withers like saltpeter in the wind."

"Where could a young girl go?" Berrin resembled an angry baby when he scowled. "Labyrinthos? Or maybe Zosi has her?"

"Labyrinthos means she's dead." I sighed, weary from the day's action. "And I think I would've noticed a shapely girl among Zosi's cadre."

We drank rose water in silence for a minute.

"If the Imperator takes the walls, we'll be fighting pitched battles in the streets," I said, broaching a new topic. "We fought house to house for months when Pasgard fell. The carnage only stopped because Zosi and the other nobles decided to join our side instead of see their city further torn apart. Edmar, you were the one who advised me to burn it all down instead."

"Why didn't you?" Edmar asked.

"Because fire is for cleansing. Fire is for hypocrites and disbelievers."

Jauz accepted his cup of rose water with an "ahh." He took a gulp, then spat it out on the table and coughed. He pointed at the shade of the tree.

A woman stood against the bark. Her eyes shimmered emerald in the fire lamp's glow. Her skin was fair and youthful and her lips perfect and red. She approached and took a seat at the table.

I beamed in surprise and glee. Not since I'd seen my daughter had there been a better sight. "Aschere." I couldn't take my eyes off her perfection.

"You look so troubled," she said. "And to think I left you so joyous."

"It's all gone down a rat hole since then." I wished she were closer so I could smell her breath. "I've been waiting for you. Unceasingly."

"I met your pet. Didn't you get my message?"

"You mean Aicard? Haven't seen him in weeks."

"Well, either way, you've done exactly what you needed to." Aschere moaned ever so gently. "Don't you feel it?"

Berrin and the rest sipped rose water and looked on uncomfortably.

"Feel…what?"

"The power coursing through you. The power that will make your present troubles so insignificant."

"I feel reborn, if that's what you mean."

"You're not very in touch with yourself, are you, Micah?" She ran a hand through her ashen hair. "Let me help you."

Aschere came close and put her hands on my new arm. Her chilly touch sent icicles through my veins. But there was something else: a wall of fire melted the icicles. The melted ice boiled so hot that sweat dripped from my forehead. I pulled away.

In her utterly subtle way, Aschere grinned. "The Blood Star hymns to you, Micah the Metal. Can you hear its song?"

Somewhere in the sky, beyond the moon, above even the sun, a star shone upon me. Its light was black and unseen, but I could feel it burning. It called to me as it filled me with darkness.

Opener. Drink from my cup. Remake the world. With the demons on your sword.

19

KEVAH

CHEERS ERUPTED AS I STEPPED IN THE MIDDLE OF THE CROWD. THE zabadar had made a circle large enough for Yamin and me to move twenty paces each way. He was bigger and more muscular, but no doubt I was faster.

We circled each other, then I baited Yamin with a slide. He lunged and found air. I grabbed his arm and twisted it till his knees thudded on the ground. I pushed his head and made him eat dirt as the zabadar howled. He growled, then kicked to his feet.

"Ru-stam! Ru-stam!" the zabadar around chanted. Rustam was their wrestling saint. Apparently, during the best matches he possessed both competitors. "Ru-stam! Ru-stam!" They beat their drums in rhythm with their chants, setting the pace of our bout.

Yamin lunged several times, but I evaded with a duck or side-step. I'd not felt this alive in ten years — this full of lightning. I darted for his leg and pulled it out from him. He slammed onto his back. One more down and I'd won.

"Ru-stam! Ru-stam! Ru-stam!"

This time, Yamin waited. He circled and eyed me, unblinking.

But no man can avoid blinking forever. I was at him when his eyes closed for that fraction of a second. I pushed at his muscled form and we tumbled together into the dirt. Three downs.

The zabadar hollered. The winners of the bets beamed as copper coins exchanged hands. Yamin pushed me off and got up.

"You...whatever you became...it's cheating!" He made a fist, then stormed off.

Aicard watched from the front of the crowd. He clenched a fistful of copper coins and smiled. "Were you this good in your youth?"

"Better. I'm still working off the rust."

He put his hand out to help me up. I pulled up and dusted off.

"Have you seen any yet?" he asked.

"Any what?"

"You know...any jinn?"

I looked around and saw a clear sky, the sun above, and the zabadar cheering, "Ke-vah! Ke-vah! Ke-vah!"

"Nothing." I said. I'd been looking for the jinn to no avail.

"So...can you snap your fingers and make the wind blow?"

Snap. Snap. Nothing happened, just like the last hundred times I tried.

Days had passed since Vaya's death. I'd planted his shrine in a patch of blue lilies that the fire and wind didn't destroy. We prayed for him, though none of us really knew him. He was born before most of our fathers and died at seventy-seven. For such wisdom to return to dust was no doubt a blow to our cause. And yes, he felt like...a friend. Death had ended more friendships than I wanted to count — such was the life of a janissary. I wondered how many friendships I'd ended — and would end. Is that all we were doing: competing to end friendships? Severing the bonds between men, forever? I sighed, knowing it better to leave such questions for when the blood had finally dried.

Our cause had taken us west toward Redbeard and his fleet of three hundred ships. We raced to make an alliance with him, and with the governor of Demoskar, who was a janissary with an army of five thousand.

We now camped a half-day from Demoskar. As the sun set, I realized I hadn't seen Sadie today.

Nesrin and a few of her girlfriends skinned rabbits by a fire. I smiled back at them. Their cheeks flushed, and they put their heads down and giggled. I'd missed that kind of reaction. I never wanted to grow old again. Although, one or two of the zabadar men had taken to staring at me as well. Thankfully, my beard thickened by the day.

"You seen Sadie?" I asked.

Nesrin poked my cheeks and pinched my nose. "Still can't believe it's you," she said. "The fat, graying man now looks like..."

"A prince from the tales of Mahal," one of her friends said.

"No, he looks like the prince from the tale of the slave prince," the other friend said.

"Oh that's such a dull story."

"Dull?" The girl hugged herself as if hugging the prince in the story. "It's the best love story there ever was!"

The other girl clearly wanted to retch. "Maybe if you're an inbred five-year-old!"

The two girls argued on.

"Sadie went with the scouts this morning," Nesrin said, flush with embarrassment for her friends. "They should've been back by now."

"Which direction did they go?"

"South."

I saddled my mare and rode south with the setting sun. Without ears, she could no longer hear my commands, which doubled the duty for my legs. I'd also adjusted the bridle to firmly wrap around the nose and head. I had to stay vigilant because she couldn't alert to wild animals out of eyeshot. Worst of all, she seemed sullen and guarded, like the other horses at camp.

I only rode a few minutes to see Sadie sitting by a pond amid a field of dandelions. She held a few and blew on them one-by-one; they puffed and withered in the air. Her horse lay behind her like a giant dog as she reclined against its pink belly. A nearby cedar had several arrows stuck into it, all on the same spot.

"Nesrin was worried," I said. "She asked me to find you."

The buzzing of cicadas evoked the perfect summer sunset.

"You're a liar." Sadie cradled a waterskin with her other hand. Her cheeks were gushing as if forever flushed. "The worst kind of liar. A 'small things' liar." She blew another dandelion into floating white strands.

"All right, you have me figured." I jumped off my horse. It whinnied and went to drink pond water. "I like everyone settled and cozy by sunset." I knelt next to her.

Her breath smelled sour and milky, like kumis. Mud stained her leather pants and shirt.

"You missed my wrestling victory. Yamin is still seething." I sat, took the waterskin, and shook it: empty. "Hmm...impolite to go drinking alone."

"I'm not alone. I have Nailer." She pointed around her horse, which had a composite bow tied to its back.

"'Nailer?' Strange name for a horse."

Sadie shook her head.

"You named your bow?"

She winced as her cheeks reddened even more. "Look at that." She gestured to the arrows in the tree and slurred, "It earned that name."

I sat next to her and picked up a dandelion. Its honey smell perked me up. "So how drunk are you? 'Topple off my horse into the mud and name my bow' drunk?"

"Not drunk enough. Not for what we're doing." Something boiled beneath Sadie's loopy glare. "I'm not made of whatever metal you think I am. I was afraid to stand up to my little brother. I trembled and cried when forced to slice my horse's ears, so much that Nesrin had to do it. What makes you think I can fight Metal Micah? The man terrifies."

"He should. He's given me sleepless nights aplenty. But you're not alone. Your zabadar are here for you. I'm here for you."

"Now that's not a small lie. You're not here for me." The venom in her words shocked me. "What if I told you I can't? What if I told you all I want is to ride around and shoot arrows at the trees? Would you accept it? No, you'd use me, like a...like a scheming harem eunuch!"

The woman darted her gaze and wrinkled her nose. Was I truly her tormentor? But that was the last thing I wanted to be. I'd been used my whole life by Seluqals, even those I admired. And yet...

"You've no choice." I blew dandelion strands into the air. "Convenient to blame me, when truly it's fate that you curse. I didn't secrete you into the womb of a Seluqal concubine. I didn't burn the wagons that brought you to the zabadar. Want to shoot arrows at the trees? Beg Lat to birth you again, this time in a village on some paltry patch far away."

Sadie's chuckle had a darkness to it. "Fuck Lat. If you really believe that jinn in the form of birds dropped us onto the earth from some faraway star, you're a fool and a liar!"

"A blasphemer — is that what you are? If you were my... I'd..."

She crawled up to me, smirking, her stinking breath in my face. "If I were your...daughter? Wife? Which is it? What would you do, janissary?"

Good question.

"Apologies." I got up and whistled to my horse, then remembered that it couldn't hear. "Fool of me to feud with a drunk. You're my khatun and princess, naught else." I took the reins and jumped on. "I'll let Nesrin know where you are." I trotted away.

WE APPROACHED Demoskar by midday and, from the overlooking hills, could see its harbor full of warships. An ancient Dycondian king had built the limestone lighthouse; for seven hundred years since, too many earthquakes rocked it, and now it seemed a husk of discolored, crumbling slate. It stood taller than the surrounding walls, which hadn't been breached since Temur the Wrathful seized the city from the Crucians hundreds of years ago. In fact, I'd come here before, as part of a janissary dispatch to quell a zabadar khagan who'd taken to raiding the suburbs. I wondered if his head was still mounted on the city gate.

But it wasn't an army at Demoskar today. Refugees from Kostany filled the tent city outside the walls. Men and women holding wooden mugs lined up and waited for soup that was cooking in a carriage-sized cauldron. The children watched us, dust on their faces as they played with rocks. Some of them laughed and ran around, while others looked upon us with vacant stares. I hoped that we could resettle them back in Kostany.

Could my father be somewhere in the tent city? I bit onto hope. After our meeting with Redbeard, I'd have to check.

To not spook the governor, Sadie had the zabadar camp an hour's ride from the wall. Only ten of us entered the city with her. I made them promise never to leave her alone. None of us would forget Lyskar.

Chanting and wailing from the towering shrine, dedicated to Saint Kali — whose remains were never found — welcomed all who entered the city by its pearly eastern gate. She'd buried her son in the sand, then went on to feed a thousand children: the perfect saint for Kostany's orphans and refugees. The limestone of the shrine gleamed whiter than the clouds. How many prayed for the believers to retake Kostany? Would Saint Kali, who despised war, take their prayers to Lat?

We needed allies more than prayers. The limestone of the White Palace glowed heavenly in the sunshine. A white dome adorned the top, and imposing white columns guarded the archways. Governor Jahan met us with his retainers in a hall with a black marble fountain and gray marble floor table. He wore a serious scowl. A thick mustache and heavy beard provided adornment to an otherwise plain face. His black turban didn't go with his flower-patterned vest.

Sadie sat to my left at the floor table, with Yamin to her left. The two strongest of her tribe would make sure no one tried anything untoward.

After we'd made our case that the Crucians would march here next, and that the governor ought to join us to save his city, he said what we'd feared, "Although I'm acutely aware that the Crucians are days from my walls, your brother Shah Alir has already taken my fealty. And as governor of an esteemed city, I knew that he was the secret heir. Therefore, and despite the dilemma, I cannot pledge my army to your cause, Your Highness."

As we talked, a beardless boy served glasses of orange-colored sherbet in ice. I sipped. The sour-sweet of tamarind cooled my throat, perfect for this sweltry day.

"And what did Ebra tell you about me?" Sadie asked. I hadn't spoken to her since our argument. Her eyes were bloodshot, as if hungover.

"He told me to welcome you within my walls on false pretenses, to arrest you, and to deliver you to him."

I looked at Yamin. He looked at me. I grabbed the hilt of my sword.

"But I won't do that," the Governor continued. "Though I am a janissary and loyal to the Shah, I am ever a man of faith. If I arrest you, it will provoke your zabadar. I'll not spill Latian blood while infidels invade our country. However..." He sipped his sherbet. "I must advise you to turn yourself over. A princess has no place leading an army. I oft sat on your father's councils. He would not have approved of what you're doing." Another sip. "The Fount have made their new home here. Shall I fetch the Grand Mufti and have him order you to stop?"

Sadie gripped her forehead as if overcome by nausea. "My father...the Fount..." She trailed off and stared at her sherbet with quivering lips. The governor shifted in his chair as the silence lingered.

"You have candor, I'll give you that," I said, unable to hold my tongue. "But as a janissary, you should want nothing more than to face our enemies. And they're all in Kostany."

Governor Jahan responded predictably: "While I want to fight Crucians, I will only do so on the orders of Shah Alir. To defeat them, we must strike as one, when the time is right. I advise you all to have patience. To be loyal to your shah, in the sight of Lat."

Sadie guzzled her sherbet. Afterward, she paced her breathing, as if trying not to retch. How could she lead us like this? How could she convince hardened men to follow her?

"And when will the time be right?" I said. "Has Ebra shared any plan with you to take back the Seat?"

This governor was trifling compared to the challenges ahead. Perhaps Sadie's heart was not in this. Perhaps she preferred to cower.

"You could ask him yourself." The governor stood and shouted, "Enter!"

The door to the meeting hall opened. A troop of janissaries marched in with shamshirs shining on their belts. We all stood. Yamin and I kept Sadie between us as the janissaries surrounded the room.

Ebra entered draped in brocade, his face pink and smug. With him was the Shah Mother, her nose imperious and blue caftan flowing like a river. And behind them, the Alanyan crown prince strutted in wearing a puffy pantaloon and his turban around his shoulders.

Ebra bent his neck. The janissaries followed. "Your Highness," he said to Sadie. He gestured for the janissaries to relax their stances. They put their hands behind their backs.

"Take ease," Ebra said. "We're not here to fight."

Three of the governor's retainers gave up their seat pillows so Ebra, the Shah Mother, and the Crown Prince could take their places at the floor table.

Though surprised, I wasn't afraid. I'd wanted to see Ebra again, if only to show him the strength he belittled when he threw me in that puddle in Lyskar. Though there were fifteen janissaries in the room, there were ten of us, and I'd take those odds.

"Why the surprises?" Sadie fumed. It seemed anger had brought her to life. "I thought you an honorable man, Governor."

"As I said, I will not allow Latian blood to be spilt on my land. If you want to fight, do it far from here."

"We don't." Ebra tapped the floor table, his jewel-studded rings rapping against the marble. With a smug grin, he glanced at each of us, quickly passing over me. "We are here, with an army, to secure Demoskar and its surrounding lands for the Shah."

The Shah Mother glowered at me. She'd been at my wedding ten years ago, and unlike Ebra, seemed to recognize my youthful appearance. It must've made little sense, but her face remained stern as she pricked me with her gaze.

"And what do you want with us?" Sadie asked.

Ebra's beard was so thin, it was as if drawn on his face by a feather pen. "The Shah has decreed that his sister be with him. I ask you to follow the Shah's decree."

Sadie snickered in disgust. "Tell me, Grand Vizier, where will you march your army next?"

"Unlike our good governor here in Demoskar, the governor of Tagkalay has been an abject failure. A peasant revolt did away with his control — and his head. The janissaries joined in the pillaging, and one of them crowned himself king, even claiming that Lat told him to. The Shah's army will put an end to such delusion and restore the rightful rule of the Seluqal House."

"Tagkalay is far east." Sadie's voice rang with impatience. I was starting to respect her again. "We can see to it after retaking Kostany. March your armies with us and let's put Kostany to siege."

Ebra shook his head and made as polite a face of disgust as one could. "You are a zabadar khatun, but you lack statecraft. If we let a province crown a king without repercussions, then the kingdom will crumble from within. We won't need the Crucians to destroy us."

"And yet, this all happened because of them," Sadie said. "Do you think the janissaries of Tagkalay would've been so bold if we still held the Seat? Defeat the Crucians, and they'll all bend their necks."

"Retaking Kostany within the year is impossible," Ebra said. "First, we consolidate our position. Then, we raise armies from every province. Only after, along with the janissaries and zabadar, as well as Redbeard's fleet, can we put Kostany to siege. And even with all that, we'd still need a fortunate twist of fate to retake it. Ask yourself, is one city worth the cost?"

"Seems you've given up." Sadie spoke in a hushed tone and sat back, as if baiting Ebra's lunge. "It seems you'd let the Crucians win." The Seluqal in her was awake.

But Ebra only matched her quiet tone. "I'm here to keep the kingdom together, not to play at war."

"I'm here to retake our capital," Sadie said, "and kill those who butchered my family."

"I was there," the Shah Mother interjected. A silver tiara glimmered in her bright brown hair. "I saw the man you speak of. Micah the Metal. He is twice what you are, Sadie, twice your cunning, experience, and strength. You may lead a few thousand zabadar who've done nothing but fight over empty plains. Micah leads fifty thousand paladins who have conquered kingdoms. You are no equal."

Sadie chuckled. "I won't take advice from someone who couldn't even control her harem."

The Shah Mother hid wounded pride with a high chin. "You're as ill-bred as your mother."

Sadie's smirk reminded me of her grandfather's wry smile. She'd baited the Shah Mother like I'd baited Yamin. "My mother was twice what you are. Twice as strong, beautiful, and cunning. You are no equal."

"Do you even have bombards?" Ebra said before the Shah Mother could respond. "Do you have engineers to build them? Do you have ships? Guns? Alchemists? Sappers? No, all you have are horses. That's not enough, Your Highness."

"We have a magus." Hope glimmered in Sadie's eyes.

"Ah yes, Vaya. Who flouted your father's laws, too." Ebra studied our side of the floor table. "And yet I don't see him."

The fuming Shah Mother pointed at me. "The magus is right there."

Ebra eyed me. "I don't know this one."

"It's Kevah," the Shah Mother said.

"Kevah?" Ebra squinted. "How could this be?"

"I killed Agneya." An exhilarating flurry blew through my shoulders, just like when I'd boasted about killing the magus ten years ago. There was no man in history — at least that I knew — who could boast of killing two magi. "And I took her mask."

"And what right did you have to kill the Grand Magus?"

"The right of dispensing the Shah's justice. It was Agneya who killed those Ethosian pilgrims, for whose death Vaya was tried."

"Ah, I'd forgotten about that mess." Ebra stroked his chin hairs, small as they were. "I must say, Kevah, your story has taken quite a turn. But no matter. One or two magi can't stand against an army."

Crown Prince Kyars of Alanya, who'd been silent, cleared his throat. "And yet a magus split the mountain of Zelthuriya, wherein we built our holy city." He seemed more serious than the drunken oaf I'd met at the pleasure house in Lyskar. "I wouldn't want to go against them."

"And yet," Ebra said with venom, "I've never heard of magi winning wars. What do they do with their magic except put on a show?"

"Just because you haven't heard, doesn't mean it hasn't happened." Crown Prince Kyars fidgeted with the blue turban he'd wrapped around his neck. "There are many things unexplained in history. Maybe a magus is the explanation."

"You are far from Alanya, Crown Prince," Sadie said. "What do you mean to do here?"

"Like my ancestor Utay, I've pledged twenty thousand horsemen, elephant riders, and gunners to fight the infidels and retake Kostany for the Faith."

"Then you'll join us." Sadie pushed her elbows onto the table, as if to close the gulf between them. "We're the only ones going there in this lifetime."

"Would that I could join with a beauty like you." Kyars grinned and raised his eyebrows playfully. "But I've let beauty distract me from duty too many times, and it's always been a loss."

"I don't ask for your help because of my beauty. If you really want to take Kostany back for the Latian faith, for the Seluqal House to which we both belong, then you'll join me."

"Oh Princess, nothing would excite me more than charging into the fray, our horses side-by-side, hair trailing in the wind, swords raised in the heat of our Seluqal blood. But, alas, I don't know you. I only know that if your father had his way, he would have invaded our lands. It was Ebra's wise counsel that stopped him, and I and my family are ever grateful."

"Then if I have none of your support," Sadie said, "I will take my leave to meet with Redbeard."

"You don't want to do this, Sadie," Ebra said. How improper for a vizier — a janissary no less — to address a Seluqal princess so plainly. "You had the correct instinct when you gave yourself up in Lyskar. It was Kevah, whispering in your ear like Ahriyya, and that renegade Vaya who turned you. You have chosen poor companions and are worse for it." Ebra paused as a dove fluttered by the window. "From this day forward, you and all your followers are no longer welcome in the Kingdom of Sirm." He covered his mouth, as if preparing heavy words, then slid his hand to his sharp chin. "At this very moment, five thousand Alanyan gholam riders thunder toward your zabadar camp. They will order your zabadar north, to the vicinity of Kostany. If you don't retreat north, they will destroy you."

"Nesrin!" Yamin stood. We'd left the camp in her hands.

I stood and approached Ebra. Two janissaries blocked my path, their hands on their hilts.

"It's just like you to only fight when you've stacked the odds," I said.

"That's what a wise commander does." Ebra stood, along with the Shah Mother. Only Kyars remained seated, his gaze downcast.

"I advise you to return to your camp," Ebra continued. "You will have three choices. Submit and surrender, which is the best of them. Flee north to the city you love so much, which means you will die, just that it will be the Crucians who do the deed. Or stand and fight. We won't be taking prisoners. Treason is punishable by death, and it will be meted out on the battlefield."

"You're the traitor!" Sadie smashed her glass of sherbet on the marble table, sending shards and liquid flying. Her grandfather liked to throw goblets at those who angered him. Better than cowering. "Where is Redbeard!? I specifically requested he be at this meeting, Governor."

Before the Governor could answer, Ebra held out his hand to silence him.

"You won't be meeting Redbeard. He's already pledged fealty to Shah Alir. Hurry back to your camp. The gholam commander has been craving a good scrap. I doubt you have much time before he strikes."

Yamin, Sadie, and I hurried out of the hall to find a place to converse. In the shade of the nearby shrine's glistening white arches, with supplicants' cries filling the air, I made my case to them. "I'll go and talk to Redbeard. You two make for camp and order a withdrawal."

"My sister is there!" Yamin paced around and fumed. "We have to hurry!"

"No." Sadie stood unbent. "I came here to entreat Redbeard. I'm not leaving until I've made my case to him."

"Let me talk to him," I said. "I know him."

"I'm of the Seluqal House. I can promise him far more than you can." Sadie took my hand. "You safeguard Nesrin and the zabadar. Lead them north. Stay along the shore and approach the villages on the outskirts of Kostany."

"Those are Ethosian villages," I said. "We won't be welcome there."

"That's why I need to convince Redbeard," Sadie said. Yesterday, this woman was drunk out of sense and lamenting her fate. Now she stood strong like a true khatun. An unyielding Seluqal. "With his fleet, we can take and hold any position."

"Nesrin..." Yamin squatted and ruffled his hair. "I have to go back for her."

"Yamin, you and the others come with me." Sadie bent down and put her hand around him, then looked back at me. "Kevah, I'm trusting you with my tribe. Promise me you won't act out of anger, like before. That you'll think carefully about every command — every life."

I bit my tongue and nodded.

"What makes you so sure Redbeard will side with us when no one else will?" Yamin asked. There was little hope in his tone. "It's clear that the tide is with Ebra."

"Redbeard is a brave man," I said. "He walked into Labyrinthos."

"Brave?" Yamin shook his head with fury. "Where were his three hundred ships when Kostany fell? He's been running from the Crucians for years!"

"He's brave," I said, "but not foolish."

"You mean like us?" He put his fist to his heart. "Because Ebra was very convincing." He beat his chest. "We are foolish."

"Look, Redbeard scarcely listened to my father." Sadie spoke like a mother trying to calm her child. "His ships are his own to command. He'll not bow to Ebra. I'll persuade him to ally with us, whatever it takes."

A supplicant's howl punctured the air. Worshippers wearing white turbans passed by, dragging sweat-stench with them. It was too hot even in the shade. I imagined that honey-apple-ice treat on my tongue, which I'd enjoyed with Melodi the day before Kostany was attacked. Sitting on the embankment and sharing that treat while laughing with her was my last happy memory. I didn't know if I'd have many more.

"Tell me, Kevah, why did we do all this?" Yamin turned to me. "Why are we now enemies of our own country?"

"Why? It's barely been a moment since I watched the life drain from my daughter's eyes. I'm done watching. We'll dispense justice for our fallen. We will take back Kostany and kill Micah the Metal."

Sadie hugged me. Her tears wet my cheeks. "Don't do anything foolish. I better see you again." Something about her — the range of emotions she showed; how she could be angry one moment and kind the next; how she could go from cowering to suddenly the bravest among us — made it hurt to let go.

"Don't forget my sister." Yamin put his hand on my shoulder. "She's all I have left."

I nodded to Yamin. "I'm going to have to borrow that horse you're so fond of."

I took the satchel with my belongings from my horse and strapped it to Yamin's gorgeous Kashanese horse. I wasted no time. The horse was so fast, the air howled against my ears. Grass, flowers, and hills rushed by as if the world spun beneath me. The gallops of the horse made a cracking sound as its hooves smashed the earth. It kicked up dust and dirt as it sped toward camp.

By the time I arrived, Nesrin had divided the riders into right and left flanks. She kept a hundred riders in the middle with her. As I slowed down to approach, the girl held her composite bow in her right hand, while her left reached into the quiver on her saddle. Once she saw it was me, she relaxed.

"Where's Sadie? Where's Yamin?" she shouted as I trotted toward her.

"They're with Redbeard," I lied. It was better than the truth. "They'll take a ship. We have to move north along the coast and meet them."

"Then why are there thousands of riders in formation, ready to attack us?"

"They are Ebra's Alanyan allies, and you can count on them being just as deadly as any zabadar. We don't have time to discuss this. Sound the retreat. I promised Sadie and Yamin I'd safeguard everyone, especially you."

I eyed Aicard, who watched us from the back of Nesrin's hundred. Was an Ethosian willing to die in a battle between Latians? Perhaps his *ruh* was good, as Vaya claimed.

Beyond the tall grass, a rider galloped toward us. His armor was bronze and gold, the colors of Alanya. His black Kashanese steed evoked a beauty and swiftness that outmatched the one I rode. I recognized him as he slowed toward us in the dwindling midday light. I'd seen him in the Lyskar pleasure house with Crown Prince Kyars.

"I am Kichak," he declared. "Commander of five thousand gholam riders, waiting just beyond the horizon. Dismount, drop all your weapons, and surrender."

I trotted to him. "We go north. None of us wants to spill the blood of kin in the sight of Lat."

"A fine beast, your horse," he said. "Each of my riders has one just like it. They say a Kashanese horse has the speed of three and the spirit of ten." He smiled at my horse, then shook his head. "My orders are to accept your surrender. Or to spill your blood."

"Ebra said we could go north."

"Ebra doesn't give me orders. Dismount, drop your weapons, and surrender."

Aicard galloped to us. "Kichak!" he said. "These riders want nothing more than to take back Kostany. They are holy warriors of your faith."

He smirked when he noticed Aicard. "Aicard!? What the hell are you doing with them?"

They shook hands and laughed like old friends.

"These are brave warriors, Kichak," Aicard said. "Your prince gave orders, not knowing truly who they were. You know the Crown Prince's character better than anyone. Would he have you slaughter men and women who mean to fight for their faith and country?"

Kichak looked upon us. He was bald and wore a thin beard over gleaming, dark skin. A Himyarite from the south of Lidya, no doubt. The gholam were slave warriors, like the janissaries, and could come from any land that slavers prowled. But their armor was nothing like ours. The man seemed royal in his bronze and gold chainmail, a shimmering golden-hilted scimitar at his belt. Was Alanya so wealthy that they fit their slaves like our kings?

Kichak studied our right and left flanks. He gazed into Nesrin's unyielding eyes.

"You speak truly, Aicard," he said. "If they are willing to charge north, into the belly of the infidel, each must be ready to die for the Faith." Kichak turned to me and pointed at Aicard. "You are lucky to have this man on your side." He paused for a moment to stare at the clear blue sky. "And yet, my gholam have not had a fight in a long, long time. Alanya is far too peaceful. The life and death decisions battle forces you to make turn you into a real soldier, capable of winning against the hardened fuckers who mean to kill you. Think of it this way, should any of you survive, they'll be stronger fighters than ten who didn't."

Aicard protested, "Kichak, please—"

"I'll give you a head start. Go. Or stand your ground. Either way, prepare to fight or die."

Kichak rode away at a speed I could scarcely hope to match.

What he'd said about his gholam applied to the zabadar. Peace made us weak. One whole survivor of battle was worth ten who'd never experienced one. Although some of our riders had fought Micah's sorties around Kostany, most were still apprentices at war. I'd told Sadie I would take care of her zabadar, and I intended to.

Nesrin shouted the order to retreat.

"Wait!" I galloped to her. "Order them to feign retreat. Then, when I give the signal, we attack."

Nesrin seethed. "Are you mad, Kevah? It will be a slaughter!"

"I hope so. We stand and fight. Or we'll be running from everyone. Micah's paladins won't be any kinder."

"What signal?" Nesrin asked.

"You'll know."

Nesrin gritted her teeth and nodded.

"I hope you know what you're doing," Aicard said as he and Nesrin galloped away.

Together, the right and left flanks and Nesrin's middle feigned retreat. They shrunk in the distance.

Minutes later, the rumble of five thousand Kashanese horses shook the world.

The horses covered the horizon. Black and white and brown. They thundered toward me. The ululating of five thousand gholam filled my ears. The dust and dirt the horses kicked up created a brown and black cloud that whirled with them. My bones shook.

I took out the little, red rocket from my satchel. I held it in my mouth as I struck the flint.

The horses were almost on me. Kichak led them, his scimitar raised high. The gholam drew and readied their golden composite bows. Riders raised their spears and swords in the air. Their ululating rang worse than the shrillest bell.

But what came next was shriller. I lit the rocket. It boomed into the air and exploded over the mass of charging gholam. A thousand and one screaming bells rang.

Kichak flew off his horse and landed a few paces from me. Five thousand horses whinnied as if on fire. Most flung their riders off; the riders still mounted struggled to steady their Kashanese horses as they darted in every direction. Horses crashed into horses, tossing riders in the air. Other horses slid to the ground and their riders tumbled with them. Dust and dirt obscured everything.

Though I could not hear it because of the ringing, I could feel the rumble of the zabadar as they neared. Not as fiercely as the gholam had, but they arrived at speed. In the meantime, Kichak regained his form and ran for me on foot. I jumped off my horse to meet him. He was right. Wrestling Yamin was only training. Fighting Kichak would really test the skills I needed to kill Micah.

Kichak lunged with his scimitar. I met his steel with mine. He grabbed a concealed dagger with the other hand and went for my neck. I stepped back just in time.

He gaped in horror at something behind me. No doubt, it was the mass of the zabadar. The rumble of their horses shook the earth. I thrust my shamshir at Kichak's head. He sidestepped, then swiped his dagger at my chest but met only air.

Now we all lived in the sliver between life and death. The zabadar roared past us, giving me a wide berth, and cut through the panicked gholam with spears and arrows. The rout was on, but the gholam couldn't outrun our horses on foot. Those that stood and fought caught an arrow in the face or a spear in the chest.

I circled around Kichak. He circled around me. I wouldn't make the first move. I had all the time to win. And all the help if it came to that. He changed his direction and fake-lunged, then backed away. His eyes never left me. We did this dance for a few minutes as zabadar surrounded us, their arrows aimed at him.

"Clever boy. You win." Kichak dropped his sword. "I surrender."

I shook my head. "Ebra said no prisoners. Earn your death." I dropped my sword and uppercut the gholam commander. He stumbled to the ground, pulled a knife from his boot, and lunged. I caught his wrist, grabbed the knife with my other hand, and stuck it in his throat.

"I'll plant your shrine here," I said as Kichak choked on blood. I plunged the knife in his heart, putting an end to his pain. "To Lat we belong and to her we return."

20

MICAH

A CLEAR DAY TURNED INTO A CRISP NIGHT AS THE SWELLING MOON smiled upon us. I would've enjoyed the breeze, but thoughts of battle consumed me.

Zosi's men were blurry outlines in the moonlight. Jauz had brought fireworks and Fallen Screams and we shot them at the sea walls to panic the seditious paladins. It didn't work. Now we had no choice but to attack. The Imperator's fleet would be here in hours, and if they sailed through the strait, my rule of Kostany would be imperiled.

I stood with Berrin and Jauz in the plaza facing the sea walls' battlements. Edmar sat in the grass. We discussed a plan. Bombs could cause chaos and send Zosi's soldiers, who were over-crowded, off the walls. But that risked damaging the walls themselves.

Aschere stood behind us, staring at the sky, whispering Paramic words.

"Are you ready, Micah?" she said.

"I'm ready to kill the traitors."

Aschere moved to my side and held my gunmetal hand. She raised our handhold in the air.

"What're you doing?" I asked.

"Close your eyes and feel it."

"Feel what?"

"Trust me." Aschere's breaths were cold and sweet — the scent of ice candy. "Close your eyes and feel it."

I closed my eyes. Something hot stirred in my gunmetal arm. Like oil falling into a lamp, it trickled from a source unfathomably far. The heat melted the ice that poured from Aschere's hand.

Aschere squeezed my hand. I saw it now. I saw the dead, dark star.

The dark star hymned in heaven a million billion miles away. Words appeared as if printed on its black horizon. Thousands of hundred-sided shapes rearranged into different forms, all in rows like script on black parchment. I remembered this strange language from my dreams — the language of the angels. But what did it mean?

The unfathomable script changed forms an uncountable amount of times. And then they disappeared from the black horizon. The dark star spat something out. Something so tiny, it was like a gnat before the immensity of the dark star: a ball of black and green fire. It sped across a backdrop of shimmering stars toward the earth. But it was so small and slow, and the earth so far, it would never reach within a million of my lifetimes. What was its purpose, then?

In front of it, something tore the fabric of heaven. A hole opened and swallowed the ball of fire.

"Look up," Aschere said.

Beneath the moon, another hole tore heaven's fabric. The ball of green fire rained through and into our world. It raged straight toward us. Berrin and Jauz stared at the sky with terror in their mouths, then sprinted to the palace. Edmar, poor fellow, hobbled away on his peg leg and cane.

Aschere came close. "They'll be fine."

As the black and green fireball neared, the sky turned from night to day. Zosi's men started jumping in the water to escape it.

"It will destroy the walls!" I protested.

"Shh," Aschere whispered. "Focus."

I quieted my mind and focused. The green and black ball of fire stilled. It hovered in the sky above the sea walls like the sun. Its fire flared and churned as if lava. And then it became even hotter.

Aschere turned to me. We kept our handhold strong above our heads. Her nose brushed mine, and I inhaled her honey breaths. "This is the best part," she said, our lips almost touching.

Zosi's men screamed. I felt like I was bathing in a cauldron of boiling water. The black and green sun flared, as if lightning raged through it, over the sea walls. The paladins beneath burst into flames. Zosi stood like a steel sculpture, staring at the fiery sun, as his armor melted and his body cooked. My little brother. My dear friend. Burned from the world.

The ball of black and green fire flickered. A hole appeared in the sky and swallowed it. The world turned back into night. The moon beamed in the sky, and a breeze provided relief from the scorch. All the seditious paladins had melted on the battlement or boiled in the water below.

I ORDERED my troops to man the walls and fire on the Imperator's fleet. But even the cannons had melted. We would have to haul cannons from the land walls onto the sea walls.

Back in the great hall, I sat on my golden seat and listened to Berrin and Edmar argue.

"The angels forbid magic!" Edmar said, almost poking Berrin's chest. "Our souls will not be saved!"

"We fight for the Archangel however we can," Berrin retorted. "You think the Latians won't use their magi against us?"

"You don't know the tenants of our faith. You are not a true Ethosian."

"How dare you question my faith?" Berrin's eyebrows touched like lightning bolts. "I was baptized in the waters of the High Holy Sea, just as you were. I'll never forget that honor and what it means to defend the Ethos."

Edmar looked to me. His eyes were heavy and red, as if holding back tears. I'd never seen him so afraid. "Do you not see the darkness in this, Grandmaster?"

I stared at my metal hand. I could feel the green fire inside. As the dark star hymned, it filled my arm with its light. I had become the darkness. Was there any way back?

"Edmar is right. The angels forbid magic. Tonight, I killed thousands of my brothers with darkness that even the Fallen Angels never wielded."

Tears flowed down Edmar's cheeks. "Grandmaster, repent and kill that woman. We can make peace with the Imperator and go back to how things were."

I approached my strongest and bravest paladin, who cried like a scared child. I brushed his hair with my metal hand. Losing a leg had truly made him gaunt and sickly — not a man to be feared. Not anymore.

"Edmar, you followed me when many others wouldn't. But now is not the time for regrets. Now is not the time for weakness. We go forward to victory with whatever power we have, whether of the light or the dark."

"Grandmaster! What of our faith? What is all this for, if not to hear the hymns of the angels across the earth?"

"It is for exactly that, Edmar, and nothing else. I am the Opener. I will spread our faith to the edge of the earth, even with a sword forged from darkness."

"No. I cannot be a part of this. Kill me if you must, but I will only die with faith in my heart." Edmar hobbled away.

Berrin came close and said in a low voice, "Grandmaster, we should not let him go."

"What can he do in his state? No one will follow him. It's not me he shuns — it's the darkness. I don't blame him." I sighed. "The Imperator will arrive within hours. Make sure we have plenty of cannons to welcome him."

Berrin nodded with determined eyes. It seemed he reveled in being the last of my five, though I'd not seen Aicard in some time. Berrin left the great hall to carry out my orders. Meanwhile, I descended into the dungeon to visit the Patriarch.

The old man huddled in the corner of his cell and hymned in a low tune. A rat sat in the other corner and nibbled on the dried figs we'd given the Patriarch for lunch. His robe was soiled and the whole place smelled of piss and worms.

"This is no place for a man like you," I said.

The Patriarch continued hymning.

"Tell me where you hid Princess Celene, and you can go free. Back to your imperator."

He paused mid-hymn and turned to me. "I swear on the Twelve. I swear on the Archangel. I will never tell you."

"This was all your plan. How sad to see you rotting here as it blossoms."

"Your plan will never work without her. And I'll never tell you where she is."

"We've ransacked every home and hovel, turned over every chapel in the city, even poured through the sewers. I don't see where you could be hiding her."

"No matter, she'll be with her father soon." The Patriarch smiled in hope. "And then your plan will turn to ash in your hands." He hymned praises to the Archangel, then asked, "Are you going to kill me?"

"You afraid to meet the angels?"

"We all should be. I've committed my share of sin."

"You'll have more time to repent. I'll crush the Imperator, then I'm going to peel you slow."

"You underestimate Josias." His chin rose in defiance. "He is the son of Heraclius, a man as tenacious as any who walked the earth. Some of that has passed on."

"He'll need more than tenacity to defeat me. Did you hear the screams?"

"My hearing is not what it once was. A mercy to be relieved of the screams of my flock."

"A mercy, indeed. Do you still think I'm the Opener, Patriarch?"

The question made him grin smugly. "Imperator Basil the Breaker called himself Opener when he marched east seven hundred years ago. He too seemed unstoppable, seizing city upon city, until one night him and his army — a hundred thousand strong — suddenly vanished in the Zelthuriyan desert. Not a trace, not a whisper, of where they went." The Patriarch let out a muffled chuckle. "You know, in the east, they call him Basil the Banished. The Fallen would not let him conquer their holy city, nor did the Archangel bless his cause, for he was not the Opener." He pointed at my black arm. "So I ask you this... was it the Archangel who remade your right hand, Micah? Or the Fallen?"

"Whoever it was, they've certainly no mercy for you."

The Patriarch nodded in resignation. "But what of mercy for Celene? She grew up beneath my gaze, you know. A little bud that I tended until she bloomed into the angelflower she is today."

How poetic — I couldn't help but roll my eyes. "And then you ripped her out of the soil and threw her at my feet, all to climb higher. Says a lot about you."

The rat in the corner finished a fig, squealed, and rolled on its side, as if too satisfied to do much else.

Patriarch Lazar said, "The vileness I see in the world, I

acknowledge in myself. But Celene is truly innocent. Do you know why she took her vow?"

Miriam, Elly's mother, had taken the same vow of celibacy. I'd never asked why, but it ended catastrophically — thanks to my charms. "Angelsong teaches us that the world is our garden — that we ought to enjoy all its fruits, within the limits of the law. Pledging 'I'm never going to eat apples' is idiocy. It's another corruption you priests inflicted upon our faith."

"Ah, a reformer, is that what you are?" Lazar waved his hands, as if dismissing a fly. "I don't want to argue theology." The Grand Mufti had said the same thing, shortly before I stabbed him. "Pendurum — remember it?"

"I almost died conquering it. Stubborn bunch of mercenaries, defending those iron walls."

"Those very same mercenaries that you crushed in Pendurum turned to plundering convents and monasteries once you took their free city. I'm sure you know what that meant for the women and boys whom they preyed upon."

"Shall I bear those sins too?"

"You are a flawed man, like the rest of us, but I don't say it to blame you." He gazed at me with a soft, almost kindly smile. "A few years ago, Celene's convent was attacked by one of those mercenary companies. They didn't dare touch her or the other nobles, but unmentionable — truly twisted — things were done to the lowborn girls and boys, and Celene was made to watch it all."

How vile. I should've never let those mercenaries go free, the day the walls fell. My mercy ought not to have overcome my wrath. I should've scattered their flesh and limbs across the icelands.

"The day she was ransomed," Lazar continued, "and returned to her father, she marched into the imperial court and, fearlessly — in front of exarchs and lords, in the presence of her father and mighty Heraclius himself — swore to the Archangel that she would never lie with a man until the order of the Twelve was made manifest across the earth."

The order of the Twelve was what we aspired to — a pure justice, wherein men and women got as they deserved, based only on faith and deeds. It could never be achieved in this world, though we ought to strive for it earnestly. Celene was a true striver, it seemed. Perhaps if I got her back, I could convince her of the justice of my cause.

"That's why I'm here, Patriarch, to bring about the order of the Twelve. Every man must get what they deserve," I gestured toward him with an open hand, "and we'll start with you."

I gave orders to the guards to rip off the Patriarch's fingernails until he admitted where he hid my wife. I'd lost my most artful torturer when Edmar walked out, so we'd have to make do with the obvious methods.

I also ordered half the active force to man the walls and the other half to search in and around the city. Without Celene, what would killing Josias gain? I would have no claim to the throne, and the lords of the Imperium would choose the next imperator from among his cousins. There would be contention and war. Finding Celene was my only way forward.

I found Jauz in the canteen he'd turned into a workshop. The room stank of sulfur. His Silklander engineers were busy mixing fluids and powders. Jauz himself heated metal to liquid at a scalding fire.

"Not as hot as your fire," he said.

"You trying to compete, Jauz?"

"Don't I have to? What use will you have for me if you have *that*?"

"What is it you're working on?"

He poured liquid metal into a cylinder. "I won't say until I can put it in your hands."

"Trying to buy time until you're obsolete?"

Jauz gawked at me as if his heart were in his throat.

I laughed to break the tension. "A joke." I smiled. "You've proven your use countless times, and I'm sure you'll do it again."

"You can rest assured I'll do anything to stay. Else it's back to building statues for the Silk Emperor."

"I can't think of a worse way to waste your talents."

"I can." Jauz banged on the cooling metal with a hammer to shape it. "My son designs the privies in the imperial castles."

"Ah yes, I think you mentioned him before. How many children do you have?"

"I have three sons and a daughter, from three wives."

"And you're married to them all at the same time?"

"Of course." He wiped sweat off his forehead and put his hammer to the side. "A wealthy Silklander should have no less. Some wealthy women, in fact, have several husbands."

"Take this however you may, Jauz, but you're no different from wild rabbits. When I conquer the Silklands, that will all have to change."

Jauz laughed in his hearty way. "If you conquer the Silklands, Grandmaster, even I will bow to these angels that breathe fire. You can hold me to that."

It was not the angels who breathed that fire, though. I returned to the great hall and napped on the golden seat.

I AWOKE to the sight of Aschere sitting next to me. She wore the green dress I'd given her in Nixos. It matched the shimmer of her emerald eyes.

"You're still consumed by such meager matters," she said.

"Has no one told you? You should never watch a man sleep unless you love him." I rubbed my eyes. "What meager matters do you speak of?"

"Your wife. It doesn't matter whether you find her. And this city. It doesn't matter if you lose it. Nor does conquering the east and giving your men some grass and dirt."

"How can you say that? These are the only things that matter."

"No, Micah. These are the affairs of men. You are ascending beyond it all."

"Was it not you who led me through Labyrinthos so I could take this city? Didn't we just burn all those men so I could keep it?"

Aschere shook her head. Her skin was paler than the moon. When was the last time she'd been in sunlight? "We did, but not for those reasons. It was all so you could become who you are destined to be."

"And whom am I destined to be? What is greater than being Imperator?"

"The Opener will not sit on a throne. He will not spread the hymns of servile angels. He will be a scourge upon the world."

"How can you say that about my faith? The Opener is prophesied by the very religion you insult!"

"Did faith bring you to this point? Did the Archangel answer your prayers? Or did someone else?"

"Who is this someone you speak of?"

"She is the Dreamer." I hadn't seen Aschere smile like this since she'd fainted after pricking my forehead. "Jinn, angels, humans — she dreamed us all into existence. And she is the only god."

"'The only god I've ever seen'," I repeated what she'd told me in Nixos.

"Yes, now let me show her to you."

Aschere held my gunmetal hand. I closed my eyes and saw the dark star unfathomably far away. Nothing could ever reach it, even if you combined the lifespans of every life of every form that had ever existed. But somehow, I floated in its orbit. I saw myself, less than a firefly against its endless darkness. While the stars burned bright in the surrounding distance, the dark star was only black. The black I'd seen in Labyrinthos that sucked light out of existence.

Aschere floated with me and held my hand. There was no sound as her mouth moved. There was no sound anywhere, only silence so complete that it numbed me.

As we floated around the dark star, cold pained my soul. Not like the cold of a chilly day, but the cold of becoming ice — the same cold I felt whenever I touched Aschere. The fire in my gunmetal arm warmed me enough to keep my eyes open. It seared through my body.

Aschere and I moved faster and faster. Something pulled and pushed us at the same time. With every second, that speed doubled, until we were moving so fast, every organ in my body pushed against my bones, and my bones pushed against my skin. And yet we went faster until I saw my own body in front of me. And then, as if fired from a cannon, we launched toward the stars.

The dark fabric around us rippled as we soared. Then that fabric tore and swallowed us. The inside of the hole was filled with light so intense and blinding it scathed my closed eyes.

Suddenly we were floating over Kostany. But it was not the city I knew. There was only a wooden wall and the most basic wood and mud houses. No palace sat on the hill by the Shrunken Strait and neither did a chapel on the second, taller hill. There were no sea walls, and the strait overflowed onto the land. The land around the strait was irrigated and sliced up by farms.

Men stood on the taller hill — on Angelfall. They chanted the word "Hawwa" and stared at the sky. Something black floated beneath the sun. Whatever it was, they bent and bowed to it. Aschere took my hand and we flew toward it.

A black metal mountain floated in the clouds. But unlike a mountain, its sides were smooth. The closer we got, the clearer its shape: a diamond.

Faces were imprinted on each side of the diamond. But they

were not human faces; they were the faces of the angels. I recognized the angel Micah, with his ten eyes down the middle. Each eye was white with a red dot for the pupil. These pupils moved — the face was alive. Micah looked upon the people on the hill.

Aschere dragged me through the sky, toward Micah's mouth. It opened and swallowed us. A black milk covered my body. I held my breath as Aschere pulled me through it. Thick, slimy, pudding-like. It would be a minute before my feet stepped on solid ground.

Now we were in a vast room lit by black light. The room was the size of a city. Thousands of pods filled with water clung to the walls, and within those pods were strange assortments of flesh. A creature with ten human legs, no torso, and four human heads grew in one of them. In another, there was a peacock with the head of a human. Each time I looked at a pod, I discovered a new horror. The pod above me contained an octopus, but at the end of each tentacle were eyes bigger than my head.

Pipes ran from each pod down to the floor and toward the middle of the room. A pod ten times the size of the other ones stood in the center. Black ink whirled within. Aschere and I approached, but nothing was visible through the ink.

I tried talking to Aschere. No sound came when I moved my mouth. I asked her, "What's in there?"

She saw my lips move and answered without sound, "Hawwa."

Something banged against the glass of the giant pod. A starfish, bigger than me, stretched its appendages across the glass. In the center of its flesh, an eye opened — a human eye the size of my head. It looked upon me with its black pupil.

Every nerve in my body wanted to wake up. I'd never felt such terror bursting through my heart. I grabbed Aschere and shouted, soundlessly, "Wake me up!" But she laughed and cried and smiled.

I wanted to run, but where could I go? Everything here terrified me. All the eyes and limbs and heads, arranged in such horrifying ways, with appendages and tentacles and the parts of animals and the parts of things I could scarcely comprehend. Terror engulfed me and I lost my senses. My eyes bulged as every part of me shook and trembled…and yet Aschere laughed and laughed.

Berrin shook me and I awoke in the golden seat. Sweat soaked my shirt and hair.

He sighed with relief. "The Imperator is here! We've already begun firing upon his fleet."

The seat next to me was empty. I sat up and wiped my sweat, but there was so much it moistened even my chest hairs, as if I'd fallen asleep in a hot spring. "What's the situation?"

"With our steady cannon fire, the Imperator cannot sail through the strait."

Cannons boomed and whined in the distance.

"We've done exactly what we needed to do, then."

Berrin nodded. "We were able to move just enough cannons onto the sea walls in time to stop him." He looked me up and down, eyes filled with concern. "I've been trying to wake you up for the last two hours, Grandmaster. I feared you'd entered an unwaking sleep, yet again."

"I don't think I was asleep. I was somewhere else."

His eyebrows curved and pointed to the ceiling. "Where were you?"

I closed my eyes. All I could see was the eye of the starfish, gazing terror into my soul.

"I was in hell."

21

KEVAH

THE ROUTED GHOLAM LEFT GIFTS. WE CAPTURED TWO THOUSAND Kashanese horses, enough for every warrior in the tribe, though we would have to cut their ears. The gholam dropped hundreds of guns and plenty of ammunition. Now a quarter of our zabadar carried a matchlock. Some traded their wooden composite bows for the metal ones of the gholam. Even the steel of their scimitars was stronger than those of our shamshirs. And best of all, we didn't lose a single rider.

We rode north until we came upon the Ethosian villages on the shore. Nesrin informed me that the zabadar had already raided these villages. And yet, as we scouted from a nearby hill-side, they seemed busy. Farmers plowed fields by the tributaries that snaked through the village. Men roamed about, engaging in trades from smithing to carpentry. Sailors unloaded cargo at the dock and loaded other cargo, most likely foraged fruits headed for Kostany.

None of it was a problem, except for the several hundred paladins guarding the village. They'd built a stone wall and placed cannons on the ramparts and even dug a spike-filled ditch — all to stop a mounted raid.

Aicard, Nesrin, and I lay on our bellies and looked down upon the village in the cool after-dawn light. The choking coastal humidity soaked the back of my neck. The sea brought other things: seaweed smells, wispy breezes, and a bulging horizon to wonder at. How many conquerors had come, eager to drench these shores in blood and bile? Dycondian treasure kings, Crucian imperators, emerald pirates, mighty khagans, Temur himself — would I join such illustrious company? Perhaps war was a song being played here, and we were the notes, plucked and strung across time.

"Let me parley with them," Aicard said. "I'll pretend to be your prisoner and negotiate their withdrawal."

"Is this the moment you switch sides, Crucian?" Nesrin said. She still didn't trust Aicard, and I wasn't sure if I did either.

"If we fight them, many innocents will die," Aicard said. "Those villagers did nothing wrong. Their faith may be different, but they are good people."

"There are no good Crucians."

"If you believe that, then you're just like Micah."

"Enough," I interjected, taking my gaze off the horizon. "Aicard, go parley with them. If they give us information about Kostany and leave their guns and ammo, we'll allow them to withdraw."

"Those are steep demands," Aicard said. "Proud paladins would rather die."

"Then they'll die."

"I'll see what they agree to. But consider what you're willing to concede."

Aicard stood and raised his hands. The paladins drew their guns as he approached the stone wall.

"He will betray us!" Nesrin punched the dirt.

"If he does, we'll kill him too. We outnumber them."

"So why not fight, then?"

The wooden gate opened and he went through.

"I'd rather get information about Kostany — whatever we can learn because we're going there eventually."

I wouldn't concede a gnat's wing, and as Aicard had implied, paladins reveled in fighting so they could die for their angel. I'd revel in giving the zabadar another challenge and testing our fresh steel. Nesrin brought them into formation while I devised a strategy: overwhelm from afar with arrows and incendiaries. Charging the ditch and wall would result in unacceptable losses, as I'd promised Sadie I'd keep her zabadar safe. We would have to whittle the paladins down and wait them out.

I was sitting under a tree on the hill, scribbling a map of the village and its stone wall, when Aicard returned.

"They've agreed to your demands...but have one of their own." He hesitated to say it. "I'm to go with them to Kostany."

"See his treachery?" Nesrin seethed. She winded her arm and almost threw the apricot she'd been munching at him. "He wants to return to his commander!"

"Think about it. Think about how useful I could be inside the walls. I could open the gates for you."

"He's lying!" Nesrin spat out a seed. "He'll go back to his master and report all that he's seen."

"What did you learn about Kostany?" I asked.

"Kostany is in turmoil. Micah has married the Imperator's daughter, without permission. In response, the Imperator sails toward the city with three hundred ships. Many of Micah's paladins have defected to the Imperator's side."

"That's our chance!" I said. "There's no better time to strike than when they are divided."

"It's a trap," Nesrin said. "Why would they fight each other?"

"We fought each other. Our worst enemies are often those near to us."

A flock of squawking seagulls glided over us and soared

through the cloudless sky. The calm sun and gentle breeze evoked the perfect summer day for pleasantry. I didn't mind sullying it with war cries and flaming arrows.

"There's another thing you should know," Aicard said. "They say Micah lost an arm and was asleep for twelve days. Then when he awoke, his arm had…regrown somehow."

Nesrin let out a high-pitched laugh. "They make up stories to scare us."

"They themselves don't know what to believe and don't want to fight you. They'd rather return to Kostany to learn what's happening."

"And you insist on going with them?" I asked.

"I'll keep Micah's trust until the time is right. Until the moment when I can help you most. Believe in me."

Aicard could be invaluable as an infiltrator behind the walls of Kostany. And if he were Micah's spy, he could be dangerous if we forced him to stay. Stories of our little band wouldn't matter to Micah, anyway.

"Go," I said. "You're our fortunate twist of fate, Aicard. When the time is right, you must act decisively to help us."

Nesrin fumed. "This is a mistake. You'd put our hopes in the hands of a Crucian? You're too naive, Kevah."

"We have no secrets. There's nothing he can tell Micah that he wouldn't have found out otherwise."

"I'll be there for you." Aicard's eyes were placid and certain. He didn't flinch, fidget, or display the telltale signs of a liar. "When it really counts."

It took several hours for the paladins and villagers to gather their supplies onto horses and carts. By midday, they had departed, along with the boats at the dock. We now held the villages on the shore, which we could use as a staging ground to siege Kostany.

Now to wait for Sadie. If she succeeded and brought Redbeard along, thirty thousand soldiers and three hundred ships would be at our command. We could take the cannons from his ships and put Kostany to siege by land. And if Aicard opened the gate for us, I could finally picture how Kostany could be ours. Once I got inside the walls, there would be no escape for Micah the Metal.

BENEATH THE MILD MIDDAY SUN, the zabadar set their yurts around the village. A sea breeze brought salty air. I found a rowboat at the dock and sat inside. I rowed offshore, figuring I would be the first to see Redbeard's ships from here — if he were coming. I hoped I hadn't thrown Sadie into Ebra's gilded cage. Would I ever forgive myself?

Surely Redbeard wouldn't turn her over. He was not easily bent and barely listened to Shah Murad. People called him the Shah of the Seas for good reason. Even if Redbeard declined to join us, he would at least help Sadie get here. And yet, why wasn't she here by now?

I reclined and broke from worrying. The calm sun soothed my face and body; I closed my eyes and listened to the seagulls chirping. Would that I could be among them, free to fly from my worries. Would that I didn't exist, that I was a drop of rain that fell from a cloud and plopped into the ocean. Truth be told, these were Taqi's words. He lamented his existence, as any man burdened with war should.

I loved his verses because they imparted wisdom. But was I wiser than the average fool? *The grief of what you've lost lifts a mirror.* I leaned over the boat's side and gazed at my reflection. A young man stared back, but his eyes were that of the dead. What need did the dead have for wisdom? Give me a war song, or give me wings.

As I ruminated, something swam toward me and jetted up water. It was a duck. No, it was much larger...an ostrich. But what was an ostrich doing in the sea? No, not an ostrich. It had the bright blue and gold feathers of a peacock.

Something about it sent shivers through my body. I squinted to confirm what I couldn't believe. The peacock had a human face.

I grabbed the oars and rowed away, straining my arms with each desperate push and pull, a child's fear thumping in my chest. But it gained on me fast; within seconds, it was next to me. I dropped the oars and stared at the peacock with a human face. The red eyes and delicate features of a young woman stared back. Then it spoke.

"I am Saran."

Surely, I'd fallen asleep in the boat and was now dreaming. I slapped myself but didn't wake.

"Why have you not traveled to Zelthuriya?" it said. "The elders await you there."

"Elders?"

"The elders of the Jann and the Efreet. They all wait for you."

"What the fuck are you talking about?"

"You are afraid." It softened its tone. "I am only a nasnas, you need not fear me."

"I've never seen anything like you."

"Of course. You've only just gained the sight of the unseen."

"You're a jinn."

"A vague word," the thing said. "The same as me calling you an animal. I am a nasnas. You are a human. I am Saran. You are Kevah."

"What do you want?"

"Are you not a magus? Do you not wish to come to Zelthuriya, to learn and train?"

"I can't go to Zelthuriya. My people need me."

"The petty needs of men are nothing in the sight of Lat."

I sniggered and shook my head. "Then why train? What's it all for?"

"It is worship. It is *fanaa*, the annihilation of the self, so that you become nothing. So that your soul itself burns as fire does, in the worship of Lat."

The creature bobbed as a slight tide pushed us toward shore.

"No, I will not become nothing," I said. "I will not go to Zelthuriya. I will go to Kostany, I will lead my people to victory, and I will kill Micah."

"That is dangerous thinking." Saran's eyes were firm as rubies. "I met a woman, not unlike you. And in her avarice, she turned to a dark path, the path of Ahriyya. Such was the corruption she wrought, it even ensnared Grand Magus Agneya. The Efreet were not pleased to be burning the villages of those who worship Lat. We cannot let that happen again. You must come to Zelthuriya."

"I will not go. You cannot make me."

"You're right, we cannot make you. But even the woman had a good *ruh* when I met her. Do not think yours cannot twist."

The woman. Who else could it be?

"I won't become like Aschere."

"Power should only be traded for one thing — the self." The preaching tone of the peacock became firmer. "We do not bestow power to those overcome by their own needs and emotions."

"Then go away."

"And yet, I cannot leave you alone. I left the woman alone, and she turned to the arcane for power. I will leave with you a shiqq. Use him as you like. But know that if you want more power, if you want to command the Jann and the Efreet, you must come to Zelthuriya."

The peacock with the woman face spread its wings. Its wing-span was longer than my boat. It flapped them with such force that it pushed my boat away and splashed seawater all over me. It soared into the heavens and flew southeast beneath the midday sun.

"What the hell is a shiqq?"

Something swam toward me. Water kicked up as it sped. Then it soared into the air and, with a splash and a thump, landed in my boat.

The child-sized creature had the legs of a chicken and the wings of an eagle. The torso of a boy and the innocent face of a child. Its feathers and skin were red and blue and green, as if these colors were painted across it with a horse's tail.

I resisted the urge to jump out and swim to shore. Though freakish, it didn't seem threatening. The claws on its chicken feet were dull like round stones, neither did it have fangs to bite. It stared at me with gray eyes and a blank face.

"You must be Shiqq," I said.

"I am *a* shiqq." It spoke in a child's tone but with the firmness of a man. Its voice resembled that of a eunuch I'd encountered in Shah Jalal's service. "My name is Kinn."

"Well, Kinn, is there a chance you could look less…strange?"

"You mean to change shape?"

"Exactly."

"I don't have that ability. I'm only eighty-eight. The youngest shapeshifter I've seen must have been at least two hundred."

"All right…what abilities do you have?"

Kinn jumped in the air and flapped his wings. So fast and powerful were his flaps that the boat moved…two feet.

"I'm a little out of practice," he said. "I'll be sure to do better. Here, let me take you to shore."

Kinn flapped his eagle wings. The rowboat drifted toward shore, but not nearly as fast as I could row.

"I don't want to go to shore. I'm waiting for someone."

Kinn ignored me and continued flapping.

"Kinn!"

"I must take you to shore, it's good exercise. I have not been moving weights much. Oh, I'm so embarrassed."

The chicken creature did not stop flapping till my boat hit the beach. I got out and stepped onto the wet sand. By then, Kinn had jumped into the air and was now flapping the boat back to sea.

"Good exercise," he repeated.

A few muscled zabadar men and women watched my boat move. To them, it must've been moving for no reason. Or maybe they thought the wind carried it to sea. Either way, only I had to suffer the sight of Kinn flapping. I watched as he flapped the boat about, changing directions as he pleased. And then, for a moment, he flapped it into the air. The boat soared a few feet and splashed back in the water. He spread his red and green wings out, as if pleased with himself.

As I watched him, I realized there was something on the horizon. Ships! Redbeard! Sadie! I ran across the sand to the dock. My heart melted with relief at the sight of ships filling the horizon. Nesrin ran to my side and panted to catch her breath. I smiled at her. She was not smiling. She looked at me with apprehensive eyes.

The ships were coming from the north, not the south. Perhaps Sadie and Redbeard had taken a different route. Perhaps they intended to throw off Ebra by sailing circuitously. But as the ships neared, my hopes shattered. The sails were purple, a far shade from the red sails of Redbeard. The only country nearby that used purple on their flags was the Crucis Imperium.

THE CRUCIAN FLEET floated on the horizon. A small galley with twenty oars and purple sails sped to shore. Nesrin and I waited at the dock as the ship pulled in.

Sailors in rough linens jumped out and tied the ship to the metal cleats on the dock. Behind them followed a more proper man. He wore silver armor enameled with purple stars, though it didn't conceal his potbelly. His dark hair flowed past his ears, which stuck out like wings. The golden hilt of a longword jutted out of the sheath on his side.

"I am Rone, Grand Duke of Crucis and Exarch of Sempuris," he said in a thick Crucian accent. Then he bowed his head as if we were shahs.

Nesrin and I exchanged a bewildered glance. I bowed back to be polite. We introduced ourselves.

Rone gestured toward the fleet as if they were a painting he'd made. "The ships you see belong to His Holy Lordship, the Imperator of Crucis. He has not come to war with you, but rather to war with the man who holds Kostany."

"We've no feud with the Imperator," I said. "Our feud is with the man who took Kostany from us."

"The Imperator would like to make landfall here. He intends to put Kostany to siege within the week."

"We too intend to put Kostany to siege."

Rone looked past me at the zabadar on the beachside. "Have you a larger force with which to do this?"

"Our force is on the way. Three hundred ships."

"Then it would be equal to ours. A battle between us would devastate. It would be just what the man in Kostany wants."

"Indeed."

"As you know, these are Ethosian villages." Rone gestured toward the hovels as if he'd built them. "The Imperator requests that you withdraw."

"I cannot do that. I intend to make use of this position."

"Then we are at an impasse. I cannot see how we could make landfall while you occupy this position."

"Do we smell that bad to you Crucians?" Nesrin said. She sniffed Rone, then ruffled her nose. "Maybe it's you who smells. When's the last time you bathed?"

I glared at her. "What she means is, this beach is big enough for both of us."

Rone guffawed, hands on his hip plates. "Not to worry, I've granddaughters with manners that would make this one seem like a queen." He shook his head, turning serious. "Alas, the

Imperator is the Right Hand of the Archangel. His presence on this land is as if an angel kissed the dirt. I say this as kindly as I can, but he cannot share any land with you."

"Then he won't be landing," I said.

"I don't see three hundred ships. I see a few thousand horsemen." Rone grunted in disgust. "We'll be landing by dawn tomorrow. If you're still here, I'm sure you know what will happen. Now, I'm off to bathe." Rone chuckled, bowed his head, and returned to his galley.

"They think they're so much better than us," Nesrin said as we watched his galley row away. "'Angel's kiss'." She spat on the sand. "I'll show him where to kiss."

"If Redbeard makes it in time, the Imperator will have to withdraw. Or do what he doesn't want to do — fight an equal force."

"You still think he's coming? You gave Sadie up, Kevah. You placed the shackles on her yourself."

"It was her decision to seek Redbeard. Have faith. They'll come."

"What's taking so long? The scouts we've sent along the coast have reported nothing. Surely if ships were coming, they would've seen them."

I didn't have an answer.

I left Nesrin and found Kinn bothering a horse. He would flutter against it, make it stagger and whinny, then do it again from the other side.

"I need your help," I said.

"Of course. That's why they sent me. To help you."

"I need you to find someone."

"Who?"

"A woman."

"What kind of woman?"

"A...princess."

"And you love her?"

The question was like a punch to the heart.

"Not important," I said. "Just fly in the air and see if you spot ships coming from the south. A lot of ships — three hundred of them."

Kinn stopped his mischief and landed on the horse's back. It seemed I had his full attention. "Is she beautiful?"

"Yes, she's plenty beautiful." I sighed. "But that's not why I'm looking for her."

"Do you want to marry her?"

"These questions are beside the point."

"What does she look like?"

Finally, an appropriate question.

"She has auburn hair to her shoulders…the ends curl upward a bit." I scratched my head. "Well, more than a bit. Amber eyes and a slender nose."

"Understood!" Kinn saluted me with his eagle wing. "I will find her!"

Kinn fluttered straight up. So high, he was a dot in the clouds. But that dot flew the wrong way. It went inland to the east instead of toward the sea.

"Wrong way!" I shouted. But he mustn't have heard me. I shook my head as I watched him fly the one direction where Sadie surely wasn't.

I thought jinn were clever creatures. Why did Saran impose this imbecile upon me? Was it meant to be a punishment for not traveling to Zelthuriya?

NIGHT CAME. I found Nesrin praying under the stars, alone, on an empty beach away from camp. She begged her saints to beseech Lat to bring Sadie back. These zabadar saints were not any I knew, but I was open to trying something new, so I prayed to them too.

Afterward, we sat in the wet sand with the tide at our feet and threw seashells in the water.

"We should return to Demoskar," Nesrin said. "What if they're keeping Sadie there?"

"We're traitors to our country. We'll be attacked wherever we go."

Tears welled in Nesrin's eyes. First time I'd seen her cry. "Was it all for nothing?" She dabbed her fingers against her tear ducts. Waiting was the worst pain. "You know, I didn't like Sadie when we first met. She was too nice, and the nice ones are usually poisonous on the inside. She was shy, and Lat knows the things shy people conceal in their hearts."

She wound up her arm and threw a seashell high, but not far, as if to release her pain. It splashed in the water, then came back to our feet with the tide.

"That first winter," Nesrin continued, "I wished she would go home, back to her palace in the sky. She was fragile and weak and couldn't hunt or even kindle a fire. When my father saw how much I despised her, know what he did, the fool?" She laughed. "He said to me, 'Nesrin, you will teach this princess all there is to know about being a zabadar. If by the spring thaw she can't skin a wolf for warmth, pitch a yurt all on her own, and fish from the ice — by Lat and all the saints, I'll feed you to a snow bear!'"

I bounced the seashell in my hand and smiled. "Your father sounds a lot like mine."

"I was twelve. She was six years older, and *I* had to teach *her!*"

"So...did you get eaten by a bear?"

Nesrin chuckled. The waves came in stronger and drenched my pants. I wound my arm and threw a shell. It plopped somewhere far.

"Sadie was a slow learner. She'd never left the harem and knew nothing about being under the sun and moon. But she was a hard worker. Everything you see in her now — she wasn't born with it. Like any zabadar, she earned her skills. She really took to archery. She'd practice day and night, in the wind and rain and snow. That's how she became the best of us. It's not because of her blood...it's not because some conqueror fathered too many children hundreds of years ago."

I put my hand on Nesrin's shoulder. She clasped it and sobbed. Her crying awoke a sadness in me. I hadn't known Sadie long, but the story of how she'd worked her way to becoming a great zabadar, despite being uncertain of herself, made me realize that she wasn't just an ornament for our cause. Those who loved and admired her did so not for her name or position but for whom she was at heart. And I missed her angry glare as much as her kind smile.

But I had no need for sadness. "We can go our separate ways," I said. "You ride south to find Sadie."

"What about Kostany? What about Micah? What was all this for?"

"I'll go through Labyrinthos, alone. I'll come out in the palace and kill Micah."

Nesrin turned to me. Even in the dim moonlight, the fear in her eyes was plain.

"There must be a better way." She squeezed my hand. "You're a magus, aren't you? Can't you learn some sorcery?"

"Only in Zelthuriya. Being a magus means little until you train there."

"Maybe then you can defeat Micah."

"I don't think I'd care to. A magus must give up all their cares, all that drives them, to claim that power."

She pulled her hand away, sighed, and shook her head. "Why's everything got to be so damned hard?"

I threw my last shell at the horizon. Didn't see it land.

I RETURNED to my yurt and fell asleep. The fluttering of Kinn and his red and green eagle wings woke me.

"I found her," he said.

I perked up and threw off my horse-hide blanket. "Where is she?"

"She rides for our camp."

"Rides? From which direction?"

"Northeast, of course."

"You imbecile." I wagged my finger at the foolish bird. "There's no way Sadie could come from there. That's Kostany!"

"I'm no imbecile — how dare you. I'm double your age!"

"I told you to follow the sea south!"

Kinn brushed dust off his feathers and softened his tone. "I may only be a shiqq, but I know a thing or two. The woman you described is coming to this camp. I whispered the suggestion to her through her dreams as she slept. She believes her allies are here and makes haste. In fact, I hear her horse right now."

I rushed out of my yurt. In the distance, a horse galloped toward us. I could barely see it in the dismal moonlight. I lit a torch on the stove in my yurt, then came back outside. The horse was here — a big red beast. A woman jumped off, her face wrapped in cloth. She removed the cloth and auburn hair dropped to her shoulders, ends curled upward. Her amber eyes were just like Sadie's, though age had hardened her cheeks.

The woman pulled someone else off the horse: a short girl, about Melodi's age, with light brown hair and eyes. Ropes bound her, and she was no doubt this woman's captive.

"Who are you?" I asked.

"Who cares who I am," the red-haired woman answered. "Concern yourself with this one."

The poor girl's eyes were strained and devoid of spirit. She stared only at the ground.

"Then who is she?"

"She is the key to Kostany," the woman said. "She's Micah's wife."

22

MICAH

CANNONS NOW SILENT, A FALSE CALM SETTLED ON KOSTANY LIKE A haze.

The Imperator's fleet had likely made landfall elsewhere. I ordered Berrin to prepare the land defenses. The city had never fallen by land assault, thanks in part to the Zari Zar Mountains, which shielded the eastern side. To attack from the east would require marching an army, along with siege weapons, across rocky and steep terrain. When Temur the Accursed tried it, he lost a quarter of his army to landslides and what he claimed were "angry jinn." Of course, what the Latians called jinn were no less than the Fallen Angels and the demons they commanded.

Berrin and I and several others he'd promoted among the paladins to take the places of my dead and lost lieutenants discussed how a siege would play. We sat at the garden's wide glass table under the cool dawn light. Berrin laid it out:

"They will focus their fire on the western wall, which is exposed to an open plain. The staging area is very muddy, with uneven and shallow ground, so should it rain, the strait always overflows and floods the area. It's likely they will first build a wall and drain along the strait. We should attack this wall unceasingly, so if it rains, they'll have to withdraw from the area."

The walls of Kostany were higher than any other, but more remarkable were the deep foundations, which burrowed like an iceberg. They made them impossible to tunnel beneath and unlikely to collapse from cannon fire and sapping. If cannons damaged the walls, the Zari Zar provided ample stone and mortar with which to replenish them.

I added my bit: "Even if the skies don't open, we'll rain bombs and rockets upon their camp from atop our high walls."

It didn't sound like the Imperator had much chance. But fortune decided sieges. If the summer rains didn't come, they'd be able to maintain their camp, and we'd have to work ceaselessly to make them suffer. Fire did that best, and in dry weather, our incendiaries would create havoc. Disease could ravage them, especially in muddy, mosquito-infested terrain, but that was a matter of fortune too. Or rather, a matter of the Archangel's will.

"Food is the problem," Berrin said. "With rationing, we can stretch food supplies to a moon, but we would not be fighting at full strength."

"Then we take the offensive," I said.

"Indeed." Berrin nodded. "Let them attack during the day and wear themselves down. At night, we counter with elite, heavy cavalry. We'll fire the Fallen Screams at their camp to ensure they never sleep. If we sustain this for a moon, with good fortune and the Archangel's blessing, we can drive the Imperator back into the sea."

I always had to remind myself that Berrin was craftier than he looked. He'd been a Sirmian noble for most of his life and had studied at their renowned university in Tagkalay. The other lieutenants didn't have much to add, as Berrin's plans were exhaustive and simple.

"Two things matter more than anything," I said. "We must find my wife, and we must kill the Imperator."

Berrin replied, "The excubitors guarding the Imperator will be tough to crack, but he will be the target of our nightly raids. As for your wife, the search will not cease, nor will the torturer."

I RETURNED to the great hall and sat on the golden seat. I'd seen the stars and been to places unimaginable. I'd looked upon our past and perhaps our future. And yet, I couldn't see where my wife was.

One girl mattered more than the earth — nay, the heavens too. I closed my eyes and pictured Celene. I made a fist with my gunmetal hand, but all I saw were those men on the hill, bowing to Hawwa. They'd called to her, when in the holy stories they called to the Archangel. And why were the faces of the angels on the diamond? What was that diamond? How did it float above the clouds when anything bigger than a bird couldn't? Truthfully, I hadn't the capacity nor desire to understand these revelations.

Nor did I want to recall what I saw inside the diamond. It was hell. It was extracted from the nightmares of all souls; my own were never so dark, so engulfed by terror. It was not the terror of death, but the terror of creation, of what could be brought into the world — things that I didn't want to imagine because when I did, madness crept through my senses as a lion creeps toward prey.

Every awful thing flashed in my mind's eye — but not Celene and her whereabouts. What use was this power if I could not use it, if I had to wait for Aschere every time I wanted something done? My reliance on her now resembled my reliance on Jauz, and I hated relying on those who worshipped strange gods.

An hour later, Aschere walked into the great hall in her wispy green dress.

"I don't like how you come and go," I said. "If you're to serve me, I want to know your whereabouts at all times."

Aschere glared at me with vast indifference. "I don't serve you."

"I tolerate such attitudes from you and Jauz because of the good you both have done. But even he is not so direct!"

"I serve the Dreamer."

Perhaps it didn't matter whom she served if it helped me. Still, I grunted in disgust. "Tell your god to find my wife. Without her, this is all for nothing."

Aschere shook her head. "We do not command Hawwa."

"Oh? Until now, it seems she's done what we asked. It seems she's given me everything I yearned for. And yet, I'm falling short because I can't find one stubby girl."

"It *seems* you misunderstand. Micah, you are the Opener. You have a destiny greater than any king or conqueror."

"Indeed, I am the Opener. I will spread the faith of the Archangel to the east."

"Do you know any Old Church Crucian?" Aschere asked. "The word 'angel' derives from the Old Church word for 'messenger,' and a messenger always serves something greater. You saw the faces of your angels. What were they except a disguise? What else did they do except obscure the truth within?"

I didn't want to recall that vision again. I didn't want to believe it. My faith in the Archangel was like a warm fire and her god the endless cold around me.

"I don't know to what hell you took me. And right now, I don't care. I have a siege to crush. I have an imperator to kill and a wife to find. If your god cannot help me do these things, then she is of no use."

"Don't you see? Not one of those things matters. Leave everything, forget this city, and come with me to Labyrinthos. You are ready."

How could she utter such words? To insist I abandon all I'd suffered for? How many brothers had died for this city with faith burning in their hearts? I would not dishonor them.

"I will not abandon my men nor this city. I was meant to conquer and rule. I was meant to become Imperator. And even if I never find Celene, I'll drag one of Josias' cousins to Kostany and marry her instead. I'll crush whoever challenges me. This is the only destiny I accept."

Aschere placed her hand on her heart and looked up at me. I could get lost in her hard green eyes were I not so angry — eyes I wished to stare into until my own melted.

"Don't you want to see your daughter again?" she asked. "I know you long for her."

My rage almost choked me. I thought of Elly with the black-on-black eyes. I thought of what she'd done on the darkest night of my life.

"She was not my daughter," I said. "I may have believed it at first, but then she—"

"I speak of your real daughter." Aschere stepped onto the dais. "The girl you slew atop the sea wall."

"What did you say?" I unsheathed my sword and put it at her neck. "If you ever utter such slander again, I'll show you first-hand that the dead don't come back."

She didn't even flinch, as if my blade were a child's toy. "The truth is just too much for you. But it's all that matters."

"I won't fall for your tricks." I lowered my sword and sang holy hymns in my mind to quiet the rage.

When all eyes will be dazzled by the bloodied sky.
And darkness devours the moon.
There will be no refuge from the angels' miracles.
On that day, toward the Archangel will be our walk.

"You'll know she's real." Aschere's pleading interrupted my holy thoughts. "You'll know from her smell. You'll know from her eyes. It will be as if she never died. I understand, Micah. You've worshipped the Archangel all your life, and now it scares you to see beyond him. I see the fear running through you, the fear of the truth. Leaving the comfort of what you've believed, it is a hard thing."

She almost sounded reasonable. As if she were calming a

scared child, reassuring him that the monsters were not real. But these monsters were. The eye of the starfish that pulsed fear through my veins — it was as real as the woman standing before me.

"All apostles needed signs to believe," Aschere said. "And sometimes one is not enough. Sometimes signs can be confused for sorcery. But you will not confuse the real Elaria for an imposter. I will pray to the Dreamer to bring her back, so all your fears will melt in the light of the creator."

"Curse your Dreamer."

"Mere words." Aschere turned her back and spoke with a tone of finality. "Should she resurrect Elaria as a sign for you, and should you refuse to believe in and follow her, it will be the end of you, Micah, and the end of everything you have ever cared about."

I TRAVELED to the western wall and stood upon the battlement to observe preparations. A pulley raised boxes of steel-tipped arrows up to the defenders. In a workshop below, Orwo's alchemists mixed vats of oil and bomb recipes to throw from above. Sulfur peppered the morning breeze.

Workers plated iron sheets on the walls. We learned this tactic from Pendurum. Its iron walls were the most formidable I'd faced, but even they came down beneath the crimson moon. We'd have to do better to defend Kostany.

Paladins dug a shallow ditch around the wall to fill with metal fragments. If Josias' army tried to charge over it, a well-placed bomb would explode the fragments and send them in every direction at the speed of a bullet. This was another of Orwo's ideas. We'd honor his memory by putting it to use.

I stared at the sky and imagined Imperator Heraclius looking down from Baladict, aghast at what I planned for his son. All his pomp and splendor, all the times he took credit for my victories, even now it boiled my blood. When I offered the service of the Black Legion to Heraclius, it was to protect Crucis, not his failing rule. And yet I'd done both, and if it weren't for the Patriarch's poison, Heraclius would be gloating that he'd conquered Kostany. Though I'd not met Josias, I imagined him as insipid as his father, and that alone was reason to end him.

Heraclius had said to me while we drank wine after my conquest of Pasgard, *"You are but my prolog."* No, Heraclius. When they write the history of my conquests, you won't be my prolog, you won't be a footnote, you and your son will be forgotten — erased from time and memory.

While ruminating, I witnessed a procession coming to the gate. They were paladins who'd been forced from the seaside villages, where the Imperator had made landfall. But why were the Ethosian farmers returning with them?

I got my answers from an unexpected man. I bid the newly returned Aicard to join me on the battlement. He'd cut his blond hair short and grew a bushy beard that almost reminded me of the Shah. He looked thinner and seemed sullen and serious.

As he climbed up the steep stairs, I recalled the time he set fire to the Ejazi fleet while it was still in the bay, saving tens of thousands of paladins and opening the island without a battle. He'd disguised himself as a Latian warrior-dervish and gained the trust of the sultan's viziers and admirals within a moon. And yet, he refused to tell me the details. Aicard was a man of results; I figured his methods were better kept secret.

"Lovely country," he said, a grin seizing his reddened cheeks. "I had the most wonderful leave."

"I don't recall granting you leave." I played along.

"A man as hardworking as me deserves some respite, no?"

We embraced. Was it time to tell him about Orwo? About Zosi? He got along well with them, Zosi especially, as they were both from the western provinces.

When we separated, his grin was gone, as was the redness in

his cheeks. "I heard what happened," he said. "May the Archangel forgive Zosi."

I shook my head. "Zosi stayed true to his faith and family. It is I who need beg forgiveness."

"Save the penitence." Aicard gripped my shoulders. "I bring news."

He reported what he'd learned: the Sirmians and the Imperator had allied against me; a magus yearned for my blood because I killed his daughter; Redbeard might be coming for Kostany. It seemed far-fetched, and yet I trusted Aicard absolutely.

During his report, a pop and burst distracted me. In the workshop below, an alchemist writhed on the floor, his hand charred. Several fingers had been seared off. A healer ran to attend to him as he screamed.

But Aicard didn't flinch. He looked at me with iron eyes and said, "Be careful, Grandmaster. Everyone out there wants your blood."

"As they should. I'm thirsty for theirs."

"But can you fight the whole world?"

I gazed at the vast plain and the bulging, sun-parched hills surrounding Kostany. Soon my enemies would fill them. Janissaries with their gaudy, plumed-helmets, zabadar wielding bows of bone, pale-faced and dead-eyed excubitors — let them come. I looked toward the Shrunken Strait, its water rheumy and placid. I'd be feeding it more bodies soon.

"If we win this battle, we can remake the world, Aicard. West and east will bow to the Archangel, the hypocrites will be vanquished, and the order of the Twelve will finally dawn."

But Aicard was unmoved, his stare filled with thorns. "Grandmaster, you may win this battle, but the war rages on."

"The Imperator's army will be bloating in the Siyah Sea, along with Redbeard's. Sirm will be opened. The exarchs in Hyperion will have no choice but to crown me, or face my unimpeded wrath. The war will be over. Your point is not taken."

Aicard hesitated with tense breaths. "Not that war."

"What other war is there? Speak plainly!"

"Have you ever asked yourself why she helped you? What price you'd pay?"

"Not this again." I turned away and sighed. It seemed Aicard was of similar mind to Zosi and Edmar. I couldn't lose another lieutenant, not now. "I know what she wants, and I've no mind to give it. Rest assured, I'll always fight for our cause, not hers or her god's." I turned back and looked him in the eye. "If ever I stray from that, then you've every reason to turn on me."

Tension thinned the air between us. I didn't want to fight another lieutenant, another friend. But hearts are hard won and easily lost.

Aicard put his hand on his heart, then got on one knee. "I've never doubted your good intentions. One thing is certain — so long as you're for our cause, I fight for you."

His loyalty reassured me. Loyalty wins wars. Good intentions don't, though. But perhaps that was better left unsaid.

23

KEVAH

Rone of Sempuris sped away on his galley to tell the Imperator that their princess was our hostage.

The girl didn't speak any Sirmian, and the zabadar and I didn't speak Crucian. Luckily, the red-haired woman spoke enough Crucian to translate. After we'd allowed Celene a bath and change of clothes, I resolved to learn more.

The Princess had asked, politely, if she could visit the chapel. I didn't even know there was one until she pointed to a stone hovel with Crucian letters painted on it. Inside, a stone likeness of the Archangel stood atop an altar. Celene bowed and sang with a saintly voice while I stared at the angel's wings. Why were there only eleven, not twelve? The lack of symmetry bothered me; I couldn't imagine a more disconcerting idol.

I sat on a stone bench in the frontmost pew. The red-haired woman sat next to me. Her name was Humayra, and she was one of Shah Murad's concubines. She'd witnessed Micah the Metal butcher the Shah's harem.

But the girl kneeling at the altar didn't seem cruel like her husband. She didn't even seem unhappy to be our prisoner.

Once done praying, Celene turned to me, a revitalized spirit in her light brown eyes. It seemed praying had given her some comfort.

"Ask her if she needs anything," I told Humayra.

Humayra said it in Crucian. The girl repeated what Humayra said but rearranged the words and added a different one at the beginning. She was correcting Humayra's Crucian in the politest way.

Humayra repeated what the girl said and, for the first time, I saw the girl smile. She began a lengthy response while looking me in the eyes.

"She thanks you for providing her with food, water, and clothing," Humayra said. "She says her only wish is to return to Hyperion, to her monastery."

The Crucians were well known for their monasteries, where men and women took holy oaths to never marry or speak or eat certain foods. During Shah Jalal's conquests in the Yunan continent, we came across many monasteries and mostly left them alone.

"Ask her what she swore never to do," I said.

Humayra translated Celene's response with one word, "Marry."

So Micah had kidnapped her, forced her to marry him, and probably wanted to kill the Imperator to claim the throne.

Celene said a few words in a hesitant tone.

"She's seen the banners of her father," Humayra said, "and asks what you'll do with her."

"That depends on her father. What kind of man is he?"

Celene gazed at the cracked stone floor, as if conflicted. She worded her response softly.

Humayra translated, "A devout man who seeks to rule justly by the laws of their angel."

"And what would her father think about allying with unbelievers?"

The question pressed on Celene's mind. Her eyes shifted with angst.

"She knows little of statecraft," Humayra translated, "and couldn't possibly comment on that."

"Does he love her?"

The Princess looked into my eyes. A hopeful smile seized her cheeks and she nodded.

Humayra and I left the chapel. Outside, the zabadar went about their tasks in the afternoon light. Standing next to a barn where mares were being milked, I asked Humayra my lingering questions.

"Is it true that Micah killed the Shah's children and consorts?"

She gazed away, sullen. "It's true."

"How did you escape their fate?"

"A Silklander in Micah's employ got a special reward for making such great weapons." Her voice cracked. "Me."

"You speak of Jauz?" Aicard had mentioned him.

Her curvy eyebrows lifted with surprise. "You know him?"

"Only of him. Is he a decent man? Could he be turned?"

"He's not the worst of them, but I wouldn't call him decent. He saved my life and yet made me live in a cage, as if I were a red tiger from the jungles of Himyar. He did teach me Crucian, though."

Humayra lowered her gaze. Behind her doggedness, I sensed a familiar emotion: remorse. Did she blame herself for what she'd witnessed?

"Surviving was the best you could do," I said.

"Was it?" She shook her head. "Just to run away?"

"You didn't just run. You brought us a princess. You may have saved us all."

Auburn hair above such kind eyes. She really did resemble Sadie. Could she be...her mother? I didn't ask, didn't want to add to her burdens. But truly, the guilt of letting Sadie go weighed on me. If Ebra had her, then I'd lost. We would never take Kostany without a leader.

"You know, we met before," Humayra said.

I raced through my memories but had no recollection. "Forgive me."

"I was running that day too. So fast I was almost flying, after I'd slipped by the eunuchs and escaped Murad's harem." She laughed, her teeth apart and tongue almost sticking out. Sadie's laugh. "I thought I was free. I'd reached the gate of the Seat...and there you were, guarding it."

The first time I stood guard at the Seat was almost twenty-five ago when I was barely a man. Still, I couldn't recall seeing her.

"You don't look much older than that day, but I guess that's how it is for a magus," she said. "Anyway, you saw my bare feet and fancy clothes and no matter what I said, I couldn't convince you to let me through. And then the eunuchs, who weren't far behind, caught up."

The memories poured in from some ancient crevice in my mind. I chuckled. "Didn't you tell me you were a pleasure girl on the run from an unsatisfied vizier?"

"I should have come up with a better story!"

We laughed as if old friends. The brawly zabadar milking the mare nearby glared at us, as if he wanted in on the jest.

"I thank Lat that you didn't let me through," Humayra said, her expression plain and serious.

I had a hunch why.

THE NEXT DAY, another galley sped to shore. A crest with four eyes in a diamond adorned its purple sails, along with Crucian letters. The wood of the ship was etched and ornate and of lighter color than the other ships. No doubt, the Imperator was coming.

Twenty bearded excubitors stepped off the boat and lined up on either side of dock, gripping their maces, axes, and guns; the

Imperator's guardsmen seemed as imposing as I remembered. In Rastergan, I used to pray to not meet one on the battlefield. A cleanshaven man in white and gold silks spread out a purple carpet. Then he opened a small bottle and sprinkled water on the carpet, all while hymning.

I wasn't prepared to welcome the Imperator. We had nothing fit for kings. I had bathed and wore fresh leathers and dabbed a bit of myrrh oil on my shoulder pads, which now smelled sappy and sweet. Nesrin had gone to scout for Sadie, so I stood alone at the edge of the purple carpet as several excubitors faced me and the scores of zabadar at my back.

I hoped he wasn't as stubborn as his father. We'd sacrificed hundreds of men for every grain of dirt seized from Heraclius, and he took much of it back. The Hated would burn entire cities than let us have them. But what is a city weighed against the life of your only daughter?

Finally, the man stepped off the boat. The four angel eyes adorned his plate mail in gleaming purple etches. He wore silk gloves embroidered with purple crosshatches. A manicured brown beard outlined a youthful, though anxious face. I always felt kinghood was in the jaw; his strong jawline reaffirmed that.

Imperator Josias walked down the purple carpet, pushed past the excubitors, and stared at me, as if expecting something.

"Your Majesty," I said. "Welcome to Sirm." I almost bowed my head.

He walked past me onto the sand. As his guard approached to follow, he gestured for them to stay back. He looked upon the zabadar who'd lined up with their fresh swords and guns. He gazed into the distance at the grass and plains. He stared up at the cloudless blue sky. Then he returned to face me.

"You are the warlord?" The Imperator had a flavorful lilt that was almost pleasing.

"As far as you're concerned," I said. "As far as your daughter's life is concerned."

314

Now I had his proper attention. His breaths quickened.

"My retainer Rone says you showed her to him. You Sirmians are known for sorcery. How do I know she's real?"

I pointed at the stone hovel where Celene prayed. "See for yourself."

Some of his guard tried to follow. The zabadar near me reached for their swords. The Imperator gestured for his guardsmen to stay on the dock, then walked alone to the chapel.

Ten minutes later, he returned to the beach, his cheeks filled with color. He seemed comforted by the short visit.

"You've treated her well, for that you have my gratitude. May I ask you a question?"

I nodded.

"Do you have a child?"

"A daughter…she has passed."

"What wouldn't you do to get her back?"

"There's nothing I wouldn't do."

"Then we understand each other." Josias nodded with hopeful energy. "State your terms."

"For a start, we happen to like this beach. Don't force us off it."

"Granted."

"But we're a bit lonely and could use the company. Make landfall here."

"We can do so up the coast." He pointed northward. "So long as you don't attack us."

"On the contrary, we want to fight Micah too. So why don't we make history and do it together."

The Imperator smiled in the same good-natured way as his daughter, then laughed politely. "Sorry, what you said reminds me of something my father once told me."

"Your father was Imperator Heraclius. I knew him as a worthy foe."

"Did you now?"

"Fought against him in Rastergan. So, what did Heraclius the Hated once say?"

"Is that what you called him?"

A westerly wind blew wisps of sand between us and carried the scent of the earth. It was getting humid.

"We despised him, the bastard. How many times did we put down his armies, only for him to raise another? You'd think the nobles would've overthrown him by the fourth or fifth time."

"My father played the long game. He clung to power through dark days, and now look at us. He tripled the size of the Imperium."

"With the sword of Micah the Metal, the man after your throne."

The Imperator flinched. Just the mention of Micah seemed to sting him. "And somehow, it is you I have to thank for denying him that throne. Strange to say it, but I'd rather my daughter be with you than with him."

"Then you can see how we're not enemies."

"For now."

"So what did Imperator Heraclius say? I really am curious."

"My father told me a story about how he secured the peace. Ten years ago, he received a desperate letter from a Sirmian royal begging for arms and gold so he could fight his cruel brother. And in exchange, this Sirmian royal promised peace with my father if he won."

It took me a few seconds to figure out whom he was talking about. "You mean…"

"My father said they were making history together. But he knew an ally one day is an enemy the next. In time, that desperate Sirmian royal would be rich and powerful and turn his bombards at us."

"You speak of Shah Murad," I said in disbelief.

"My father and the Shah honored their secret alliance…until it became inconvenient. I don't mind doing the same with you."

I kicked at a rock on the sand, sent it toward the sea. "All I care about is killing Micah the Metal."

"And the fate of Kostany?"

"If you want your daughter back, you'll return it to us."

The Imperator breathed deeply. Too much stirred beneath his laden expression. "The day we'd heard that Micah captured Kostany, was a day when every Crucian cried out in joy. Parades marched through cities and towns, flying kites with the likenesses of the angels. Hymns burst from the chapels. Angelsong filled the streets, and faith glowed in the hearts and eyes of everyone — lowborn and high. How can I, then, hand it over?"

"As you said, we'll be allies until it's convenient."

"And then what? We'll gut each other in the streets?"

"If it comes to that."

"You're the leader of two thousand horsemen, who happens to have my daughter in his custody. You can't hold Kostany even if you wanted to."

He wasn't wrong. The zabadar standing in the distance were lionhearted, but to hold a city of that size, we'd need Redbeard's fleet and army.

I stopped myself from spitting on his words. Instead, I held his gaze and solidified my tone, as if I were a king too. "I'm the leader of two thousand horsemen, but you're the father of one daughter. Make landfall. Prepare your siege. Attack Kostany, *with* us. When Micah is dead, you'll get her back. If you break these terms — poor girl — she'll pay."

Josias forced a smile to hold back the fear that flared through his eyes. "And the Sirmian in you shows true. We'll do what you ask. Just know that Kostany is the one thing I can't trade for my daughter's life." He turned his back to leave, then said, "When the time comes, you might find I have something more to offer."

"What does that mean?"

He kept silent and walked away.

· · ·

A DAY LATER, the Imperator's forces landed a few miles up the beach.

Meanwhile, the zabadar butchered the game they'd hunted and hung the meat to dry in the sun. A group of women on the beachside fletched and sharpened arrows while chatting and laughing as if we weren't about to attack the most fortified city in the world. The horse archers drilled, so every nearby tree was covered in arrows.

Sputtering out of the sky like a drunk bird, Kinn fluttered his way down to me. "There's something out there," he said.

"Something? What is it?"

"A lone ship drifts in the sea yet keeps its distance."

"Could it be Sadie? Guide me to it."

I took the rowboat. Before I could start rowing, Kinn landed on the back of the boat. The creature's feet seemed to stick onto the wood. He flapped his wings, faster and faster, until they became as rapid as a hummingbird. The boat moved by their speed, and Kinn fluttered us out into sea.

"So this is your power," I said. "I was hoping to work out my arms, actually."

"I need the practice too. Else I'll be useless to you."

I gawked at how much he'd improved. Every minute, a feather would fly off his chicken body as he glided the boat on water. But even as the shore became distant, I couldn't see the ship.

"You sure we're going the right way?" I asked.

"I spent most of my eighty-eight years flying around Lidya. I know these waters. Although, I sometimes confuse this part for the Siyah Sea."

"The Siyah Sea is a glorified lake," I said. "This is the fucking ocean."

"Can't you read a joke?"

"This isn't the time for jokes. Tomorrow we could all be dead."

"Ah, but that's the best time for jokes. Don't you want to die with a smile?"

I could scarcely believe I was arguing with a creature part chicken, part boy.

"If you can find Sadie, that will make me smile."

Calm water surrounded us. An ebbing tide lifted the boat ever so gently. The sea had always meant war for me. The only boats I'd been on were warships. It was a welcome change to be gliding toward something other than battle.

Kinn grinned. "So…" He chuckled with some chicken clucks mixed in. "When are you two getting married?"

"I can't marry her. I'm twice her age, and she's twice my station."

"You're a magus. You're forever young."

"Truth is, I'm done with love. Hate is better fuel for what I need to do."

The bird clucked. "But is love done with you?"

I shook my head and grunted to dismiss the topic. "I've been wondering — what does it even mean to be a magus?"

"It means you put on an enchanted mask."

"I had one ten years ago. I brought it to my face once, but it didn't turn me into a magus."

Kinn looked at me with placid, thoughtful eyes. "For it to transform you, you have to have killed the magus it came from."

"But I did kill that magus."

"Saran mentioned that you have the right to command both the Efreet and the Jann. Normally, a magus commands only one tribe. Maybe that explains it."

"What are these tribes?" I asked.

"The Jann like to live in the plains. Lat gave them dominion over wind. The Efreet like to live in the desert. Lat gave them dominion over fire."

"The magus ten years ago…he turned air into ice. Almost froze us all…in the dead of summer."

"He commanded the Marid tribe, who live in the frozen wastes."

"So do I have the right to command that tribe, too?"

"I don't know...I'm just a lowly shiqq. Truth be told, I'm not meant to know any of these secrets, but I overhear what I overhear."

I sighed in frustration. "Truth is, I can't *really* command any tribe."

"You must go to Zelthuriya for that."

"Why?"

A nearby gurgling alerted me to a dolphin. The curious thing poked its head above water, then dove with a squeak and splash. I'd never seen one so close.

I scanned the horizon for the ship, to no avail.

Kinn sighed in a high pitch. "First of all, the Jann and the Efreet don't respond to Sirmian. You'll have to learn Old Paramic to command them. The same Paramic in the Recitals of Chisti, who was the first magus, who commanded all tribes."

"Thank Lat that you speak Sirmian."

"Us shiqq are not like the others. We enjoy being around humans and animals, if only to make mischief. Ever had your shoes go missing after using the privy? It was probably a shiqq. We love to steal shoes and laugh as the human searches for them. Once I put his shoes in a tree — oh that was the best — he threw rocks to knock them down, and when that didn't work, he even tried to climb it! And then I kept moving the shoes higher and higher up the tree — oh that was a hoot." Kinn's laugh was half chicken, half boy. "Alas, Lat did not give us dominion over anything, so we made shoes our dominion."

I tried to forget the number of times I'd mysteriously lost my shoes and asked, "Why serve me, then?"

"I aspire to a little more than the average shiqq. My mother was a nasnas, but they say my father was a human. I've always been interested in humans, more than just for japes. I hope one day I'll find my father, if only just to see him."

"So you're half human? How is that possible?"

"I'm sure you've heard stories of jinn mating with humans. Most were nasnas, some were also likely silat. Sometimes a nasnas just likes what she sees and so takes the form of a beautiful woman and seduces a man for his seed. It cannot work the other way, though. A human womb cannot birth a jinn."

"But you can't change your shape."

"It's not an easy thing. To change your shape and remove the veil that covers the unseen is something most shiqq never learn to do. It takes hundreds of years of practice." Kinn's tone turned grim. "There will always be something that the shapeshifter cannot mimic. Usually, it's the eyes. Don't let the shapeshifters fool you — they are often the worst of us."

WE'D BEEN at sea for some time and hadn't seen any ship.

"It was here," Kinn said. "But now…it's not."

"Perhaps it went farther out to sea."

Kinn stopped flapping. Our rowboat rocked on gentle waves. Salty air filled my nose as the afternoon sun beat down.

"I can't take you any farther," he said.

"What? Why?"

"Beyond here are the waters of the Yunan continent. We don't go there."

I laughed. "You afraid of the Crucians?"

"Not the Crucians, but whom they worship."

"The angels?"

"Beyond here is the realm of the angels. We do not enter it."

"You can't be serious? The angels are false."

"Are they? The veil of the unseen has lifted for you. You may yet see one."

"Have you seen one?"

"No, I've never crossed into Yuna."

"So you're just going to leave me here? You said you were different from other shiqq."

"It's not just the shiqq that fear the angels. All the tribes do. There's one rule that no jinn ever breaks. We do not cross into Yuna."

The water below was foamy and green, as was the water in the *sea of the angels* ahead. I'd traveled the Yunan Sea with Shah Jalal and never seen any angels. Overhead, seagulls soared. Would the angels' seagulls drop stones upon us? Would the dolphins spray us with acid from their snouts? Absurd. What was the danger?

I grabbed an oar, pushed it into the water, and pulled it inside the oarlock. "I'll search for her on my own."

Kinn stared into me with anguished eyes. "But I can't leave you in the middle of the ocean. I was sent to serve you."

I stretched my arms — up high, then across. "I'll not return until I've found her."

"You love her that much?"

"It's not about love. We need her to win."

"I've been around plenty of humans in my eight-eight. I know love when I see it. I hope my father looked at my mother with those lovey-dovey eyes of yours."

I did miss her. But love? I'd not the time nor space in my rage-filled heart.

"I'm going now."

Kinn jumped off the boat and landed in the water like a duck. I rowed away. Ah, my arms got much-needed action. The tide had turned a tad forceful, so I put my back into it — just the exercise I'd been yearning for. I hummed a janissary song to keep my rowing in rhythm, as if I were on a mighty galley speeding to raid a Crucian city.

By Temur's sword,
A thousand noble souls,

Sacrifice themselves.
O' Lion of Lat,
Prince of Men,
There is no hero but you.

I imagined the war drums beating to the song's brutal rhythm. How we marched through Yuna to its beat, terrorizing Crucian hearts. With every repetition, we'd replace Temur's name with each shah of Sirm until we reached Shah Jalal, and then we'd cheer so loud even the mountains trembled.

I was getting into it, but then there was sputtering and a jet of water and a chicken landed on my boat. "If a nasnas and a man could work, then you and her can work. I'm going with you."

Kinn waddled to his position at the back end.

I eased my grip on the oars. "You'll enter the realm of the angels?"

"I've never been one to follow rules. Besides, I'm just a lowly shiqq. Perhaps they won't notice...I pray they don't."

Kinn flapped us farther into the ocean for another thirty minutes. A hazy dot appeared on the distant horizon. He flew into the sky to get a better look.

"It's the ship!" He glided back onto the boat and fluttered so excitedly that the boat lifted into the air. We sped toward the ship, the boat lifting and splashing.

"Easy, bird!" Nausea swam through my stomach as seawater soaked my clothes.

I recognized the red sails. The eight-pointed star shone on them in gleaming gold, with a scimitar resting beneath it — the standard of Hayrad the Redbeard.

Kinn stopped before we got too close. A medium-sized galley with twenty oars on each side floated upon placid water. The perfect vessel for ramming the enemy sidelong, and quite mobile. The sailors had noticed us, and now a troop of gunners aimed at me.

"Don't shoot!" I shouted. "I'm friendly!"

Sadie appeared on the bow. Seeing her, I felt like a thirsty traveler spotting an oasis.

"Kevah!" she shouted.

The gunners lowered their weapons.

Kinn dug his fangless chicken feet into my shoulders. With a great flapping, he lifted me into the air.

"What the hell are you doing!?" I shouted.

"Lat gave me eagle wings for a reason. This will impress a princess!"

"Oh no, please don't, bird—"

Salty air assaulted my eyes as Kinn flew me to the ship. He dropped me on the bow; I landed with panging pain as my hands and knees hit wood.

"That was easy," Kinn said. "I'm getting stronger."

Sadie and the sailors glared at me with open mouths. To them, I must have literally been flying.

"Don't be too surprised," I said. "I am a magus."

Sadie shook off her shock and hugged me. I breathed the sweetest relief as our cheeks touched.

Kinn fluttered near my ears. "Don't disappoint me, young man." He soared onto the mast.

"Sorry I didn't come to shore," Sadie said. "I intended to, but we feared capture by the Imperator's fleet."

The sailors around us chattered in Paramic. I even heard what sounded like a Kashanese dialect and a deeply southern guttural tongue. Redbeard's crews were known to be motley. Khazis journeyed from every land that worshipped Lat to serve under him. Filled with zeal and given to meditation and prayer — even during battle — they were like the holy warriors from the poems of Utay and Temur.

Someone slapped my back: Yamin, beaming and overjoyed to see me.

"Word reached about how you crushed the gholam," he said. "How's my ill-tempered sister?"

"The gholam left her a Kashanese horse of her own. We all have one now."

"That so? Mine's still the best." Yamin laughed in his ferocious way.

Sadie took me to her cabin, a bare room with a floor table and a mattress, so we could talk alone. Maps and a brass astrolabe cluttered the table. Kinn fluttered into the room before I could close the door.

"Go away," I whispered to him.

"I risked the wrath of the angels. No way I miss this." He plopped himself on the table and sat the way a chicken lays eggs. "Do your best. I won't say a word."

"Who are you talking to?" Sadie's unbrushed and wild hair disarmed me — very sailor-like.

"Well…a jinn."

"You can talk to jinn?"

"Only this one jinn. He helps me out…sort of."

"So that's how you did it. Are you…becoming cold and distant like Vaya, too?" Her amber pupils became small. I yearned to brighten them.

"Now you've made her sad!" Kinn said. "You need to make her smile!"

I shot Kinn an angry glance.

"No, not at all," I said to Sadie. "They say I have to travel to Holy Zelthuriya to train, but we have more important things to do."

"About that…Hayrad the Redbeard has agreed to join us." It was joyous news, but Sadie said it with heavy breaths.

"Where is he? Why are you alone, on a single ship, in the middle of the Yunan Sea?"

"He went to Rastergan. Their count wants to help us retake Kostany. He's pledged ten thousand men. I believe they're only a day behind me."

"They're Ethosians…can we trust them?"

"They don't want Crucis to rule them. My father at least allowed them freedom, so long as they paid tribute. Hayrad promised them the same terms if they helped us."

"What gives Hayrad the right to promise anything? He only rules on the seas."

Sadie swallowed and took a deep breath. "Not anymore. Should we retake Kostany, Hayrad the Redbeard will ascend the throne and be declared Sultan-Regent. That was our agreement."

"Impossible," I scoffed. "Hayrad's mother and father were Ejazi merchants. He doesn't have a drop of Seluqal blood."

Sadie met my gaze in silence. She seemed to be choosing her words carefully. "I've the blood."

My heart sank into a pit of thorns when I realized what she meant. "You married him."

"I agreed to marry him once we retook Kostany. It was the only way he would join us." She looked as if she'd swallowed a bitter melon.

Kinn covered his face with his wings. "I wish I'd stayed outside. Can I go now?"

It hurt...more every second. Regardless, I was used to biting down on pain.

"You did the right thing," I said. "He's a capable commander and brings with him a large fleet and army. With the Rastergani forces and the army of the Imperator, we have close to eighty thousand men. Micah has barely half that. We will win."

"The Imperator?" Sadie wrinkled her nose and glared.

"I also made an alliance of necessity. Imperator Josias has agreed to siege the city with us."

"Why would he ever?"

"One of the Shah's consorts survived and escaped to our camp. She brought with her a gift — the Imperator's daughter."

"Consort? What's her name?"

"Humayra."

Sadie gasped. Tears welled in her eyes. "My mother!" She sighed in relief.

I'd hoped as much but didn't want to assume. Didn't want to give false hope.

"Is this a dream?" Sadie pinched her cheek. "Is this real? Is she really alive?"

I wanted to hug her, but it didn't seem proper to touch another man's betrothed.

"Your mother is alive and well," I said. "And because of her, we have the upper hand. Once Redbeard arrives, we can take back Kostany, kill Micah, and win this war."

Sadie nodded. Bittersweet feelings of our reunion swam through my stomach. I quelled them with fiery thoughts of vengeance. Still, the sensation that everything I wanted was so near, yet infinitely far, overcame me.

Sadie broke through my thoughts with a touch on my shoulder. "I'll send Yamin with this ship to inform Redbeard of what you've told me. You and I will go to your camp in the morning."

"We should go now. I imagine you've waited long enough to see your mother."

"It's sunset, we'll not make it before dark."

I looked to the chicken and smirked. "Oh, we'll make it."

Sunset bled in the sky. The ruddy horizon foreshadowed the blood to come. I helped Sadie into the rowboat. Redbeard's sailors, who seemed so comfortable in their hodgepodge outfits, used a pulley to lower it, and then we untied the rope.

Kinn glided onto the edge of the rowboat.

"You know," he said, "she could still see you on the side. You don't need to marry her. Or maybe I push this Redbeard fellow down a well?"

"Don't you dare. Now *flap-flap* us home."

Sadie stared at me with one eyebrow raised. To her, I was

talking to the wind. She gasped as our rowboat moved and sped through the water.

"So this is your power!" She clung onto the sides of the boat. "What else can you do?"

"Send messages through dreams...I think."

The boat lifted in the air on the crest of a wave, then splashed as it whipped on the water. Sadie gasped again.

"Not really used to boats." She gripped her seat as if she feared flying off. "Much less used to boats propelled by jinn."

I wished I could hold her. I wished I could be the one to keep her steady. Was Kinn right about my feelings? I crushed such thoughts with the iron fist of reality.

An endless and open sea surrounded us. We could pick any direction, go anywhere. But instead, we charged toward war.

"I wasn't either." I had to raise my voice to be heard over the splashing. "Now I'm not sure I can do without it."

"You know, I've always wanted to see the islands to the south. They say Ejaz is like an emerald floating on a turquoise sea."

"Why don't we?" I joked. But half of me wanted to. The other half wanted to see the insides of Micah's throat. "Bird, how far is Ejaz?"

"My name is Kinn. And no way I'm taking you to Ejaz. I won't have any feathers left after such a journey."

"Too far," I said to Sadie. "Any place closer you know of?"

Sadie stared up, as if into her own head. "Oh! Jesia isn't far. Their cheeses are divine. Or how about Rupat? I've heard so much about their snail pancakes."

"Snail pancakes?" I could almost taste the slime. "That doesn't sound very appealing. But I did once eat my shoes, so..."

Sadie laughed. "How did they taste?"

"I'd been wearing them for months. It was like eating my own skin."

She laughed some more. Her laughter made me laugh, too. I couldn't recall anything more fulfilling than being the reason for her smiles. And when she beamed, I adored the chipped tooth in her top set. A somber warmth flowed through me.

"I've got a surprise for you," Kinn said. "Grab on tight...to each other...heheh."

Kinn dove and swam under the boat. With his newfound strength, he lifted the boat above water. Sadie grabbed me and screamed. The boat lifted ten feet. I screamed too.

"Kinn!" I shouted. "We don't have time for—"

"You know what you have to do!" he said. "Here we go!"

A burst of wind lifted us twenty feet in a second. Now fifty feet, a hundred, two hundred, five hundred. My stomach rose faster — I barely kept from retching. I lost count of how high we flew as the sky darkened.

Frigid air chilled my bones. Sadie and I hugged for warmth while howling protestations. And then we were in heaven.

The ocean below stretched forever. The setting sun filled the sea with an orange glaze. Above, the cloud wisps were close enough to touch, and a blazing tapestry of stars cut across a deep firmament.

"Is this happening?" Sadie whispered.

"It's f-freezing," I said, unable to fathom it.

The stars burned furiously as the sun sank beneath the sea. We sat there, clinging to each other and staring at the unbelievable. When I was a child, I thought one day I would climb the Nocpla peaks and see the earth as a bird would. Another childish dream exceeded.

Sadie giggled. "This can't be real." She pinched my cheek, which I'd nestled on her shoulder.

"Ow! Why'd you do that?"

"To wake up."

"You're supposed to pinch yourself, not me!"

"I tried earlier. What if you're the dreamer? Maybe you need to wake up."

"That makes no sense."

We watched heaven in silence for a minute. I stared up at the firmament, each star like a shimmering diamond. What was beyond them? And what was beyond that? We'd journeyed so high, and yet there was ever higher to go. Sitting here embracing Sadie, both cold from the air and warm from her body heat, I wondered if this was the best moment in my life.

Sadie hugged me tighter and said, tenderly, "You know... while we were apart, I thought a lot about what you said. I'd been cursing my fate — my birth and all it entailed. It seems a Seluqal is destined to either rule or die. To kill or be killed. Nothing scared me more, in both respects, and all I wanted was to be free of that curse." Her tears moistened my cheek and smelled warm. "But there's no escaping it...that's why I agreed to marry Redbeard. I'll do what has to be done, so we can win." She looked me in the eyes, our noses touching. "I'll be strong...for everyone...and for you." Her breaths warmed my face as our lips neared.

"All right!" Kinn's shout startled me. "That's all my tiny muscles can take, down we go!"

I felt weightless as we descended, held in place by Sadie's hug. She too was trying not to retch. The boat was like a cannon-ball gliding down toward a rippling, blue wall. As the air screamed by, I knew I never wanted to ride a cannonball again.

We landed with a splash that doused us in seawater. If we weren't freezing, wet, and an inch from spilling our insides, I guess it would've been amorous.

Sadie clutched her arms, teeth chattering, then smacked her left ear until water flew out the right. I did the same; my ears popped, and I could hear the breeze brushing against them. Falling so fast had left me nauseated and yearning to do anything but move.

Sadie, too, held her stomach. She sank into the boat, reclined, and stared to the side. What had happened up there? Was it a dream, or was she really about to kiss me? Did it matter?

Of course not. Whatever happened was a flight of fancy, literally and figuratively. All that mattered was to get to shore. Where the hell had Kinn gone?

The little chicken jumped on the boat, a stupid grin on his face. He chuckled with clucks. Then his face turned grim.

"Oh no, there's something on the water," he said. "We shouldn't have flown. We should never have come here. Lat have mercy…"

I turned my head eastward, toward whatever Kinn was staring at. At first, the waning sunset seemed to obscure it, but the longer I looked, the clearer it became. The head of a mountain-sized jellyfish floated above the water. I could see through it, as if its skin were crystal. And as I stretched my gaze left and right, I failed to find where it began and ended. A thousand tentacles dangled off its head and dipped deep in the water, lightning flickering between them. It blocked our way to shore.

"What is it?" Sadie asked, still shivering.

"You don't see it, do you?" I said, strangely fearless. Perhaps my mind, after just witnessing heaven, was now unafraid of such wonders. Or perhaps it had not quite hit me yet.

Sadie gazed into the distance and shook her head. "I just saw the earth as an eagle does. What's left?"

Amid the pores and strands in the thing's head, an eye opened — a human eye with a black iris, bigger than a galleon. As it gazed upon us, deathly terror flowed through my bones. I couldn't look away from the eye and couldn't bear the fear that seized me.

I shut my eyes and saw an egg. Upon it were a thousand mouths, each with a thousand fanged teeth. The mouths hymned something incomprehensible, and then trees shot out of them. Upon each tree branch, angels sprouted. They grew a thousand times larger every second, until they burst from the trees and soared across a burning white sky. The angels were…made of faces…human faces, each screaming, eyes popping out, tongues vibrating with shrill cries. A sea of anguished human faces melted and dripped off the angels, until—

"Kevah, what's wrong?" Sadie asked, putting her hand on my shoulder and snapping me from the vision. Still, the giant eye would not cease glaring.

I looked upon my trembling hands. I hugged myself, but couldn't stop my body from quaking, as if the eye pulsed tremors through me. Sadie grabbed and hugged me, but still I shook against her.

"What the hell is happening?" she cried.

Kinn stared into the eye, utterly entranced. "Angel." Feathers flew off him as he shook. And because he shook, the boat shook. It shook so violently that it nearly overturned. With my arms and legs and body shaking, I kicked Kinn into the water to keep the boat from overturning.

"What do you see!?" Sadie shouted.

The eye closed. The giant jellyfish disappeared. My body and breathing calmed. A tiredness overcame me. Every limb yearned to melt, as if I were pudding. Would that I could melt into the sea and annihilate, instead of witnessing such terrors.

Kinn jumped back on the boat and began flapping us toward shore.

With both of us wet from the splashing, Sadie wrapped her arms around me. We stayed like that until my heart calmed.

24

MICAH

ASCHERE STOOD IN THE MOONLIGHT AT THE PLAZA WHERE WE'D roasted thousands of paladins. Where we'd cooked my little brother with a green flame. She prayed, her hands outstretched in the way of the Latians. But she was not one; they did not worship Hawwa — the Dreamer. It was a name not heard in any religion I knew. And yet, this woman devoted herself. Not out of faith, like everyone else. No, she was like the apostles — like Len and Benth. What she'd seen and experienced compelled her to believe.

I didn't feel shame in interrupting an infidel's prayer. "What is it you ask for?"

Aschere ignored me and whispered under her breath. Old Paramic had a strange, wavy sound to it. One word seemed to breathe into the next.

"Why does your god speak the language of the Latians?" I asked. "Church Crucian is as old and obscure. Does she not understand it?"

I huffed at being ignored. But a true believer would not interrupt her prayers for anyone. I subdued my anger with a grudging appreciation.

I sat at the broken fountain where I'd parleyed with Zosi. He was a good man, loyal to his faith and flag. That was all I asked of my men...and yet, I'd allowed myself to stray so far. In Angelsong, there were portents about those who lusted for power. Stories of the kings of old, whom the Archangel destroyed for their arrogance and avarice. Was I on such a path?

Aschere sat next to me. "The Dreamer understands all tongues. But not all languages can convey what Old Paramic can. She speaks to me in an even older language, one that tongues cannot utter. And in this way, I pray for your daughter."

"You think I'll believe in her if she brings Elly back?"

"If she brings Elly back, then you cannot deny her. Then denial becomes a crime. And on the day the Dreamer is brought into our world, all souls who don't submit will be sent toward the Great Terror, wherein they will be remade in fire."

"You speak of a wrathful god." I clenched my black hand, as if it held my heart. "I love my faith. I love the Archangel. Do you know why?"

"Because you were raised to."

I shook my head. "My life hasn't been straightforward. I've lost far more than I've gained. I'd rather be raising my daughter than conquering countries, or tending my father's inn than an army. It's only the high holy hymns, and the hope they inspire, that keep me going. If you were to cut me open, you'd see nothing inside but my love for Ethos, for the religion the Archangel gave us, to guide us away from hellfire and toward paradise."

Moonlight shimmered in Aschere's zealous eyes. "I was like you, once. But it was not love for god that kept me going. It was love for my son." She looked out at the seventh sea wall, the one she'd partially destroyed, sadness in her gaze. "The tribe commanded me to carry him through the desert — alone. One day, not a drop was left in our waterskin, and he screamed and cried. No matter what I did, he wouldn't stop. So I…" Her pupils enlarged as her lips quivered. "I put him on the ground. I piled the sand on his head and body. Only his heel remained to be buried…" No matter how much she slowed her breathing, she couldn't quell the trembling. "…and then a spring burst forth, right where his heel was." She bent her neck backward, stared at the sky, and opened her mouth, as if tasting that spring water. "A cruel jinn's jape."

Hunger and thirst turn men to beasts…but to bury your son in the sand? Still, she seemed penitent, and all sins were forgivable. "Cruel? Did that spring not save your lives?"

"We drank from the water and journeyed on for several days. Then we arrived." Her pupils almost burst out of her sockets, as if in terror. "When I saw the Palace of Bones, I wished I'd buried him instead." So much stirred beneath her eyes.

I yearned to know more — to know everything about her. "What happened to you?"

"It doesn't matter. Once I completed my training, I ascended above it all. To love what is not eternal is to throw precious jewels into a fleeting tide."

"I disagree." I took her hand with my gunmetal one. The oil inside made a fire that melted her ice. "How long has it been since you held someone's hand?"

She stared into me. "A long time."

"Haven't you craved the touch of another?"

I pushed the hot oil from my gunmetal hand into her. She closed her eyes and breathed deeply. Her face twitched as she suppressed pleasure.

Then she pulled away and stood. "Hawwa is enough for me. I don't need anyone else."

A predictable reaction. Disappointing, nonetheless.

"The Archangel never ordered us to love him to the exclusion of others. Love is a holy emotion, no matter its obsession."

"When I pricked your forehead in Nixos, I saw all the women you'd bedded in your village." Oh yes, she already knew everything about me. "You wear your faith now like a raiment, but beneath it, you're the same as you were. Chasing one thing, then chasing another, and another, until the whole world is yours." She gazed into me and shook her head. "But until you love Hawwa, I'll never be."

Aschere walked away, staring only at the ground in the darkness of the night.

THOUGHTS OF LOVE and loss weighed on me as I visited Berrin in his quarters. I loved him as a brother because he'd lost as well. His family was killed and yet faith burned so brightly in him.

"Sorry, Grandmaster," he said as I entered. He stood up off his mattress. The man had never gotten used to sleeping on a raised bed. "I'm just resting briefly. I'll be preparing all night."

Candles and the moon lit the room in a faint blend of cool and warm light.

"I'm sorry for disturbing you. You've earned some respite."

Berrin kept simple quarters: a small table for meals, a grimy lantern, and a stack of books written by one bishop or another. Cards were strewn about on the floor. Each card was named for a different star, with glimmering paintings of those stars on the faces.

"Wealthy man's game — cards," I said. "At our tavern we only had dice."

"I could teach you." Berrin gathered the cards. "Zosi and I would…" He shuffled them, his gaze low.

"I miss him too." But I wouldn't mourn him, though it would grant solace. As his killer, I didn't have that right.

I inspected the book stack. At the base were tomes with wavy Sirmian or Paramic letters on the binding. Berrin noticed me glaring at them and said, "Research. I've learned much from reading their books."

I pulled out a book from the base, careful to keep the stack intact. The letters might as well have been the swirls of a daydreaming blind man. I flipped through it: full of circles and triangles, drawings of the moon and the earth and the stars. "What did you learn from this one?" I asked to humor him.

Berrin's eyes lit up. The man loved knowledge. He'd often sit with Jauz and talk about things that to my low intellect seemed the mutterings of mad men. They'd both attended great universities and possessed knowledge weightier than gold.

"A real curiosity. That book was written by a polymath named Tengis. He claims to know the next twelve eclipses."

I was right: mad mutterings. "Eclipses are a sign of the Archangel's glory. Eclipses are miracles that yet beget more miracles. No man can have prior knowledge."

Given what I'd seen, you'd think I'd be receptive. But my journey with Aschere made me cling ever more to the Archangel's truths.

"We'll find out soon. He claims there's going to be one — next month."

I slammed the book shut and handed it to Berrin, shaking my head. There was a crimson moon when we sundered the iron wall of Pendurum. That night, a Rubadi astrologer had told me the crimson moon was an emissary of the Blood Star and portended the end. I sent him away because our faith said different. That eclipse brought the miracle of a fiery victory…what would the next one bring?

I took another look at the stack of books. The wood-bound tome at the top was titled *The Tear of the Archangel: Its Description and Miracles*. Finally, something I could appreciate.

"Ever since I was a child, I dreamed of seeing the Tear of the Archangel," I said, fingering the lettering on the book's cover. "I always imagined it as a shining stone with the purest light. Sometimes I think all of this is just to fulfill a child's dreams. Tell me, what was your dream?"

"Like many children in Sirm, I wanted to be Shah."

Of course he did. I chuckled. "If I become Imperator, you won't be far off. But it seems no matter how close we get, our dreams are always in the fog ahead, forever out of reach."

He offered me a stool and slid back onto his mattress. "You know, you're not bad with words. I think you'd make a good priest."

My laughter was embarrassingly loud. "Absurd."

"I still don't know why you hate them."

I'd never told this story. But it seemed a night for firsts. "My daughter's mother, Miriam, was a sister at a convent. Dazzling place in the mountains, a day's hike from my town. When the priests learned she was with child — well — they wanted to make an example of her. There was this priest — I'll never forget him, he had one eye..." I cupped my eye as if my hand were an eyepatch. "One Eye locked Miriam in a windowless room and didn't let her out until she'd birthed. Back then, I was not the man I am now. I couldn't stand up to someone who'd been conse-crated by the Church. Nine moons later, when I came to get the baby, I finally saw Miriam again. All the light in her was gone. The last thing she said to me was, 'her name is Elaria.'

"Anyway, a short while later, I learned that One Eye had himself fathered a bastard with some wench in town. Instead of punishment, the local bishop transferred him to a seminary in another province. Tell me, does that sound like justice?"

Berrin bellowed in disgust. "It sounds like goatshit."

"That's when I looked at the world for the first time. I didn't like what I saw. It was no place to raise a child as pure and good as Elly. But I was merely an innkeeper's son whose only virtue was that he could read. And read I did, the only book any man will ever need. When I finished Angelsong, I knew then of the world I wanted to make. One united under the order of the

Twelve. Where a beggar and a lord are equal, where no man or woman is property, where good triumphs over wickedness. But is that the world I'm making?"

Berrin looked upon me, his expression stern and doubtless. "You, Micah the Metal, are the sword of the angels. You are the Opener. Only you can spread the true faith to the east and bring about the order of the Twelve. Not some priest. Not the Patriarch. Not the Imperator."

I sighed, unable to bear the weight of those words. "You're so certain about all this. It's as if you've placed your faith in me and not the Archangel."

"If you want an unthinking supplicant, know that you roasted many alive the other night. They'll turn on you, like Edmar and Zosi, because your purpose leads you out of the bounds of their comforts. But if you want someone who will help you build the world you dream of, no matter what, then look no further."

I tried to find solace in his answer. I brushed the smooth metal of my black arm and shook my head. "I appreciate it, but I don't understand it. Why follow me when there's so much at risk?"

"I have nothing left to risk but my life, and I decided long ago that my life was yours. The men loyal to you decided the same. When loyalties divide, soldiers make a calculation. Most soldiers want to be on the winning side, and you win because you do what others won't. They see you dance with darkness and know, despite their faith and all that the priests have taught, you'll be the one left standing."

"And what if I lose?"

"I've become a simple man with the years." Berrin grunted and laughed. "I'd be honored if my bloody carcass was thrown in the same ditch as yours."

Though his loyalty was reassuring, it didn't put to rest the doubts that bubbled through me. I ascended to the one place where I could find solace.

· · ·

THE COURTYARD of Angelfall lay empty. Inside, dried blood from the fighting still stained the underside of the pews and the grouting of the stone floor. The bodies had been buried and the place hurriedly cleaned, but the stench of death lingered.

I knelt at the altar. There was no likeness of the Archangel, as the sculptors hadn't finished it. It was to be made of solid gold, the Patriarch had told me, to rival the one in Nixos. They would ship it from a workshop in Hyperion, where artisans I'd captured during my conquest of Dycondi labored to create it. But the faithful did not need a likeness to worship. When we bowed, we did so with the image of the Archangel in our hearts.

We all had a personal image of him. That was the beauty of faith. I'd always imagined a pure angel, his head in the clouds and his wings august over the world. But now when I imagined the Archangel, all I could see was that floating diamond with the faces of the angels printed on it. All I imagined was the black milk that surrounded me, that went inside my bones as the mouth of Micah the angel swallowed me. I saw the eye of the starfish, its slimy body immense against the glass of a giant container, gazing fear through my veins. There was nothing more unholy, nothing darker, than that eye.

I prayed to the Archangel to save me, to spare me the trials of the Fallen. Had I not been baptized in the High Holy Sea? Was I not protected by that water until the life drained out of me? Then why had darkness cradled and nurtured me with unholy succor? Why had the darkness given me this gunmetal arm and rekindled my fire when it had gone out? Was it all a trial? Did I still have a choice?

Faith had brought me too far to turn away. Faith could be the igniter that lights the oil of ambition, so long as ambition doesn't drown out faith the way thick oil douses an infant flame. I could not let my ambition outstrip my faith, for then what would it be for? I did not mean to be a king. I did not mean to be a conqueror. I raised my sword for the Archangel alone and had brought his praises to the tongues of millions. That was why I breathed.

"Zosi...forgive me. I let my darkness consume you. Consume so many of our brothers."

I cried for forgiveness. I shouted repentance until my lungs heaved. Though the Archangel heard my silent thoughts, I wanted even the Fallen to know that I was sorry. That I would not drink from their cup anymore. I wanted to scream and rip my shirt and beat my chest, but the sensation that I was being watched overtook the sadness I felt at the state of my soul.

Aschere bathed in the darkness behind me. The full moon beamed through the stained-glass windows, but she did not grace its light.

"It is done," she said. "My prayer has been answered."

Words that I feared more than any others. And yet words that I desired more than the cleansing of my soul.

"You cannot bring the dead to life, Aschere. The Archangel will not allow it."

"He has no power except what she gives. The dream doesn't exist without the Dreamer."

"Your demons will not beguile me. My Elly is dead, and will be until the cool breeze of the Fountain quickens her soul on the Day of Resurrection."

Aschere laughed. "Your Elly is indeed dead. Hawwa's wisdom is far beyond my own. It is not Elly she brought back as a sign for you."

"What are you saying? Who did she bring back?"

Aschere emerged into the red moonlight, joy glistening off her rosy cheeks. "The sign awaits you in the great hall. Once you witness it, the line between faith and disbelief will be drawn on your soul. You will have to choose, Micah. Will you be her apostle? Will you be the Opener?"

Who waited in the great hall? I didn't want to know.

I finished my prayers.

Outside, a crimson moon stared upon the city, casting the world in red. Darkness ate at it. Low in the heavens, it seemed like a giant red eye, baring its malice upon mankind. Berrin's book was wrong — the eclipse was not next month; it was this day. What miracle would it bring?

If not Elly, then who? There was none more worthy of life than my sweet daughter. She would have been strong and noble — an angel feather plucked from a raven. And yet, it was by my wicked hand that she—

I smacked my head to still the thought. I didn't wait to admire the crimson moon and climbed down the steps of the hill. A chilly wind swept through the world. At the palace, I found the outskirts deserted. No guards at the entrance, either. And in the hallways, which had now been painted white and purple, no guards stood.

They were all in the great hall. It was full of paladins in the red and black, kneeling before the golden seat in reverence of a miracle. I waded through them, toward the one who sat upon the seat. An old man with gray hair, his body gaunt and tan. A thin hazel beard was the only bright color on him. He wore a night-gown, as if he'd just woken up. Well, he had. So this was the sign meant to move me. This was whom the Dreamer brought back from death instead of my daughter.

Imperator Heraclius gazed down at me, as he'd done all my life. He sat on the throne I'd won like it was meant for him. I climbed the dais and looked into his stern, hazel irises. He looked back at me, wordless, but with the serenity of an imperator who'd ruled longer than I'd lived. I'd treated his death as a trifle, but his resurrection I could not ignore.

He leaned forward, and in the iron tenor that only befits true kings, looked into my eyes and said, "Kneel."

25

KEVAH

Nesrin kissed Sadie on the forehead and hugged her. The overjoyed zabadar danced and hollered in the glow of the crimson moon, flowers in their hair and henna on their hands. Our faith taught eclipses were signs of Lat's power, that they brought fortune to the faithful. Sadie's return was hopefully a portent of victory to come.

Humayra stood with me on a small hill. Her auburn hair matched Sadie's, as did her amber eyes. They both had a ferocity to them, though Humayra's lay well hidden. To spirit away Micah's wife from under his nose...

She gazed at the crimson moon, whispered a prayer, then placidly looked upon her daughter in the distance. Did she not want to hug her?

"Fine girl you raised," I said.

"You think a goat herder's daughter would ever be allowed to raise a princess?"

"Fine girl you made."

"She was raised like the other children, by those miserable eunuchs. She was fed the finest food, tutored by polymaths and

343

philosophers from the eight corners of the world...and yet, look at her. Destiny pushed her into the plains because that's where she belonged."

Sadie whispered something in Nesrin's ear, and then Nesrin pointed at us. I wondered how long it'd been since Sadie saw her mother. The zabadar made way as she crossed the beach toward us.

Sadie was in tears. Humayra's cheeks tightened as she tried to contain herself. Then she sobbed and cried. Mother and daughter embraced.

"Are you well?" Humayra asked.

Sadie nodded. "I gave up praying long ago...I'd despaired of Lat's mercy...and yet, here you are."

Humayra clutched her daughter's thin wrist and frowned. "You're skinnier than a mountain monkey. Why haven't you been eating? I'll cook you something tonight."

"That's the least of our worries." Sadie laughed in between sobs. "Though I do miss the apricot pudding you used to make."

Some good had been done this day. Desiring rest before the battle, I returned to my yurt.

Kinn sat atop the brightly colored chest where I kept my battle clothes, as if laying an egg. He'd been quiet since we returned. He barely gave me a look and just stared at the embers of the stove's dying fire.

"You reunited a mother and daughter," I said. "You saved us from the Imperator. Go out there and steal someone's shoes."

"I broke the cardinal rule. The angel saw me. And now the moon is bloody!" He flapped his wings, agitated, feathers flying in all directions and disappearing when they landed. "And worse, I bruised muscles taking you both to heaven and you failed to kiss her!"

"Sadie's engaged to the future regent. I need to put her out of my mind, not deeper in it."

Recalling our trip to heaven reminded me of that eye. I didn't care for a mountain-sized jellyfish. The thousands of porous tentacles I could dismiss as merely a nightmare. But that giant human eye that pulsed fear through my soul...I tried to block from my mind. The more I tried to block it, the more I saw it, until I found myself staring at the fire, my very spirit trembling.

Nesrin strode into my yurt with roses in her braids and red henna on her neck. She carried a hookah pipe and plopped next to me. Just the distraction I needed.

"I like to ease my nerves before a scrap," she said, kumis on her breath.

"Never saw you smoke."

"And I never saw the moon so gushing. It's a night for new." She gestured with her eyebrows at the hookah. "It won't set itself up."

I took the bowl from the base of the hookah, cleaned it with a bit of water, and wiped it dry. The hashish came in a tin container and smelled of smooth cherry. I pressed a few thimblefuls into the bowl, then put the bowl into the hookah. I took embers from the stove and placed them beneath the bowl. Finally, I removed the pipe and blew into it; the ash from its previous use flew out.

I reattached the pipe and gave it to Nesrin. She bubbled the water with a deep inhale, then exhaled cherry smoke.

Kinn sniffed and his eyes enlivened. He waddled next to Nesrin and looked her up and down.

"This one is nubile," he said. "Is she married? Why don't you take her? I can whisper your name in her dreams."

"No," I said.

Nesrin glared at me. I didn't feel like explaining.

"I might do it anyway," Kinn said, "just to see what happens. I've set up many happy couples that way. You wouldn't believe how many marriages and love affairs are because of us bored shiqq."

Nesrin filled the yurt with the calming scent of cherry smoke. She passed me the pipe.

"So I heard Sadie is to marry Redbeard," she said, twirling one of her waist-length braids. "Must be hard for you."

"He has three hundred ships and thirty thousand men. I can't think of a wiser choice. She may have saved us all, and saved Kostany, by bringing him into the fold."

"That's all you care about — Kostany. But you won't get anything if we take it back."

I pointed to an empty spot above my straw mattress. "I'll get Micah's head to hang on my wall."

"You're all business, all the time." Nesrin chuckled. "But when I first saw you, you were an old man covered in your own blood and filth, digging graves with fingers swollen like cucumbers. Now look at you. You may not realize, but every unmarried woman in the camp dreams about sharing your yurt."

I let cherry smoke rest in my lungs, then blew it out. "This isn't the time for such thoughts. Tomorrow—"

"Tomorrow some of us will be dead. Our last memories will be of tonight."

I couldn't ignore what her heavy eyes said.

"Here we go." Kinn waddled toward the yurt flaps. "Anyone who tries to come in, I'll blow them into the sea!"

Nesrin took the pipe from my hands and pushed me down. She inhaled cherry smoke, then slid over me and nestled her nose over mine. I reached inside her shirt and rested my hands on smooth, slight hips.

She pushed her lips on mine and breathed the smoke out. I tasted cherries in her mouth. But her tongue had an earthy, wet taste that I liked even more. I slid my hands up her abdomen and found the softness of her breasts, then the hardness of her nipples. She tugged on my tongue. She bit my lip. I lifted her shirt off. She pushed her pants to her slender thighs.

Nesrin broke from plowing her tongue through me. She looked me in the eyes. Hers were dark and deep-set and as intense as I'd ever seen.

"I can see the sadness in you," she said. "You don't want this."

"Every part of me does. Except one."

"The one that matters most."

Nesrin got dressed.

"She's a princess of the Seluqal House and will always put duty first," she said. "Even if she might feel the same way as you."

"Does she feel the same way?"

"You're that clueless?" Nesrin laughed. "It doesn't matter. Why do you think Ebra wanted to exile her? She can make an ambitious man king. And now, one of those men has claimed her."

"Then there's nothing to be done."

"Are you completely daft?" She stared into me with all the fierceness she could muster. "Are you a warrior? Would the great warlord Utay have sulked like you? He would have taken what he wanted, whatever it was."

"What I want is to kill Micah."

"You can only kill a man once. What will you want afterward? Have you given it a thought?"

"What I'll want afterward doesn't matter."

"It will." Now Nesrin looked upon me with pity. "You will want her. But it will be too late. She will honor her pledge and marry another."

"I came to this land as a slave. I, least of all, deserve her."

Pity gone, her cheeks turned fiery red. "Did Micah deserve Kostany? Who cares, he took it. But you're no conqueror. You're the same scared old man we rescued in the forest. Scared of everything that isn't death."

She stormed out. Kinn waddled in, as disappointed as ever. I slept a few hours.

· · ·

I WOKE before dawn and rode to the Crucian camp. Earless horses grazed by a pond. A group of excubitors, with the yellow hair and beards of Thamesian northerners, sharpened axes and swords at spinning grindstones they mechanized with their feet. The four eyes in a diamond sigil adorned their armor, as it did the armor of the Imperator.

I found Imperator Josias with the bombards. They were as large as the ones Shah Jalal used against his father Heraclius during our conquests in Yuna. It seemed they'd learned that with siege engines, the bigger the stronger. Encased in fresh gray metal, each bombard was the size of two horses. The cannonballs were larger than my torso.

The Imperator sat on a muscled, white steed. "What did your diviners say about the eclipse?" He bit into an apple redder than blood.

"We don't have any with us. But I know it augured victory."

"Ours say the crimson moon brings miracles. But it wasn't a miracle my scouts reported early this morning." He spat out a bit of apple at my feet. "You neglected to tell me about Redbeard."

"I didn't know myself until late last night."

"The man is a corsair who plunders our towns and then turns tail. I'm now forced to keep an eye on my back as I go forward. Redbeard would see us throw ourselves at the city and himself barely lift a finger. Then when we are spent, he will swoop in and take it. Do you think me a fool?"

"It's our city, Imperator. We've had it for three hundred years."

"And we had it for seven hundred before that."

"I will ensure Redbeard does his part. I doubt we'd succeed with your swords alone."

The Imperator puffed his chest and hung his chin high in the air. "I'll be keeping count. If I sense him doing anything false, our alliance will be at an end."

"Then your daughter's life will end. Don't think I won't bring you her head."

"Don't think I prize her life more than Kostany. Any man can father a daughter. Only the greatest can rule the largest empire on this side of the earth. Don't doubt who I am."

That only made me doubt him more. But the greatest doubt was upon me: was I a "good man" as Aicard claimed, or would I do what had been done to me? I shuddered at the thought of cutting into that polite, rosy-cheeked girl's throat. War urged savagery, but vengeance oft demanded it.

Shortly after, the Imperator ordered the march, so I returned to the zabadar camp. Sadie had put the zabadar into formation and took the lead on her pink-bellied horse. We were to do what zabadar did best: attack and retreat. If Micah sent flankers out the walls, we had to be ready to counter. With battle-hardness, fresh guns and bows, and Kashanese horses, I had no doubt we would prove crucial to the success of this siege.

Sadie looked radiant. She tied her hair into a knot and wore mail of hardened red leather, buckled tight on her chest. A pair of brown gloves had a parched, smooth look and would assist her in drawing her composite bow.

I tried not to smile too widely as I trotted next to her. "You know, I'm still dizzy."

"I threw up three times last night." She rubbed her stomach. "Definitely worth it."

"So how'd your mother take the news that you're to marry a fifty-year-old man?"

"He's forty-four. She didn't like it."

"Should've offered yourself to the Alanyan prince. He had a bigger army, as well as youth and good looks."

"Too bad Ebra married him first."

I laughed at the thought. "They do seem good for each other. A pair of 'well-fed ninnies', my father would say."

The rider to my left tossed an apricot over my head. The rider to my right caught it, chomped down, and gave the rest to his horse. Talking to Sadie, it was easy to forget we were in a sea of zabadar.

"What kind of man was your father?" she asked.

"Tengis was a man of many talents, which your father and grandfather liked to squeeze as if he were an orange to be juiced."

"Why do you call him father, anyway? Wasn't he your teacher?"

"A teacher is the closest thing a janissary has to a father, especially when that teacher cares for you as he'd care for a son. I pray he's survived — somewhere, somehow. I must avenge Melodi, not just for myself but for him."

Sadie glared at me. "You still haven't told me, Kevah."

"Told you what?"

"What did you see on the boat?"

I stopped my horse. Sadie stopped too. The zabadar horde trotted past us. I closed my eyes and tried to picture what the giant jellyfish's eye showed me. But they had no colors or sounds or shapes. Only terror — pure.

"I saw the eye of Ahriyya. It whispered to me…but I can't describe what it showed me. I can only feel what it's done to my mind, to my soul."

"I wish I could've seen it too." Sadie trotted closer and rested her hand on mine.

"I would not wish such a thing even on Micah the Metal."

"I don't want you to suffer alone."

"I put this mask on. I've no choice but to see what it's unveiled. Besides, I imagine you'll suffer plenty when you're the wife of the Regent."

"We'll both suffer alone, then. We should have taken that boat and gone elsewhere."

"It's too late for that," I said. "But one day, when you're staring out the tower of your castle, and I'm lost in the caves of Holy Zelthuriya, we can imagine that we did."

We trotted on. I wanted to laugh at our sacrifices, but they seemed too serious on a day when so many lives could end.

"Where would we have gone, anyway?" I asked.

"Anywhere. Everywhere." Seeing Sadie smile was like swallowing a mouthful of honey. "Just not Kostany."

I smirked. "Maybe I'll see you 'anywhere' and 'everywhere,' someday."

"We'll have to survive this day first."

"You won't be dying today. I've let enough people I love die."

Sadie's voice hoarsened. "And in what way do you love me?"

I toyed with various answers. Perhaps I loved her as my princess or my khatun — or better yet, as a dear friend. But my heart spoke first.

"The wrong way."

Sadie fell silent. At least she'd heard it from me. I trotted forward with the rest of the zabadar, my heart the heaviest thing on me.

THE WALL of Kostany came into view. It was twice as tall as any other on the continent. That didn't make it stronger, but it doubled the distance you had to stay clear to avoid its cannons and arrows. It seemed Micah had plated the areas closest to the strait and around the gates in iron. Those gates were made of ten-inch thick steel, utterly impossible to pound through.

Few showed it, but all were afraid. Even the hardiest zabadar, the cockiest excubitor, or the most-seasoned janissary would feel tremors in their hearts looking upon that wall. Nothing killed like a determined heap of stone. The zabadar around me raised their hands, begging their saints to take their prayers to Lat. I preferred to save my prayers for the moment of the fight, my heart shaking, because that's when they were truly earnest.

An oppressive midday sun beat down. These Crucians, no doubt accustomed to northwestern climates, must not have liked it much. But if they wanted shade, I hoped the Imperator made clear they could only find it within the wall we needed to break.

The Imperator kept his heavy cavalry on the left. These knights wielded lances and longswords, and even the horses wore plate. But he didn't have as many gunners as I expected. They formed the frontline, and the guns didn't look different from what Imperator Heraclius used fifteen years ago. They wouldn't fare well against Micah's fast-firing guns.

Engineers began constructing stone walls on the shore. If it rained, these lowlands would get swept by muddy water, and that would be a disaster we could ill-afford. The walls would hopefully block the strait from overflowing.

Sadie positioned the zabadar on a hill southeast. If Micah sent out cavalry from the southern gate, it would be the zabadar's task to engage so they couldn't hit the Imperator's exposed right.

Word came that Redbeard had begun landfall and was bringing a force of forty thousand to the field. He could occupy the hill we were on and attack the southern wall. Faced with a barrage on two sides, Micah would have to divide his force, and that could prove decisive if fortune went our way.

No doubt, the question of who would control the city lingered in the back of everyone's mind. Allies would become enemies once the wall fell. Sieges were easy compared to a street-to-street, house-to-house struggle for control. What awaited us, should the siege succeed, was far messier and horrific. But that bloodbath was months, if not years, away.

"Doesn't that seem odd to you?" Sadie squinted and pointed at the walls.

The battlements were empty of defenders.

Sadie continued, "Usually when an army creeps upon your city, you fill your walls with archers and gunners and militia and anyone who can hold a bow, gun, or throw a bomb."

"Something is amiss. I'll consult with Josias."

I began to trot away.

"Kevah, wait," Sadie called, her voice hoarse and trying. Her hand trembled. "I..." She squeezed it and it stilled. "Just...be safe."

I galloped down the hill toward the Crucian camp.

Imperator Josias stood amid white and purple tents adorned with his insignia. Around him were his commanders, who themselves wore white and purple armor, but with shinier metals than the average soldier. Once again, the excubitors blocked my approach with their pikes and guns. The Imperator shouted to let me through.

"Do you notice these undefended walls?" I said as I jumped off my horse.

Rone of Sempuris pressed his gray mustache and answered before the Imperator could. "Of course. And have you noticed the ditch that Micah built, full of metal bits? He means for us to approach the walls, then he'll light his bombs and we'll all be picking metal out of our flesh for the rest of the year."

"You think it's a trick?"

"Why else would the walls be unmanned?"

"Perhaps his paladins don't want to fight yours."

The Imperator silenced Rone with his hand and said, "Unlikely. He butchered all the paladins that would have rallied to my cause."

"By the way," Rone said to me, "have you any of that Sirmian drink in your camp — what do you call it — *fermented barley water*?"

I could certainly have used some barley water to steady my nerves. I pointed at Kostany. "Plenty of the stuff in there, last I checked."

Rone's eyes lit up. "Another reason to bring down those walls, posthaste. You know, I did enjoy it once on a diplomatic mission to Ejaz. Relaxing concoction, I must say. You Sirmians do know how to brew."

I supposed I could spare a minute to chatter with this strange

Crucian man. "We've no shortage of the zabadar drink — fermented mare's milk."

Rone grunted in disgust. "The Rubadi make the same. Not to my taste, not at all."

Meanwhile, Josias shook his head and turned away. All business, all the time, it seemed.

"I thought so too," I said, "but the kumis grew on me."

"Hmph. I'm an old man with set tastes. Now, have you ever tried the Rastergani drink?"

"Once or twice. Far too gingery."

Rone's whiskers flared in shock. "In Sempuris we say that ginger is the angels' root."

How could an angel have a root? Were they trees, now? Bizarre.

"I do like ginger, just not in that amount."

As we talked, grating sounds came from the western gate. Its portcullis was being raised.

"Does Micah mean to fight us in the field?" I said. "Is that why the walls are empty?"

"Or perhaps he wishes to parley," Rone said. "They tremble before the resolve of the Imperator!"

The gate stood open. A single rider galloped out on a rusty-colored steed. He wore the black and red of Micah's paladins. His gray hair flapped in the wind; I'd think he were a man of age, but he rode the horse as a young zabadar would, his body forward as the horse charged.

The soldiers in the vanguard opened the way for him to reach our camp. As he galloped by, they watched with awe, as if he were one of their angels made flesh.

The genuflections of the excubitors as he rode past startled me. It seemed to frighten Josias, who gazed with bulging eyes at the man, seemingly shocked at the reverence his army showed.

Now there was clamor as soldiers talked among each other like gossiping girls. When the man pulled the reins and halted his horse at our position, I swore to myself that I'd seen him before. He descended with the swiftness of wind and landed with the grace of a holy warrior. I knew this man, I realized. I knew this man long ago.

"Did the crimson moon bring this?" Josias said. "Or did sorcery?"

The lords that Josias had assembled stared motionless, mouths hanging, as the gray-haired man walked past them. He stood in front of Josias and looked upon him with eyes of iron, the lines on his chiseled face hard as steel. I'd seen this man when he was younger. I'd seen him at the head of armies. I'd seen him outside Rastergan, as his bombards pounded us. I'd met him in the fields of Yuna, almost a lifetime ago.

The man was Heraclius the Hated, the deceased Imperator of Crucis. I didn't understand his Crucian words, but he spoke them with a tone of certainty that even Shah Jalal never reached. While I watched, Kinn glided out of the sky and fluttered near my ears.

Kinn said, "He's telling them he came back from the dead!"

"You understand Crucian?"

"Of course. I spent much time in Crucian-speaking villages. Their shoes may be plain, but they use some of the hardiest leathers."

"What's he saying?"

Kinn whispered into my ear what the man said.

"The Archangel has made me a sign unto you all," Heraclius said. "He brought me back, beneath the crimson moon, to sit upon the holy throne of Kostany."

"This is sorcery," Josias responded. "The dead cannot come back."

"What's that, son? Speak up!" Heraclius walked toward his son with one hand on the hilt of a silver sword. "A true believer knows the difference between a sign of the Archangel and the guiles of sorcery."

"I bathed my father's body." Josias seethed and clenched his teeth. "I buried him myself!"

"What did I say the last time we spoke? I said that you would rule a larger empire than me, but because you hadn't won any of it, your heir would rule a hamlet."

Josias backed away, trembling.

"And Rone!" Heraclius turned to face Rone, who stared back like a lost child. "What did I say to you at your grandson's wedding? Did I not complain about the taxes you'd collected that year? And did you not complain that the pox had spread through your lands?"

"That is as it went," Rone said. "You are the image of our Lord Imperator. By the angels, is it really you, Adronikos?"

"Indeed, I am sent to test your faith. And what about my faithful excubitors?" Heraclius continued. "You who are supposed to taste every morsel before it goes down my gullet. Which one of you died from the poison that killed me? Or was it in fact one of you who administered that poison?"

The excubitors knelt. Perhaps for these simple-minded outlanders, just the sight of Heraclius, not even a day after witnessing an eclipse, was enough to believe. I, however, suspected something else.

I asked Kinn, "Is he a jinn?"

Kinn fluttered toward Heraclius, flew around his head, sniffed him, and returned.

"That's a man," Kinn said. "The eyes are a man's eyes. The smell is a man's smell. A shapeshifter couldn't do this."

None of it made sense. I needed to tell Sadie about this. I jumped onto my horse.

"Where are you going?" Heraclius pointed at me. He spoke Sirmian without a hint of accent. "Disguise yourself in horseman's attire, but I know a janissary when I see one."

The excubitors surrounded me, brandishing axes and maces.

"I'm here to help retake Kostany," I said. "Let me go back to my people."

All the archers and gunners aimed at me.

"Retake Kostany?" Heraclius scoffed. "The city is open! All are welcome, provided they submit to my rule. Is that what you mean to tell your zabadar on the hill?"

"And what of Micah the Metal?" I asked.

Heraclius' laugh was like the plucking of iron strings. "I sent Micah to ponder his sins in the dungeon. There are repercussions for burning and imprisoning holy men, stealing my granddaughter, and waging war against my son."

Kinn fluttered near my ears and continued translating.

Josias breathed deeply, then said, "But all of that happened... because of your death."

"Yes, I've been dead a while. But the angels told me everything." Heraclius unsheathed his silver sword and pointed it at me. "You'll not be taking Kostany as long as I'm alive, which may be a long time, seeing as I was just rebirthed. Go and tell Redbeard as much."

I was about to spur my horse when Josias shouted, "He's not allowed to leave. He'll kill Celene!"

"She's already dead," Heraclius replied. "Or rather, she will be. In all my years, the Sirmians have never let treachery go unpunished."

"I have Shah Murad onboard my flagship," Josias said. "I had intended to trade him for her but was waiting for the right moment, once we'd seized the upper hand."

Heraclius raised his eyebrows and nodded as if impressed. "Hmm...a clever gambit. But if he's on your flagship, Redbeard might attempt a rescue. Better he doesn't find out."

Rone came close to Heraclius, as if he needed to inhale the man's essence. "It is not just his image. I have known him since we were youths, drinking and debating philosophy amid the wine gardens of Lemnos. You have his mind. You are either a ghost...or you are Adronikos Heraclius Saturnus, Lord Imperator of Holy Crucis, in the flesh." He dropped to his knees, trembling. "The crimson moon has brought us a miracle! Archangel be praised!"

"Archangel be praised!" The chant rippled through the entire army. Everyone looked to the sky in praise of these angels that supposedly brought back a dead man. And then, as worldly matters returned to concern, all eyes were on me, a disbeliever in a faithful sea. Guns and sharp steel surrounded me. No way through, so I climbed off my horse.

Kinn stopped translating and said, "Too many guns and arrows. You'll die if I try to fly you out."

I focused and said the only thing that mattered, "Make sure Redbeard knows that Shah Murad is on the Imperator's flagship. He can't let that ship sail through the strait, beyond the sea walls. And Kinn...keep Sadie safe."

"Leave it to me." Kinn soared into the air and flew toward the coast.

"Talking to the wind, janissary?" Heraclius approached, sword forward.

"The wind's on our side, dead man."

I looked upon the distant hill where Sadie and the zabadar waited.

"Worried about your friends? Don't be — we'll get the message to them."

Heraclius shouted something in Crucian. A horn sounded. The surge of armored cavalry shook the earth. They charged toward Sadie's position.

An excubitor threw a sack over my head. I struggled to free myself, but more excubitors grabbed me, and now a rope leashed my arms. They tied the rope around me and I fell to the ground, writhing in place.

"There's a cell in the dungeon just for you, janissary," Heraclius said. "You and Micah can rot together."

26

MICAH

THEY THREW SOME ZABADAR WITH A SACK OVER HIS HEAD IN THE cell across from me. What was the logic in taking prisoners? The zabadar knew what I'd done to the prisoners after Kostany fell, including how I slaughtered the Shah's family, so they killed every paladin they captured. They even massacred the Ethosian villagers that they didn't enslave. Surrender was not an option for anyone; I made sure of that. That way, it was cleaner. A fight to the death — how war ought to be.

I wondered what Heraclius would do with Berrin, Aicard, and Jauz. He never liked Berrin and saw him as a shifty Sirmian who converted out of spite. Aicard was slinky enough to get by. Would Jauz serve a man so deluged in vainglory? Heraclius was as pompous as he was accomplished. I didn't know if he delighted in showing superiority or just believed it was how things ought to be.

So there I sat, next to a pile of hay. Maggots coursed through the hay the way lice courses through hair. Subjected to this because I refused to kneel to the man on my throne. To a man that should be dead. To a man that was dead when I conquered this city. And yet, Heraclius knew things that had happened while he was dead, as if someone had whispered to his soul while it waited in Baladict. He even knew it was the Patriarch who'd poisoned him. Despite this, he freed the Patriarch and threw me in his cell instead. It was as if he'd been resurrected to slight me and destroy everything I'd worked for.

Aschere had said a *"line would be drawn on my soul."* But really, it had been drawn on the souls of my paladins. Now Heraclius could claim an apostle's miracle and wield both earthly and divine authority, unlike any imperator before. It forced those loyal to me to choose between faith and country on one side and their grandmaster on the other. An obvious choice for even the most obvious fool. Now they would never be free, in lands of their own. I lamented my shattered promise.

Thus ended the story of Micah the Metal. I wanted to close my eyes and drift away, but the zabadar was screaming in Sirmian. He'd managed to get the bag off his head and now stared at me, enraged.

"Micah!" he shouted along with some Sirmian nonsense. "Micah!"

He banged against the iron bars. He kicked them. He shook them every way. But there was no breaking through. I'd pounded them with my metal hand earlier, to no avail.

"Micah!"

What had I done to this poor fellow? He was a curly-haired and dark-eyed man with a distinct Ruthenian look. I'd never met a Ruthenian who didn't like to scowl. Even as he calmed and rested his back, he wouldn't take his eyes off me. It was touching to be so loved by someone, but we didn't share a language, so our courtship would have to wait.

I closed my eyes and thought of Elly — the demon Elly, with black-on-black eyes, who smelled of lilies and nothing else. Seeing her was the happiest moment of my life because even though I knew it wasn't her, I let myself believe it. That's why faith made so many happy, too. But just like black-eyed Elly, I now realized that my faith was a skin of truth piled onto a body of falsehood. It was a tunnel lit by a dismal light and the deeper you went, the more lost you got.

If the Archangel was real, then where was he when I drowned the Shah's three-year-old daughter? A just, true, and good god would have stopped me, for the sake of her soul and mine. And yet, it was in that moment when I'd finally felt I avenged Elly, only for the anger to rekindle. And that anger still raged within, but now I had no one to blame but myself.

The young Ruthenian fell asleep. Even anger needed rest. Maybe I needed sleep too. Maybe in the darkness, Elly would visit. More likely, she'd already gotten what she wanted and I was alone. Except for one person, whom I knew would come, if only to check on the line she'd drawn on my soul.

"Why?" I said to Aschere as soon as she arrived at my cell.

She looked down on me, her face a blank slate. How could this girl be the only one who knew god? How were the rest of us, whether Latians or Ethosians or worshippers of some wheel, so deluded?

"Why what?"

"Why didn't she bring my Elly back!? My Elly was full of light and would have lived a good, full life. Instead, she brought back a man at the end of his years, who clings to his throne the way fungus clings to feet."

"If she brought Elly back, what would you have done?"

"I would've loved her! She would've loved me. There would be another good soul to enlighten this world instead of one that sucks light out of everything."

As we argued, the Ruthenian snored softly.

"You would've become weak." Aschere lowered her gaze and sighed. "You would've clung to this broken world even more than you already do." She looked me in the eye. "Come with me to the Dreamer, and we'll fix everything."

"By doing what? By burning the sin off the world? By freezing it to death? I don't want to be a part of it. I won't be manipulated anymore by vengeful gods!"

"The Dreamer doesn't want to kill her creatures. She wants to create. She wants to dream so much more, so many new creatures, and she wants us all to share this world. Together, you and I will be the apostles that make it possible."

Like those things in the floating diamond. Like the peacock with the human head. Like the starfish with the human eye. I wanted no more of that in my world. But Aschere surely did. The light of faith gushed out of her when she spoke of her god.

"You've made a huge mistake, Aschere. I am not the apostle you seek. I refuse to be. I would rather die and be forgotten than be remembered as a prophet of your god."

"The Dreamer stripped you bare, took everything, so you had nothing left to lose. She prepared you for this, from the moment you were born. You are the Opener."

"I'm not! I reject your god! I reject my god too, for the part he played in all this! I reject all the gods! If there will be a god, then I will make one myself. I will build one from metal if I must, a better god, one worthy of worship. But that god will be nothing like the one you showed me!"

My shouts woke the Ruthenian. He stood against the iron bars, mouth agape in wonder. But it was not me he gazed at. He fixed his dark eyes on Aschere, then trembled and whispered something. Aschere turned and whispered something back.

A guard had heard my shouting. He ran down the corridor. Aschere touched his cheek, and he collapsed on the ground with icicles for eyes.

"I will not leave you, Micah," Aschere said. "I will wait for your heart to digest the truth."

"You said we all get to choose. That's what I'm doing. I'm choosing to stay here, to be punished by men I fought and served with...for my many crimes, rather than go with you to god."

"I won't give up on you." Aschere put her hand through the bars. "Let me touch you."

I grasped her hand with my gunmetal one. But the fire within had withered. Now her touch made it cold, and that cold crept from my hand, up my arm, and to my shoulders. Still, I did not let go. Though I despised her god, I liked her, more every time I saw her. Behind all the preaching and sorcery was a woman with a heart as shattered as my own.

But then the cold reached my face and stung my brain. I recoiled and left her hand dangling.

"Why does that happen, Aschere? Why do you spread cold with your touch?"

She almost smiled — the kind of slight smile that masked sadness. Still, I'd take any kind of smile on that face.

"It's a curse placed on me by the Marid tribe of the jinn," she said. "So I would never be loved."

"Why'd they do it?"

"Because I turned away from them. Because I made a pact with the jinn of the Deep, who dwell within Labyrinthos."

"Why?" I almost reached to cover my ears, as if I were a child trying to drown out a frightening tale. "Why make a pact with demons?"

"The same reason you did. To get what I want."

"And what is it you want?"

"I'm not like you — I don't want power. I'm not like this broken man." She turned to the Ruthenian. He was still staring at her, but now he was crying. "I don't want love. Nor vengeance. Nor redemption. All I want is the truth."

"Then you're not like anyone I know. Truth to the rest of us is something to bend and shape, like metal, into whatever suits our purpose."

"When truth becomes your purpose, all else falls away. I could already see beyond the veil of the unseen, just like you can now. But that only created more questions. Who were these jinn that controlled wind and fire and water? Where did they come from? We feared them, but what did they fear? And what did those they feared, fear? Whom do the angels fear, Micah?"

"Why would the angels fear anyone?"

"Everyone fears their creator."

"Then whom does the creator fear?"

"The Dreamer fears no one."

"Are you so sure?" I asked. "If she dreamed us into existence, then what does she want with us?"

"I don't have all the answers. But I know if I follow this path, I will get them."

"What if there are no answers?" I laughed to distract from the dread spreading through me. "What if the world is as dismal as it seems?"

"Then at least we'll know it. We won't be lying to ourselves. We'll drown in the truth, our eyes wide open."

She spoke with such sincerity. Her face shone with faith and her eyes glimmered like a smitten girl.

"I wish you and I had met in a different time, different place," I said. "Can you imagine it? What if we were a pair of minstrels, traveling the world, uplifting hearts with our songs? How fun. Or perhaps we were birds that met somewhere in the sky, so high above everything that the world and all its miseries ceased to exist." I prepared to say what I really wanted. "Truth is, I may not like your god, Aschere. But I like you."

"You don't have to like her. She brought a dead man back. She is greater than anything we know. Should we find something greater along the way, I promise you, we'll seek the truth rather than cling to falsehood."

The Ruthenian's sobs grated. I wondered what he was mumbling.

"I'm not so different from him," I said. "I cry a lot, too. I'm moved more by love than truth, and I can't serve a god I don't love."

Aschere said something in Sirmian to the crying man. Her words caused him to hunch over and crumble.

"Hawwa must have brought him here, too, for a reason. It cannot be a coincidence."

"Who is he?"

"He is a magus who has not yet learned to use his power, otherwise he wouldn't be stuck here."

"Why the hell is he crying?"

"It's a long and sad tale," Aschere said.

"Does it look like I'm in a hurry?"

"You may not believe it."

"I saw an imperator come back from death. I saw a black star shoot out a fireball that roasted men alive. I traveled hundreds of miles through a tunnel—"

"You've made your point." She sighed in defeat. "I told him where his wife is."

The Ruthenian reached out through the iron bars. But Aschere did not touch him. I realized I knew nothing about her. All I knew was that she'd lost a son.

"So you'll find his wife," I complained, "but not mine."

"His wife is a bit easier to find."

"And why is that?"

Aschere's pupils shrunk. She stared at the ground, where sad memories seemed to play. "Because she's standing right in front of you."

27

HERACLIUS

THE ARCHANGEL BROUGHT ME BACK FOR A PURPOSE, NOT TO SIT around in Kostany. Yes, it was my throne, the holy city of the Ethosians, and would be the center of the empire I would build. To build that empire, I'd have to bring my army to the gates of other cities. But first, I'd have to crush the wretches at the gates of mine.

A man who lives a second time doesn't have patience for sieges. Doesn't have patience at all. Though I'd come back, I was old, and it would take a tub of dye to cover my gray hair. I'd have to swat pests like Redbeard to achieve my destiny.

My eldest Alexios — crowned with the name Josias — was youthful but was only my eldest because his older brothers died, one to dreaded consumption, coughing flesh and bile till he stilled, and the other from an arrow to the eye. A janissary fired that fateful arrow during Shah Jalal's invasion of our lands, outside the walls of treacherous Rastergan, as my son led a charge at a part of the wall we'd collapsed.

Far from that bloody battlefield, now I sat upon the golden seat of Kostany — the first imperator to do so in three hundred years. I had dreamed of this day, prayed for this day, died for this day. Everything I'd done during my long reign was to strengthen Crucis so we could smash the Sirmians and retake this great hall, which the Patriarch had redecorated in the Crucian colors of white and purple. Paintings of the angels Cessiel, Principus, and Micah surrounded us. Here, I spoke with my son.

"Redbeard made landfall with forty thousand troops," Alexios said. "We are surrounded."

My son eyed me as you would a bear on a mountainside: afraid, but uncertain if the animal meant harm. That depended — would he submit?

"Have you not come to terms with this miracle, Alexios?"

He obviously preferred to sit on this golden throne rather than stand beneath it.

"The Sirmians are known for sorcery," he said.

"And you think me a Sirmian machination? Come closer."

He stepped on the dais.

"Closer," I said.

He came close enough to smell me and see the spots on my neck.

"I washed your body," my son said. "I saw you entombed."

"And I saw Baladict. I remember where they kept my soul. Imagine the sun. Take a piece of it and mold that into a castle. Now imagine that castle is beyond the sky, beyond every heaven, in a place unknowable. The angels came to me there and spoke of all that had happened to the Imperium, to Kostany, to you. They always meant to bring me back."

My son turned away. Of course, it hurt that I'd taken over. Had my father done the same, I would have pulled out his innards, although my father was never Imperator. I was of low-noble blood and married the former imperator's cousin, so I understood the yearnings of ambition and felt them more acutely than my son, who tended to obey his father: a trait I appreciated but struggled to admire.

The lieutenants that assembled were from Alexios' excubitors, Micah's paladins, and the regular army. They sat at white marble tables that the Shah used when entertaining western guests. Together, we discussed how to break the siege.

"It's well past dawn," I said. "Why aren't they shooting the walls?"

The leader of Alexios' heavy cavaliers looked more statue than man. Chiseled and hard, not just on the body but on the face. He wore armor that must've weighed more than many men.

"We hit them earlier," he said. "They were slow to react. Perhaps they lack a leader."

"It would be Redbeard, would it not?" asked Rone, my childhood companion and steady ally, at least in every matter other than the overdue taxes of his fiefs. I was planning to make an example of him before I died...truthfully, I was surprised it wasn't Rone that had me poisoned. But taxes were a trifle compared to the present challenge, and I had little patience for trifles since resurrecting.

Alexios shook his head and said, "My flagship did not make it to the city. That means they've captured it and the prisoner I kept there — Shah Murad."

"You foolishly left your ships undermanned," I said, "despite knowing Redbeard was coming. You turned your back on a rabid cur. A blunder I never would have made."

Alexios seethed in silence. Had the weight of the Imperium not wizened him up? No matter — I would have to.

"In what state did you leave the Shah?" I asked.

"I treated him as a guest, as our faith teaches," Alexios said. "I fed him. I allowed him his prayers and gave him decent lodging."

"Then he would be their leader," I said. "Murad and Redbeard are no fools. They know the larders here are bare, that's why they're fighting on, despite that we outnumber them."

A cannon shot sounded and whined through the air. It hit the city wall with a faint crack and rumble. We all waited for the next one and soon they followed in rhythm.

"I expect the cavaliers to put a stop to that," I said. "Do not allow them rest because they won't give us that comfort. We will not starve in this city. We have the numbers. Open the gates and rout them."

My lieutenants fell silent. Good. It was time for great deeds, not words.

"They have Celene," Alexios said. "Our priority must be to get her back."

"Why, Josias?" I made sure to use his crowned name. One day, he would reign and needed the reverence of his men. "Why is it a priority? She swore herself to celibacy, your daughter. Her marriage to Micah is voided, and she cannot marry another."

"She is my daughter," my son said.

"And you are my son and heir, but I'd still throw you out there just the same because kings do not keep thrones by cowering behind them. We end the siege first. Then, we can parley for her release from a position of strength."

I dismissed everyone and traveled by carriage to the land wall to watch the battle. Cannon shots glowed and roared. Redbeard had assailed many of our coastal towns with his monstrous bombards. They didn't have strong walls, so the bombards would break them within hours. Redbeard would kill, pillage, and enslave. I often wondered how these Sirmians had a god.

The corsair's flag waved in the distant wind. How proud he was of that standard. He'd litter the towns he sacked with it: the scimitar beneath the eight-pointed star, said to symbolize the eight points of the world. But any fool knows that the world has four points, so how did they conceive the other four? I once asked a wise man in my court that question. The world of the jinn, apparently, constitutes the other four points. What a heap of nonsense.

Sieges are dull, but I enjoyed the view. I marveled at how the enemy filled every flat land between the sea and hills. And yet, we had more than they. Soon our sorties would begin. I looked forward to defeating Shah Murad.

I'd enjoyed cordial relations with the man. Peace on my eastern border allowed me to expand north, west, and south. I added Dycondi, Pendurum, Pasgard, Ejaz, and other great nations to my own. A wise king takes advantage of peace on one front to make war on others, something the Shah had failed to do. This siege would be another failure he'd rue.

Our heavy cavalry began their sorties as I enjoyed a glass of Lemnosian wine. Lemnos is a gorgeous, hilly region north of Hyperion. I spent several years there in my youth, under the tutelage of the local exarch. Drank more wine than I cared to admit. Good of Alexios to have brought some.

The wine tasted all the sweeter as our heavy cavalry routed the zabadar. The armor that covered our horses was mighty steel from the mines of Camok. Not a place I cared to go, no wineries, but settled by a hardworking and indispensable people. Whatever guns the Sirmians used, they had trouble breaking the armor at a distance, and a thunderous cavalry charge sent their gunners scurrying to the back of their lines.

Using hurled bombs, we destroyed several of their cannons, too. Our heavy cavalry pulled back to the gates and inside the walls just when the Sirmian lines started to reform and rebuff. Perfect.

I TIRED of battle and strolled through the gardens. The Seluqal House was renowned for their pleasure gardens and the birds that sang in them. But Micah had not maintained them. I'm sure he didn't have an inkling how. Overgrown bushes crowded the pathways and shrubs stuck out like an unkempt beard. They hadn't even trimmed the trees, though that made them better nests for birds. Beautiful black drongos perched on the highest branches. When the siege was over, I'd have to make this garden fitting for pleasantry.

Next, I visited Angelfall. The Patriarch held a vigil in the holy halls, and supplicants sat in the pews and hymned. He preached what I told him to preach if he wanted to live.

"The Archangel brought us a sign beneath the crimson moon," the Patriarch said at his pulpit. The poor fellow had no fingernails and the tips of his fingers were swollen like grapes. Half an ear was gone, too. "He has made faith an easy choice for us all. The flesh and soul of our imperator have been brought back to this world, so he can lead us in a final battle against the wicked infidels of the east."

After his sermon, we met in the chapel's crypt. A dusty place. The Latians had replaced our apostles' coffins and holy relics with Paramic books and scrolls. Nothing disappointed more than hearing that our holiest relic, the Tear of the Archangel, was missing.

"Have you learned where they took it?" I asked.

Patriarch Lazar was proof that age doesn't diminish ambition. Oh, I knew he gave the order to poison me. A holy duty, he'd told the excubitor who did it. But I didn't come back for vengeance. I enjoyed punishing treachery and had done so in ways some would describe as cruel, but most of all, I enjoyed putting men on the path to redemption. I would redeem the Patriarch first and then get to Micah, for whom I still had great plans.

"Lord Imperator," the Patriarch said, "my priority is to find the Tear. My priests have poured through this room and all its contents, and we have discovered where they sent it."

"Where?"

"They did send it to Zelthuriya, as we expected. But then, for some reason, they moved it to Tagkalay, to the vaults of their great university."

"Good, it's not as far away. They say that the Tear can scorch the darkness and shield a holy warrior from sorcery. I believe it is meant for me and that the Archangel shall guide me to it."

"I'm afraid it's not that simple. Several traders have reported that there was an uprising in Tagkalay after Kostany fell. The vaults were plundered and now sit empty."

"Not very good vaults, then." I guffawed, hoping to bring some color to the Patriarch's face.

He managed a weak smile. "Not at all, my Lord." His gaze wouldn't leave the floor, as if too ashamed to look me in the eye.

"My son thinks you're innocent of all this," I said. "He thinks Micah forced you to marry his daughter, though we both know the idea was yours. I have not yet told him, nor anyone else, that you had me poisoned. I will lock up these secrets in my own heart, Patriarch."

"Your mercy is, as ever, inspired by the Archangel's own."

"But you must not cease your ministry. My son doesn't believe I've come back. He clings to the notion that I'm the work of sorcery. Now, Rone and the holy warriors have eaten it up, but the other nobles at court will be, like my son, more suspicious."

"I will not cease to proclaim the miracle of your resurrection until your name rings in the hearts of all Ethosians."

Tears poured down his cheeks. I hardly cared if they were real.

I AWOKE the next day to a breakfast of fried okra cakes in bitter verjuice sauce. Yet another reason to break this siege. The reports of the night's skirmishes left me pleasantly optimistic. First, we shot rockets that exploded with maddening screams at their camp, so they'd get no rest. After a few hours of that, we assailed them with heavy cavaliers and Rubadi light cavalry.

Ah, the Rubadi. Hundreds of years ago, they surged through the plains and invaded Crucis from the northeast. Decades of fighting got us nowhere, so we resettled them in the less populated regions of the Imperium. They were cousins of the zabadar by blood and just as fierce and skilled on horseback. Though they converted to our religion, they combined it with elements of their old one, and many bishops insisted they were still unbelievers because of how heterodox it was. Some Rubadi tribes even preferred to worship the angel Saklas because he, with his tree-like limbs, resembled their earth god from the Waste.

What did I care how a man worshiped? I did care whom a man worshiped, but I cared far more how a man fought. And the Rubadi were skilled, though lacked discipline.

We sent ten thousand Rubadi, gunners, and armored lancers pouring through the walls at midday. Though the Sirmians repulsed us, their bodies piled up on the battlefield by day's end — so many that it was difficult for them to maneuver. We lost more, but so what? We had a wall and a city.

The next day, rain came. Hard. At dawn, we sent sappers to fire rockets at the stone wall they'd built along the shoreline. A resounding success. Rain muddied the ground, and without the wall, the strait overflowed and crept into the lowlands. We watched, from the comfort of our walls, as the Sirmians rushed inland to keep from getting stuck in the muck.

That's when the Shah showed his baseness. His engineers wheeled a wooden platform to the front. Atop it, they hung a noose from a pole. A gallows. And then they marched a young girl onto it and tied the noose around her neck. For a time, the battle stopped as we waited to see what they intended to do with my granddaughter. But all I saw was the desperation of the defeated.

My son's desperation was difficult to ignore. He came to me as I sat in the garden, his breaths filled with the panic of a father about to lose his only child.

"They have given us until tomorrow to surrender the city, or they will hang her," my son said. "They will kill her when the sun is halfway to its zenith. We have to do something!"

"Offer them Micah. Offer them the janissary we captured and all the gold in the vaults. We've nothing else."

Alexios went himself with these offers.

He returned to the great hall a while later, howling for succor. He begged at my feet, in tears, that I do something to save Celene. As if I worked miracles like the apostles.

"Alexios, you know I love Celene. And I love you. But they will not relent unless we give them this city."

"Then give it to them!" he screamed in-between sobs. "We already have a city. We have Hyperion. This place is not our home!"

"A hamlet compared to Kostany." I climbed off the Seat and grasped my son by his cold and trembling cheeks. "I watched your brother charge into the fray and take an arrow to the eye. That was a hard day. It will pass."

I envied my son's relationship with his daughter. Some poet once said *love is suffering*. That's why as imperator, you cannot love your children too much. Whatever you love will always be used to hurt you, so an imperator must not truly love anything but the Imperium and the job. It was a cold reality that my son had to learn.

"No, I'm not like you," Alexios said. "I didn't want this. After your death, I ordered Micah to return to Hyperion rather than waste treasure and lives seizing this city. Don't you see? We can't hold Kostany. There are too many Latians on this side of the sea!"

"Micah had the right idea." I returned to my throne as my son groveled. "Fewer Latians."

A DAY PASSED WITHOUT FIGHTING. My granddaughter knelt for much of it. They threw her a few pieces of bread and made her drink from a bowl like a dog. The Sirmians were beasts. It was said that their ancestor Seluq spawned from the consorting of a wolf and a Fallen Angel. Their inhumanity proved as much.

I visited my two prisoners that night. The dungeon smelled ungodly. I stuffed cotton bits up my nose, but even that barely held the stench of feces and worms. I didn't want to stay long but had to see if the janissary was pliable. And perhaps I could begin Micah on his path to redemption.

I hadn't appreciated before that the janissary was young and strikingly handsome. He was a Ruthenian or Thamesian, from the look of his golden hair and fair complexion. I would've been interested to hear his story if it didn't smell so wretched.

"Do you remember your homeland?" I asked in Sirmian.

He quietly mumbled poetry, his curly hair covering his forehead.

"No, of course you don't," I said. "Our missionaries have converted most of Ruthenia and Thames to the Ethos faith. Had the Sirmians not enslaved you, you'd be one of us."

"You think I care what I would have been?" He spoke with more bitterness than the verjuice sauce.

"My excubitors are all Thamesians. You could have served me, in another life."

"I struggle to conceive a greater dishonor."

"Oh, that's what you believe, young man. But we are all products of our birth and raising. You believe in your country, in your shah and false faith, only because they raised you to. But it's not the way of your blood."

"I piss on my blood and yours."

"As angry as you are, we are not enemies. Convert to the faith of your real kin, and perhaps I'll let you join me. Think on it."

He spat at my feet. Uncouth barbarian. I turned to Micah, who seemed even more dejected and trodden upon. If only he'd knelt, I wouldn't have thrown him in here. No question: he was the sharpest military mind among us, though we didn't need cleverness to defeat the Sirmians. Our numbers would do that.

Micah scratched at the ground with his black metal arm. What darkness created that? Was it as the paladins whispered? Did a sorceress bestow upon him the powers of the Fallen?

"I'll never forget that day, Micah, when you knelt and offered the service of the Black Legion to me. I was afraid of what it would cost. Our treasury had dried up as our borders shriveled. But when you said your allegiance came free, that all I would have to do was punish a few minor lords and priests that had wronged you and your men, I could scarcely believe it."

He kept clumping handfuls of dirt with his black hand. Even his complexion had turned dark, as if his vile deeds had extinguished the light of faith. A rotting man — within and without.

"I should've known," I said, "that free is never free. You thought Kostany would be your payment. You believed the Imperium itself would be yours, that the title of Imperator would be recompense for your service. The Archangel has humbled you. He has shown you your limitations and how to serve within them — as a sword, not as the crown."

Micah's laugh was as dark as his arm. "You are even less than that, Heraclius. You were sent by a darkness so vast and deep, that you could never comprehend it, even if you lived a thousand more times. And you were sent for one reason — to test me."

"Indeed, the Archangel sent me to test all souls that would see me. To be a sign of his sovereignty over the earth."

Micah's dark laugh turned demonic. "Sovereignty? Oh Heraclius, you have no sovereignty and neither do the angels. Just wait and see what she has in store for you. I won't serve her, and I definitely won't serve you. I'll be here to watch and laugh as everything you touch crumbles."

He fell silent and turned away. The man needed time to come to sense. He spoke dark, blasphemous words of despair. I decided to forgive it.

· · ·

THE CHIRPING of all kinds of birds greeted me on the following bright morning as I had breakfast on the battlement. My granddaughter still knelt at the gallows. They'd left her there all night. Alexios went again and again to the gates to parley, but nothing came of it.

I felt true sadness for my granddaughter. A heavy heart is a sign of one's humanity, but an Imperator must hold the realm higher than his heart.

I enjoyed a pouch of cherries and waited for the sun to reach halfway to its zenith. A hangman stood next to Celene; he tightened the rope around her neck. Once he opened the false bottom, the girl would be dead in seconds, and we could end this drama and finally resume the battle.

The sun reached its midpoint, casting a brilliant glow over the Zari Zar. Alexios shivered next to me and plunged into a hysterical fit of weeping that was barely befitting a woman, let alone my heir. I ordered him inside so he wouldn't have to see or be seen.

The sun continued to ascend, but the Princess still knelt at the gallows, unharmed. Shortly after, a young, red-haired woman escorted her off it. It seemed the Shah had lost his nerve. I respected barbarity and ruthlessness more than hesitation and false threats. What is weaker than a threat that goes begging? The Sirmians drowned in their weakness. I preferred to drown them in steel.

With the Princess out of sight, I ordered the entire army out the gates to assail their narrow position. I hymned as my men poured through like a sea of steel. And the sea washed over the Sirmians, scattered them, drove them deeper inland until they routed. Weakness begets weakness, and strength begets strength. The siege was won.

I proceeded to the gate. My son was there, saddling his horse and having his sword sharpened at a nearby workshop. He did not share in our joy. His cheeks were red and heavy with sleep-lessness.

"You cannot go," I said.

"I must get my daughter back."

"You are in no mind to lead men. Would you sacrifice our armies for her? I will lead the charge. You stay and govern Kostany." I spread my arms and looked around. What a dirty and despondent city. And yet, it was all that mattered. "One day, you're going to inherit all this."

Alexios pushed his face into his horse's side, wetting its fur with his tears.

"If they couldn't kill her today, they won't kill her," I said, as resolutely as possible, to fill my son with a hope I didn't share. "Let the angels bear witness — I'll get her back."

I organized my troops. Heavy cavaliers and Rubadi light cavalry would be the vanguard and cut down the retreating Sirmians. We would burn their ships to prevent a retreat by sea, then destroy them in the grassland. Thus began my conquest of Sirm.

28

MURAD

SELUQ THE DAWN WAS LOOKING DOWN FROM BARZAKH, WEEPING AT
the failings of his son. How else to explain this unending rain that
turned grass and mud to sludge beneath our boots? The river we
were to cross — the Syr Darya — had flooded its banks, and now
it coursed at frightening speed, its water cold as the gaze of
Ahriyya. We could either fight or drown. It seemed the god of the
Crucians had defeated ours.

Heraclius must've told his men as much. The angels had
brought him back, and they'd defeated us at the gate of Kostany,
torched our ships to prevent escape, and now would deal a decisive blow that would seal my kingdom's fate. What hope was left
for the warriors who revered me?

Things had happened so fast. One moment, I was a prisoner,
living at the pleasure of Imperator Josias. He brought me along
on his flagship, hoping to use me as a bargaining piece. And then
Hayrad — of all people — freed me and imposed upon me the
burdens of rule and command…as if these were mine by existence, despite that I'd not been in my country for many moons
and barely knew what the hell was going on.

But shahs have commanded under worse pressures. These failures were my own, and nothing could mask that it was under my rule that Kostany fell and under my command that we failed to retake it. If Lat did not favor us, I would be the last Shah of Sirm. Perhaps I should not have been Shah at all. Would Selim have failed as I did?

Heraclius' cavalry had menaced our retreat. The Rubadi barbarians were as fast and fierce as the zabadar. They ran down our infantry and made setting camp as difficult as planting flowers in a windstorm. On last count, only half of the forty thousand soldiers we started with remained.

Heraclius' heavy cavalry was slower, but no sight was more frightening than them thundering at us. Lance, man, and horse seemed a unified, steel monster.

Now we camped under heavy rainfall, well clear of the furious river. The thick mud stank of dead grass, and already enough of us were weary and ill.

Last night I dreamt that the Syr Darya overflowed. Its water turned into boiling blood and its rocks to charred bone. The shadowy hands of Ahriyya pulled my children into its surging current, as the black drongos from my garden pecked their flesh and eyes. The blood poured over our armies and cities and every field and even the mountains. It extinguished hope and doomed our country.

From the northern sky flew a flock of birds as big as elephants. The feathers of these simurgh were colored like a rainbow, and they picked us out of the blood and carried us by their claws to Kostany.

What did it mean? Could we still be saved?

Hayrad, whom the fawners liked to call Redbeard, the Count of Rastergan, and my daughter Sadie sat together in my yurt around a fire-breathing stove. Sadie argued with Hayrad like a scholar scolding an unruly seeker. Aye, there was Papa Jalal in her, a bit of me, but mostly Humayra. And there was something none of us possessed: a deep sea of compassion. During this ordeal, she cared for the zabadar as if each was her child. She'd lost a thousand children and mourned enough for ten thousand lifetimes. I certainly could relate.

"I swear to you, the magus made the rain and wind stop." She snapped her fingers. "As if he'd just…" *Snap-snap.*

If only she knew that Hayrad couldn't be taught anything — Lat knows I'd been trying for a decade. The man sat on a stool in the corsair way: his legs spread with little regard for his audience. His clothes were a mishmash of all the places he'd been. I hated his necklace with the pelican sigil of the Sultan of Ejaz molded in mother-of-pearl. He'd received it upon freeing the isles of Ejaz from the garrison Micah had left there. That was what he'd been up to while I was imprisoned.

And yet, I didn't regret choosing him to command my largest fleet. It was among my first acts upon ascending. The man had tormented my father by ceaselessly plundering our shipping, but I always believed the worst enemy could become the best ally. With me funding him, he turned to raiding Crucian ships and towns. Hayrad often walked with death and knew best how to outlast it.

"Listen, woman," Hayrad said, "I've sailed every sea and never seen a sorcerer change the weather. Besides, there're no sorcerers here."

"I don't care how many seas you've pissed in!" Sadie fumed. I'd never known her to be vulgar, but she had been living with the zabadar. Their maroon leathers suited her. She wore them with the grace of a Seluqal. After all, hundreds of years ago, we Seluqals were zabadar too, living in yurt villages far to the east, worshipping strange Rubadi ice gods.

"A magus can fly!" Sadie pointed to the ceiling. "Kevah could get here faster than a bird."

"Again with Kevah?" Hayrad said. "He's all you talk about!"

"Seems we've gone beyond desperation," I said. "And you…"

I pointed to Hayrad. He closed his legs when he realized his shah spoke to him. "As long as I'm alive, you'll refer to my daughter as 'Your Highness.'"

Hayrad scowled. "Your Glory, sorcery won't save us. Only Lat can now. Lyskar is a few days march past the river. If only it would—"

"Again with Lat!" Sadie coughed and spat. "If she's real and cares about any of us, then why won't the rain stop and the river calm!?"

"Our own swords then," Hayrad said. "We can hold out until the river stills enough to cross. Men have survived worse odds."

"Aye," I said, ignoring my daughter's blasphemy. "But men as shaken as ours?"

"You're their leader," Redbeard said. "Inspire them."

"Am I? Last I counted, we had zabadar, Rasterganis, and your khazis too, Hayrad. You've all been leading them longer than I."

"You're the Shah," Hayrad said. "Either we risk the Syr Darya, or we draw our swords and fight. Your decision."

"An easy one," I said. "Prepare to fight. I'll not be killed by a river!"

The Count of Rastergan grunted his approval. He was an experienced commander who had repulsed my father until he agreed to be our vassal. And then he spent his days fighting Crucians and had even expanded Rastergani territory. If we failed, the Crucians would punish his family and install someone else to the Rastergani throne. He had as much to lose as anyone.

Hayrad and the Count hurried out of my yurt.

"Hold on," I said to Sadie before she did the same.

I didn't show it, but I'd never seen a brighter light than Sadie grown up. Nothing made me joyful anymore, but I praised Lat in my heart for letting me see her again. Nothing scared me more than the thought of her screaming, like my other children. Each was as precious to me as Sadie, and yet I'd let it happen. The moment of their slaughter had never ended and never would. Would I let it happen to Sadie, too?

"Father?" She didn't look at me with reverence. I sensed pity beneath those amber eyes — her mother's eyes.

"You shouldn't be here, Sadie."

"I won't leave your side."

"I watched the Crucians kill your brothers and sisters. You and Alir are among the few children I have left...I will not let you suffer the same."

"Alir is safe and will carry our house into the future. My place is with the zabadar, and their place is with their shah."

"I know you grew up and became strong out of my sight. But as your father, I cannot allow you to die in service of your shah." Not again. Not ever. I'd tried to digest the pain all these moons while a prisoner of the Crucians. Was there a way I could have saved them? Should I have proclaimed my faith in the Archangel? Surely Micah, in his crazed bloodlust, would have killed them anyway. Surely...

Already, Sadie nursed a wound on her shoulder. A gunshot had grazed her before she put an arrow through the gunner's eye. I'd watched it happen: as the Rubadi girl galloped toward her, gun forward, Sadie barely reacted. It was almost as if she let the Rubadi shoot her. The healer had cauterized the wound, but rain doused her in her weakened state, and she coughed and sneezed constantly. She'd been taking cinnamon and poppy but still didn't look well. Though she was energetic in the morning, at night the fever would worsen and leave her bedridden — typical of sweating sickness.

I touched her forehead: too warm. "You shouldn't be fighting. You should ride to Alir."

"And how long until Alir has to fight them?" She trembled. Though she put on a brave mask, fear laced her words. "Will we run forever? Would grandfather have run?"

She was a daughter of Seluq the Dawn. The blood of Temur

the Wrathful would never run, except toward the enemy — that's why we ruled three countries. These were not thrones built on cunning plots; they were thrones built by swift horses, true arrows, and blood-stained steel. And yet...

Sadie sneezed and shivered. Her brown skin had turned ruddy like her hair. I didn't want to be her shah. I wanted to tuck her in a thick blanket and feed her hot soup. In that moment, I would've given the kingdom to see her healthy and happy. But the blood of Seluq ran hot through my veins, and it was time to fight or die.

The horn blew three times: Heraclius was coming.

Before I could leave, Sadie tugged my arm. "Umm..." She cleared her throat. Something weighed on her, but she hemmed and hawed.

"I'm your father. Out with it."

She stared up at me with guilty eyes. "Do you ever think about the men we kill out there?"

"The Crucians?"

"They have mothers and fathers too. Are they not just like us? What's the difference, save our faiths?"

"Lat's mercy — is that why you let that Rubadi shoot you?" Though she resembled her mother, she was too much like me on the inside. I had asked the same question to my father, long ago. "The difference is, this is our land, and they're not welcome." That wasn't the answer my father gave me.

"But they believe it's their land. Wasn't it, before our ancestors took it from theirs?"

My father's voice took over. "Lat gave Seluq and his descendants dominion over the earth. All land is ours, by right."

"Then we're no different." She gazed at the floor.

I grabbed her wrist. Too damn thin. "The truth is, we fight so we don't die. I can't make it any clearer. Our blood is a death sentence — it might as well be poison. The antidote is to kill, and keep killing, until all our enemies are in the grave." I squeezed her wrist so she wouldn't look away. "Out there, when you see the whites of a Crucian's eyes, you put an arrow into them. Understood?"

Sadie sneezed. She swallowed her remorse and nodded.

OUTSIDE, gunners took position on a small hill that formed our center. Most of the zabadar were divided between left and right flanks. I kept some zabadar, including Sadie, to act as a reserve strike force. But really, I meant to keep her away from the thickest fighting. Although nowhere was safe anymore.

Heraclius waited on a larger hill across the plain. His forces were three times ours. His heavy cavaliers did not seem bothered by rain and mud. The armored beasts they rode were used to being slowed by heavy loads, and so had stronger legs to break through mud, though they had to lighten their loads somewhat. Worse, Heraclius had more guns and fast-firing ones at that.

He ordered his light cavalry to charge our gunners. His Rubadi galloped swiftly through the mud and rain. Our gunners fired furiously, and the Rubadi failed to assail the hill and retreated. I ordered our gunners, most of whom were soldiers Hayrad had recruited from far-off lands, to hold position.

Artillery rained on our gunners holding the hill. They'd dug trenches and built light fortifications of wood and stone, but as artillery fell, many of them became chunks of burnt flesh. The healers carted the dead and wounded back to camp, where they piled around my yurt. Though I didn't have the deep compassion of my daughter, I knew that each had a mother. I imagined my mother weeping for them as she'd wept when my baby sister passed. I deserved nothing less than the deepest hellfire for allowing this to happen. They called me the Shadow of God for a reason — because I ruled in Lat's name. And to rule as badly as I did…

I pushed such thoughts aside. I couldn't lead an army

dwelling on crying mothers and Lat's punishment. I didn't know how long Heraclius could sustain the bombardment, as I didn't know how many cannons he'd managed to haul through the mud. I assumed it couldn't be too many.

Hours of sustained bombardment proved that assumption wrong. I ordered the right flank of zabadar to attack and silence the artillery, knowing that Heraclius was baiting me.

Crucian gunners and archers rained fire onto our riders. Bloodied horses and screaming men littered the battlefield. The zabadar returned having lost fifty. They'd destroyed a few exposed cannons, so the artillery barrage became lighter, but not light enough to bear much longer.

Heraclius broke our front line and claimed the hill within hours. While trying to counter, our center was reduced to a ditch full of men with spilled entrails and smoking gun wounds. Sadie counterattacked with her zabadar, but the onslaught was too much for her weary force. I ordered Hayrad's men and the Rastergani forces to collapse on their vanguard, but the Crucian guns fired too fast. Fighting entered my camp by midday.

I knew things were dire when Heraclius himself, surrounded by his Thamesian excubitors, perched his camp atop the hill overlooking us. Heavy cavalry rode through our line of yurts and clashed with the zabadar. Sadie put down three heavy riders with perfectly aimed arrows at the legs of muscled horses. Her zabadar encircled me, and their endless arrows created a torrent that Heraclius' overstretched cavalry found difficult to resist.

But this only bought time. Numbers would dictate the winner, not tactics or bravery. Still, I didn't renounce hope.

By day's end, Heraclius brought more forces to our camp that had been freed up after cutting through our flanks. They encircled us. I watched hundreds of my soldiers wade into the Syr Darya, but almost none made it across the raging current, which swept them into downriver rocks. The setting sun cast a dismal red glare upon us. It seemed Heraclius was tired too; fighting ended for the day with the final whimpers of steel on steel.

Sadie and the Count came to my yurt plunged in despair. Hayrad less so.

"Some of my lieutenants have already surrendered to the Crucians," the Count said. "Others took their chances in the river. Our camp could be empty by morning."

Sadie was more determined, though rain had drenched her clothes and she was shaking. "We should hold out as long as possible. The zabadar are ready to die."

Hayrad seemed unfazed, as if no stranger to hopeless situations. "My khazis are getting cut down. But we'll survive. We always do."

I knew then that it was over. By retreating for the night, Heraclius had denied us the dignity of dying. I raised the white flag above camp. Perhaps I could save some lives by placating the Imperator and giving him mine in a felt-lined box.

ON HORSEBACK, I climbed the hill to Heraclius' camp with Hayrad, the Count, Sadie, and a few zabadar. The excubitors took our weapons, and Heraclius invited us into his tent. He gave us water and seated us on wooden chairs at a great oak table. One of his sycophants recited his titles and added one I'd never heard: *The Resurrected.* Finally, we were invited to speak.

Out of respect for the victor, I spoke in Crucian. "I am defeated, but my fate should not extend to my daughters and son. Micah, your general, slaughtered the rest of my children. When I tried to look away, he forced my eyes open. Is there any mercy in you? In the Archangel?"

Heraclius peeled an apple with a curved dagger. "Had I been alive and on the throne, I would never have allowed such savagery. Our dogs sometimes stray far from their leashes." He pointed the dagger at Hayrad. "Your dog is responsible for many atrocities on our shores."

Hayrad spat on the floor. "I'm no one's dog. And I—"

"Silence, Hayrad!" I gave him a seething glare.

Heraclius' laugh rang deep. "Even a wicked dog listens to his master." He crunched his apple. "Help yourselves to some fruit. We picked plenty on the way down."

We were all hungry, but not enough to eat the enemy's fruit. Heraclius' lieutenants, who it seemed were not allowed to speak, helped themselves to apples and figs and apricots. The guards surrounding our table eyed the fruit too; had he picked enough for them? Perhaps their force was wearier than it seemed.

"I still have your granddaughter," I said. "You'll get her back. But I ask you to pledge that my daughters and only son, so long as they don't revolt against you, will be safe."

"I have thought at length about what to do with your family. Yours is a great lineage, brought to heel only by the will of the Archangel. It was not my genius or anyone else's that led to this victory. We are all humbled and see that. The Archangel bids us to be merciful, whenever we can, if mercy does not impugn upon justice. As your children are guilty of little, I will allow them to continue as heirs of the Seluqal House of Sirm. On certain conditions."

"And what would those be?"

"We will reclaim most of the land that your father and his father and so on took from us. I will allow the Seluqal House to have dominion over Lysithea — Lyskar, as you know it — and Tagkalay, but only as a client to me at fifty percent of collected taxes. If the Alanyans invade, then I'll rely on your children as the first line of defense."

Hayrad came close to my ear and whispered, "That's a shit deal."

I eased him away, gave him another glare.

"I object to none of that," I said, returning my attention to Heraclius.

The Imperator smiled the way a drunk man would at a beautiful woman. "Did you dream of fighting to the last man, Shah? I had such dreams when your father routed me. I wanted to stand and die before another inch of Crucian land was lost. But now look at me. The astute are those who survive, and by pledging to these terms, your house will go on. And who knows? In a few hundred years, your progeny could rise again."

"And that doesn't concern you?"

"What concerns me, Shah, is of no concern to you. Shadows of God, your litter will not be. Shadows of the Imperator of Holy Crucis — now that rings like redemption for all the wickedness you and your ancestors have wrought."

Was that the destiny of the blood of Seluq? The successors of Temur and Utay? To collect taxes for this bastard and his progeny?

Sadie sneezed. She slouched in her chair as if too weak to sit up. This defeat had crushed what was left of her spirit, and now the sickness was taking hold.

"Your daughter has caught the sweat," the Imperator said. "Shall I have my healer see to her?"

Hayrad leaned over and whispered, "Their healers know as much about medicine as I know about crocheting. Don't do it."

Why did this pirate think I needed his voice inside my head? Yes, he was more worldly and knowledgeable than I, but these were my decisions.

"Defeat has stung on her soul," I said to Heraclius, "but she's stronger than she looks."

The Imperator nodded and waved his dagger at Sadie. "Indeed, there isn't a soldier in my camp who doesn't fear her arrows. If you had ten more of her, I'd be the one surrendering."

"I will surrender at dawn tomorrow. Once the sun appears on the horizon, you may ride into our camp and take whatever prisoners you may. If the Archangel allows you to be merciful, then whoever that mercy falls upon, allow them to go freely. As for my daughter, she will ride to Lyskar with a small accompaniment."

"I agree to it all. But I have a question. We've been fighting for weeks, and I've seen so few janissaries. Where are they hiding?"

"Some are with my son, Alir, whom I'm told is leading an army to retake Tagkalay from rebels."

"And how many are in this army?"

"Not enough to resist you. And Tagkalay is far."

Heraclius nodded and smiled smugly. "Thank you for your honesty, Shah Murad. You may go."

We returned to camp. I prayed alone in my yurt, then visited Sadie, who'd taken to bed.

A healer knelt at her bedside and mixed bitter herbs. He placed Sadie's right hand in the mixture and then rubbed some of it on her forehead and beneath her nose.

"You will ride away at dawn," I said to Sadie. "Go and don't think on what happens here."

"What about you?" Sadie sat up. "I won't leave you to your fate."

"Whatever fate awaits me is as I deserve for my failures. You are the future of this house. And the future is bright, so long as you live."

The healer bowed his head and left.

"Where will I go? Alir would just imprison or send me away."

"Go wherever your heart beckons. I say this not as your shah, but as your father. Is there nothing...or no one you have to live for?"

Sadie's face flushed, but not from fever. I knew that gaze — I'd seen it on many smitten girls. Sadie never looked at Hayrad that way. I didn't ask who it was for. I'd barely been her father and didn't have the right to know her heart. "I made a promise to someone...and to myself...that I wouldn't cower. That I would rise to my duty as a Seluqal and a zabadar." She shook, but not from sickness. "And yet, I've been afraid from the first. I don't want to run, but—"

"There's no shame in it. I order you to take your mother and go. If you're not welcome in Lyskar, then the Alanyans will have you. If they refuse, go to Kashan — your sister is married to a prince there. If she wants nothing to do with you, ride to the Silk-lands, so long as you live. Understood?"

She nodded and stared at the ceiling bells, which chimed somberly. "Father...why did you have so many children...if you knew what would happen to us? What we'd have to do to survive?"

I sighed. Even I was never so bold to ask my father that. "I'm just a man, Sadie. I tried to change things, I did. Gave the Fount the authority to decide who lives and dies in our family, so we wouldn't bear that burden."

She turned away, as if my answer wasn't good enough. I searched my thoughts and tried a more fatherly tact. "Six hundred years ago, a thousand miles away on a frozen plain, our father Seluq was born beneath the Glorious Star. The Waste was a bare place — tribes would war over a goat." I chuckled at the thought. Though during the siege of Rastergan, we fought to eat rats. There was nothing humorous about scarcity. "Seluq had a vision of a billion crows devouring the sun as it set in the western sky. So with a billion arrows, he conquered a hundred cities between Kashan and where we sit." Sadie turned to face me, then sat up on her mattress and rested her head on clasped hands. I continued, "But even great men must return to Lat. The conqueror had three sons whom he loved, and on his deathbed, carved three kingdoms between them.

"As soon as his shrine was planted, those three brothers raised their swords — against each other. The fighting outlasted them, raging for a hundred years — it was said that tulips turned red from blood in the soil — until Temur the Wrathful unified the three kingdoms with the dream of pushing farther west, beyond the Syr Darya." Every Seluqal had heard this tale a thousand times, but it never lost relevance. "Only Kostany stood against his horde. Temur caught the death sweat planning his second attempt to take it. His was the largest empire ever beheld — imagine what would happen if it fractured like Seluq's. So on his deathbed, Temur appointed a secret heir and declared that, once he'd breathed his last, all his other sons and daughters be put to death." I couldn't begin to imagine doing the same. "He was a hard man, true, but he loved his family as much as he despised his enemies. It was not an easy thing, but he did it to save lives."

Sadie gazed at me with bated breath. I used to recite bedtimes tales when she had trouble sleeping — though none so grisly. A fussy child she was, prone to tantrums. Staring into her expectant eyes — my child's eyes — I almost forgot the point of this story.

"We die, Sadie, so others don't. We kill each other so others don't have to kill for us. We go willingly into exile to spare our subjects the suffering. What else can I tell you? This is our curse." I held my tears. "I had you and your siblings hoping things would be different. But—" I couldn't say another word, lest I weep in front of my daughter.

She nodded, her smile weak and tender. "Thank you, Father. Though it's been awful, I'm glad we had this time together."

I squeezed her hand. I could hardly feel her squeeze back.

THAT NIGHT, another dream blazed through my mind. A simurgh trampled my yurt and seized me. It had the iron claws of a lion, the majestic wings of a falcon, and the head of a menacing wolf. It flung me onto a giant nest that sat on a tree taller than two stacked mountains. I'd imagined this exact place from a bedtime story I'd heard as a child. Golden eggs bigger than my body were spread around the nest. They glistened beneath a cloudless sky.

I touched one of them and brushed its smoothness — hard

like brass. It cracked open and out popped a chicken with the wings of an eagle and face of a boy.

"Pick up your sword." Its gray eyes were as bright as a full moon. Its voice was like a eunuch I once knew. "When the sun reaches its midpoint, the succor of Lat will come."

He pricked my forehead with his fingernail. I couldn't move. He whispered in my ear the words he'd just said. So powerful was his voice, I felt the words being chiseled onto my soul.

When the sun reaches its midpoint, the succor of Lat will come.

I woke up reciting these words. I rushed out of my yurt. Dawn already painted its dismal blue across the sky; Heraclius would arrive when the sun appeared. It was nearly time to surrender.

Fires glowed around camp in the dim light as soldiers awoke for breakfast. So little food would be split among so many. We were short on everything: gunpowder, horses, morale. Everyone nursed a wound, whether of flesh or spirit. If there wasn't blood on your armor, there was char, and often both. Gunners had to make do with a handful of bullets. A quarter of our spearmen were using wood, their metal spears having dulled. With no bombards, our artillerists threw crude incendiaries that tended to explode in their faces. The standard bearers had dropped their flags during the rout and had taken to playing drums, the beat of which truly grated.

Worst of all, the rain hadn't ceased. The plains were known for summer rains, but did they have to go on and on at a time like this?

I looked for Hayrad. Even I could admit I needed his advice at a time like this. One of his lieutenants mentioned he was with Sadie. As long as I lived, they would never marry, no matter what oaths she swore. I could grudgingly concede that Hayrad was a great man and deserved to be called Shah of the Seas, but he was the son of an Ejazi merchant. And that was without mentioning his age, which neared my own.

I found him in her yurt, sitting at her bedside and watching her sleep. I sat with him and looked upon my daughter, who breathed weakly.

Sadie shifted in her bed. "Kevah, that you?" She opened her eyes and yawned, then squinted at us. "Don't you two have more important things to do than watch me sleep?"

It was clear she'd sweat through the night. The healers said that was a sign of the body fighting, but she still had the complexion of rusted iron.

Hayrad and I went outside to let her rest. We left earshot of the zabadar, who were busy tending to their horses. In a bog by the river, with its thunderous current, I told him what was on my mind.

"I am considering fighting on," I said.

He raised his bushy eyebrows and pulled at his famous red beard. "Your Glory, I'm ready to forfeit my life, as you are yours. I thought it a shit deal, but it's done, and Sadie and many others have a chance at life. If you break that whoreson's terms, a cruel end could await your house."

"I believe help will come."

"Help? We're hundreds of miles from help. Had you sent your swiftest rider days ago to Tagkalay, help would not have reached by now. Unless you can beg of the jinn."

"I had a dream. Lat told me to wait until the sun was midway to its zenith...that if we just lasted until then, succor would come."

"You would gamble your daughter's life, and the future of your house, on your nighttime fancies?"

Hayrad was right. It was the most foolish thing I'd ever considered. And yet...

"Hayrad, didn't you say that you had a vision before you rescued me?"

"Who told you that?"

"Sadie mentioned it. She said that you attacked Josias' fleet because of a vision you had."

He nodded. "I saw a ship made of gold with purple sails. Within it was a mountain of treasure, the like of which I've never seen in all my travels, and the ruby-eyed golden peacock that adorns your throne room." Hayrad's eyes were entranced by images of his vision. He shook them off. "But that's not why I attacked. I did so because it was obvious. Josias — the fool — had made landfall, and his ships were undermanned or moored. Many of his Ejazi shipmen defected to our side, so his flagship was easy picking. When I heard of his treachery, I had to punish the Crucian mongrel."

"Mayhap the river will calm by the midpoint hour. Is it too much to hope Lat is directing us toward something?"

Hayrad guffawed. "History is filled with men who hoped the same. They're all buried in a ditch somewhere."

"Such faithlessness from a man who commands a swarm of warrior-dervishes."

How Hayrad could find the ease to smile within this crucible, I'd never know. I despised that grin. Each tooth was a different shade of gold. "The legend is iron..." He tilted his head and pointed at himself. "But the man is water."

I shook my head, reminded once more why I couldn't stand this pirate. "There are a thousand and one ways you could have phrased that. You picked the stupidest."

He bellowed a laugh. I laughed too. Perhaps for the last time.

The sun poked its head out of the horizon, and the sky filled with rays. The Imperator would be here shortly. His mounted scouts already gazed at us from their hill.

Madness. All of it. I wasn't immune to making decisions from portents, but I couldn't imperil my family after I'd secured mercy.

Humayra came to me in the spare moments I had to make my decision. She was emaciated from all that we'd been through. The sight of her still sent flutters through me. I'd loved this daughter of a goat herder more than the Sultan of Abistra's sister, whom I married. When I looked upon her, I saw the same quick-tempered girl I'd met almost thirty years ago.

We spoke in my yurt as the rain pattered. I told her my dream. I sought her wisdom, as I always had before our hearts hardened against each other.

"I must give the order, either to surrender or fight," I said. "Your daughter's life…" I choked on the words. I couldn't muster the courage to even finish the thought.

Humayra smiled at me like she had during the days of our passion. Days that seemed a lifetime ago yet had the fragrance of yesterday.

"You used to tell me the story of your father at Rastergan," she said. "How he refused to surrender, even though he had no food and was outnumbered three to one."

"Rastergan had a wall we could hide behind."

"Your brother Selim was there too, wasn't he?"

I nodded.

"Let me ask you, then," Humayra said, "do you think your father was ready to die? Ready to sacrifice you and Selim?"

"Knowing my father, certainly. But I'm not like him. I only became Shah because I didn't want to die, didn't want my children to die, didn't want you to die. Seluq is looking down, weeping at what I've done to one of his kingdoms."

For the first time in years, she didn't pull away when I touched her cheek. Though I could tell from the sorrow in her gaze that she hadn't forgiven me. The things lovers do to each other, you'd scarcely need enemies.

"Seluq isn't crying." Humayra took my hand. She pressed it closer on her cheek. "If we live our lives afraid of death, we will never cease being afraid."

"I can't do it. Heraclius will allow you and Sadie to go free. I can't give him a reason to kill you."

When her amber eyes warmed, they comforted me like cherry sherbet on a hot day.

"I had your love, once, but I never had your name. And still, I find it impossible to run. I would gladly exchange freedom for death. Let my shrine, and the shrine of our daughter, be planted on the battlefield than in some distant land where you and this kingdom are a faded memory."

Staring into my lover's unyielding eyes, I decided our fates.

I ORDERED the army to retrench at the river's edge. The fierce rain had turned into a drizzle. We had to hold out several hours, and if the succor of Lat did not come, there was no question our shrines would be planted on this battlefield.

Rastergani gunners marched through the camp and took positions at the front. There were only a few thousand left. A man named Yamin now commanded the zabadar, who numbered only seven hundred. He brought them into one formation at the right. How many would I sacrifice? Surely their mothers would curse my name and lament that I'd sat the throne.

Hayrad's men numbered several thousand; he commanded them from a pocket to the east. Many were zabadar seeking pillage, but most were khazis who spent their days swaying their heads in prayer instead of drilling. Some even wore mirror plate inscribed with saintly verses. Though they didn't lack bravery, they seemed to take their orders from Lat rather than Hayrad and that often got them killed.

Amid our planning, everything started exploding. A cacophony of death deafened the ears as the ground sundered. Cannon blasts scattered limbs and flesh across the muddy bogs. Char and ash and shrapnel swept through the air and into our eyes and lungs. I stared it down while barking orders that no one could hear, least of all myself. My lieutenants were dead or screaming or huddling for cover. Even my horse had exploded, its head at least a mile from its body.

Heraclius had awoken to our treachery. He was coming.

I turned to see the Syr Darya, where some Rasterganis were fleeing. I didn't blame them. Normally, I would order death to deserters, but the river's angry current already did that.

Sadie and her zabadar galloped to my side, waking me from my shock. She wore her maroon leathers and carried her composite bow around her shoulder. But she seemed ready to retch, and I could tell from her reddened eyes that she wasn't better.

I wanted to order her to lie down, but how could I? I had not acted as a father and had endangered her life.

Heavy cavalry charged down the hill and flattened my forward line of guards. They broke through as easily as a bullet through flesh. Gunshots, clanging steel, and screams now filled the surrounding air. From every side, armored cavalry dashed through our ranks and scattered men.

I unsheathed my sword. The zabadar surrounded me and didn't cease loosing arrows and firing guns. Could we last till the midpoint hour? Did it matter?

A heavy cavalier surged through the wall of zabadar and impaled one of them on his lance. Sadie shot the foot of his horse and it flung the cavalier off. I ran toward him and swung at his neck. My sword did just enough to pierce his gorget and leave a gash that sputtered with blood.

The earth shook as more heavy cavalry neared. Zabadar fell to lances and gunshots, and all around horsemen fought horsemen. Sadie rode to my side and beckoned me onto her horse.

"Redbeard's line is holding east of here." She held out her hand. "We must break through and join them."

I didn't want to run, but we had to carry the fight as far as we could. If I fell now, morale would collapse, and the entire army would rout. I climbed on and we thundered away along the riverside, her zabadar securing our escape with endless arrows and bravery.

I clung to a daughter who was half my size but twice my fortitude. Sulfur tasted bitter in the wind and a choking smoke covered the battlefield. Fire and steel and blood and flesh mixed into each other like paint colors.

Rasterganis fought sword to sword with Crucian paladins. Steel shuddered against steel as we rode by. But there was no escape. A wall of paladins, their fast-firing guns drawn, marched along the riverside in the direction we were going. Sadie shot her arrows and killed several but couldn't create a gap for us to break through.

A gunshot screamed and hit our horse. It flung us off and onto the riverbank. I pulled Sadie on top of me to break her fall. We landed with a splash in thick mud. Pain cracked through my bones. Had it been solid ground, they'd be broken.

Sadie jumped to her feet and pulled me up. She picked up a bundle of mud-dripping arrows that had fallen out of her quiver, put them back, then loosed them on paladins as they charged our position. A beast of a man ran at me with a spear, but Sadie shot his eyes out. Another paladin missed us with his gunfire and Sadie sent an arrow into his neck. Then a third thundered at me with a greatsword; Sadie found both his cheeks with her arrow. It all happened too fast for my sword arm, which was as useless as me — a shah who forced others, even his sick daughter, to fight for him and his absurd dream.

We ran along the riverside toward Hayrad's line. The ascending sun beamed through cloud cover. It was not yet at its midpoint.

A squad of heavy cavaliers rushed toward us. Sadie loosed arrows at them, but they bounced off steel armor. She reached into her quiver, and there were no more arrows. The cavaliers surrounded us. They inched closer and closer as Sadie shielded me with her body.

The river was at our back and a wall of cavaliers at our front. The cavaliers made way and a white horse trotted through. Upon it rode a man with silver armor draped in purple regalia. Heraclius.

He pointed his longsword at me and shouted to be heard above gunshots and screaming steel. "I was generous with my terms, Shah, but the infidel in you showed true."

I kept my silence. What was there to say? Would I plead for my life? For my daughter's life? I would not dishonor us so.

Heraclius seethed. His scowl seemed permanent. "I swear by the Archangel that you will watch each of your remaining children die screaming. And we'll start with this one." He pointed his sword at Sadie, who still shielded her shah and father.

"How shall we do it?" Heraclius looked to his cavaliers and paladins. "I offer baptism in the High Holy Sea to the man who comes up with the best way to repay treachery."

"I'll kill her with my cock!" a paladin said. Laughter erupted and drowned out the noises of battle.

But Heraclius' scowl only hardened. "Who said that?"

The paladin lowered his head as the others pointed him out.

"You'll be whipped for such obscenity," Heraclius said. "I want suggestions befitting our great faith!"

"Trample the horse bitch!" a cavalier shouted. Cheers erupted.

Heraclius forced a smile. "Not bad, but trampling a 'horse bitch' is a tad banal. Let's make it a sight the Shah will never forget, even while he roasts in hell's fire!"

"Stone her!" someone in the back shouted.

As the Crucians cheered, Heraclius nodded and smiled, chin high. "There we go!"

Two paladins pulled Sadie away. She writhed in their grip. I rushed to free her, but two other paladins grabbed my arms and pushed me to the mud.

They made Sadie kneel and held her in place. Sweat dripped from her forehead. Tears gushed from her eyes. She prayed with quivering lips. I looked on as I'd done when Micah slaughtered my family.

A shah must never relent to the enemy, even to save his family. A shah must uphold the honor of a nation and ensure his country's future. But had I done any of that? No, I'd thrown it all away. What kind of shah was I? What kind of father was I?

"I'll throw the first stone," Heraclius said.

One of his paladins handed him a water stone. Rounded and smooth. Imperator Heraclius flipped the stone in his hands and squinted. He threw the stone. It smacked into Sadie's forehead and clacked against her skull.

My daughter screamed out in pain. She clutched her forehead. Blood seeped through her hands. The Crucians cheered and cheered. I could not hold my silence.

"I piss on your angel," I said. "If I survive this day, I'll disembowel each Crucian child. I'll spare no Ethosian from a boiling and let the birds have their fill!"

The paladins laughed. Heraclius beamed.

"Can you throw harder than me?" he challenged his paladins. "Baptism in the High Holy Sea to the one who throws the killing blow!"

As the paladins passed around water stones, Sadie's body went limp. She slid into the muddy grass. Blood seeped off her forehead into the mud.

"Wake her up!" Heraclius ordered.

A paladin lifted her body. He slapped her across the face, but Sadie didn't wake. Tears filled my eyes. The paladin slapped Sadie again and let go. Her body fell limp into the mud, dragging with it all hope in my heart.

The frown returned to Heraclius' face. "I did not expect her to go so easily. What a disappointment. Slit her throat."

A paladin approached her. His sword glistened under a ray of sunshine, which had just broken through the clouds. I tried again to push away those who held me. Too weak. Too late. I didn't want to see it. I didn't want to watch another of my children leave this world. I stared up at the sky.

The sun shone through a patch of clouds — halfway to its zenith. The world stood still.

Then a low rumble pulsed through the earth. The Imperator, paladins, and cavaliers looked around and at their backs. That rumble turned fierce. The world quaked. It could be nothing other than the thundering of horses. Thousands of them. Tens of thousands of them.

Ululating. No one ululated like that except the Alanyan gholam. So high pitched and grating. But it was the sweetest sound I'd ever heard.

Heraclius and his paladins and cavaliers turned to face another foe. I dashed toward Sadie and grabbed her. Faint breaths still lifted her chest. I hugged her. I sheltered her with my body as she'd sheltered me.

With what little strength remained, I picked her up and carried her into a trench by the riverside. I watched hundreds of paladins and cavaliers and Rubadi run by into the Syr Darya to drown. The screaming rockets sounded, but the gholam ululated louder — apparently unaffected, as if their horses were without ears too. As the battle raged, the ululating did not cease.

A LITTLE BEFORE SUNSET, the gholam found Sadie and me. She hadn't woken up, but her heart still beat, and I did not cease praying. Towering, dark-skinned soldiers in bloodied gold and bronze armor helped us out of the ditch and brought us on horse-back to their camp. They put her to bed with the attention of several healers, then took me to their commander.

The man wore the simurgh sigil on his turban, along with three plumes of red, orange, and green. He seemed too at ease to be a commander and barely filled the armor of his gholam. But why was a prince of Alanya roving through my lands? He bowed his head and did not look up until I'd addressed him.

"My daughter's life is in your hands," I said.

"My healers will not sleep until she's well."

"Tell me, Prince, what are you doing on my land with so many gholam?"

The Prince grabbed prayer beads from his pocket and flicked at them. "I was with your son, your wife, and Grand Vizier Ebra. We put Tagkalay and its rebellious janissaries to siege...and it was going badly. We could hardly dent its wall, as wormrot carved its way through our camp. Then I had a dream. A simurgh told me to ride south, to the most fertile bank of the Syr Darya. I saw my father, the Shah of Alanya, drowning in a sea of blood. It was an ill omen, and though I've never been one to care for omens, this one I could not deny."

I nodded and fully understood what he meant. Lat had not forsaken us.

"Send a rider to Ebra. Command him to march to Kostany." I cracked my knuckles. "Now take me to Heraclius."

They'd chained him and kept him outside with the other prisoners. The gholam herded thousands of Crucians into wooden pens while Heraclius sat alone in the grass. He looked up at me, as proud as he'd ever been. He pushed his chin so high he might as well have been staring at the sky.

"What will you do with the prisoners?" I asked the Alanyan prince.

"We need strong slaves to work the metal mines. Their lives belong to me now. But as you are a king, this king's life is yours."

The Alanyan prince unsheathed his sword and handed it to me. I placed it above my head and lined it up to Heraclius' neck.

"You once sent me weapons and gold so I could fight my brother, and I promised you peace. I kept that peace. That was my greatest mistake. I should've invaded your lands and put Hyperion to siege. I'm going to make good now."

"My granddaughter," Heraclius mumbled, "I promised my son I would bring her back."

"It was my daughter, the girl you stoned, who convinced me not to hang her. She reminded me that a 'king sets the character of his kingdom.' From this day until my death, I will cherish her words. I will no longer allow my kingdom to be as cruel as yours — even as I burn yours down."

Heraclius did not retort. Unlike him, I didn't care for memorable deaths. I didn't care to show my power over another king. I preferred to relieve the earth and air by ending his life.

"I am the Shadow of God, and I sentence you to die. May you never return."

Heraclius whispered a prayer, but I brought my sword down clean before he could finish. Blood sprayed as his head rolled onto mud.

29

KEVAH

LAT BROUGHT ALL THE THINGS I PRAYED FOR SO CLOSE, THEN PUT iron bars to stop me from taking them.

I wanted to bludgeon Micah, then wipe his blood off and hold Lunara and tell her how much I missed her. But I plunged my hands in the dirt, then brought them to my face. I covered myself in dust and dirt because what else could I do?

Lunara bent down, but never close enough to touch. It was the second time she'd visited. She looked so young, like the thousandth time I'd fallen in love with her at Tengis Keep. Tengis had said they unloaded us off the same slaver ship, though she was Thamesian and I Ruthenian. We were too young to remember our prior lives. But all I did remember, all my first memories, were filled with Lunara.

In those days, Tengis trained scores of janissaries. He didn't get many girls but trained them the same as the men. Women janissaries were not unheard of, especially in the days of Shah Jalal before the Fount strengthened their grip. My fondest memories were of Lunara and I sparring in the yard before we were ten.

What started as serious sparring became a dance of reasons to touch each other as adolescence painted over innocence.

She was all I would think about. When they sent me to fight Shah Jalal's wars, I survived on those thoughts as much as water or food.

The day I returned to her was the only time Lat ever gave me what I wanted. From that day we stayed together, fought together, got married, and lived together.

"What is it you want to say?" Lunara asked. Though she looked mostly the same, I struggled to see her as Lunara. The woman that bent down at my cell had witching eyes devoid of kindness. The color had drained from her narrower face, and her hair was shades lighter.

"That man killed Melodi!" I shouted. "Free me so I can kill him."

"Let it go, Kevah," she said. "You and Micah are crushed by such meager burdens."

"Of course you'd say that. You had as much to do with my daughter's death as him."

"Calling Melodi 'daughter' doesn't make it true." I didn't recognize Lunara's venom-filled chuckle. "If only you knew what you really lost, the day I put on the mask of the magus I killed. The day I walked out on you."

None of it made sense. I couldn't handle the lies. Not at a time like this.

"What are you saying? I killed the magus in the valley, not you."

"Did you? Do you remember the shards of ice that hailed on us as we fought him? We were as good as dead. My teeth were chattering as the air thinned and froze, yet I prayed. But it wasn't Lat who answered. An angel appeared on the horizon, a hundred times greater than the mountains around us. As I raised my hand in the air, the angel raised its sinewy hand to claim the magus' soul, seconds before your blade severed his head. It was my prayer — the prayer of the apostle-to-be of the creator — that killed him."

I laughed from the madness. "A prayer can't kill anyone."

"My prayers brought you home from Jalal's wars," she said tenderly. "Prayers, when made truly, can achieve everything that armies and guns cannot."

"Your prayers are to a wretched god!"

"Want to know what's really wretched?" Acid filled her tone again — ever sharper. "I was pregnant when I left you. I gave birth to our son on my journey to Holy Zelthuriya. They said I was the first magus to ever give birth, that the boy was a miracle. But my love for him interfered with my training. You can't achieve *fanaa*, you can't annihilate yourself, until you love nothing. So the jinn of the Marid tribe commanded me to walk hundreds of miles into the desert, to a place filled with the bones of the dead, and leave our son there.

"I refused to do it. But then Hawwa spoke to me. Reassured me that she would take care of his soul. I gave him to her, and she guided me to the truth."

I wanted to cut my ears off rather than hear anymore. I closed my eyes so I wouldn't have to see her.

"Look at you," Lunara said. "Cowering before the truth. But it's all I owe you."

"What truth could make you sacrifice so much?"

"If only I could show you. But you are not chosen." Lunara pointed at Micah, who was sitting against the wall with his arms crossed. "He is."

"Let's see how your god feels when I kill her chosen one."

Lunara looked at me as she never had, flat and unattached. But she struggled to keep a straight face, as if she dammed a tidal wave behind her eyes.

"Why did you leave me?" I asked.

"Don't you get it? It's simpler than you think. I was called to something greater than our love."

Lunara stood up. She gave me a pity-filled glare, then walked away, her green dress trailing in the dirt.

"Where're you going!?" I shouted.

"To Labyrinthos." She stopped to look at me one last time. Now I saw her. I saw Lunara behind that sullen gaze. "He had your hair." She trembled. "And your smile. Melodi would have been a loving sister. The old man would have adored him, too."

I pulled myself up and stuck my hand through the bars. "Lunara…all we dreamed of was having a family. All we wanted was to be free of our janissary vows, so we could live together in a peaceful place."

"No, that's all you dreamed of. You went with Shah Jalal to war, while I waited. Every night as I slept, I'd see the Archangel picking you off the battlefield and swallowing you whole. And after you returned, do you think Jalal just dropped dead? Do you think we just happened to be in the valley when the magus moved against Murad? It was as Hawwa planned — I was merely her instrument."

"This is too much. How can you say these things? You're not the same woman. You're not the woman I loved."

Her face hardened. Then she let out a freeing sigh and shook her head. "No, I'm not."

I spent days in the dungeon with Micah. Not that we could talk. The only things that cheered me up were the cannon blasts and gunfire. Redbeard had sieged the city, and for days the bombards raged. The sweetest sound was stone exploding. It made a lovely crumbling crack, as a clay pot does when you smash it. I fantasized about the holes in the wall growing bigger with each crack of the cannonball. How the walls would come down. The city would be saved, I would be freed, and I could strangle Micah.

I wondered what my son was like. I imagined him with my curly hair and Lunara's warm green eyes. An innocent boy, who like my daughter, deserved a happy life. The life we would've had in Tombore — far from the wars for which we were fodder. But without someone good and strong to protect him, he was another sacrifice to the causes of wicked gods or kings.

A wicked king visited me during the siege: Heraclius. I told him to fuck off.

One day the wailing of cannons stopped, and the cheers of paladins echoed through the halls. I knew then that we'd lost. I covered my face in dirt that smelled of my shit because what did it matter anymore?

That day the guard gave us more food than usual. I devoured half a dried fig and a stale date. If only I'd gone to Zelthuriya and learned the ways of the magi, I'd never feel hunger again. But I was only a magus in name and appearance. The arrogant jinn wouldn't help me. It seemed even Kinn had forsaken me.

The next day, the only man who hadn't forsaken me walked into the dungeon holding a lamp. His yellow hair had grown and curled, and stubble clung to his chin. I'd never seen Aicard beard-less, but he was a man of appearances. Whatever he looked like was intended to make you believe he was one of you. When he rode with us, he trimmed his hair and grew a beard fitting the zabadar. Now he did the opposite. Who he truly was, I feared only he knew.

He walked past Micah, who took interest by standing up and rattling the bars. Aicard bent down at my cell and handed me a bit of soft, warm bread. I plunged my teeth into it.

"Sorry I didn't come sooner," Aicard said. "It wasn't safe."

"What happened outside?"

"Shah Murad besieged the city with Redbeard's forces, as well as those of the Count of Rastergan. It seemed to be going well, but on the final day, Heraclius hit them hard with a cavalry charge, forcing their retreat."

I let out breaths of relief that the Shah was free. Kinn had done some good. Everything else was the worst I'd feared.

"So it's over," I said.

"Not quite. Heraclius has taken most of the army and now pursues them. Sixty thousand men. If he wins, city after city will fall, and he'll rule this land too."

"Is Sadie all right?"

"I don't know. I know you're fond of her, but my information comes from paladins." The man spoke softly, with a sincere tone. Was he an actor? Did he really care? "I got to know her one night, on the journey from Lyskar. We shared a waterskin of kumis. Awful drink, but great company." He laughed. "If only there were more people like her in the world, we wouldn't be constantly at each other's throats. I truly hope and pray she's all right."

Hoping and praying wasn't enough. "Aicard, can you free me?"

He shook his head. "Josias has the key. He holds Kostany while his father chases the Shah. He still hopes to trade you for Celene."

Micah shouted at Aicard. Aicard gestured with his hand for him to wait.

"What does he want?" I asked.

"He wonders why I'm talking to you. I'll make him think I'm just plying you for information."

"And what if you're fooling me too?"

"Have I given you reason to doubt me?"

"You didn't help us win the siege."

"I couldn't have." Aicard sighed, annoyed and sharp. "Heraclius and Josias don't trust me. I have to be careful about what I do beneath their eyes, or I'll end up worse than you two."

"What good are you, then?"

"I'll bring you information. Often, that's all I'm good for."

"Vaya vouched for you, Aicard. He said you had a good soul. But I can't see your soul. I can only see your acts. Make your choice. Whose side are you on?"

"You fail to realize, there are more than just two sides." He smirked. "'Beyond truth and falsehood, there is an ocean. My sails flutter in its wind.'"

The man knew his Taqi...too well for a Crucian.

Aicard left me and spoke at length with Micah. Perhaps his loyalty lay only with the victor. He'd planted his seeds in different gardens and now waited to see which tree would grow tallest. A man like that used cunning to get ahead, whereas I relied on strength. And even that had failed me.

I thought of Sadie a lot. I regretted everything. I should've fought for her, as Nesrin had implored. But though I looked like the man I once was, I was not that man. I was a man who'd failed to protect those he loved. If Sadie were hurt, I'd never forgive myself.

I wondered what regrets Micah had. I often watched him cry. It warmed me. What better comfort was there than the sight of tears on his face? He'd scream a name: *"Elly! Elly!"* Who was this "Elly" that hurt him so?

And yet, as time went on, I began to feel sorry for him, the way I felt sorry for myself. The sight of him crying would remind me of my own pain, and the two of us would weep together and bring music to this dark dungeon. But when my tears dried and sadness left me, only anger took its place, and I hated him all the same.

Aicard returned after a few days...or weeks. I wasn't certain. He hurried to speak to me.

"There's been an abrupt development." He suppressed a sigh of relief with one of trepidation. "The Shah has won!"

Aicard described how the Alanyan gholam had ridden south to save the Shah, just as it seemed defeat was certain. It sounded too good to be true, but Aicard assured me it was real. The Shah was coming.

"Thank Lat." But a tension still choked me. "Did you hear anything about Sadie?"

411

"Nothing. But listen and listen well. The Shah is coming. Josias doesn't have enough men to hold the city, and there's little food to feed the men he does have. He'll flee to Hyperion with you as his captive, and once there, will likely try to trade you for his daughter. This is your chance to escape."

Aicard slipped a dagger with an ornate sheath through the iron bars. I pulled it out: a sturdy piece of steel, sharpened and curved.

"I'm giving him one, too." He gestured his head at Micah, who was asleep, back against the wall and head drooped to the side. "Excubitors are no trifle. You'll need his help."

"What makes you think I won't stab him?"

"Do what you want. Just know that I did my part."

"And yet, in trying to please so many masters, have you satisfied any?"

"I serve one master," Aicard said. "My heart — and the good it implores."

"Always with the platitudes," I scoffed. "You're an impossible read, but I'm sure you revel in that. I'll ask you one last time — who are you truly, Aicard?"

He breathed deeply and didn't exhale, as if preparing his answer. Then he stared at the ceiling and let out a resigned breath. "Everyone, even Micah, believes that I'm Aicard from Sargosa, but I'll tell you a secret." He came closer and hushed. "It's just another part I'm playing, in a far grander war — one of a scale you can't conceive."

I smelled goatshit on his tongue. "Is that all you have to say? How many layers of deceit will you shamelessly pile upon yourself?"

He covered his mouth and whispered, "Here's the truth. I was born on an island not on any map. I'll never forget how seven times a year, pillars would appear in the sky — beams of light that stretched from the sea to the highest heaven. It was a language, you see. Something deep in the ocean was speaking to something floating in the clouds."

I almost shook my head off. "What the hell are you talking about?"

"You want to know who I am, don't you?"

"That's not what I meant. I want to know whose side you're on. Save your life story for when we've a hookah to share."

He grabbed my bars, pushed his head through, and said without blinking, "I'm on the side of man."

A guard clanged his hilt against cell bars in the distance.

"I don't have much time. Hide the blade." Aicard bowed his head, as if I were a shah, warmth on his face. "I hope to see you when the wars between men are over. When peace can truly reign."

Shah Murad's words came out of my mouth: "Peace is a disease."

Aicard shook his head. "Only because we don't trust each other."

He spoke with Micah for some time and slipped him a blade too.

30

MICAH

I HID THE BLADE AICARD GAVE ME IN A CREVICE BENEATH A PILE OF worm-ridden hay. That way, none of the guards would touch it.

I hoped the Ruthenian, whose name I learned was Kevah, was as clever. He didn't like me much, but I hoped he'd put survival above his desire for vengeance. Then again, violent impulses tend to overwhelm sense.

Aschere had told me everything. His daughter's name was Melodi. I'd killed her atop the sea wall after she cut off my hand. And Aschere was Lunara, his wife. Funny, how connected I was to a man I'd never seen until I ended up in this dungeon. And yet, that's what fate does: connect us, even across the boundaries of empires and faiths. This was a cruel fate, though, built on deception. If there were gods, they were laughing at us — him boiling in his hatred, and me in my self-loathing for all I'd done in the name of an impotent angel.

The Crucian reconquest had ended in disaster, and it was because some laughing god resurrected Heraclius. To chase an army so deep into their territory was a blunder I never would've made, which is why I'd won wars that changed the fate of more countries than I had fingers. No matter how it ended for me, Crucian fathers would tell my story to their sons, and their sons would say that I not only defended the faith but took back our holy land, only for some vainglorious old man and his insipid son to lose it. And yet, the thought left me hollow.

One day — I didn't know if it was ten days after I'd been imprisoned or a hundred — the excubitors descended into the dungeon. The four watchful eyes of the angel Cessiel adorned their silver armor. The eyes were arrayed in a diamond that reminded me of the black diamond in the clouds. What was worse than the realization that these angels were just servants of Hawwa?

The excubitors were Thamesian tribesmen from outside our country, holding no allegiance except to the Imperator. And they were known to be the most ferocious and skilled fighters. I'd once said that a single janissary equaled ten men. One excubitor might have equaled three janissaries, and that was no embellishment. But the real question was: how many excubitors did I equal?

I didn't realize how weak I was until I stood. A mere bundle of sticks with a bag of skin thrown over it. My Ruthenian companion didn't look much better, but he had curly blond hair to adorn his sorry state.

When the guardsman entered my cell, I plunged the knife in his liver. Then I grabbed his short sword and sliced his neck.

Down the hall, a squeal sounded and a body thumped onto the floor. Before I could look, three excubitors rushed me.

I blocked a sword with my metal hand and sliced a head off clean. The next excubitor was bigger than me, and no doubt skilled with his ax, but I turned his brown beard red by sidestepping his lunge and slashing his eyes.

As the remaining excubitor sprinted to get reinforcements, the Ruthenian hollered in agony. A guardsman strangled him against the wall, and he struggled to punch free. I picked up an ax from the ground, aimed, and hurled it into the guardsman's back.

That wasn't enough to placate the Ruthenian. The hateful fire in his eyes flared, and he charged at me with an excubitor's mace. I met his swing with my metal hand and lunged at him with my sword. He backed away, then smashed down on me as if his mace were a hammer and I a nail. I caught the mace with my black hand. Whatever metal the darkness had molded it from was better than any weapon.

The Ruthenian dropped the mace and tackled me to the ground. Punched my jaw bloody. My blood tasted metallic and sour, and I was choking on my teeth until I kneed him in the groin.

I crawled away, but he grabbed my foot. I kicked his head; before I could rise, he threw himself on me. We wrestled — his strength against mine. Metal against flesh. I squeezed his arm with my metal hand, twisted it, and pulled myself over him. Then I smashed his head into the floor.

The bearded, blond-haired sack of skin and bones lay limp. Fearing reinforcements, I grabbed a lantern off a dead excubitor and ran into the stony stairwell.

Josias and his excubitors controlled the upper floors, which comprised the workshop and storage chambers. Higher than that was the great hall where Josias held court. There was no safe way but down, so I descended the spiral staircase. Lower and lower, until the chilly air of Labyrinthos brushed over me. Before I knew it, I was at its black mouth and through the iron gate that locked the tunnels away. Real darkness lay beyond, but there were no fireflies to guide me.

Did I really want to go? Some days, I swore that I'd never left Labyrinthos. That all that had happened since were just shadows dancing on its ancient, tar walls against the light of green fireflies. There was no place I wanted to be less, and yet it whispered to me so sweetly.

I couldn't even finish my thought when the Ruthenian ran down the stairs, clanging his mace against the wall. Would he chase me into the depths? Would he find his wife and daughter at the gateway to hell? Or would we be two lost souls, wandering the winding caverns until our skins withered off our bones?

A bloody and swollen head didn't stop the Ruthenian. He charged with the mace and swung at my chest. I jumped to the side and grabbed his neck, then dragged him down and crushed the air out of him. The mace fell from his hands as he struggled against my strength. I braced to twist his neck.

A fiery pain erupted in my side.

"Fuck." I released my grip and stumbled to the floor. He'd stabbed me with a concealed dagger, right in the kidney.

Blood spurted in the bare light of my lantern. The Ruthenian dipped his hand in the blood pooling from my side, as if he needed to be sure it was real. It smelled like the metallic heavy water of the High Holy Sea. My blood became a river on the cold, hard ground. A fatal wound, no question.

He brought his knife to my throat.

"Kevah!" called a voice from the darkness. Sweeter than strawberries. Elly's voice.

I headbutted the distracted Ruthenian, cracking my nose. The knife flew from his hand as he stumbled outside the iron gate. I closed it and tied the chain around to lock it.

The gasp of strength in my body faded. I fell to my knees. The scowling man crawled up the steps, then looked back at me, cleareyed and plain faced. He got on his feet and rushed upstairs.

I got back on my feet too. Clutching my wound, I staggered through the tunnels. Moments later, the clanging of steel on steel reached my ears. The Ruthenian must've been swinging an ax against the chain that tied the iron door. Fear forced me to hurry into the darkness of Labyrinthos, praying to no one that I'd make it far enough before he broke through.

31

KEVAH

I SUNDERED THE CHAIN WITH MY AX. THE DOOR SWUNG OPEN. THE last time I'd been at the entrance to Labyrinthos was hours before Micah killed Melodi. And yet, I'd just heard her sunny voice in the cave. Was it real, or were the jinn playing tricks?

I hoped Micah was bleeding in agony. It was what he deserved. But leaving him like that was not final enough. He'd survived many battles, and I wanted to ensure he wouldn't survive this one. I could follow his trail of blood, ax him to pieces, and be out in minutes.

As I stared at the black mouth, I recalled that these were the winding caverns that led to the gate of hell. All souls — good and evil — went to Barzakh first, and then Lat adjudged them to one of the thousand worlds of paradise or hellfire. But I'd descend to the coldest hell before any of that if it meant I could ensure Micah's end.

And yet, my feet wouldn't move toward the darkness. I knew if I followed Micah's blood trail that I would never leave Labyrinthos — that I would succumb to the madness that seized all who walked into it.

I forced my feet forward. Why did I hesitate? Why were my feet laden like a blacksmith's hammers? It wasn't fear that stopped me.

I wanted something that could not be found in that tunnel. That could only be found under the sun and stars of the living world. I thought of how she pinched me while we were floating in heaven. I wished she were here to snap me out of this nightmare. To pull me back from the precipice.

But rage drove my feet forward. The memory of Micah choking Melodi — of him stabbing her throat — could push a mountain. I hurried into Labyrinthos, lest I change my mind.

And then I stumbled. Collapsed onto the ground. I'd caught my boot on a rock, and the fall stung. On my knees and covered in tiny rocks and dust, I looked in front. There was nothing there. Just an empty depth. I turned my head and looked upon the entrance, which was growing distant even though I wasn't moving.

I imagined Sadie standing there, holding her hand out, begging me to come back. That was my reason not to go. My reason not to sacrifice myself for vengeance. Sadie. I wanted to see Sadie more than I wanted to kill Micah.

As I dashed to the entrance, it was as if it were running from me. As If I were chasing it. In my mind, something chased me too — a fire jinn from a children's tale, its horns made of lava and its split tongue ravenous for my flesh. But Sadie was there, cheering me on, her kindness like a lighthouse. The entrance was near now. I thrust forward and grabbed onto the bars. I heaved and coughed and regained my breath. I'd come back from the bridge to hell — thanks to her.

Before I ascended the stairs, I looked back one last time, resolute that the darkness would not have me.

I needed to hide.

The next level up was the canteen. I climbed the stairs and approached the entrance at the end of an unrecognizable hallway.

The Crucian purple covering the walls would give any Sirmian eye blisters. Even stranger, dead excubitors lay scattered at the canteen doorway, gun wounds smoking through their enameled plate.

I peeked through a bullet hole in the door. A group of gunners had barricaded themselves. If the excubitors were their enemy, then perhaps I could be their friend. They fired at me, exploding another hole through the wood door.

"I'm a prisoner from the dungeon!" I shouted after backing up against the wall. "I'm looking for a place to hide. Can you help me?"

"Drop your ax and approach, slowly!" a heavily accented voice shouted back. I couldn't place the accent.

Was that wise? Or should I take my chances on the higher floors?

I settled my ax on the floor and approached the men. On the left, someone aimed a matchlock at me from behind an over-turned cabinet. And on the right, another man lay flat on the floor beside an overturned table, his long barrel aimed in my direction. Right in front of me, a Silklander stood up and put his gun in my face.

"You're that zabadar they captured." The Silklander gestured for me to take cover behind the barricade. "You do anything stupid, and I'll shoot you." He handed me a matchlock. It was typical of Micah's matchlocks, with a rotating cylinder that stored four bullets. "Aim at the entrance."

"Why are they after you?"

The Silklander frowned. He was bald with thin, wavy eyebrows and a thick, even wavier mustache. "Because none of us want to go to Hyperion. You want to go to that shit heap?"

I shook my head. His gun had a longer, thinner barrel and more holes in its smaller cylinder, enough to hold seven bullets. Most surprising, the trigger didn't have a slow match.

"I've never seen a gun like that," I said.

"Because it's the only one like it."

It took genius to innovate in matters of fire and metal. I then remembered what Aicard had said: Micah had a Silklander engineer who made weapons for him. Humayra had also told me of him, though I couldn't recall his name.

"You're the Taqi of guns," I said. "You'll have to explain that new gun to me."

"I don't know what that means. And I don't see why I should."

"If we survive this and the Shah retakes the Seat, I'll put in a good word for you."

The Silklander sighed as if regretful. "We'll be gone before the Shah arrives."

"Don't you want to see your wife?"

"Which one?"

"The one you held in a cage."

He grunted in shock. His nostrils flared. "Is she all right?"

"She was well last I saw her. She told me how you kept her alive and even taught her Crucian."

"Humayra was a fast learner." The Silklander's eyes softened. "I had no idea you knew her. My name is Jauz."

"Well, Jauz, I'm sure the Shah would value your service. And despite the strange way you did it, he may also be grateful that you saved the mother of a princess."

"The Shah was there when it happened. I watched Micah butcher his family and didn't do a thing to stop it. No man would forgive that, let alone a king."

"Could you have stopped it?"

Jauz seemed to watch the memory in his mind. Then he said, "In war, the better butcher wins. The one with the weak stomach usually finds it slit open. But killing the family of a king — it's not something I would've advised." He shook his head. "I thought it, and many more mistakes, would be Micah's undoing. Then I watched a ball of green fire melt a thousand armored soldiers in seconds." Sweat dripped off his strong forehead, as if he still felt that fire. "Darkness blesses that man, and I fear you haven't seen the end of it."

We held this position the rest of the day and repulsed several assaults by paladins and excubitors. During the downtime, I got acquainted with Jauz, who also patched up my headwound. He was dumbfounded to hear that Aschere was my wife.

As we shared a few underripe dates while crouching behind an overturned table, Jauz told me what he knew about her: a horrific report of a woman beyond recognition. I tried to connect the Lunara I knew to the one in his story, but the task left me bewildered. Was there something I'd missed? Had Lunara secretly always been so cold, so uncaring, so malevolent? Perhaps my love had obscured her true nature. I thought back on our childhoods and on the blooming days of youth but couldn't find a moment when Lunara had been cruel. Could the years have changed someone so thoroughly?

They had changed me. Turned me from a hero into a coward. Perhaps it was the loss of a son — our son — that changed her. A boy I never had the opportunity to know, and never would. Another child taken from me. I didn't want to think on it because it filled me with poisonous rage, and I needed my sharpest wits to survive the present ordeal.

"Was there ever a moment when she was kind?" I asked Jauz.

Silklanders ate dates in an odd way. Instead of spitting the pit while chewing, he would squeeze it out with his hand. "You want to know if there's still good in her? I didn't see it — ever. Don't take this the wrong way, but if she were in front of me now, I wouldn't take that chance. I'd fill her with holes."

Those words cut me. The thought of her dead hurt, as it always had. She still held a piece of my heart, one that bled each day since she left.

"I'll tell you this," Jauz continued, tossing a date pit. "In the Silklands, we like to understand how things work. Why the days grow long in summer. Why the tides get stronger under a full moon. Why does saltpeter cure meat and also help charcoal burn? But were I to try to understand the things Aschere could do..." He shuddered. "I fear we are not meant to know."

To think she was so far gone...the sorrow choked me. If what he said was true, then my Lunara was dead.

Jauz twirled his mustache. "I don't know if it's worth mentioning..." He twirled it faster. "I saw her feeding the birds once. The black drongos in the garden."

Kindness to animals...and yet she left our son to die in the desert. Birds never go hungry anyway — what a fruitless gesture.

BY THE THIRD MORNING, there were no more footsteps on the floors above. No more shouting and clamor. The Sublime Palace was as still as a crypt.

Before he left the Seat, Jauz handed me his special gun. "I don't need this where I'm going. For whatever it's worth, tell Humayra I'm sorry."

"Where will you go?"

"The Silk Emperor has been waiting a long time for his statue."

"So while we sow our fields with blood, the kings in the northeast build statues."

"It will be greater than the Colossus of Dycondi." His bored tone contrasted with the grandeur of the Colossus. "Hopefully I can finish it before I die."

Once the Silklanders had left for the dock, I went up to the great hall. The Crucians hadn't held it for that long, but it was unrecognizable. The golden peacock with ruby eyes was no more. White and purple paint covered the walls, and straight Crucian script in black replaced wavy, golden Paramic calligraphy. Worst of all were the paintings of angels, with their insect eyes and legs and protrusions. They had too many wings and eyes. One even resembled the giant jellyfish I tried my best to forget. I couldn't fathom worshipping these bloodcurdling creatures.

The sight of the throne comforted me. It was as we'd left it: a golden divan with cushions embroidered with magnificent birds. I'd never gotten this close to it. I brushed its silky texture. I sat on it.

For the hours before the Shah's army retook the city, I was the ruler of Kostany...which meant nothing as the palace was empty.

I left the great hall and stood upon the palace wall. The midday sun hid behind a thick, black cloud. A drizzle and breeze cooled me. These would be the last summer rains before the dry season that ushered autumn.

Much of the city had been burned. What remained was an unplanned mashup of stone, mud, and wood buildings huddled along the city's cobbled streets. I descended the steps of the Seat and made my way to Tengis Keep.

I arrived at the estate near the lake. The roof had collapsed through the second and third floors. The courtyard where I'd trained with Lunara was overturned and filled with broken stone. This was once my home, and now it lay as a ruin. If Tengis survived, he wasn't here.

I knelt amid the rubble and made a fist. "This was all your fault. You taught me to be dutiful. I should have stayed in Tombore. I should've never answered the Shah's summons. I should've never come back." I dabbed my fingers against my eyes to stop the tears. How pathetic: a forty-year-old's resentment toward the man who taught him everything. Who taught him to survive in a world that crushed the slightest weakness.

"The Seluqal House is your shield," Tengis would say, *"be dutiful to them, and they will never forsake you. Be mindful of Lat, and she will never forget you."*

"Liar!" I screamed at the rubble of his house. "I've suffered enough for them. I'll take Sadie and go far from here. I'll spit on what you taught me." I heaved and shouted, "Say something, old man!"

"*You're a soft, well-fed ninny who reads too much poetry.*" That's what he would've said. I recalled his scolding when I washed my shoes in the lake, so many moons ago. If only he were here today, he would've laid bare my unsaid truth in that agitated tone of his: "*Ten years ago, you ran from your father and daughter. And then when you had a second chance to be a good son, to be a good father, Micah took it all away. Because you were weak.*"

I put my forehead to the ground, tears gushing onto cracked stone, and prayed, "Please be alive. I want to see you again, Father. Please."

I returned to the Seat and bathed in the Shah's private bath-house. A painting of a different bird adorned each marble tile. Water and steam, heated by a stone-filled fire, cleansed weeks of filth and decayed skin. Afterward, I slept in the great hall on the floor beneath the throne.

I awoke to the sound of fluttering. Kinn stood on the throne as if he were the shah of the shiqq.

"You left me," I said. "You left me to rot in that dungeon."

"I did what you commanded me to do."

"Where were you all this time!?"

"I helped us win. Who do you think whispered to the Alanyan prince to ride south with his gholam? Who inspired the Shah to keep fighting? Me."

Around Kinn's neck, a pendant shone with a milky light. For some reason, it made me sad.

"The city is about to be retaken," he said. "But...there's something I have to tell you. It's Sadie..."

Blood drained from my face. "Take me to her."

Janissaries and gholam poured through the gates and retook

the walls. Kostany was reconquered. What a struggle it had been, and yet I hardly cared. What matter was a heap of mud and stone when Sadie was in trouble? I hurried out of the south gate and followed Kinn toward the camp. The zabadar on guard recognized me and let me through. It was some comfort to see these horse folk, who'd rescued me from the worst despair of my life and given me a home. They pointed me toward Sadie's yurt.

She slept as if at peace. Faint breaths moved in her chest. A man in the gray garb of a healer knelt and prepared incense at her bedside.

"When will she wake?" I asked.

The slant-nosed healer hunched his shoulders. "The girl suffers from a fever, made worse by the blow to her forehead. Her body fights its own battle — when it wins, she'll wake."

I knelt at her bedside and touched her hand. Her skin was clammy and blueish. When I'd last seen her, she sat radiant upon her horse. I caressed her hair. A purple bruise and sewn gash stuck out on her forehead.

"What did this?" I asked the healer.

"Best I let him tell you."

Shah Murad had slipped into the yurt. He wore the dirty and scuffed chainmail of a warrior. His beard seemed a lion's mane. I didn't stand for him; I didn't want to let go of Sadie's hand. Not yet.

"You lost weight." The Shah knelt beside me. "And quite a lot of age. No wonder she likes you." He raised his hands and said a quick prayer. "Heraclius caused that wound. I cut him down for it. But the sickness is from Lat."

"You're her father. Is she not more precious than the world to you?"

"You think I didn't want to take her somewhere safe?" Murad's eyes were bloodshot and watery. "I'd give everything to have seen my children grow rather than butchered before me. We did not choose to be of the Seluqal House, but I'm sure you've come to realize, magus, we don't choose our fates."

"I'll choose whatever fate I want."

"Is that what you think? Do you know why I summoned you from Tombore? Because of a dream. Nay, a vision. Many moons ago as I slept, I saw you with that magus' mask around your neck. Except it wasn't just one mask. There were so many masks, all dangling from your neck, all of them your prizes."

"My prize? Is that what you call this curse?"

The Shah nodded. "Power is a curse. You can use it to kill — slaughter all you want — fill your plate with bones and your goblet with blood. But to save those you love? Hah!" He took his daughter's other hand, trembling, and squeezed his eyes shut. "I wanted to show my power when Hayrad freed me. I had nothing in me but the blood of Temur, who built a tower with Crucian skin and skulls to avenge his fallen. The Crucian princess...I would have ended her. It would have sated me, barely, but she —" He swallowed bitterly. "Sadie said that if I killed Celene, that she would ride away and I would never see her again. That if we were no different from those we fought, she could not be one of us." With a twitch and twist on his face, the Shah began shaking. With laughter. "I should have tossed Celene into our biggest bombard and shot her back to her father. That's the way of Temur. That's the way of my blood. Had Sadie left me because of it, all the better. She wouldn't be lying here at death's shore."

One of the Shah's retainers beckoned him and he left. What a glorious day for the blood of Temur, for the Seluqal House. They'd reclaimed Kostany and smashed their greatest foe. But I'd trade the whole kingdom to see Sadie's eyes open.

Sadie's mother entered a few minutes later. She covered her face with a veil, but that didn't hide her tears. Hunched over and sickly, she would turn her gaze away, then look back at her daughter, as if hoping she would awaken between glances. What could I say to her? How could I offer her comfort when I had none to give?

My heart was sinking into quicksand. I didn't notice when Nesrin entered. She wouldn't look me in the eye, as if she were a child who'd failed her teacher. But I knew she'd done everything to keep Sadie safe. The girl sulked and pressed her hand against her forehead.

"Nesrin," I said. "I'm relieved to see you well."

"What does it matter that I'm well?" She sobbed and heaved. "I can't do anything for her. Just like I couldn't do anything for my father."

"We're all just children when it comes to life and death."

Nesrin's tears wet the carpet.

"Kinn!" I called.

The chicken waddled into the yurt.

"Go and tell every jinn you know that they had better do everything in their power to save this girl. And tell those jinn to tell the same to every jinn they know, until all the jinn in heaven and earth have heard."

Kinn scratched his head with his rounded claw. "I don't want to be insensitive, but the jinn won't care about some human girl… princess or not."

"You're wrong. The jinn told Magus Vaya to free her back in Lyskar. They care about her. Now go!"

Nesrin looked up at me, her cheeks wet. She couldn't see Kinn, but she didn't seem confused. "You didn't see her, Kevah. They'll tell stories about how many armored riders she brought down. About how she shielded the Shah with her furious arrows."

"No, Nesrin. They'll tell stories about how she awoke from her sickness and married some prince. How she had fat children and grew gray and wise."

Nesrin tried to swallow her laughter. It mixed with her sobs. "That doesn't sound like her."

"After all the battles have been fought, isn't that what we all want?"

"Some of us must die so others can have it."

"Then let me die. But not her. Not her."

The more I looked upon Sadie, the angrier I got. The resentment boiled. Why was this happening — again? Was it Ahriyya who cursed me, or Lat herself? I was certain I'd kill everyone on earth to break this curse. I left the yurt, lest I explode in furor.

An unexpected man stood in the mud outside: Grand Vizier Ebra, flicking prayers beads and reciting praises to Lat, as was the fashion.

He didn't notice as I lunged and smashed my fist into his forehead. He fell into the mud, and I climbed on top. Before I could bash his face into lumps, janissaries pulled me off. One elbowed me in the chest, so hard I felt my ribs would fly out my mouth. They pushed me down onto my knees.

A stunned Ebra sat up and flung his prayer beads into the distance. Back on his feet and clutching his forehead, he spat on the ground. "A lover's rage is hotter than hell. You were always a dashing man, but enough to woo a Seluqal princess?" He shook his head. "No matter how high our legends soar, we'll never be more than servants in this land of theirs."

I couldn't break the janissaries' grip. "Fuck you."

"I was right. You did want to marry her, but the Shah of the Seas said the words first. Seems like you were the coward all along. What is a hero without valor?"

"You were right about goatshit. We reconquered Kostany. We defeated Micah. Without any help from you."

Ebra's silks dripped mud. A janissary brought him a wet cloth for his eye, but he threw it on the dirt. He came close to my ear and whispered, "Was it worth it?"

The janissaries pushed me flat on the ground. Ebra whistled, and they released their grip. I turned to watch them walk away.

· · ·

THE HEALERS MOVED Sadie to a room in the Sublime Seat with a verandah that let in fresh air. Nesrin and I slept that night on its silky, patterned carpets. Healers placed fresh incense every few hours, mostly chamomile and arrowroot. When they washed Sadie's body, I saw the swelling. It was as if water filled her ankles and turned her skin blue.

I prayed to every intercessor. I prayed to Saint Nizam, Saint Kali, Saint Chisti, and dozens of others whom I only knew by name. I asked them to beg Lat to let Sadie wake. And I prayed to Lat herself, though that'd never gotten me anything. Perhaps it was as the Fount taught, that she only listened to those that dwelled near her throne — that only the prayers of pure hearts reached her. But had she ever created a purer heart than Sadie's?

The next day, I awoke to chirping birds. A cool dawn shone through the clouds as a subtle breeze brought warm sea air.

But Sadie lay so still, her head tilted on her pillow as if serenely asleep. Her chest did not move. I put my ear to her heart and held my breath. I kept holding it, praying to hear a rhythm, until my face must've turned purple and I gasped and coughed and choked on a familiar dread.

"I shouldn't have given you a choice." I threaded my hands through her hair. "I should have caged you in my love and put you away somewhere."

Where could I have put her? A man as weak as me? I wasn't a king. I had no power. Whatever I loved were like eggs in a bird's nest, ever ready to be snatched by the next vulture. And the vultures were everywhere: I imagined them filling the room and carrying Sadie away. No matter how firmly I clung to her, I was not enough to stop them from whisking her to the next life.

I wished they'd take me too. Why was I cursed with life? It wasn't fair, to always be biting down on pain. As the imagined vultures carried Sadie out the window, the thread of light between us snapped. Severed forever — until the world turned to cinders.

I shrugged off the imagery. Sadie still lay in the bed. Maybe she wasn't dead. Maybe someone could save her. I shouted. I wailed. Nesrin awoke and rushed out of the room.

The healers came in their night robes. They checked Sadie's heart. A white-bearded healer raised his hands, palms open, and recited the death words, "To Lat we belong and to her we return."

I wanted to bludgeon them as they put her on a litter. How could they take her away? Were I the Shah, I'd behead them, and their families, for daring to call themselves *healers*. But what of those who called themselves *saints*? How worthless was their intercession? And the one called *god*? If Lat heard our prayers and did nothing, then she was wicked like Ahriyya. If she couldn't hear or was powerless to answer, then she wasn't worthy of worship. If I could, I'd tear down every shrine, burn the holy books, and disembowel the sheikhs. Extinguish this hopeless faith.

The scholars said Ahriyya was driven by hatred toward Lat and her worshippers. They never said what Lat did to make him so angry. Swallowing despair and rage, I now had some idea.

IN ACCORDANCE WITH OUR FAITH, they planted Sadie's shrine the next morning in a garden at the Sublime Palace. Humayra wept as they lowered her shroud in the dirt. The Shah, though he was busy reestablishing control over the city, took the time to attend the ceremony, which some sheikh presided. Even Redbeard was there, and behind his unruly beard and corsair facade, scowled with genuine grief. The Alanyan prince hadn't known Sadie, but the moment overwhelmed him as he pulled his orange turban over his eyes. Ebra seemed smug as usual, but now a bruise adorned his perfumed face. The Shah Mother veiled herself, most likely to hide her delight. I raised my eyebrows in surprise upon seeing Princess Celene in the garden, wearing a black frock as sullen as her expression. I supposed she was the Shah's hostage and would be until peace was restored.

Tens of thousands perished while I was in the dungeon. I'd had an easy time, it seemed. Men buried their brothers. Wives buried their husbands. Brothers buried sisters. Daughters buried fathers. But most were not buried because their bodies were baking in the mud somewhere. Many prayed to see their loved ones again, and Lat would answer few of those prayers. Kostany had been reclaimed...but as Ebra had said...was it worth it?

As the sheikh read from the Recitals of Chisti, the zabadar crowded the garden with Nesrin and Yamin at the head. Though most remained stone-faced, many covered their faces with their hands to hide their tears. Nesrin cried in the arms of her brother. The tears in his beard seemed like pearls of grief.

Sadie's death was the last star in the sky burning out, leaving me in darkness. But I did not cry. I knew what I had to do. Once dirt covered her shroud, I strapped on my weapons, walked into the palace, and descended its spiral steps into its deepest part. Before long, I stood at the black mouth of Labyrinthos. Micah's blood stained the ground. Had the darkness claimed him? Would it claim me?

Lunara had spoken of her god. All I knew was that this god had brought back a dead man. That was the only god worth talking to. All the jinn, all the intercessors, and Lat herself...none cared enough to save Sadie. Perhaps they couldn't. Perhaps they were powerless before death. Perhaps Lunara's god was the only true god.

I'd been staring at the entrance for minutes now. The darkness whispered. It blew an icy wind that thinned the air.

Nesrin ran down the stairs in her mourning gown. She gasped with relief at the sight of me.

"Don't go!" She grabbed my arms and tried to drag me up the stairs.

I pushed her away. "The god inside brought a dead man to

life. I'm going to make her bring Sadie back too. No matter what it takes. No matter what she asks of me."

"Why you?" Nesrin pleaded. "Why do you bear all these burdens?"

"Because I have nothing left."

"Sadie wouldn't have wanted you to do this. She would've wanted you to be happy. She would've wanted to die to make the world better, not worse."

"She died for her country. But it was not worthy of her. I would rather see this country, and all others, erased — if it would bring her back."

"She would not want that trade. You know she would not want it." Nesrin clung to my arm. "I won't let you do this. You have much to live for."

An icy gust torrented through and made us shudder. It screamed my name as it passed my ears. Or had I imagined it? No matter — the gateway to hell seemed more welcoming than another day sunken in grief.

"Nesrin." I held her cheeks and looked her in the eyes. "If there's anything left, Lat will take it away." I sniggered. "I'm cursed."

"Sadie wasn't your possession!" Nesrin reared back, as if to strike me. "She chose to die for her country, not because of some curse placed upon you!"

Nesrin was right. I loathed my powerlessness. If it were a curse, I could blame fate. But it was Sadie who chose, just like Melodi had. Just like Lunara chose to leave me and follow a dark god. They made their choices, and yet I felt so slighted. I didn't want them to have the power to choose; I wanted that power for myself. I wanted to pick who lived and died. I would choose better souls to inhabit this earth than Lat had.

Kinn fluttered down the stairs. His little eyes bulged at the sight of Labyrinthos. A feather shed off his thighs as he landed next to me.

"She's right," he said. "You mustn't go in."

"Don't tell me what to do, chicken. Your kind has proven useless."

Nesrin raised an eyebrow. "You're talking to your jinn again?"

I turned away from them and walked a few paces toward the mouth of Labyrinthos.

"Is there no stopping you?" the little chicken pleaded. "Are you so determined to meet your end?"

"Either I get what I want in there, or I die. I've never been given a better choice."

"You're wrong," Kinn said. "In that place are fates worse than death."

"Then let it be. I'll accept any fate, but not this one. Not the one Lat chose for me, where I watch everyone I love die. Down there, at the gate to hell, fates are written by darker gods. By Ahriyya. By Hawwa. Let them listen to my prayer and write what they will. I'll cherish it. I'll do whatever they ask. Be whatever they desire. But I won't accept Lat's cursed fate."

Kinn fluttered onto my shoulders. He put a thin chain around my neck. A pendent glimmered on it — the one I'd noticed him wearing earlier. A white crystal shone in the pendant, within which throbbed a somber, pearly light.

"The hell is this?" I asked.

"I don't know. Saran told me to give it to you if ever you entered Labyrinthos."

"Saran...the peacock lady?"

White light twinkled within the crystal like a star. For some reason, it made me sad.

"Don't touch the crystal with your hands," Kinn said. "It burns."

I tucked it under my shirt. "What else does it do?"

"I'll protect you from sorcery. You think the jinn above have powerful magic...wait till you see what the jinn below can do."

Nesrin hugged me. "You better come back." Her tears wet my

neck. "I'll pray for you. I won't stop praying, not until I see you again. But whatever you do, don't come back astray," she sniffled, "like that fire magus. Because if you do, then I won't stop until you're buried too."

I pulled out of her embrace, turned away from her forlorn eyes, and began my descent.

32

MICAH

I AWOKE IN THE DARK WITH A BLOODY MOUTH, A BOULDER PRESSING on my chest. My lungs wouldn't fill, and I wheezed as soon as I inhaled. The pain was as if a sword cut through my belly, and another through my back, and yet another through my side. Oh yes, the Ruthenian had stabbed me — right in the kidney.

I moved my hand to check the wound. I felt the softness of cloth tied and wrapped over it. Who had tended to me?

I tried to push the boulder crushing my chest. But there was nothing there. The crushing came from within, from my bones and muscles. I felt the ground beneath me and the wall behind. Cold. Smooth like a water stone.

This was true darkness. Not a glimmer or a shimmer to be found. If it weren't for the hard ground and the pain, I might suspect that I didn't exist. That I was merely a thought that flickered into god's mind — whatever god really created us.

When I tried to get up, the pain in my chest and sides and belly flared as if I'd swallowed boiling water. I settled and sat still.

At least I wasn't dead. Or was this death? Was I in Baladict?

I didn't know whom to pray to in those nauseous moments. I wished I'd died with faith on my tongue and heart. A believer's death. But then my soul would pass to Baladict, and it was clear who the master of Baladict was: a god I refused to serve because I couldn't serve what I couldn't love.

As children, we were taught that the Archangel and the Twelve Holies were merciful, just, and good. They loved us even when we sinned. And they would send punishments upon the sinners to clean them of sin, the way fire cleanses gold. So if any were suffering because of life's viciousness, it was out of love.

To those who did good deeds, the rewards would be in the next life. After the resurrection at the Fountain, the angel Principus would judge us. He recorded our good deeds and our sins into two books and would weigh them on a scale.

A folk tale that my father told me — though not canon — was that the angel Cessiel would hide a piece of lead in the book of good deeds so that when Principus measured, the book of good would weigh more, even if the good deeds were lighter than the sins. And Cessiel would not do this on her own. The Archangel, in his infinite mercy, would ask her to so he could welcome more into his paradise.

No one knew what that paradise was except that there would be twelve levels, the highest of which would bring you near to the Archangel. But even the lowest level was a blissful place that no one could comprehend. I always aimed for that lowest level and hoped I'd get a chunky piece of lead in my book. But now, what did it matter? What were all the prayers for? Should I cling to a god that was powerless before another, greater one?

Light shone in the distance. A warm glow came toward me with footsteps.

"Thank the angels you're awake." A Sirmian accent.

"Berrin? Where are we?"

He knelt next to me and put the lantern to his face. An

unkempt beard puffed around his cheeks. "We are near the gate to hell."

"And what? You're looking for a way out? We'll never find it."

"I'm looking for that girl."

"For Aschere?"

"Not Aschere...the girl," Berrin said. "The young girl. The pregnant one. She led me this way, and now I don't know where she went. Every tunnel seems to lead to an opening with four or five more tunnels, all going in different directions, which lead to their own openings, that also have their own tunnels, going in different directions. This place makes no sense."

"We only made it through last time because of Aschere's fireflies."

"The girl said she knew the way."

"What fucking girl!?"

"The thing pretending to be your daughter!"

I was hoping it wasn't her: the demon Elly, who'd given me the gift of this arm, restored me to health, and took as her payment my seed.

"Did you carry me all this way?" I asked.

Berrin walked around to the different openings. Dark suffocated his lamplight. I barely saw it from a few feet away.

"You're a tall fucking man." He chuckled with a hoarse throat. Somehow his spirit had not withered. "But the dungeon made you scrawny."

"What've you been doing all this time?"

"I knelt to Heraclius...then I picked up a gun and defended the wall."

"Clever. But not clever enough. You should've left me and ran."

"Where would I go?" Berrin's tone descended into melancholy. "Where would I be welcome?"

"Certainly not this place."

Talking hurt, as if my lungs couldn't gather enough air for my tongue. Spikes stung all over my chest. This was how the Archangel left his devoted servant — dying at the gate to hell.

"Our religion is false, Berrin."

He knelt at my side, then sat against the icy cave walls and put the lamp between us.

"Does it have to be true to matter?" he said. "I studied different religions at the university. They are all true and false, in their own ways."

"So it's true what they say about you? That you never believed?"

"I believed and I didn't, like everyone else. Praying felt good, and it was nice to have hope."

"Sounds like an unbeliever to me. Good to know I'm not alone." I wheezed out a bloody cough. "Aschere said that a line had been drawn on my soul. That if I did not serve her god, everything would be taken away. Now look at me. I lost the city and my army. I lost my country and faith."

"We're more similar than you know, Grandmaster. There's something I ought to tell you."

"Just call me Micah. I'm not the master of anything anymore."

"Micah…I lied. I'm no Sirmian noble. I only said that so you would accept me."

"Berrin, what do I care if you're lowborn?"

"I'm not lowborn. My name isn't Berrin. It's Sulaym…eldest son of Selim the Cruel, the chosen heir of Shah Jalal."

"Then that means—"

"I delighted in the butchery of my cousins."

I laughed at the thought. Although it wasn't funny, not at all. Nothing hurt my lungs more than laughter. "I was going to say, it means you have a claim to the throne of Sirm."

"Claim — hah! What did it get my father? He hid his weaknesses behind his cruelty. I hid mine behind yours." Berrin pulled at his beard, his hand shaking. "The day after we massacred the harem, I went to Angelfall. Know what I did?" He coughed, then spat to his side. "I prayed for everyone we'd slaughtered. They didn't behead my father, nor did they abduct your daughter. The real killer — Murad — is coming to reclaim his throne. And it is *his* — not my father's, not the Imperator's, not yours — know why?"

"I don't know anything anymore."

Berrin laughed soundlessly. "I've read every religions' holy books. One theme resounds through them all — the gods direct affairs as they see, as they will, for reasons only they know. Pray with every breath, feed every orphan on earth, raise a million-man army if you can...but some god laughs at your plan, and before you know it, you're lugging your dying friend on your back through the gate to hell." Now his belly shook with laughter.

I laughed too — oh did it hurt. Were we going mad in this abyss? "You're a good man, Berrin. And a good friend. But this is where it ends. I don't see us getting out of here."

"I do." A voice came from the darkness. Sweet and melodic.

"Elly!?" I shouted. That was a mistake. It ripped my insides apart. I coughed bloody phlegm.

Berrin walked the length of the open area, looking for the source of the voice. "I don't see her." Then he turned back to me. He gawked and pointed to my left.

Elly sat next to me. Her black-on-black eyes always seemed so malevolent, but she smiled and still smelled of lilies. She wore the same white lily-patterned dress, but now her belly swelled: with my seed.

"Elly..." I wanted to hug her, but the pain was too much to move.

"I'll make you better, Papa." Elly put her hand over my heart. Somehow, it warmed my insides.

"But you're not Elly," I said as the pain lessened. The warmth was like a massage on my heart. "Who are you, truly?"

"Don't I make you happy this way?" she asked.

Berrin held up his lamp and squatted next to me. "You said you'd help us get out."

"I will," Elly said. "I'll take you exactly where you need to go."

"And where is that?" I asked.

"You'll see." Elly chuckled. The sound of her laugh healed my spirit as her warm hand healed my body. A numb tingling replaced pain.

"I don't want to go to Hawwa," I said.

"Fuck Hawwa," Elly said. "The moment I saw you marching through these caves at the head of your army, I knew I wanted you all for myself. If only to torment."

"So you don't serve Hawwa, but you keep me alive to torment me...what are you?"

"Your people call me Fallen Angel." She turned to Berrin. "His call me Ahriyya."

Both of us gasped, as if we'd come face to face with evil incarnate. Well, if her words were to be believed, we had.

"But Ahriyya is male," Berrin said.

Elly laughed. How could this dark creature make a sound so beautiful? "All your stories about me are wrong. Just know that I don't obey the angels. I don't obey Lat. And I definitely don't obey Hawwa."

"Why do you take my daughter's form?"

"What's worse than being mounted by your own daughter?" Elly chuckled. If she didn't consider toying with humans evil, then what *did* she consider evil?

Berrin's eyebrows were lightning bolts. I shook my head so he wouldn't ask.

Elly lifted her hand from my chest. "All better now."

It was true. I stretched my arms. I pushed off the wall and stood painlessly, a lightness in my body. How had Elly healed me so fast? Where did the Fallen Angels get such power?

441

Elly put her hand to her swollen belly. "Our child is coming." She smiled the way a mother would.

"Will our child be human…or one of you?"

"I have many half-human children. I try to have one every hundred years or so, all from the seeds of kings and conquerors. Some are more like you. Some are more like us."

"And you all live here? What even is this place?"

"Curious, are you? I'll just say this — I'm far from the worst thing here. Men gaze up at the night sky in awe of its mystery. But they don't consider what lurks below — things that even I fear, existing a thousand thousand layers deeper than where we sit. Things so old, born from seeds before time, that were I to glimpse even a shadow of their shadows, I'd be burned from presence and memory. And yet, we tarry upon the shell of an egg that will one day rebirth them."

My shudder almost paralyzed me. Was this truly such a cursed place, or was she toying with me some more?

Elly stood. Despite sitting on the cave floor, her dress remained white and pure. She walked toward a tunnel. "Some-one's coming. He's just above us." She suppressed a chuckle. "He has a gun!" What was so amusing about that?

Berrin and I looked at each other, concern awash on our faces. Neither of us was armed. Could it be the Ruthenian? His hatred for me would never abate.

Elly smirked. "Don't worry." She held out her hand, then pulled away when I reached for it with my flesh hand. "Your other hand," she said. "Your black hand is like the mask of a magus. If you learn to use it, you'll gain unimaginable power. That's why I gave it to you."

I held her hand with my metal one, and an invisible oil seeped through our handhold. What was cold and dry became moist and hot. It reminded me of my handhold with Aschere that summoned the fireball that burned Zosi and thousands of paladins alive. I recalled the terror on my brother's face as the searing flame melted him out of existence.

I pulled my hand away. "Let's talk to him, then. I know he hates me, but we can at least try."

"The man with the gun hungers for your blood," Elly said. "His is a hatred that will never sate until you're gone from this world, and I think you know why. Hawwa is guiding him here to punish you. If you don't kill him, he'll kill you." She put her hand to her belly. Her cheeks reddened and she smiled. "Don't you want to see our child?"

The child of a demon? Could I ever love such a thing, the way I loved Elly? And yet, she wasn't wrong. I wanted to be a father, more than a conqueror or king. I wanted to live, if only for that chance.

I took Elly's hand. Within seconds, my metal arm simmered with her darkness.

"He is a magus," Elly said, "who wears two masks. Kill him, and you can put them on. What will you do with such power, I wonder?" She chuckled.

If I ever had power again, I would do what I couldn't when the slavers snatched Elly in the night, all those years ago.

"I won't fight for false faiths." A crackling lightning suffused my metal hand. It yearned for release and cried for explosion. "But to see my child born and prosper, I will fight even the gods."

33

KEVAH

WOULD THIS TUNNEL EVER END? MY LAMPLIGHT BARELY SHINED IN the suffocating depths of Labyrinthos. All I'd brought was Jauz's gun, a pouch of ammo, and Aicard's dagger. Even through my boots, the cold ground chilled my feet. I was chattering and wished I'd worn a thicker cloak.

Instead of praying, I opened my heart to Hawwa and hoped she would see I was willing to do whatever she wanted. Not because she was true, nor because I loved her, but because she could bring Sadie back. If she were all-powerful, my private thoughts would be as clear as ink on parchment.

One thing I knew: a powerless god was not worthy of worship. Whether that god was good, I no longer cared. But if Hawwa were the one true god, why did she hide in this dark place?

Maybe we were wrong to think god was merciful and good. Maybe god put us in this world to suffer. Still, I'd strike a deal with such a god.

A green firefly clung to the ceiling, dropped, and hovered

toward me. When I passed it, another one appeared, and then another. The fireflies led me to an open area and down a winding cavern. By now I must've been deep in the earth.

Coiling tunnels. Winds that whispered and shrieked. Tar walls that stunk like the mucus of demons. Labyrinthos seemed as unholy as in the stories. The air thickened the deeper I got; my lungs strained to breathe the fog. But I pushed onward, ignoring fears of what may lurk in this beast's core.

Another open cavern lay before me. But the darkness here… danced. Like birds, shadows seemed to flutter in patterns. Almost alive — they looked like the black drongos from the Shah's garden. As I gaped in terror, the bird-like shadows surged together, coalescing into a monster — a massive jinn with hateful, eyeless sockets. My matchlock shook in my trembling grip; surely gunpowder would be futile against such a hell spawn. Surely my fear-drenched mind was painting childhood nightmares upon Ahriyya's canvas. I blinked and blinked, hoping the hateful jinn would vanish. To my relief, it faded like smoke wisps blown from a dying hookah. Was it real…or a portent of madness?

I regained some calm and followed the fireflies through a tight, fog-filled corridor. Then I turned a corner, and there he was, a true nightmare: Micah the Metal. Fireflies clung to the walls of the cave, bathing us in green.

I aimed my gun at his head and fired.

Micah punched the bullet with his metal hand; it whizzed by my head and hit the wall behind me. What kind of dark power was this? Where was the stab wound that sputtered and oozed?

I quelled my trembling and fired lower, at his stomach. With the speed of a hummingbird's wings, he caught the bullet, crushed it, and grinned. That same grin — the grin of Ahriyya himself — as when I fought him on the sea wall. As when he killed Melodi.

"Why won't you just die!?" I shouted.

Whatever darkness blessed Micah, I wished would bless me. Then I could kill him, avenge my daughter, and bring Sadie back.

Micah bent his knees, ready to charge. But he had no weapon. His eyes were bloodshot and hungry. He made a fist, then opened it. A ball of yellow light the size of a marble appeared in his hand, growing until it was as big as a melon. Then it raged toward me as lightning.

As if it were alive, the pendant Kinn gave me lifted forward and absorbed the lightning. The force of light it released sent me flying backward, onto the hard cave floor.

I rolled to my feet and slid behind a cave wall for cover. The pendant still floated on the chain around my neck. What the hell was it? Kinn had said it would protect me…

A white light glowed off the pendant. Brighter and brighter.

Micah approached. I peeked out of cover and fired. He swatted the bullet away. His metal hand glowed with a spectral hue, as if lit by black light.

How to fight a man who treats bullets like flies? I ran down the winding cavern I'd come from as Micah neared, hoping to find a hiding spot to calm my heart and figure out how to kill this bastard. Green fireflies clung to the walls, lighting my way. I backtracked to the opening I'd been in earlier.

Somehow it was different. Perhaps I'd taken a wrong turn, though I felt confident I'd gone back the way I came. I was in a huge open space — as if I were standing atop a mountain under an utterly black sky. Only my pendant and the green fireflies buzzing about provided any light. I walked until I reached the edge of a cliff, over which I could see nothing.

I hardly had a moment to breathe when Micah appeared. I shot twice, and he flicked the shots away with his forefinger. He grinned — but up close, it seemed so false. Now I realized why: he didn't enjoy this; he was baiting me. He took a low stance like a wrestler and gestured for me to come.

Fuck him. I dropped the gun, unsheathed my dagger, and ran

at him. He punched the ground.

Rocks shattered, and lightning hurled me in the air. I smashed onto my back near the edge of the cliff. My dagger flew beyond it. I coughed dust. A searing pain erupted across my back.

Before I could push myself up, Micah stood over me. My pendant floated between us, as if pulled like a magnet toward him, only kept from flying away by the chain around my neck.

Micah muttered something in Crucian. He stared at my pendant with big, reverent eyes. Tears gushed out of them. He bent down, then grasped the pendant with his black hand. White fire flared from the crystal. His arm ignited. Micah screamed while I pushed up and ran for my gun.

Footsteps — hurried. Dashing out of the darkness, another man appeared and shoulder-charged me in the chest. I landed, again, near the edge of the cliff — my ribs crying. I forced myself to my feet.

"Why do you have it!?" The man was Sirmian and familiar, though I couldn't place where I'd seen him. He resembled a younger Shah Murad, and his eyebrows pointed down with palpable fury. "Why do you have the Tear of the Archangel!?"

He picked up my gun and aimed at me. Micah still wailed — such a satisfying noise. The white fire burned on his arm but dissipated as he grinded against the ground.

I pushed up and rushed forward as the Sirmian man fired. The bullet screeched by my ear. I slammed into him, taking us down, and the gun flew from his grip and landed a few feet away. I punched the man in the jaw. I raised my fist to punch again, but Micah — now at my back — caught it with his metal hand, twisted my arm, and then flung me away. Toward the gun.

I picked it up, fired at Micah. His metal hand was burnt and missing a finger, but still he blocked the bullet with a backhand smack. Then he grabbed his head with his other hand and pulled his hair, as if overcome by pain. Sparks coursed through Micah's black arm. Another ball of yellow light formed in his palm. He crushed it; fiery bolts engulfed his fist.

I opened the loading cylinder of my gun. Empty. Instead of reaching for my ammo pouch, I reached for my pendant. The Tear of the Archangel, the Sirmian man had called it. I shattered the glass and allowed the tiny crystal to fall into the loading cylinder.

Micah lunged to finish me with a lightning punch.

I fired. His black hand caught the crystal bullet and combusted. He howled as his metal arm disintegrated in a blaze of lightning and white fire.

I didn't notice the Sirmian man. In the chaos, he'd gotten behind me and now put me in a chokehold. My throat felt like it would pop out of my neck. I headbutted him with the back of my head until he let go and stumbled. I grabbed my gun, loaded a bullet from my pouch, and aimed at Micah.

The gunpowder in the cylinder ignited, lighting the gun on fire. Had my face been closer, it would've burned. I dropped the flaming metal before it charred my hands. Fucking guns.

The Sirmian man smashed into me. We tumbled off the cliff's edge. Air zipped. A long fall. I screamed. Then crack, into the water. Agony overtook my arms and legs and body. Water filled my eyes.

Ignoring the pain, I swam upwards, gulping loads of water that stung my nose and throat.

Something pulled on my leg. The Sirmian man. I kicked his head. He climbed up on me, dragging me down. I pushed against him, but he was too big. He squeezed my neck. Suffocated me in this watery grave.

A firefly twinkled. Behind it, my dagger descended. I waited a second for it to be eye-level, grabbed it, and stabbed the Sirmian man's throat. Blood spurted, reddening the water. The man died with a lolling tongue.

Dagger in hand, I swam and swam until I hit air and gasped for breath.

The water tasted of rusted steel. Of iron and onyx. The flavors of the metals assaulted my tongue. I spat. My gums stung.

I took a few moments to regain myself. Had I fallen in one of Kostany's aquifers? But our water didn't taste like rust. I tried to see, but there was no light. So I picked a direction and swam.

A green firefly appeared. It dropped down in front of me like a falling star, then zipped by in the opposite direction. I turned to follow. More and more fireflies fell and zipped toward something in the distance. They throbbed green against a dark metal structure. As more of them shimmered on the thing, I began to see its form...or rather, its face. The metal monster had ten eyes in a vertical line. The fireflies swirled around it and combined to make a furious light. Then the fireflies poured into its open mouth, leaving me alone with the eyes. The eye at the bottom watched me.

As I pushed out of the water and onto dry ground, I trembled at the thought of going through that mouth. What was I doing here? What madness had possessed me to enter this place? Was there any way back, or was my soul trapped forever? Could even Lat pluck me out of this hellish chasm?

Perhaps hell was neither hot nor cold. Perhaps that mouth was the door to hell — a place of living terrors. An endless array of mouths, swallowing me for the rest of time — deeper, deeper, bowels within bowels, each new darkness a thousand times more hateful than the last.

I slapped myself. Bleeding, bruised, and broken — I couldn't stop now. Sadie needed me. I mustered every shred of bravery and walked inside the mouth of the metal creature, to wherever the green fireflies led.

Upon entering the mouth, the path descended into water. But this water was thick like milk and didn't reflect against the fireflies' light. I waded through this dark milk and climbed out to find another open cavern. The fireflies clung to the walls, floor, and ceiling, illuminating everything.

My boots crunched on broken glass. It covered the ground the way sand covers a beach. Metal pipes jutted out of the walls. Some slithered toward the ground, while others ended in the air as if cut partway. The pipes on the floor led to something in the middle of the room.

A broken glass wall. No, a glass cylinder, half-shattered. Lunara stood in front of it and watched, expressionless, as I approached. She stared at the ground when I got close enough to touch.

"I hoped it would be Micah," she said. "Or anyone but you."

I wanted to backhand her across that blank face of hers. For ten years, I prayed ceaselessly to see her again. But she'd forsaken me.

"I didn't come to shatter your hopes. I came to speak with your god. The god that brings back the dead."

"Indeed, you have seen her signs. You have witnessed truth."

"Truth? What truth is here, amid all this shattered glass?"

"The truth of where we came from. Our forms were all created here — angels, jinn, and mankind. But our souls are even older than that. Older than time itself."

"I don't care about truth. If your god will answer my prayer, then she can have my soul. She can have my service, my adoration, my worship — for as long as she wants it."

Lunara came close. She raised her hand to touch my cheek. She brushed my beard hairs, then lowered her hand.

"The Dreamer did not speak of you," she said. "I tried to turn Grand Magus Agneya, but she lost her mind when she heard the hymns. Still, Hawwa used her. I know not how she will use you."

"Where is Hawwa? Show her to me, so I may look upon god!"

"She's not here."

Laughter overcame me. "Not here? Are you saying I came all this way for nothing?"

"The Dreamer rules over Barzakh. I prayed for her to bring Melodi back, but she brought back another."

"Melodi? What right do you have to pray for her? It's because of you that she died!"

"Melodi is Micah's daughter."

My laughter turned dark. "Now you've truly succumbed to madness!"

"Is it madness? Or is it the Dreamer, directing all souls to their proper places?"

Lunara took my hand. Hers was colder than an icy rain. I winced and pulled away.

"I can't even touch you anymore." She shuddered and wiped a tear off her cheek.

"Forget about Micah. I will serve the Dreamer. I will be the instrument she wants. But only if she brings back what I've lost."

"And what have you lost?"

"I lost you. I watched the life drain from Melodi's eyes. Yesterday I woke up and the woman I loved didn't."

"Oh Kevah, you're softer than the nutmeg pudding we used to eat on hot, dry days. I once loved that about you — your steel shell and tender core. But you can't serve the Dreamer if a few deaths torment you so."

Fireflies swarmed. More and more. A whirlwind of green light surrounded us. Then the fireflies ascended into the air. They formed shapes. These shapes had many sides and points, and they kept changing.

Lunara stared at them, transfixed. The green of the fireflies' light shimmered against the green of her irises. "The Dreamer has heard your prayer. She will answer it in exchange for your service and bring back the one you love."

"I accept," I said. "Bring Sadie back, and my life and service are hers."

The shapes of the fireflies changed in the air. Patterns emerged among the shapes. These were letters, far more complex than any I knew. This was how Hawwa spoke to Lunara. How could she read such a strange language? What had turned her into this? When had she become so inhuman?

Lunara pierced me with her gaze. There was a time when that stare would ensnare my heart and either light it on fire or shatter it. When I'd listen to her talk in her sleep, and I'd laugh and cry because we were on this earth together. Did she still feel it, too?

"There is a condition." Lunara pushed a smile onto her face. "To prove your service."

Something was coming. It surged through the darkness and sliced the air like a thunderous wind. Then it crashed into the glass a few yards away and sent shards flying around the room. The fireflies shielded us from the shards, burning them with emerald fire.

Lunara and I approached the metal and glass coffin that landed like a meteor. The green light of the fireflies lit what was inside: Sadie. Her cinnamon skin seemed so fresh, as if it had never turned blue from the sickness that killed her. Slow breaths filled her chest as she slept.

I put my hands on the smooth glass that covered her. Hot, as if it'd just been forged. Whoever made this was a true god, that I couldn't doubt. I knew that I could never be with Sadie, but at least she would light up this world, if only because of my dark deeds.

The fireflies danced in the air, once again forming different shapes, each with many sides.

"Are you ready?" Lunara asked.

I nodded, unsure what she meant.

A large hole appeared in the air above Sadie's coffin. Within it was black, as if the air had been torn out and replaced with the darkest sky. A light flashed within the hole. Now it showed the image of a city. No, not an image — the people on the streets moved. I recognized the zabadar yurts at the wall and the resplendent green dome of the Seat. The Blue Domes shimmered in the sunshine, higher than everything. This was a window. It showed us what was happening above.

Lunara took my hand. She raised our handhold above our heads. Feeling her again, even like this, was a mad relief.

And then a fire within my arm melted her ice into hot water. It surged through me. Steam billowed from that water and filled me with insatiable power.

"Close your eyes."

I did as told.

In my mind, a black sphere bigger than a million earths churned. As it did, wisps of green light churned with it. Those lights formed shapes with hundreds of sides, changing their configuration every second. And then the black sphere shot out an egg: a pearl swimming through a dark sea. The egg cracked, and an angel pushed out. It soared across a starlit background, toward a hole that swallowed it.

I opened my eyes and looked upon the window to Kostany. The angel hovered above the city. It had eleven arms and eleven wings. "Archangel," I uttered. Its dragonfly wings — translucent and patterned like stained glass — flapped against the sky. Gunmetal encased its body, upon which were bulging veins. It gazed upon the city with a single human eye. The eye I'd seen in the giant jellyfish. The eye of Hawwa.

I wanted to stop it. I wanted to let go. But I couldn't resist Lunara's touch and the power that flowed through it. The power to eradicate a city.

The people of Kostany stared at the sky, transfixed. Others stampeded toward the gates. Within that city were all those that mattered to me, that mattered to Sadie: Nesrin, Yamin, Murad, Humayra, Redbeard.

"But all the people will—"

Lunara kissed me. She rolled her tongue around my mouth and squeezed my hand. Her saliva tasted of ice and honey.

I pulled my face away. "Is it really you in there, Lunara?"

"Of course, my love. Do you remember the day you came back from the war?" Lunara giggled. Whenever she did, dimples would form in her cheeks. "We hadn't seen each other in ten moons."

"I'll never forget," I said, straining to hold back tears. "You heard Jalal's army was returning to the city, so you rode to head us off and see me."

"I'd waited almost a year and yet couldn't wait a moment more."

"I sighted you on your black horse, galloping toward us. I tossed my spear and shield and everything I was carrying and ran to you."

"Being in your arms again was the sweetest relief."

"Shah Jalal was furious that I'd left my position. But when he saw it was you, he plucked a rose from the ground and put it in my hair!"

"They called you 'janissary of the rose' the rest of the way home!"

Giggling overcame us. We were children again, simply enjoying each other's existence.

"You're the sight of that day," I said, drowning in her eyes. "You waited ten moons to see me. I waited ten years."

A sword taller than a mountain materialized in front of the angel and hovered above the Sublime Seat. The blade glimmered like a diamond in the sun.

I looked at Sadie asleep in the glass coffin. I thought of her smiling. I pictured her riding her pink-bellied horse, her auburn hair trailing in the wind as she leaned forward. I'd not heard it enough, but I loved her laughter and how it revealed a chipped tooth.

What wouldn't I do to have her light up this world?

"The wait is over, my love," Lunara said, her voice tender like a rose. "We'll be together forever. We'll serve Hawwa — you and me. Now I know why she chose me. It was not for Micah. It was always for you. Together, we will open the gate to the Blood Star and bring the Dreamer into our world."

A green fire radiated around the Archangel's sword, swirling and churning so fast it would explode and annihilate Kostany. How miserable would Sadie be to return to a world without her loved ones? A world of anguish and sorrow. Such a world was not worthy of her.

"Lunara, we must stop this!"

Our handhold remained high and firm. I pulled. It would not break, as if our hands were melded together.

Lunara faced me and caressed my hair. "I gave up everything. I annihilated myself. And yet, no matter how hard I try, I can't help but love you." As if a dam burst, tears gushed down her cheeks. "But I am a servant of Hawwa, and there's only one way out."

The Archangel grabbed the sword with a sinewy hand. He raised it above his head. The green fire crackled like lightning, ready to torrent upon Kostany with a swing of the sword.

On tiptoes, Lunara pressed her cheek on mine. Then she rested her head on my chest. "It's your heart I love," she said, "and you must follow it."

As the angel swung, I unsheathed my dagger. I gazed into my wife's adoring eyes and plunged the blade between her ribs.

Lunara released my hand. A spasm seized her legs, and she fell upon the sea of glass shards. She smiled sweetly as she aged twenty years in a second. "I'll keep waiting...janissary...of the..." My wife trembled her last words and became still.

The massive sword shattered into a million metal pieces. A black hole swallowed the Archangel. The window to the city vanished, taking Sadie's coffin with it.

I dropped the dagger and fell on my knees, glass shards cutting them.

It was over. And I was alone.

I closed my eyes. When I opened them, I was not on earth. I

floated in a black sea. Stars twinkled everywhere, as if the night had swallowed me.

In front of me, the dark star churned. Wisps of green swirled and scalded me with their light. In this ghostly dimension, I saw her. Hawwa floated above her throne in a form I struggled to understand. She was shaped like a starfish, but a porous black milk bubbled through her body, as if she were not fully formed. A thousand and one eyes popped out of the milk and gazed at me. She was less a thing and more a coalescing of truths and nightmares. As I gazed at each eye, I felt that truth, I experienced each nightmare. I saw Lunara slip out in the night, mask in hand, never to return. She buried our son in the sand, then left him in a pyramid of bleeding skulls. I heard my daughter's cries as Micah strangled his own daughter. I felt Sadie bleed from her forehead and fall limp into mud. I saw eggs give birth to a thousand angels, and a jellyfish the size of a mountain, and creatures with limbs that sank into the sea and eyes that drifted in the clouds. I realized why she was the Dreamer: she brought her nightmares to our world.

In that moment of clarity, bursting with truths, drowning in love and sorrow, I said to her, "I will not serve you!"

Everything became white, and then black again. My body disappeared. I floated in a sea of nothing — starless, airless. I didn't have lips or hands or feet. I couldn't swim or scream.

An eye opened. The pupil was a star the size of a million suns. Fire jets screamed off it, arcing and coalescing back in. A billion years passed in a second, and the star began to shrink. It ate itself to smaller than a gnat, its fire compressed to explode.

A boiling lightning burst and torrented over the endless black. Blue and green and white and yellow firebolts raged through time. It boiled, it eviscerated, it melted, it annihilated. A thousand and one worlds, spirals of light, seas of stars, and clouds so bright — burned out of existence.

It washed through my soul and scathed it with truth:

I am the darkness and the light.

The beginning and the end.

The first and the last.

· Once the light had gone, all that remained was a spinning darkness. But that darkness was alive. It seethed.

And I am coming.

34

MICAH

Sunshine brightened the cave mouth. It had been too long since I'd seen sunshine, and it blinded me with its beauty. The moment I felt it warm my aches, was as if I'd entered paradise. Such a simple pleasure I hoped to never take for granted.

"Here's where I leave you." Elly stood in the cave mouth. "You sure you don't want me to fix your arm again?"

I brushed my metal stump. "After everything, I think I'd rather keep out of trouble." It was cool, like metal ought to be. "What about our child? You said—"

"I will carry him to term, then I'll find you."

"So...eight moons from now?"

"Closer to eighty moons."

"That's...quite a term," I said. "Where are we, anyway?"

"Walk a few minutes." Elly smiled, warmer than even the sunshine. "You'll know."

I wished Berrin could be here to enjoy the sunshine, but he'd sacrificed himself so I could go on. Another of my friends, dead because of me. I hoped to become worthy of their sacrifices, to earn the right to go on living.

Right or not, here I stood, a survivor of things I could scarcely believe. I'd witnessed the Tear of the Archangel, held it in my hand, and then it melted my black arm. Burned it off me.

Elly walked into the sun and scowled. "I don't know how you people find joy in this light. You call us evil because we live in the dark, but to us darkness is comforting." Her sigh was like an old woman's. "See you in eighty moons...or perhaps sooner."

Elly descended into the cave and disappeared.

The thin air and blistering wind on this mountain path were typical of the highlands. Even in summer, snow covered the mountain peaks and cold hardened the mud. As I walked to a lower elevation and looked upon the stone hovels that wrapped around the cliff-side, I whispered to myself, "I know this place." I'd always loved how the red roofs clashed with the leafy trees. A warm familiarity fluttered through me. "It's her convent."

I came here sixteen years ago to pay a debt my father owed to the parish. On that visit, I sinned with a sister in the convent. Our sin created the greatest light of my life: Elly.

I approached the stone chapel on the outskirts. Graves dotted the flowery pathway. I read the names on the tombstones out loud, hoping not to read hers. But just before I entered the chapel lawn, there it was: "Miriam." Elly's mother. She'd died not long after Elly was born.

I knelt at her grave and wept. I shuddered when my knees touched the frigid mud. I tried to tell her about her daughter, but in that moment, I couldn't remember anything about Elly — about what she'd been like before the slavers kidnapped her. I said the only thing I knew for certain.

"I killed our daughter." I didn't want to cry; I didn't want to sob. But the despair at finally ingesting those words broke me. "I killed her with my rage. With my hatred. With my wickedness."

Gunshot. Searing pain. Right in my belly. I fell against Miriam's tombstone, bloodying her name. I touched near my belly-button. Blood colored my fingers.

I sat against the tombstone as if it were my throne. A boy no older than ten appeared, with curly blond hair and green eyes. He wielded a matchlock with a smoking barrel. A damn good shot.

A man ran toward us. He wore a thick black coat with red accents and wielded a long-barreled gun. He aimed it at my head.

"You company dogs think you're so sly," he said. "This is our mountain."

"Company?" I croaked. "Isn't this a convent for holy sisters?"

The man spat. "Playing the fool? This hasn't been a convent in years. Not since Micah smashed Pendurum and sent us hirelings scurrying for the hills. It was the last free city on the continent — a bastion for us low fools — oh how I miss it."

The man did look like a mercenary — unwashed, soot peppering his face. Even his coat was made of carded wool, the kind that chaffed the skin.

"I like your colors," I said to placate him.

"You don't know the colors of the Black Front? Did that shot hit your belly or your brain?"

"Black Front?" I hesitated, then said what was on my mind, "Couldn't come up with a more original name?"

The mercenary patted the boy's head, as if to reward him for downing me. Then he studied the charred metal stump of my right hand.

"The hell is that mess?" He wrinkled his nose in disgust.

"I'm Micah the Metal." I raised my metal stump. "This was my metal hand, bestowed upon me by the demons of Labyrinthos."

He gaped in shock, then laughed like a drunk hyena. "And I'm Imperator Josias!" He rubbed the boy's head. "And this here's Patriarch Lazar!"

I laughed too. It hurt like hell. "Care to do me a favor, friend?" I pointed to my erupting wound.

He wiped his slobber with his sleeve. "We got no healers back in those hovels. Best favor's a quick death."

"I have a better idea. Go down this path and up the mountain till you find a cave. Yell the name 'Elly' down the cave mouth."

The mercenary burst into laughter. Even the little boy laughed.

"You're a funny one," the man said. "No healer could sew a hole that big. I'll do you in the heart. How about it?"

The pain was as if my blood were lava burning my insides. Still, I shook my head.

"All right then, die slow." He walked toward the convent, laughing the while. The boy looked at me with pity, then followed.

I HOPED to live till sundown. Maybe then Elly would find me and heal me as she'd done twice before. I passed time by talking to Miriam. I told her about my conquests, my victories, and my only defeat.

Night came, but Elly didn't. I bled a puddle now and wheezed blood. I screamed her name, each scream more painful than how I imagined birthing to feel. I imagined Miriam giving birth to Elly in her windowless room, tended to by people who despised her. Her last moments probably weren't any better. And utter terror drenched my daughter's last moments...because of me. Her garbled screams as I choked her on the sea wall would surely haunt me in death. Turns out, I was what I hated all along.

To die with sad thoughts seemed wrong, so to cheer myself up, I thought of all the women I'd bedded. There was the baker's daughter, the butcher's niece, and the moneylender's suspiciously young wife. There was Miriam and Alma — Zosi's sister — and the demon...that's it. I never touched Celene. But it was Aschere whom I really wanted. I recalled the scent of her ice and honey breaths, her impassive expressions, and the time she smiled onboard my flagship, all those moons ago.

Footsteps. A light patter on the grass.

The boy from earlier stood in front of me. He clutched a knife twice the size of his hand.

"What's your name?" I smiled — best way to go.

He hesitated, too bashful to answer, then said, "Princip."

"Ah, your namesake is the angel Principus, the judge of souls. A great and mighty angel."

He nodded proudly and puffed his cheeks. I was once proud too, to be named after one of the Twelve. Micah — the angel that reset the world.

I showed the boy where the heart is. "You can tell everyone — 'I killed Micah the Metal.'"

The boy bent down. His green pupils...they were like Aschere's. I gazed into them as he brought the dagger toward my heart.

Then I shut my eyes and imagined my father and Miriam and Elly and me, together on a patch of green. Berrin was there too, reading a book beneath a tree. Edmar and Zosi wrestled while Orwo stirred a big pot. Aicard put his arm around me and grinned. We were together and beholden to no one. Free.

35

KEVAH

THE WARRIOR-POET TAQI COMPARED LOVE TO BEING DRUNK. LOVE made us fools as it made us happy. And when love wore off, we were left weakened, stinging, and hollow.

That's how I felt for having loved Lunara. For having loved Sadie. For having loved. Half of me still longed for those I'd lost. The other half hated myself for it.

I'd been in Labyrinthos six days. I drank the metal-tasting water to survive, not forgetting I'd killed a man in there. I chewed on the leather from my boots, eating bits a day, while jinn climbed the walls. They were skeletons wrapped in shadows, with eyes of white in black. They'd watch me from above but never approach. At first, I trembled in fear. Now, I appreciated the company.

The metal creature with ten eyes watched me too, but only with the eye at the bottom. I didn't want to enter its mouth. Lunara's body was in there, rotting amid broken glass. Wherever else I went, I would end up back here. It was as the legends said: Labyrinthos was a place of no escape.

I considered ending it all. I could stab my heart with Aicard's dagger, but I didn't want to go to Barzakh, knowing who tended it.

So there I sat, sickened by metal water, chewing on leather, and shivering from biting winds that howled through the cavern. What did I want most? No question: a hookah with the finest hashish.

I recalled a time, long ago, when I was wandering through the spice bazaars of Kostany. A pirate-looking fellow with a braided beard called me to his stall and tried to sell me a flavor of "otherworldly molasses, never before known." He told me a story: he was sailing to Kashan and, out of nowhere, a whirlwind seethed and swallowed his ship. Luckily, he awoke on an island, bruised but breathing. He looked around; to his astonishment, he was surrounded by colorful trees that grew bizarre fruits. *"There was one that resembled a strawberry, but it was blue and bursting out of its pores was a type of honey that tasted like sweet wood. Another was like a fig, but within it were tiny diamonds that when crunched between your teeth exploded with mouth-burning spice."* I listened to this guy go on and on, and then finally succumbed and bought the "otherworldly molasses." Later that day, I pressed it together with some hashish and smoked it from my hookah. It was like nothing else — as if you took sunshine, melted it, and mixed it with sugarcanes.

The next day, I returned to the bazaar to buy more, but the man was gone. No matter whom I asked, none recalled knowing or seeing such a man. If I had one wish in this moment, it would be for some hashish pressed with that otherworldly goodness.

She came as I was daydreaming. The peacock with the face of a woman descended. Her wingspan was longer than my body, and her bright colors clashed with the darkness that surrounded me.

"I took a great risk coming here to find you," Saran said upon landing.

What did I care what risks this bird took? "What do you want?"

"I want you to go to Holy Zelthuriya, to train and become what you were meant to be."

I laughed.

Saran extended her wing and placed it around my body like a cloak. Warmth soothed me for the first time in days. But not just warmth...within seconds I no longer thirsted nor hungered. I didn't even feel sick from ingesting the metallic water. A tingling energy surrounded my heart and lungs and muscles and I felt as strong as ever.

And yet it made me sick with anger. "If you can do that, why didn't you save Sadie!?"

Saran glared at me with piercing ruby eyes.

"I don't want your succor," I said. "I won't go to Zelthuriya. A slow death sounds better than being your pawn, or the pawn of any king, god, angel, jinn. Fuck all of you."

Saran said in the gentle tone of a mother, "You need not speak. I can feel your heart as if it were my own. I've tasted your suffering and know it to be great. That's why you must come to Zelthuriya. The training will free you of dependence on fleeting things. You will not need food or water or sleep. Love, hate, grief — your heart will be free of it all. You will achieve *fanaa* — total annihilation of the self. Doesn't that sound better than dying here?"

I wished I'd been born that way: uncaring and unfeeling. But even Vaya said he felt things. Though he didn't show it, he seemed to care about us. Lunara was the opposite. Her training truly made her cold...at least until the end, when she seemed to love me again. Right before I stabbed her.

Sadie had mentioned how I would stay young and watch those I love grow old and die. But they never had a chance to grow old because I'd failed to protect them. Had I been a true magus, I would've never allowed Heraclius to capture me, and perhaps then I could have protected Sadie. Protected everyone.

"What happened in Kostany?" I asked.

"Some were killed in the stampede, but everyone you know is fine."

"I killed them."

"You did, but you saved many more. You slew the apostle of Hawwa." Saran no longer spoke in the gentle tone of a mother but rather in the iron tenor of a queen. "The gate to the Blood Star will not open, and our world will not hear its maddening song. You saved us all."

"But the star said it was coming."

"Perhaps...but not in a thousand of your lifetimes. The gods have been fighting longer than man has walked the earth. Though our war will not end soon, you've struck a blow for the light. And I take care of those who fight for me."

The way she spoke...so satisfied. As if it were all her doing...

"You used me." It became so clear now. "That's why you gave Kinn the Tear of the Archangel. You wanted me to enter Labyrinthos. You manipulated me into killing Lunara. That's why you let Sadie die!" I pushed out of Saran's embrace and onto my feet.

"I gambled that you would do the right thing. The choice was always yours."

"You don't strike me as the gambling type." I looked upon the peacock and made a fist. "Tell me, Saran — who are you, truly?"

Saran spread her wings. Her feathers and human face turned into wisps of light, then reformed into something else.

Now a woman stood before me, though she had peacock wings on her back. She wore a crown upon which was the eight-pointed star. Her curly black hair fell to her waist, and she looked upon me with ruby-colored eyes.

"I am Lat," she said, "and I cannot let the most powerful magus alive die."

Wisps of light coursed through her hands and a scepter materialized. Before I could speak, her scepter emitted a blinding aurora.

I AWOKE outside the mouth of a cave. The icy breeze of Labyrinthos blew out of it while a scorching sun beat down. Dry air and sandy winds trailed across my face. Strange, to feel so hot and cold at the same time.

I got to my feet and surveyed my surroundings. Or lack thereof. An endless desert lay in all directions, covered by dunes that rolled with the sandy winds. The only shade was in the shadows of the dunes when they clumped and piled high.

"Zelthuriya is that way," a voice said. Saran's voice. No, Lat's voice.

She stood at the mouth of the cave, pointing her scepter toward the wind.

"Then I'll be going the other way!" I faced the opposite direction. Sand blew into my nostrils and mouth. I coughed and rubbed my eyes.

"To where? Your anvil in Tombore? Heat it enough, and you can shape metal however you like. But the world is not the same. No matter who you are, it will not bend. You thought strength would save you when prayers failed. And when strength failed, you despaired. But in the end, the only way was to digest your pain and serve. You never needed a reward for that, but this time you're going to get one." Lat banged her scepter on the sand. "I'll bring her back."

I glared at the woman who claimed to be god. "I don't believe you. You're nothing but a shapeshifter."

"I won't deny it. You saw the true form of Hawwa with your own eyes...mine is no better. We of the veil were not born in the light of your star, but in the light of the Blood Star. We are

467

refugees from its death, that erased our world and bathed yours in fire."

"Why care for us then? Why not kill us all and be done?"

I stumbled. My bare feet sank into the hot sand and burned. I staggered back toward the cave mouth, wishing I could soak my soles.

"Would you kill every ant on earth? Would a king slaughter all his subjects? What is a god without worshippers? A thousand years ago, I created the Latian faith and chose Chisti to guide and prepare mankind to fight the darkness. Now I choose you for that same purpose." She pointed her scepter at me. "Hawwa took a soul from Barzakh and brought it back. Barzakh owes me a soul, too. If you'll agree to go to Zelthuriya and train, I'll bring back Sadie."

"You mean to say that Hawwa doesn't rule Barzakh?"

"You've only seen one set of truths, Kevah." Lat's ruby eyes glistened in the sunlight. "What did Taqi say about how blind men would describe a simurgh?" She recited the poem:

One felt the claws and said it was a lion,
The other felt the wings and said it must be a falcon,
And another felt the head and said surely it's a wolf.

"All of them were right and wrong," I said. "You know your Taqi." I struggled to hide how astonished I was. I dropped to my knees, ready to pray. "I'll do as you wish. Please bring Sadie back. And my daughter too."

"Your daughter's soul has already moved on to the formless sea, which the Silklanders revere as the Wheel. She is at peace. When Heraclius died, Hawwa trapped his soul in Barzakh. She did the same with Sadie, hoping to use the promise of her resurrection to ensnare you."

I would never see Melodi again. I'd already accepted that, and despite the pain, it was comforting to know she was at peace. Though I'd failed to recover her body, I would never forget that patch amid blue flowers where I'd planted her shrine. "What of my father?"

"Alive."

That was a gust of hope on my heart. I almost slipped onto the scorching sand again as I shuffled closer to god. "Where!?"

"Demoskar. You barely missed him. I promise you'll see him again."

My heart steadied. If Lat herself was promising our reunion, who was I to doubt? There was only one thing left to say. "Bring Sadie back."

A tense silence floated between us, until Lat said, "I'm sure you realize that if you're to serve me, you cannot be with her."

I nodded. In a world this harsh, it seemed like the best deal ever made. "Will you let me see her, one final time?"

THOUSANDS OF YEARS AGO, the jinn carved Holy Zelthuriya out of mountains. Today, the Shrine of Saint Chisti stood radiant out of the largest of those mountains. Bright, sand-colored pillars guarded an entrance taller than a palace. The holiest site of our faith exceeded my expectations.

Every structure in the city was carved out of mountains, between which were sandstone streets. The people of the city covered their faces with bright scarves as they endured the never-ending sandstorms.

Within the Shrine of Saint Chisti, a thousand candles burned. The hollowed-out cave was larger than the entire Sublime Seat, and Paramic calligraphy covered the walls. Every supplicant would light a candle, raise their hands, and pray for the saint's intercession. But it seemed I needed no intercessors anymore.

I waited in a small chamber. The hum of supplicants coming through the walls alternated between mellow and passionate. It calmed me as I sat on one of the sofa pillows spread around the room. They had tiny mirrors sewn into them — a very Alanyan style. Though I'd rarely met an Alanyan who didn't irritate me in some way, I couldn't deny they knew how to decorate.

I pondered what Lat had told me when we arrived here. I would be trained by the Disciples of Chisti, an army of warrior-dervishes that served only the city, until the jinn tribes that controlled wind and fire and water sent for me. It seemed I wore three masks: Agneya's, Lunara's, and Vaya's. Though I hadn't killed Vaya, his mask had been infused into Agneya's when she killed him. Lunara's had been infused into mine. I was, according to Lat, the most powerful magus alive.

I had no idea how to use that power. Not yet. So I sat in this chamber, with its brightly-painted walls and ornate carpet, and waited. Waited for the fulfillment of a prayer.

Kinn waddled in. "I'm not missing this." He sat next to me in his egg-laying posture.

"You got here fast."

"In case you didn't notice, I can fly."

"I'm just shocked you didn't get lost, or steal someone's shoes along the way."

"I did steal the Alanyan prince's shoes." Kinn covered his face with his wing, as if embarrassed to admit it. "But who could resist shoes like that? The toe-end curls upward — I'd love to meet the sage who came up with that!"

I chuckled. "You're too late to steal mine...I already ate them."

"That's disgusting. You're disgusting."

"Well, it's not like I enjoyed them. I did it to survive."

"Shoes are a gift from Lat herself. How dare you justify your crime?"

We bickered for a while.

EPILOGUE
SADIE

IN MY DYING DREAMS, I HEARD KEVAH CRY. HE WAS AFRAID. EACH tear melted his emotions onto my soul. I tasted his love as if it were honey dripping off a spoon. His grief was a whirlpool, dragging me into a dark sea. And then his anger scorched my soul like an exploding star.

I was afraid, too. I hadn't prayed since I was a child and thought little of where my soul would go. In truth, I didn't believe in an afterlife as much as I didn't believe I would ever die. If Lat were real, I never needed her — until the day they stoned me.

Barzakh, where all souls go after death, was not how I'd imagined. A saint spoke to me while I lay encased in a bubble of water that hung above the world. Not just one world, but an endless cascade of worlds. And from those many worlds, souls floated to and from Barzakh as bubbles float to the surface of the sea.

The saint told me that I would go back — whether I wanted to or not. That I'd already gone back a thousand and one times, each time to a different world and as a different droplet, but that now I would go back to the same world. I would inhabit the same body, with the same memories and cares. I would not rejoin the form-less floating sea, which shimmered and churned in the sky above Barzakh. The saint told me of our victory, our reconquest of Kostany, but she said nothing about Kevah.

That's when a strand of red light appeared. It dangled above me like a rope and led into a tunnel filled with starlight. I pulled on the strand until I burst out of the water droplet and through a starry hole. Then a thousand more red strands appeared, each leading a different direction. I didn't know which one to pull, where it would take me, to which world, to which rebirth.

Until I heard Kevah crying. Until his emotions stirred through me. Until his love pulled me home.

I woke up with a metal taste in my mouth. I felt as if I were a freshly forged sword. I was in a room with sandstone walls, naked, standing before a woman who wore the eight-pointed star as a crown.

"You never believed in me," she said.

It all felt like a moment. Heraclius' stone struck me on the head. I died, went to Barzakh, came back, and now was standing here — all one moment that raced through my soul.

"Who are you?"

"The one who brought you back."

Her red eyes reminded me of the golden, ruby-eyed peacock in my father's great hall.

"I killed and died fighting for my country. All you've done is ensure I'll have to kill and die for it again." I covered my breasts with trembling hands. "Instead of waiting for me to thank you, at least get me a robe."

"I'll do you better." She pointed to two chests: one delicately patterned in bronze, the other simple and wooden. Before walking out the door, she said, "The choice has always been yours."

Inside the wooden one were fresh zabadar leathers and a cotton vest that fit perfectly. While putting them on, I heard his voice. Kevah was in the adjacent room, talking to himself about...shoes?

I rushed out of my room and into a sandstone hall with a ceiling fit for a giant. Where the hell was I? I didn't wait to consider it and pushed open the wooden door to the room where Kevah's voice came from.

I melted at the sight of him. Sickly and skinny as he was, his hug was warmer than a horse-hide blanket on a snowy day. He said he wanted to show me something and took me by the hand up a flight of stairs, to a balcony that overlooked a city carved out of mountains: Zelthuriya.

The horizon was dark with the promise of a sandstorm. But for now, sun warmed my shoulders while a breeze sifted through my hair.

"Let's go," I said.

"Go?"

"To Rupat island. To eat snail pancakes."

Kevah chuckled. "We're far from the sea."

"Then we should get moving."

His yellow hair was so wispy and straw-like. It was uncaring of me to insist on travel when he didn't have his strength back. I'd been dead and was healthier than him. I knew nothing of the struggles he bore while I was gone, of what had happened after Heraclius captured him. And yet, I didn't want to waste a moment on the past, on all the suffering we'd endured. I'd already died for my family, for my tribe, for my country, and didn't mean to again.

"I'm not going anywhere, Sadie." He couldn't look me in the eyes. "I promised my service to Lat in exchange for your life."

"No, you've served enough. You've bled for enough masters. Fuck your promise!"

"I can't defy god."

"Isn't that what we just did? Wasn't it a god that resurrected Heraclius? And still, we fought back."

"That god was evil."

"They're all evil! They want us to bathe in each other's blood — for what? For prayers that go unanswered?"

"But my prayer was answered. This one time, it was answered." He gazed into me, tears glistening on his eyes. "I've lost everyone I loved. One day, you're going to grow old, and I'm going to watch you die. I know I won't be able to bear it. I almost destroyed a city to see you again. That's why I need to detach, like the magi. I need *fanaa*."

I shook my head. "You helped me be brave. Now let me help you not be stupid. Next time I die, I want you to mourn me...and then I want you to move on and love someone else. Even if you live ten thousand years. Even if you watch this world end. Don't waste your life on the dead."

"*Fanaa* is death." He smiled somberly. "My death. I choose it so you can live. Be free and happy, Sadie. For the both of us."

Kevah hugged me as if it was the last time. I pushed him away, then pulled him close and kissed him. That red strand of light that guided me home — it flowed between us, connecting our souls as one.

I whispered in his ear, "I love you, Kevah."

He squeezed my hand and whispered, "I'll always love you."

We didn't stop kissing.

And then a rowboat, floating by itself, appeared at our balcony. Kevah and I stared at it, perplexed as ever.

"You brought that all this way!" Kevah said to the invisible jinn carrying it. "Is that so? You better be telling the truth." He turned to me. "It appears I have a month before I start my service."

Kevah climbed over the railing and jumped onto the flying boat. He held out his hand for me.

· · ·

WE SAW THE WORLD. We toured the islands of Pilimay and admired its giant stone faces stuck in mud, then joined the descendants of the warlocks as they danced beneath them in the crescent moon's light. Afterward, we threw up snail pancakes in Rupat and smelly cheeses in Jesia, then ate more. We stayed a week outside Qandbajar, the capital of Alanya, searching the palm forests for the mythical simurgh, which Kevah's jinn swore he'd seen. Too bad we didn't find it. So we went to Harijag, a city in the jungles of Kashan, to swim beneath cascading waterfalls and dive for lavender pearls — I begrudgingly admit Kevah found the brightest and biggest. Gumong, the city of metal in the Silklands, was our next stop. Its palaces were metal towers molded from the steel of an underwater mountain. We watched the stars set from the tallest one.

We did in a month what most couldn't with a thousand and one lives. Most of all, we loved each other fiercely.

A few days before Kevah would begin his unending service, we flew to the outskirts of Demoskar. To the house of an old man who lived by the sea. I had not seen Kevah cry since we found him burying bodies in that forest, but when his father embraced him, his weeping did not cease until they pulled apart. I thought of my father and mother and zabadar and how cruel it was that I'd let them grieve. And yet...would I ever go back? Had dying not freed me of all that I feared?

Watching Kevah's tearful chuckles while his father praised him — impishly — for slimming down, the weight of our looming separation crushed me. How many lifetimes would Kevah give? How selfish was I, to think that dying once was enough? And yet, he'd done it so I could be free.

As the cheerful old man and his son approached, I smiled to hold back tears of goodbye.

WANT MORE?

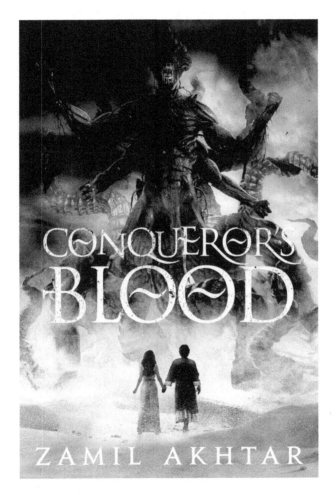

The gods are not done with Kevah, nor with you. The story goes on. Get *Conqueror's Blood* (Gunmetal Gods Book 2) at Books2Read.com/CBlood

QUICK GLOSSARY

Ahriyya
A dark god, scorned in the Latian faith

Alanyans
Denizens of the Kingdom of Alanya

Baladict/Barzakh
Believed to be where souls go immediately after death

Crucians
Denizens of the Holy Empire of Crucis

Ejazi
Denizens of Ejaz, an island kingdom south of Sirm

Ethosians
Worshippers of the Archangel

Excubitors

Loyal guardsmen of the Imperator of Crucis

Fanaa
Paramic word meaning "annihilation" of identity and desire

Gholam
Loyal slave soldiers of the Shah of Alanya

Jinn
An invisible spirit said to be the source of magic

Kashanese
Denizens of the Kingdom of Kashan

Khazis
Mystical warriors of the Latian faith

Latians
Worshippers of the goddess Lat

Lidya
The eastern continent, home to Sirm, Alanya, and Kashan

Paramic
Liturgical language of the Latian faith and common tongue of the
Kingdom of Alanya

Pasgardians
Denizens of Pasgard, a territory of Crucis

Rubadi
A clan of nomadic horse warriors, related to the zabadar

Ruh

Paramic word for soul or spirit

Ruthenians
Denizens of Ruthenia, a country north of Crucis

Seluqal
The royal house of Sirm, Alanya, and Kashan

Silklanders
Denizens of the Silk Empire

Simurgh
A giant bird from myth

Sirmians
Denizens of the Kingdom of Sirm

Thamesians
Denizens of Thames, a country north of Crucis

Janissaries
Loyal slave soldiers of the Shah of Sirm

Yuna
The western continent, home to Crucis

Zabadar
Horse warriors that live in the plains of Sirm

ACKNOWLEDGMENTS

Thanks to Salik, Tim, Sophie, Chirag, and Colton for their contributions. Special thanks to my Reedsy editor Fiona McClaren. Shoutouts to Abdullah and Salik, who inspired me to write this.

And thanks to Miblart for an incredible cover!

ABOUT THE AUTHOR

Zamil is a fantasy author based in Dubai, where he lives with his loving wife and his badly-behaved pet rabbit. Of Pakistani heritage, he grew up in the Middle East and moved to Massachusetts when he was thirteen, and his varied upbringing colors his fiction. He's an international relations junkie, horror movie binger, and avid traveler.

Make sure to stay updated about future releases by following him at the links below. Join the mailing list at ZamilAkhtar.com to get DEATH RIDER, a prequel novella to Gunmetal Gods, FREE!

facebook.com/zamakhtar1
twitter.com/zamakhtar
instagram.com/zamilakhtarauthor
amazon.com/author/zamilakhtar
goodreads.com/zamakhtar
patreon.com/zamakhtar

Made in the USA
Middletown, DE
23 December 2022

20297322R00276